Through her marriage to Reggie Kray, Roberta Kray has a unique and authentic insight into London's East End. Born in Southport, Roberta met Reggie in early 1996 and they married the following year; they were together until Reggie's death in 2000. Roberta is the author of many previous bestsellers including *Broken Home, Strong Women, Bad Girl* and *Streetwise*.

NO MERCY

ROBERTA KRAY

sphere

SPHERE

First published in Great Britain in 2014 by Sphere

Copyright © Roberta Kray 2014

The moral right of the author has been asserted.

A CIP catalogue record for this book
is available from the British Library.

ISBN 978-0-7515-5376-5

Typeset in Garamond by M Rules

An Hachette UK Company
www.hachette.co.uk

www.littlebrown.co.uk

NO MERCY

Prologue

Lucy Rivers stood under the railway arches, sheltering from a thin, drizzly rain. Her shoulders were hunched, her face pale and tight. She shivered. It was getting dark now and the hope was seeping out of her. He had to come. He must! She peered along the narrow street, willing him to appear through the gloom. Please, she silently begged, her hands clenching into two tight fists. Please, God, let him come.

She checked her watch again. Already it was half an hour after the time they had agreed, and with every minute that passed she felt the knot in her stomach grow tighter. Her mouth was dry. Her heart was racing, thumping in her chest. Briefly she closed her eyes, but when she opened them again, the street was still empty.

There was the rumble of a train as it approached and slid smoothly into the station. She thought of the travellers mingling on the platform, beginning their journeys or ending them – people leaving and people coming home. Tonight she was supposed to have been starting on a journey of her own.

What chance of that now? Tears pricked her eyes and she roughly brushed them away.

She glanced at her watch again. She looked down at the pavement. All her meagre possessions, everything she owned, were packed into the small, shabby suitcase standing by her feet. Her hands had been trembling with fear and excitement as she'd packed the case in the early hours of the morning before slipping out to the yard to hide it behind the bins. At work, she had barely been able to concentrate, her fingers clumsy on the keyboard, her mind a million miles away from the words she was typing. And with everything she had done, every simple action, every routine chore, she had thought, This is the last time I will be doing this.

There was a sound, footsteps, and her heart gave a leap, but it wasn't him. She shrank back into the shadows as a tom with her arm linked through a customer's tottered by. The clicking tap of the prostitute's heels echoed on the pavement. The woman's voice was high and brittle, her artificial laugh carrying on the damp evening air.

Gradually, the quiet settled around Lucy again. From somewhere behind came the light, steady drip of water. There is no point in waiting, she thought, but still she couldn't leave. Another five minutes. She would give him that. Half an hour was nothing. He could have been held up. Or an accident, perhaps. What if he was lying in hospital, unable to get in touch with her? What if he was— No, she would not allow herself to think of it. A world where he did not exist was too painful to imagine.

The minutes dragged by, five, ten and then fifteen. She rummaged in her pocket for loose change. She could go to the phone box at the station and call him. But what if he came while she was gone? Anyway, she knew that it was pointless. She would get no answer if she rang. Either he was on his way or he wasn't coming at all.

Although the street was empty, she still felt self-conscious, as if the very bricks in the wall, the pavement slabs and even the air that she breathed bore witness to her humiliation. She hung her head in shame. It was obvious what had happened. He had changed his mind. He had weighed up the pros and cons and decided she was not worth it. In the final reckoning – for she would not be the only one who was leaving everything behind – the price had proved too high.

As soon as the thought entered her head, she tried to push it away. It *couldn't* be so. All the things he had said, the promises he had made. Surely they must have meant something. He was the one who had suggested they run off, who had made all the plans, who had convinced her that this was the only way they could be together. *We can do this, Lucy.*

But men lied and that was the God-honest truth. They gazed into your eyes and swore that black was white. She only had to look at her dad to know this for a fact. He lied about money, about where he'd been and what he'd done, about all the cheap little tarts he slept with. She would smell the perfume on his clothes when he came home, the overly sweet scent mixing with the ugly stink of fags and booze.

She paced ten feet to the left, turned and went back to where she had started. She shifted unhappily from one foot to the other. 'Where are you?' she muttered under her breath. 'Why? Why are you doing this to me?' She lifted her eyes to the darkening sky and knew that she couldn't wait any longer. It was almost an hour now. People didn't turn up an hour after they were supposed to.

If she didn't go home soon, she'd have trouble explaining where she'd been. There would be questions, an interrogation. She would get a grilling from her stepmother, Jean. She had promised to be back from work by six and already it was past the hour. Her emotions welled up inside her, a swirling pool of

3

grief and pain, of shame and shock and anger. How could he have betrayed her like this? He had taken her love and trust and thrown them both away.

With a heavy heart, she picked up the suitcase and began to walk. As she trudged along the street, her legs felt leaden. She glanced back over her shoulder, still hoping even though she knew it was hopeless. She couldn't help herself. In her mind, she had an image of him hurrying towards her, his mouth full of apologies, his arms reaching out . . .

But no, that wouldn't happen now. She realised that. The dream was shattered. She had envisaged the two of them together for always, but it wasn't going to be. It was over, finished. She had been cut adrift. The breath caught in her throat and the tears began to flow.

As she passed the station, she stopped and looked in through the entrance. There was nothing to prevent her from leaving on her own. She was eighteen, old enough to take care of herself. She could buy a ticket, get on a train, go anywhere that her money would take her. Except that wasn't very far. And what then? To be alone in a strange place would take more courage than she currently possessed. An hour ago, she had thought herself brave, fearless, a woman rather than a girl. Now she felt like a child again, small and defenceless and scared of her own shadow.

A lad walked past and grinned at her. 'Cheer up, love. It may never 'appen.'

Lucy, jolted from her introspection, gazed blankly back. Yesterday she would have been ready with a smart retort, but at this moment she had nothing. 'Fool,' she murmured, although she was not entirely sure if the comment was directed at the boy or herself.

Her gaze shifted towards the row of three phone boxes, one of them empty, and she wondered again about calling him. She

4

was clutching at straws, but that was all she had. What if something *had* happened and he was waiting for her to make contact? It was possible. Anything was possible. Before she could change her mind, she rushed over, pulled open the door and stepped inside.

Dropping the case down by her feet, she grabbed a couple of coins from her pocket. She picked up the receiver and dialled the number with a shaking hand. It began to ring at the other end. 'Come on,' she urged, as she pressed the phone to her ear. It rang and rang and rang. Long after she knew that it would not be answered, she continued to stand there with the sound echoing in her head. Eventually, she put the receiver down, gave a sigh, wiped the snot from her nose with the back of her hand and wearily set off for home.

Crossing the road, she was careless of the traffic and deaf to the protests of honking horns. She went to the corner and began to walk up Kellston High Street. The rain was coming down harder now, soaking into her coat and drenching her long, fair hair. Most of the shops had closed, their iron shutters pulled down for the night, but a light was still shining from Connolly's. As she passed the café, she peered in through the window, automatically scanning the faces of the customers in case he was sitting there. But of course he wasn't. Why would he be?

She traipsed along the street until she came to Rose Avenue. Here she stopped again, her face twisting as she gazed down the row of identical terraced houses. She could see the light on in number 26 and knew that their visitor must have arrived. The front room, the parlour, was only ever used for special occasions.

A part of her wanted to turn round, to retrace her steps and hurry back to the station. Anything was better than what awaited her at home. She hesitated, aware of the sound of her own lightly panting breath. What now? She still had a choice, but her emotions were too tumultuous, too confused, for her to think straight.

A bus went by, heading for Victoria. That was near to where he lived. She could go to his flat, see if he was there, demand some answers to the endless questions that were rolling through her mind. But he wouldn't be there. Or if he was, he wouldn't come to the door. And by the time she got there and back – probably with nothing to show for it – it would be *really* late and she'd be in even more trouble than she already was.

She stood for a minute, paralysed by indecision. As her eyes darted left and right, she worried about seeing someone she knew. How would she explain the suitcase? Her fingers tightened round the handle. In these parts, the women had nothing better to do than gossip; they took pleasure in other people's misfortunes, in other people's mistakes. She could imagine their eyes, shiny with malice. She shuddered at the thought of being ridiculed, of her humiliation being exposed to the world.

In the end, aware that the longer she stood there, the more likely she was to be observed, she made the choice and set off for home. She felt sick inside, hot and cold, almost dizzy. She wished she had the strength to go it alone, but she didn't. As she cut down into the alley that ran along the back of the terrace, she recalled the tom she'd seen earlier. Perhaps once, years ago, that woman had dreamed of something better too.

It was dark in the alley, only a faint light slipping from the kitchen windows. She heard the rattling of dinner plates and the muffled sound of voices. Keeping her head down, she walked as quietly as she could, desperate to escape the notice of the neighbours. The rain was starting to gather, forming puddles on the uneven surface of the path. In her haste, she stumbled, twisting her ankle.

'Damn it!' she cursed, before quickly limping on.

When she came to the open gate of number 26, she paused again, checking that no one was watching from the window, before hobbling into the cluttered yard. She slid the suitcase in behind the bins, then leaned down to rub at the swelling flesh of her ankle. She was glad of the pain. It helped to distract from the grinding ache in her chest, from the knowledge that her life was in ruins. But then, as she approached the back door, she had another rush of hope. What if he had left a message? Something cryptic that no one else would understand. Maybe he had pushed a note through the letterbox. Or got someone else to do it.

She burst through the door, eager now to get inside. The kitchen light dazzled her for a second and she raised a hand to shield her eyes against the brightness.

'Sorry I'm late.'

Her stepmother, Jean, a thin, waspish woman, was placing the lid on the best china teapot. 'Oh, decided to honour us with your presence, have you? What time do you call this? You were supposed to ... And the state of you! Jesus, you look like a drowned rat.'

'It's raining,' Lucy explained unnecessarily. 'And I had to ... to stay late at work.' She wondered if the lie showed on her face. 'There was nothing I could do about it. A last-minute order came in and we all had to stay. And then I had to wait ages for a bus. I got back as fast as I could.'

'He's been here half an hour,' hissed Jean, glancing towards the front room. 'Tidy yourself up, for God's sake. What's he going to think?'

Lucy gave a shrug. She didn't care what he thought. And she didn't give a damn how long he'd been waiting. She slid out of her wet coat and hung it over the back of a chair. Her eyes raked the room, searching for a note, but there was none in sight. She was desperate to ask the question on her lips, but equally afraid of the answer she might get.

'Er, did anyone call round for me earlier?'

'Like who, for instance?'

'Anyone.'

'No.'

'Are you sure? No one came round?'

Jean's eyes narrowed with suspicion. 'Who you expecting, then?'

'Nobody.' Lucy gave a quick shake of her head. 'It doesn't matter. I was just wondering. We're supposed to be going out Saturday, me and the girls. I thought one of them might have—'

'Well, they didn't. No one did.'

Lucy stared hard at her. Was she lying? Jean was more than capable. It was ten years now since she'd married her father and the evil cow had started sniffing around before poor Mum was even cold in her grave. It hadn't taken her long to get her claws in. Still, the one consolation was that neither of them had got what they'd bargained for: he had found himself hitched to a nagging harridan who made his life a misery, and Jean had been landed with a no-good bastard who squandered his cash on tarts, booze and gambling. The two of them deserved each other.

Jean glared back at her. 'What?'

'Nothing.' Lucy slumped down at the table, a wave of exhaustion washing over her. This morning, over breakfast, she'd been convinced that it was the last time she'd ever have to see the woman, the last time she'd ever have to listen to her vile grating voice. So much for that! So much for all her stupid dreams! She felt a lump growing in her throat and quickly tried to swallow it. She mustn't cry. If she started, she might never stop.

'So what's with the face?'

Lucy put her elbows on the table and rubbed at her eyes. 'I'm tired, that's all. It's been a long day.'

'Well, don't just sit there. Get upstairs and smarten yourself up. And put some lippie on. You look like a bleedin' ghost.'

Lucy wished she was a ghost. To be dead and buried was all she wanted. The dead couldn't think, couldn't feel, couldn't weep. Slowly she got to her feet, wincing at the pain in her ankle.

'And I wouldn't go making any plans for Saturday,' Jean said. 'You play your cards right and there could be a much better offer on the table.'

'Maybe I don't want a better offer.'

Jean's lips pursed. 'Don't start that again. We agreed, didn't we? Or do you want to see us out on the street without a roof over our heads?' She glanced towards the front room and lowered her voice. 'You should thank your lucky stars that he's taking an interest. Most girls would be grateful.'

Grateful, Lucy thought with a shiver of revulsion. The man was over twice her age, a gangster and a thug. It wasn't her fault that her dad owed him a fortune, but she was still the one who was expected to pay. And it wasn't money that Brendan Vasser was after. Sure, he expected the debt to be repaid, but not in hard cash. What he wanted was *her*. He had made that clear from the first day they'd met. And the more she'd resisted, the more determined he'd become.

'Well?' Jean said. 'What are you waiting for? Get a move on.' She made a flapping gesture with her hands. 'Sort yourself out and get back down here. Five minutes, yeah. Don't take any longer or he may change his mind.'

Lucy gave a small shake of her head; she knew he wasn't going anywhere. Once Vasser set his mind to something, he didn't give up until he got it. She was the prize and he intended to have it. A feeling of dread enveloped her. Her chance of escape had gone. If only she'd had the nerve to get on a train, a bus, to run away from it all ... but it was too late for regrets now. She limped out of the kitchen, glad at least to be free of Jean's scrutiny. Had she suspected anything? It was hard to tell.

As Lucy passed through the narrow hallway, she gazed hard at the phone as if by sheer effort of will she could force it to ring, but it remained silent. Naturally it did. The phone had been cut off months ago when the bill hadn't been paid. The rent was overdue too. Other final demands were piled up on the table, gas and electricity and water, all of them unopened.

Male laughter drifted from the front room, a harsh, dirty sound that set her teeth on edge. What kind of man pimped out his own daughter? She glanced at the front door, tempted to open it, to step outside and keep on walking. But she couldn't find the strength. Instead she climbed slowly up the stairs, resigned to her fate and too tired to fight it.

Jean leaned back against the sink, a self-satisfied smile playing around her lips. She lit a fag and breathed out the smoke in a long, narrow stream of relief. She'd been on pins all day, worried that something would go wrong, but one look at the girl's face had been enough to put her mind at rest. He hadn't shown up and that was all that mattered. He was out of the picture and that was the end of it.

She reached for her handbag and pulled out the letter that had come a week ago. It had been typed and sent to her anonymously from a 'well-wisher'. *I think you should be aware that your step-daughter is planning to elope.* A hot flush of rage burned across her cheeks as she read the man's name, address, telephone number and the date that the two of them were intending to leave.

'Ungrateful bitch,' she muttered. All the years she'd skivvied for her, washed her clothes, cooked her meals and this was the bloody thanks she got. The slut had got herself a fancy man and

10

had been planning on running off, leaving her and Charlie high and dry. It was all there on the page in black and white.

A thin hiss escaped from her lips. The dirty little tart deserved a slap. Still, she'd managed to scupper their plans good and proper. It had taken her a whole morning to construct the brief note, but when it was done, she'd been well pleased with the result: *I'm so sorry but I can't go through with it. It's over. Please don't try and see me. I won't change my mind.*

The writing had been perfect, an immaculate forgery, but Jean had still been worried that the man might ignore the response and turn up as arranged. That had been the big problem, the fact that she'd known when but not where they were meeting.

Jean shoved the letter she'd received back in the envelope – she would burn it later tonight – and returned it to the bottom of her bag. She took one last drag on her cigarette before jabbing the butt into the ashtray. Then she painted a smile on her face, picked up the pot of tea and carried it through to the front room.

'Sorry about the wait, Brendan. She won't be long now. She's just powdering her nose.'

Lucy stood in the bedroom, gazing at her reflection in the dressing-table mirror. The person who looked back felt like a stranger, someone she had never seen before. She studied the oval face, the wide blue eyes, the bloodless lips that were slightly parted. Was this really her? An odd kind of numbness was spreading through her body, a sense of dislocation that she couldn't shake off.

'Lucy Rivers,' she murmured.

She ran a brush through her wet fair hair and listened to the sound of the rain against the window. It had been raining the last time she had seen him. They had decided not to meet again until this evening – no unnecessary risks, no chance of anyone seeing them together – but perhaps that had given him time to reconsider. She wondered at what precise moment he had stopped loving her, or at least stopped loving her *enough*. And why hadn't he let her know? It had been cowardly and cruel to leave her waiting there. She had not believed him capable of either of those things.

'Why?' she whispered, her lips barely moving.

There was still a chance, she thought, that someone or something had prevented him from coming, but the idea was a stale one now. No, if he had wanted to contact her, he would have found a way. She threw the brush on to the bed, went over to the window and looked down at the street. She wrapped her arms around her chest and rocked gently back and forth. The gaping emptiness of her heart was suddenly shot through with rage and bitterness. She wished that he was dead! Better that than he'd betrayed her. She would rather grieve for him than suffer this kind of pain.

Outside, the street lamps cast a soft orange glow. A middle-aged couple walked by, the man holding an umbrella protectively above the woman's head. Abruptly she pulled the curtains across and turned away. She went back to the mirror and stared at herself again. The simple blue dress was creased, but she wasn't going to get changed – she had nothing to get changed into. All her decent clothes were in the suitcase, and the suitcase was out in the yard. Anyway, it didn't matter what she looked like. She didn't care. She didn't give a damn.

Slowly she limped down the stairs, her hand gripping the banister. She paused for a moment when she came to the bottom of the flight, took a couple of deep breaths and then walked into the front room with her head held high.

'There you are,' said Jean, as if she'd been gone for hours rather than minutes.

Lucy glanced from Jean to her father to the monster that was Brendan Vasser. He was sitting in the armchair by the fire with his legs splayed and his hands resting on his heavy thighs. She knew what he was feeling without him having to say a word. She could see it in his cold reptilian eyes, in the way he stared at her. It wasn't love – brutes like Vasser didn't understand the meaning of the word – but it was obsession. He wanted to possess her, to own her body and soul. And she suddenly thought, What difference does it make? She had already lost everything. Lucy Rivers was dead. Whatever happened next was irrelevant.

Her stomach flipped over, but her voice remained calm. 'Here I am.'

1

Maddie Layne shifted the rucksack on to her other shoulder as she passed through the tall wrought-iron gates. It was half past eight and a thin morning haze still blurred the outlines of the graves. She liked this time of day best, when everything was fresh and new. The constant burdens of her life, the responsibilities, the worries and financial difficulties, seemed to weigh less heavily in the peace of the cemetery.

Dressed in jeans and a black T-shirt, she strolled along the main thoroughfare before turning left by the weeping willows and heading down a narrower path. It was almost a year now since she had placed the advert in the *Kellston Gazette* offering her services as a grave tender. It didn't bring in a fortune, but every little helped.

She had twelve clients on her books, and most of them lived away from the area, making it difficult to visit the cemetery on a regular basis. Her duties involved washing down and polishing the headstones, tidying the plots and putting fresh flowers in the urns. To prove that the work had been done, she would then send a photo from her mobile. Once a month was the most common arrangement, but sometimes it was quarterly, and in one unusual case it was every week.

It was this latter client who interested Maddie the most. The man, Mr Cato, had contacted her six months ago, and the cheques came regular as clockwork. The voice on the phone had been neither young nor old, but it had been terse, gruff even, with the merest hint of a London accent. He had provided the name on the grave and the number of the plot, given her instructions, taken her address and then hung up without saying goodbye – all in the space of a couple of minutes.

The grave, which she was now approaching, was situated on the edge of the older, wilder part of the cemetery. Here, nature had reclaimed the land, with weeds and wild flowers establishing themselves in every nook and cranny. Deeper into the undergrowth lay weathered tombstones and crumbling mausoleums covered in ivy. Grey stone angels rose from the foliage with their hands clasped in prayer.

The grass, still damp from the morning dew, brushed against her ankles as she walked. She could hear the birds in the trees and from across the other side of the graveyard the low rumbling sound of a mower. She checked her watch – she had to be at the garden centre for her shift at ten o'clock – before coming to a halt beside the white marble headstone.

'Hey, Lucy,' she said, softly patting the top of the stone with the palm of her hand.

She stood and studied the inscription for a moment. Lucy May Rivers had died over thirty years ago when she was only nineteen. So young, *too* young. Maddie drew in a breath and released it in a sigh. She found herself wondering, not for the first time, what had happened to the poor girl. Her gaze travelled over the brief and by now familiar words – there was only the name, the dates of her birth and her death, and then *Rest in Peace*.

Maddie swung the rucksack off her shoulder and dropped it on the ground. She crouched down, took out a bunch of red roses and placed them on the grass. The flowers had come from her back garden, and before leaving the house, she had cut down the stems and wrapped the ends in wet cotton wool and cellophane. Next she removed a bottle of water from the rucksack and a couple of cloths. She dampened one of the cloths and stood up again, leaning over the stone to wipe away the film of summer dust before giving the surface a polish.

As she worked, she pondered on Cato's connection to Lucy. Who was he? A relative? A friend or lover? But if this was the case, she didn't understand why the grave had been neglected for so long. When she'd first started tending the plot, it had been clear that no one had visited for years. Or if they had, they'd made no attempt to tidy it. At the start, it had taken her half an hour just to clear away the tangle of weeds.

'So what's the deal?' she asked softly. 'Who is this guy, then?'

Maddie didn't even know his Christian name. The monthly cheques, sent by a local firm of solicitors called Crosby, Link & Chatham, only added to the mystery. Why didn't he send them himself? Perhaps he was living abroad. But the mobile number she had was for the UK. She thought of that voice again, gruff and insistent, but still couldn't attach an accurate age to it.

'Cato,' she said, rolling the name on her tongue.

She tugged the old flowers out of the urn, discarded the water, refilled it with fresh and then set about arranging the roses. She always took extra care with this plot, and it wasn't just because of the money. Lucy Rivers had died at the same age as her own sister, Greta, and she felt an emotional attachment to the grave that she didn't feel towards the others.

Maddie paused for a second, her fingers hovering over the smooth red petals of the flowers. She couldn't visit Greta's resting place because there wasn't one. Her sister had been murdered – there was little doubt about that – but her body had never been found. The police reckoned that it had probably been swept out on the tide from the Thames to the sea. It was six years now since she'd gone missing and Maddie was still struggling to come to terms with it.

She gave a shake of her head, trying to free her mind of the horror of what had happened.

It was no good dwelling on it – that wouldn't change anything – but the lack of closure, of not being able to bury her, to properly grieve for her, meant that it all felt unfinished. Greta's life was like a book with the last few pages torn out.

She finished arranging the roses and stood back, inclining her head to view the effect. 'Not bad,' she murmured. The different shades of red looked striking against the cool white of the marble. She took a photo and checked her watch again before sitting down on the rucksack. The sun was getting stronger and she could feel its rays warming her bare arms. She would stay for a while and have a few minutes to herself. Time alone was a precious commodity these days.

There was a kind of solace in tending Lucy's grave. Maddie was able to do for her what she wasn't able to do for Greta. It might not be much, but it went some way towards filling the void. In front of the headstone was a small oblong marble kerb filled with white quartz chips and she began to pick out the pieces of twig and leaf that had gathered there. As her fingers worked, her thoughts revolved around her sister. Where had it all gone wrong?

As kids, they'd been close, allies in the face of their mum's manic restlessness. Never staying in one place for more than a year had been a strange, nomadic way to live, but Kim Layne had always believed that the grass was greener someplace else. They'd travelled the length and breadth of the country, settling in cities, towns and country villages only to be quickly uprooted again.

Maddie had soon learned that there was little point in making new friends and she and her sister had relied on each other for company. With Greta being four years younger, she had always felt protective towards her. They'd rarely disagreed, shared the same sense of humour and had a common understanding. They even looked the same, with their long, glossy chestnut hair – an inheritance from their frequently absent father, Conrad – and the slender frame and hazel eyes of their mother.

But later it had all changed. Maddie frowned, her brows bunching together. When was that exactly? After she had gone to university, she thought, when Greta was left on her own. At Christmas everything had been fine, at Easter too, but on returning for the summer holidays, Maddie had found a sister she barely recognised. She hadn't just become sullen and argumentative, but downright hostile.

'It's just a phase,' her mother had said dismissively. 'Teenage hormones. She'll grow out of it.'

But Maddie hadn't been so sure. There was something reckless, something hard and brittle about Greta that hadn't been there before. She had a sudden image of her leaning against the kitchen sink with her arms folded across her chest, her chin jutting out, her eyes flashing with contempt.

'Archaeology,' she'd said sneeringly. 'I mean, why are you even doing that? What's the point? It's just old bones and dirt and bits of pot and stuff.'

'It's more than that.'

Greta had curled her lip. 'Oh yeah? Who cares about all those dead people? It's boring.'

'It's not boring.'

'*You're* boring.' And with those words, delivered as smartly as a blow, Greta had given a snort and flounced out of the room.

Maddie winced at the memory, wondering why that particular moment had stuck so vividly in her mind. Perhaps it was because it marked the beginning of the end of their closeness. Old bones, she thought, raising her face to look around the cemetery. Well, there was certainly no shortage of those around here.

It was a year or so later that their mother had made the ultimate mistake of moving to London and, more specifically, the East End. Why had she chosen Kellston? Maddie still didn't know. Something to do with one of her causes, probably. She was keen on causes – feminism, human rights, animal rights, anti-racism, anti-war, global warming – but her enthusiasms were as changeable as her postcode.

It wasn't long after the move that Greta started bunking off school, smoking and drinking and hanging with the other local drop-outs from the Mansfield estate. Then, when she was sixteen, she'd had the misfortune to meet Bo Vale. He was twenty-three, a tall, black, handsome, cocky guy who liked to flash the cash. Anyone could see that he was trouble, but maybe that was what Greta was looking for. It wasn't long before she fell pregnant, and nine months later she gave birth to a son.

Maddie smiled as she thought about Zac. He was the one good thing, the *only* good thing to have come out of the relationship. She had no idea if the pregnancy had been planned or not – Greta was barely talking to her by then – but the child had probably been conceived in the same careless way in which her sister appeared to do everything else. Anyway, Greta had moved in with Bo on the Mansfield estate and two years later she was dead.

Maddie's smile quickly faded. Not just dead but murdered. And whose fault was that? A gangland killing, the cops reckoned, but she placed the blame firmly at Bo's door. He'd worked for the Streets, a local family of villains that by all accounts pretty much ran Kellston.

She'd never liked him. What was there to like? They say never judge a book by its cover, but that's all there was to him – a man who lived outside the law, who was all show and no substance, a man who had managed to get Greta murdered.

Angrily she pushed deeper into the white quartz chips, churning them up. She wanted to shake him, scream at him, make him tell her what had happened, but it was too late for that. He was dead too, shot through the head, his corpse rolled into the Thames. He had died on the same night as Greta. His body had snagged on the tow rope of a boat, but hers had never been found. There was blood, though, *her* blood as well as his, on the path where they must have been standing.

Maddie didn't like to think about those last few seconds of her sister's life, of the terror she must have felt. It made her feel sick inside. What had Greta got involved in? What was she even doing there that night? The police had found out nothing. The investigation had dragged on for months, but no one had been arrested. There was, she knew, little chance of the truth ever coming out now.

She took a few deep breaths. As her anger subsided, she withdrew her hand, sighed and began to smooth out the chips. It was then, in the far left corner of the kerb, that she noticed a tiny glint in the sunlight. A piece of foil or shiny paper, she presumed, as she casually reached across to retrieve it. But what she pulled out was something quite different. For a moment she stared at it, astonished. It was a gold ring, a wedding band, and judging from the size, it was a woman's.

Maddie held it up between the thumb and finger of her right hand. She examined it some more, holding it closer to her eyes and squinting. Engraved on the inner rim were just two words: *For ever.* What was the ring doing here? It was hard to tell how old it was, but it didn't look thin or worn. She couldn't figure out when it had been put on the grave. She was sure, absolutely sure, that it hadn't been here six months ago, when she'd first starting tending the plot. She had removed all the chips to clear out the debris that had gathered between them and would have spotted it for sure. And it couldn't have been dropped – it would have been lying on the surface – so someone must have buried it.

She placed the ring in the palm of her left hand, wondering what to do next. Intrigued, she glanced over at the headstone. Perhaps it had been Lucy's. From the inscription there was no indication that she'd been married, but then there was nothing to say that she hadn't been either. But not to Cato, she thought. The name on the stone was Rivers. Should she mention it to him or keep it to herself?

After a moment's reflection, she decided that the best thing, the right thing to do was to simply put it back. If someone wanted the ring left there, it was none of her business. She'd push it down between the chips and pretend she'd never seen it.

She was leaning forward, about to bury the ring again, when she heard a movement behind her. First there was a small rustling sound and then the distinctive crack of breaking twigs. She got to her feet, turned and peered into the undergrowth, but it was too dense for her to be able to see anyone.

'Hello?'

She was greeted by silence.

'Hello?' she said again.

Nothing.

Maddie took a few steps along the narrow curved path. 'Rick?' Rick Mallory was one of the cemetery workers. Although a pleasant, easy-going kind of guy, he had a questionable sense of humour and was more than capable of trying to put the wind up her. 'Come on, stop messing. I know it's you.'

She thought she caught the whiff of a cigarette. Not Rick, then. He didn't smoke. Or had she just imagined the smell? She sniffed the air again. Perhaps she'd been mistaken. But she wasn't wrong about the feeling that was rolling through her body. There was someone out there, someone watching her. She was absolutely certain of it.

She stopped dead in her tracks, a thin shiver rattling down her spine. Warning bells were going off in her head. She held her breath and listened. The air seemed unnaturally still, heavy with foreboding. She wasn't usually the nervous sort, but this was the loneliest part of the cemetery; even if you cried out, it was unlikely that anyone would hear. For a moment she remained frozen, her feet glued to the ground, but then the adrenalin kicked in.

Instinctively, she turned tail and fled, snatching up the rucksack as she passed the grave.

She sprinted towards the main path, her feet barely touching the ground. She ran as if she had the Devil at her heels, her lungs pumping, her heart thrashing in her chest. Panic had engulfed her and her single thought was flight.

She reached the central thoroughfare in record time and it was only then that she glanced back over her shoulder. No one was following her. As soon as she realised this, she slowed to a jog before making her way to the nearest wooden bench. She threw the rucksack on to the seat, leaned forward from the waist and waited for her breathing to get back to normal.

What had happened? She wasn't entirely sure. Now that she was on safe terrain – there were people walking through the cemetery on their way to work – a wave of relief flowed over her. Then she began to wonder if she'd overreacted. She'd got spooked all right. Someone or something had been lurking in those bushes, but it could have been a cat or even an urban fox searching for a meal. Maybe thinking about Greta's murder had made her overly jumpy.

She stood up straight again and stared in the direction she'd come from. No, she'd been right to run, to follow her instincts. You never knew who was hanging around. There were rumours of homeless people living rough in the crypts, of junkies and drunks, of devil-worshippers who gathered at night to try and raise the dead. Granted, most of these stories had come from Rick Mallory, so there was no accounting for their veracity. Personally, she had never experienced anything to worry her – well, not until now.

It was only as she leaned over to get the bottle of water from the rucksack that she realised she was still grasping the ring in her hand. Unfolding her fingers, she gazed at it again. The plain gold band, still mysterious, seemed to have acquired a darker quality, as if it was in some way connected to what had just happened.

She rolled it in her palm, frowning as she pondered on what to do next. The ring belonged with the grave, but its return would have to wait until her next visit. She was not prepared to take the risk of going back there today. With the decision made, she slipped the gold band into the back pocket of her jeans, picked up the rucksack and set off towards the exit.

Maddie glanced at the cemetery office as she went past, wondering if she should mention anything to the manager. She thought not, but then had a change of heart. What if some psycho *was* lurking in the bushes? What if another woman came along who didn't get away in time? She would never be able to forgive herself.

She stopped, retraced her steps, pushed open the heavy glass door and went inside.

2

The walls of the office were painted a utilitarian shade of magnolia. There was a wooden floor, two desks, a few chairs, a bank of filing cabinets and a potted palm standing in a pale blue pot. It was cool inside, the fan already whirring in preparation for another scorching day. The chill air made Maddie's bare arms come out in goosebumps.

There was no sign of the manager, Bob Cannon, but his secretary was standing by the photocopier as a stream of A4 sheets rolled out into the tray. Delia Shields looked to be in her early fifties and had a thin face, cropped brown hair and a pair of shrewd grey eyes. She was the type of woman who if not perhaps embracing middle age did nothing to try and disguise it. Her clothes were smart but not stylish, and she wore little make-up. Maddie didn't know her well. She had introduced herself when she'd first started working at the cemetery, but since then they hadn't had any contact.

Delia moved away from the machine and came over to the desk. 'Good morning. Lovely day, isn't it?'

'Lovely,' Maddie echoed.

'What can I do for you?'

Maddie noticed her gaze slide sideways towards the machine and knew that her presence was if not exactly unwelcome, certainly an interruption. She hesitated, in two minds again as to whether to say anything. Ever since Greta's murder – when the whole family had been under the intrusive glare of the media – she had developed an aversion to making a fuss or drawing attention to herself. Still, now that she was here, it would be stupid and possibly irresponsible to leave without reporting the incident.

'Look, it could be nothing, but . . . ' Maddie, not wanting to look a fool, embroidered the truth a little. 'Well, there's a bloke hanging around by the old path that used to lead down to the chapel. I thought you might want to check it out.'

'Oh,' said Delia, her brows arching. 'Was he . . . ? Did he . . . ?'

'No, no, he didn't do anything. He was just kind of lurking in the bushes. I wouldn't have mentioned it, only he seemed to be acting a bit suspiciously.' Maddie gave a light shrug of her shoulders. 'I'm not sure. It might all be completely innocent, but . . . '

'Better safe than sorry. Absolutely. You were right to let me know.' Delia looked over Maddie's shoulder and made a beckoning gesture with her right hand. Maddie turned her head and saw Rick Mallory striding towards the office. He came through the door with his usual swagger and that familiar grin on his face.

'Morning, ladies. And how are we today?'

Maddie saw Delia Shields frown at the trail of grass that his boots left on the floor. However, seeing as she was the one who'd invited him in, she could hardly complain about the mess he was making.

'Rick, do me a favour and take a look round D Section, will

you? I think there might be a man hanging about. This young lady, er ... '

'Maddie,' Maddie reminded her.

'Yes, of course. Maddie. She was tending one of the graves and there was someone hiding in the bushes.'

Rick gave a nod. 'Sure. No problem.' He glanced at Maddie. 'You okay? You get a look at the geezer?'

'I'm fine. Sorry, no, I didn't see him clearly.' She wasn't about to admit, especially to him, that she hadn't set eyes on the bloke at all. The last thing she wanted was to come across as some hysterical female who jumped at the sight of her own shadow. 'I got the impression he was trying to hide. It was over by the old path, near the Rivers grave.'

Delia gave a start, flinching at the name, and her forehead furrowed into a frown. '*Lucy* Rivers?'

'That's the one.'

'Oh, I didn't realise that anyone was taking care of it these days.' Delia paused for a second, visibly flustered, but then rapidly recovered her composure. 'Well, I'll leave it to you, Rick. Let me know if you think we should call the police.' She gave Maddie a thin smile. 'Nice to see you again. Thanks for the tip-off.'

Maddie, having been dismissed, followed Rick out of the office. She was simultaneously bemused and intrigued by Delia's reaction, wishing she'd had the nous to ask a few more questions when she'd had the opportunity. It was too late now. 'That was odd,' she murmured.

'What's that?'

'How does she know about the Lucy Rivers grave? It's been abandoned for years. I had to clear away the weeds just to find the name.'

Rick Mallory placed his hands on his hips. He was a tall, good-looking man in his early thirties, his skin tanned brown

27

by the summer sun. 'Are you kidding me? Delia Shields knows everything about everything. Well, about this cemetery at least. She's worked here for years.'

'But there are thousands of graves. And she seemed sort of . . . I don't know, kind of surprised that it was being tended.'

Rick's shoulders lifted and fell in a casual shrug. 'Did she?'

'Yes, she did.' Maddie studied his face for a moment, wondering how he could have failed to notice. But then again, men failed to notice all kinds of things. 'I thought so, anyway.'

'Do you want to come with me, point out exactly where this bloke was?'

'Why? Are you too scared to go on your own?'

Rick's mouth slid into a grin again. 'What if he's a flasher and gets his bits out? It could scar me for life.'

'I'm sure you'll cope. You're a big boy now.'

'Well, I've never been one to brag, but . . .'

Maddie raised her eyes to the heavens. 'Spare me the details! I'd like to keep my breakfast in my stomach if that's all right with you.'

Rick laughed. 'Come on, then. Let's get over there before he does a runner.'

She was pretty sure that her own hundred-metre sprint would have been enough to make the bloke take off in the opposite direction, but she was still curious to find out if he had left any evidence of his presence. Although she wouldn't have dared to go back on her own – not this morning, at least – now that she had company, it didn't feel so daunting. She glanced at her watch again. 'Okay, let's do it, but we'll have to be quick. I've got to be at work by ten.'

They set off at a smart pace towards the older section of the cemetery, Maddie having to trot to keep up with his longer stride. 'So where's Eli today?' she asked. 'I thought you two were joined at the hip.'

'He's around someplace. Up top, I think, measuring out. We've got a couple of burials tomorrow.'

Suddenly, Maddie found herself wondering if Eli Glass had been the man in the bushes.

He was a small, strange, furtive sort of bloke and had been working at the cemetery for even longer than Delia. She didn't think he'd spoken more than ten words to her since she'd first started tending the graves, and all of those had been a muttered 'Morning', his mouth turned down at the corners and his gaze quickly sliding away as if her very presence in some way offended him. 'He doesn't say much, does he?'

'He's the quiet type.'

'He's that all right.' But didn't they say that it was the quiet ones you had to watch? Maybe Eli got his kicks out of lurking in the undergrowth and spying on women. 'What do you two talk about all day?'

'Oh, you know: world peace, the state of the economy, the usual chit-chat.'

'That must make the time pass. What about beer, women and football?'

'Ah, now you're just being sexist. There's a law against that, you know.'

Maddie smiled back at him. 'You're right. Please accept my heartfelt apologies.'

'Apology accepted,' he said, as they turned on to the side path. 'And you'd be surprised what Eli talks about. Sometimes he even tells me what the voices are saying.'

She raised her eyebrows. 'Huh? What voices are those?'

'The voices of the spirits. All those dead people chattering away, trying to make themselves heard. Now, some folk can't hear them, but to Eli, they're as clear as a bell.'

Maddie looked up at him, her eyes widening. 'Jesus, tell me you're kidding.'

'Straight up.'

'Don't you find that a little worrying?'

Rick laughed again. 'Nah, he's harmless enough. Anyway, who's to say he's wrong? Maybe he's one of those psychics, able to tune in to the other world.'

She kept her gaze on his face, wondering if he was actually being serious or if this was just another of his wind-ups. 'For real, or are you having me on?'

Rick put his hand on his heart. 'Swear to God. He reckons he can hear them, and who am I to call him nuts?'

Maddie gave a shudder as they approached the grave of Lucy Rivers. 'Bizarre,' she murmured.

'And the voices are especially strong round these parts. So Eli reckons. Men, women, kids – all of them with something to say, and most of it none too pretty. Yeah, it's real busy round here. Seems like the spirits aren't resting too easy.'

'You don't really believe in that ghost stuff, do you?'

Suddenly, he stopped dead in his tracks, his body becoming rigid. 'What's that?'

Maddie started, her heart missing a beat. 'What?' she asked, her eyes darting frantically from side to side before finally coming to rest on his face again. He was grinning from ear to ear. 'You bastard,' she said, slapping him on the arm. 'Cut it out. I don't scare that easy.'

'You just jumped three feet off the ground.'

'Did not.'

'Yes, you did.'

Maddie gave a snort. 'Anyone ever tell you how annoying you are?'

'Frequently.' He walked past the grave and on to the narrow, winding path that was so overgrown as to be almost invisible. There were tall stinging nettles, clumps of buttercups and wild briar roses. 'This where you saw the geezer?'

30

'Yes, in among the bushes there.'

Maddie followed behind, her gaze shifting between the undergrowth and Rick's tall, lean body. Today he was wearing faded jeans and a dark blue shirt with the sleeves rolled up. Through the thin cotton, she could see the contours of the muscles on his upper arms. His hair, usually the colour of wheat, had been bleached by the sun so that now it was streaked with a paler blond. She took all this in, aware that she was paying more attention to him than the job in hand. Well, she could look, couldn't she? A girl deserved a few small pleasures in life.

Rick veered off to the right, strolling round the old ivy-clad mausoleum of the Belvedere family. It was about seven feet square and built of a grey brick that had weathered to a silvery colour. There was a heavy arched door and he pressed against it with the palm of his hand. 'Could have been someone checking out a place to kip.'

She pulled a face. 'Do people actually do that? I mean, isn't it full of coffins?'

'Gets cold at night, even in this weather. Beggars can't be choosers.'

'I guess,' she said, wondering what it would be like to be so desperate that sleeping with the dead became a viable option. A thin shiver ran through her. The mausoleum had been built in the nineteenth century, and she read through the inscriptions, the list of six Belvederes interred in the tomb. Once, she thought, they must have been a prominent family, wealthy enough to afford the more ostentatious kind of burial place. Now, all of them were long gone, all of them forgotten.

'Still locked,' he said, moving away. 'And there's no sign of anyone trying to get in.'

Maddie was pondering on the transient nature of life when she glanced at the ground near the foot of the door and saw a

31

couple of cigarette stubs partly crushed into the earth. She crouched down and picked one up with her fingertips. 'Look at this,' she said, straightening up again and holding it out.

Rick shoved his hands in his pockets as if to indicate that he had no intention of removing the item from her fingers. 'It's a fag end. So what?'

'It's a fresh fag end. Don't you think? I thought I smelled cigarette smoke when I was here earlier.'

Rick looked dubious. 'It hasn't rained for ages. That butt could have been there for weeks.'

'I reckon it was his. And there are two of them close together, like he was standing here for a while.' She withdrew her hand, brought the cigarette end close to her eyes and studied it carefully. 'Which rules out your theory about him being a homeless person.'

'How do you figure that out?'

'What kind of down-and-out smokes packet cigarettes like these? They cost an arm and a leg these days. Wouldn't they be more likely to roll their own?'

'Unless he picked them up off the street.'

Although his line of reasoning was perfectly viable, Maddie refused to accept it. 'No, this wasn't a tramp. I'm sure of it.'

Rick gave a small shake of his head, his expression one of amusement. 'Okay, Miss Marple, so what if you are right? Now we know our lurker likes a smoke, what next? Should we call the cops and get them to run a DNA test on the evidence?'

'Oh, mock me if you like, but I bet it's true.' However, being certain of this made her feel more nervous rather than less. A random tramp searching for shelter was one thing, but a man deliberately hiding was quite another. She stared back along the path. Yes, you could just see Lucy's grave from here. The guy could have been watching her from the moment she'd arrived. This gave her an uneasy feeling, a shifting in the pit of her stomach.

'Well, whoever it was, he's obviously scarpered. I'll keep an eye out, check back every now and again.'

'Sounds like a plan,' she said, chucking the cigarette end into the weeds. 'I'd better get off or I'll be late.'

They walked in single file back to the start of the path. As they went past Lucy's grave, she noticed the discarded flowers still lying on the grass and bent to pick them up. As she did so, she felt a light blush rise to her cheeks, wondering if Rick would guess at her reason for having left them there. Would he realise that she'd taken off like a bat out of hell, or would he simply presume that she was the type of lazy grave tender who didn't bother to take away the rubbish? On balance, she wasn't sure which of these options was worse.

'Oh,' she said, trying to make her voice sound casual. 'I forgot about these.' And then as soon as she'd spoken, she wished that she hadn't. Now it sounded like she was making excuses.

'There's a bin down the way.'

'I know,' she said, more sharply than she'd intended.

He gave her a sideways glance, but didn't pursue the subject.

They were silent until they hit the main path and then he said, 'So, you got any plans for Friday night?'

Maddie shook her head. 'Nothing special.'

'You should come down the Fox, have a few drinks.'

'Maybe,' she said. It wasn't the first time he'd suggested it and she was never sure whether he meant the invitation as a date or was simply being matey. It was ages since she'd been asked out by a guy. She was out of touch with courtship rituals and found it hard to interpret the signals. What had once come so easily to her – there'd been a time when she was never short on offers – now felt like a complicated dance to which she'd forgotten the steps. 'I'll have to see if I can get a babysitter.'

'How's your Zac doing, then?'

Your Zac. Even after all this time, Maddie hadn't quite got used to hearing those words. Six years ago, when she'd first started taking care of him, she had always told people that he wasn't actually her son. It had felt disloyal to Greta to claim him as her own. But now she no longer bothered to explain. The story was a long and painful one, and somehow it was easier – and less upsetting – to let the presumption lie.

'He's fine,' she said. 'He's going to one of those daytime activity camps at the moment, so that keeps him out of trouble.' Without the extra cash from the grave-tending, and especially from the mysterious Cato, she would have struggled to afford the fees. 'My friend Shauna picks him up in the afternoon and drops him off at his grandparents'. They look after him until I get home from work, but they're getting on a bit, so I don't like to impose. It's hard work taking care of an eight-year-old.'

'It must be tough,' he said, 'bringing up a kid on your own.'

They went past the bin and she dumped the wilted flowers in it. 'I'm not completely on my own. Like I said, I've got help.' In truth, without Bo's parents – Winston and Alisha – she would have struggled to cope. Her own mother had taken off to Portugal shortly after Greta's death, making it clear that her child-raising days were over and that she had no intention of taking on another. And as for her father, well, when it came to family responsibilities, he hardly qualified as Dad of the Year.

'Enjoying the camp, then, is he?'

'Yes, loving it, but not as much as I am. He's so worn out by the time he comes home I barely get a peep out of him.'

'Now that's worth paying for.'

'Every penny,' she agreed. She was on the verge of asking if he had any kids of his own, but then thought twice about it. What if he thought she had an ulterior motive, that she was sussing him out as possible boyfriend material? That wouldn't be good.

It might make her look desperate, and no girl wanted to be placed in that particular category.

They arrived at the main path that led in a northerly direction to the top part of the cemetery and in the southerly to the high-street exit near Kellston Station. Rick stopped and there was one of those slightly awkward pauses as if neither of them was quite sure what to say before they separated. Maddie looked at her watch again even though she already knew the time.

'So . . .' he murmured.

'I'd better go,' she said, 'but thanks for being so brave.'

'No problem.' He rocked back a little on his heels. 'We gravediggers are renowned for our chivalry and courage.'

'And modesty,' she said. 'You mustn't forget modesty.'

'Well, I didn't like to mention it, but . . .'

She smiled. 'See you around, then.'

'Sure. See you around.'

She had only gone a few feet when he called out to her again.

'Oh, and, Maddie?'

She turned, wondering if he would mention the Fox again. 'Yeah?'

'Take care, huh?'

'You too.' She gave him a wave and continued along the path, aware of a mingling sense of disappointment and relief. Quickly she brushed the feelings aside. What was the matter with her? It wasn't as if she even had time for a boyfriend. No, she definitely didn't. With two jobs to do and a child to take care of, with all the washing, cleaning and cooking, there were barely enough hours in the day as it was.

Maddie raised her face to the sun and felt the warm rays spread across her skin. There she went, making excuses again. When it came to relationships, she was always full of them: reasons why she couldn't, why she shouldn't. It was years since she'd even been out with a man. And yet other women managed it. There were plenty of single mums out there who didn't stay home alone every night.

'What's the matter with you?' she murmured.

But she already knew the answer. It was fear that prevented her from getting involved, fear of loving someone and losing them. Greta's death had shaken her to the very core. The only person she allowed herself to love was Zac, but even that love was shrouded in anxiety. She was not his real mother and never could be. What if she got it wrong? What if she let him down? Sometimes she woke up in the middle of the night, her heart racing, her skin clammy with dread. Staring into the darkness, she would clench her hands into two tight fists, praying that nothing bad would happen.

Maddie had almost reached the tall wrought-iron gates that led out on to the street when she heard the sound of footsteps hurrying behind. She flinched and turned sharply, her nerves still on edge after the episode at the grave. But it was only Delia Shields.

'Sorry,' Delia said, catching up with her. 'I didn't mean to . . . I was just wondering if I could have a quick word?'

'Of course.'

Delia hesitated, the tip of her tongue snaking out to dampen her dry lips. Her hands did a curious dance in the air. 'Er . . . I hope you don't mind me asking, but I was . . . I was just curious as to who'd employed you to tend the Lucy Rivers grave.'

Maddie gazed back at the woman. Delia's face had a tight, strained look. 'Lucy Rivers?' she repeated, playing for time. Although there was nothing strictly confidential about the work she did – she was hardly a doctor or a priest – a part of her still felt that the question wasn't appropriate. Mr Cato paid her and that, as far as she was concerned, gave him the right to privacy unless he told her otherwise. 'Why? Did you know her?'

Delia hesitated again, a red stain appearing on her cheeks.

'Er ... no, not exactly ... Only ... the family ... the family are curious.'

Maddie frowned. She was pretty sure that Delia was lying. And if Lucy's family were so interested, why had they ignored the grave for so long? It didn't make any sense. 'I'm sorry,' she said, 'I don't really think it's my place to say.'

Delia's eyes narrowed. 'What do you mean?'

'Exactly that. I can't give out the names of my clients.'

'Oh, don't be ridiculous!'

Maddie gave a thin smile. If she'd had any doubts, her mind was now made up. 'Look, I really have to go. I'm sorry I can't help.' She turned and walked off towards the street.

'It's him, isn't it?' Delia called out after her.

Maddie glanced over her shoulder. 'Who do you mean?'

'That bastard! That bastard Cato!'

Maddie stopped, almost jumping at the viciousness in her voice. The sensible, polite middle-aged secretary had morphed into a snarling harridan. She stared at the woman, shocked by the transformation. Delia's mouth was slightly open, a gob of spittle resting in the left-hand corner, her eyes blazing with fury. What was going on? Well, whatever it was, she didn't want to get involved. Without another word, without even bothering to reply, she hurried through the gates, eager to escape the madness.

3

Maddie tried to maintain a pleasant expression as the couple in front of her changed their minds for the third time about whether they wanted a striped or plain parasol to go with the bench set they'd decided to buy. The girl, who had pink sunburned shoulders, pulled a face as her gaze flicked indecisively from one to the other.

'What do you think, babe? Which one's gonna go best?'

The bloke nodded towards the red-and-white-striped version. 'That one. Yeah, let's get that one.'

'You reckon?'

'Yeah.'

But the girl still dithered. 'I dunno. Maybe. I do like that one – the colours are nice – but I'm not sure if . . . '

Maddie had to make a conscious effort not to raise her eyes to the heavens. For the most part she enjoyed working at Marigolds – being surrounded by plants usually had a calming effect on her – but today she'd been consigned to the garden furniture section and her patience was starting to fray. Where she longed to be was in one of the greenhouses or in among the roses with the peaty smell of the earth in her nose. Instead, she was stuck out on the hot concrete with the sun beating down on the top of her head.

Maddie found her attention wandering. The events of the morning kept revolving in her mind, first the incident at the grave, then her conversation with Rick and finally the confrontation with Delia Shields. What had made the woman turn like that? There was clearly some kind of history between her and Cato. And she was still no closer to knowing what his connection was to Lucy Rivers. Automatically, her hand went to her back jeans pocket, checking that the wedding ring was still there.

'Do you have this in yellow and white?'

'I'm sorry?' said Maddie, preoccupied.

'Yellow and white,' the girl repeated. 'Or pink and white? What other colours do you have?'

With an effort, Maddie painted the smile back on her face. 'Just the ones that are on display, but we can order other colours if you like. It'll mean waiting, though. It usually takes a week to ten days.'

'Nah, we don't want to wait,' the guy said. 'Let's take the red and white.' He glanced at his girlfriend. 'Yeah? Shall we do that, babe?'

The girl shrugged. 'Maybe we'll have another look round.'

Maddie would have left them to it if she hadn't noticed her manager, Paul Spencer, hovering by the sun loungers. He had an anxious, twitchy look, as if he was planning to intervene before she let an easy sale slip through her fingers. Quickly she got her head into gear. Money was tight and she couldn't afford to lose this job.

'It is nice, isn't it? The red's very striking. It's the last one we've got in this colour.' She had no idea if this was true or not –

there could be another twenty sitting in the stockroom for all she knew – but she was determined now to make the sale. 'I think it's a really good choice.'

'You see?' the bloke said. 'If we don't get it now, then ...'

'I suppose,' the girl said.

'And we deliver,' Maddie said. 'That's no problem. If you'd like to come inside, I can take all your details.' She began walking away, praying that they'd follow her.

Amazingly, they did. Three minutes later, the deal was done, the bench set and parasol were paid for, and her indecisive customers had left.

It was cool inside and Maddie lingered for a moment, appreciating the air conditioning. She gazed through the window and saw Paul giving his salesman's spiel to a bloke standing by the barbecues. Personally, she didn't like pressuring people into buying stuff – in her opinion, they either wanted something or they didn't – but she had no desire to get on the wrong side of her manager. If she lost this job, she might not get another in a hurry. There wasn't much call for archaeologists in Kellston, and she wasn't qualified for anything else.

Maddie's heart sank as she returned to the concrete forecourt with its hot metal tables and chairs, its arbours, gazebos, water features, pots and planters, and endless rows of solar lights. She remembered the job she had been forced to give up and how once upon a time she had always looked forward to going to work.

It was six years now since that fateful phone call had changed her life for ever. No, she wasn't going to think about that. She plumped up the cushions on a swing seat and shifted the deckchairs back into line. She tried to think about something else, but the memory refused to go away.

She had been twenty-three, working on a dig in Cornwall, when the call had come from her mother. Not the kind of news that could be absorbed easily. Murder. That didn't happen to families like theirs. It happened to other people, other sad, unfortunate people. Cold – that's what she'd felt, like someone had plunged an icy dagger through her heart.

'You have to come home,' her mother had said.

And of course she'd had to, wanted to, needed to. But what she hadn't realised then was that once she'd returned, she wouldn't be leaving in a hurry. Six years later and she was still in Kellston. It was the longest time she had ever lived anywhere and sometimes she yearned to be on the move again.

Maddie's fingers tightened around the top of a deckchair as she had a sudden vivid image of the last time she'd seen her sister. It had been at the flat in Carlton House, a few months before she'd died. Greta had been standing at the window, staring down at the grey, sprawling walkways of the Mansfield estate. Zac, who must have just turned two, was playing by her feet. What had they talked about? She couldn't recall. All she could remember were Greta's short bitten-down fingernails with their chipped black nail varnish. And that expression on her face, sullen and bored, as if Maddie was an unwanted visitor who, for the sake of politeness, had to be endured.

A thin sigh escaped from between Maddie's lips. She should have tried harder to heal the breach between them. She should have made more of an effort. Although she had long since ceased to understand Greta, she had never stopped loving her. Their lives had gone in different directions, but if she'd taken the time to talk to her, to reach out, then maybe the relationship could have been salvaged. Instead, irritated and bemused by her sister's attitude, she had made her excuses and left. Jogging down the nine flights of worn stone steps, she had felt only an eagerness to get away from the estate and the pall of despair that hung over it.

Now it was too late for reconciliations. The clock couldn't be turned back. Maddie closed her eyes for a second and blinked them open again. It made her angry and frustrated that Greta's killer was still out there somewhere. Maybe she had walked past him on the street. Maybe he drank in the Fox. Maybe he was one of the young hooded men who hung around the Mansfield with their cold, angry faces and their pockets full of smack.

She felt an ache in her chest, a longing for justice. It wouldn't bring Greta back, but at least it would provide some kind of closure. There must be other people who knew the truth about what had happened. The police, she suspected, had lost interest in the case. Officially, it remained open, but the files were stacked up on a dusty shelf by now, abandoned and forgotten. The trail, if there had ever been one, had long since gone cold.

Maddie released her hold on the deckchair and took a step back. Her hands felt damp. Although Zac had the right to know why his parents had been murdered, it seemed unlikely that he'd ever do so. She feared for the effect this history would have on his future. If she could have wrapped him up in cotton wool, protected him from the horror of it all, she would have, but nothing could change the past.

She peered up at the clear blue sky, squinting against the sun. All she could do was carry on, one day at a time, hoping that the worst was over. Yes, that was something to cling on to.

And yet she couldn't quite believe it. A part of her still lived in fear of what the future might bring. An odd chill feeling crept into her bones as if someone had just walked over her grave. She gave a shiver, lowered her gaze and glanced uneasily around her.

4

Lena Gissing made some final adjustments to her fine blonde hair before pausing to gaze more intently at her reflection. The long gilt-edged mirror in the hall told her two things: one, that she wasn't a young woman any more, the other that she didn't look as old as she actually was. Surgery, Botox and cosmetic fillers were her constant allies in the battle against ageing, and it was a war that was waged with stubborn determination. She refused to give in, to give up her beauty. It was a defence, a shield against all the crap in her life. So long as she had her looks, she could survive. She could do *anything*.

Lena gave a small satisfied nod. Yes, she could easily pass for forty, she thought, even late thirties in a more forgiving light. She took a few steps back in order to view the bigger picture. The short white sleeveless dress she was wearing showed off her long, shapely legs as well as her tan. Her body, on the whole, was still slim and firm, her curves still inviting enough to attract admiring glances. Only her upper arms were showing some signs of wear, a slight crinkling of the skin just beneath her shoulders.

She lifted her arms and dropped them again. She frowned. She considered getting a jacket, but decided against it. It was too hot, and anyway, the person she was going to visit didn't need impressing. She put on her Prada sunglasses, picked up the car keys from the hall table and walked over to the living-room door.

'I'm off. See you later.'

Tony Gissing looked up from the paper he was reading. He was knocking on sixty, a short, stocky man with a thick neck, a pronounced beer gut and the squashed ugly face of a bulldog. What remained of his greying hair was cropped short, surrounding the ever-growing bald patch on the top of his head. He came from a long line of East End villains, all of them vicious and none of them smart. 'Where are you going?'

'Out.'

'Where's out?'

'I've already told you. Delia. Don't you ever listen? I'm going for a coffee with Delia. I won't be long.'

Tony's expression shifted to one of indifference. Women like Delia Shields didn't interest him. Unless a female was under twenty-five with breasts the size of melons and a butt worth slapping, she didn't merit more than five seconds of his attention. 'Ah, right. See you later, then.'

Lena walked out of the flat, got in the lift and glided smoothly down from the penthouse apartment to the ground floor. The foyer, filled with palms, leafy ferns and small citrus trees, had a Mediterranean feel to it. Her heels tapped on the polished marble tiles. As she left the air-conditioned space, she felt a rush of heat, as if the door to an oven had suddenly been opened.

Quickly she climbed into the red MG and pulled across the seatbelt. Driving through the gated community of Silverstone Heights, she gazed out at the detached houses, the semis, the rows of smart terraces and other smaller blocks of flats. These were all surrounded by landscaped gardens – the sprinklers were on, shooting thin jets of water across the grass – and these, in turn, by high brick walls designed to keep out the less desirable residents of Kellston.

It amused Lena to know that she was one of the 'undesirables'. The Heights had been built to protect the respectable, the law-abiding from the common riff-raff of the area. But the enemy was already within. Once, Tony Gissing had been nothing – the youngest son of a family of third-rate villains who never learned from their mistakes – but Lena had changed all that. Now he was rich, feared and respected. Now he was a force to be reckoned with.

And force, she thought with a sigh, was all he actually brought to the partnership. She didn't love Tony, didn't even like him most of the time, but they had made a deal and for the last ten years she had stuck to her side of the bargain. The marriage wasn't a particularly happy or fulfilling one, but divorce wasn't an option – they were joined by secrets, by a devilish pact that bound them together.

Still, she had made the best of a bad job. Her husband wasn't the sharpest knife in the drawer, but unlike his brothers – both of whom were currently residing at Her Majesty's Pleasure – he had the sense to realise it. When it came to business, she called the shots.

Lena had an eye for an opportunity and over the years she'd built up several thriving businesses. The best and most lucrative of these was a high-class escort service for the more discerning kind of client. MPs, judges and top corporate bosses were all on her books. When it came to sex, the weakness of men never failed to amaze her. They'd pay more for a shag with a desirable woman than most people earned in a month.

Lena never advertised her services. She didn't need to. Her

clients came by word of mouth and she always ran a check before agreeing to take them on. Her girls – all of them smart, stylish and beautiful – were able, if required, to fit into any social situation. They could be taken to lunch, to dinner or parties, without fear of their true profession being exposed. Of course, most of them never got beyond the bedroom. The majority of her clients were married men who had no desire to be seen in public with a woman who wasn't their wife.

She pulled up by the electric gates and slid her card into the slot. It had been a good choice, she knew, to come and live here. The penthouse apartment provided everything they needed. It was spacious without being grand, comfortable without being ostentatious. There was no point in drawing unnecessary attention to themselves. Other villains liked to flash the cash, to buy mansions with swimming pools, but she preferred not to advertise their wealth. So far as the taxman was concerned, Tony and Lena Gissing made their money from two legitimate car lots and a luxury car-hire service.

The gates swung smoothly open and she swept the MG forward into Silverstone Street and then down on to the High Street, where she swung a left and continued south. Delia had called her this morning, her voice sounding tight. She hadn't said what it was about, only that it was important.

'You have to come over. We need to talk.'

'What's wrong?' Lena had asked.

'Not now. I can't . . . Later. Come after five. I'll be here on my own then.'

Lena, who was generally fearless, felt a stirring of unease as she entered the cemetery and pulled up on the main thoroughfare. It was odd for Delia to summon her like this. Usually they met for coffee once or twice a month, engagements that she found tedious – they had little in common these days – but which she felt obliged to continue. They had known each other since school and some ties were hard to break.

She got out of the car, locked it and walked over to the office. Delia was waiting by the door, her arms folded across her chest, her expression one of an anxious parent waiting for a child to return home.

'Where have you been? It's almost a quarter past. I thought you weren't coming.'

Lena raised her eyebrows. 'Nice to see you too. And you know what the traffic's like at this time of day. It would have been faster to walk. Anyway, I'm here now. What's the panic?'

'There's no panic. I just ... Why don't you sit down?' Delia stood back and flapped a hand towards a desk by the window. 'I'll make coffee. Do you want coffee?'

'No. I can't stay long. What's going on?'

Delia's face twisted a little, her hands lifting and falling through the air. She walked over to a table in the corner. 'It's already made,' she said. 'You may as well have one.'

Lena tried to stem her impatience, but there was no point in trying to rush her. She had learned from experience that Delia always did things in her own good time. She pulled out a chair and sat down, watching as the other woman organised mugs and milk and sugar with her usual brisk, tidy movements.

'Is it all right if I smoke?' asked Lena, taking a pack of cigarettes from her bag.

Delia glanced over her shoulder. 'I'd rather you didn't. Not in the office. It's not allowed. Bob would have a fit.'

'Bob isn't here. I won't tell him if you don't.'

Delia's gaze flicked between Lena and the cigarettes. 'Do you have to?'

'I'll go outside if you'd rather.'

Delia waved a hand again, turning back to the coffee. 'No,

no, it doesn't matter. You go ahead. I can give the room a spray before I leave.'

Lena lit up, sat back and crossed her legs. Not for the first time, she wondered why Delia didn't do more with herself. They were the same age, both forty-eight, but nobody would have guessed. Delia was the typical spinster in her plain skirt, prim white blouse and flat, boring shoes. Her hair, a dull shade of brown, was already streaked with silver, and her make-up was minimal. If that was what was called growing old gracefully, then Lena intended to do it with as little grace as possible.

'Why do you stay here?' Lena asked.

Delia brought two mugs over from the table and placed them on the desk. She frowned at the question. 'What do you mean?'

Lena gave a low, almost inaudible sigh. Life was for living, but Delia chose to spend it surrounded by the dead. How many years had she been here now? Too many to count. She looked out of the window at the endless rows of graves. It was a morbid, depressing place. 'I mean, you could get a job any- where, somewhere more . . . I don't know, more *cheerful.*'

'I like it here.' Delia sat down, picked up her coffee and blew on the surface. 'It suits me. Why would I go anywhere else?'

Lena gave a shrug. There were lots of things about Delia she didn't understand. Her old friend's life seemed dull and con- fined. There wasn't even a man on the scene so far as she was aware. In fact, had Delia ever had a boyfriend? Still, maybe she was better off without one. In her experience, all a man ever brought was trouble. And perhaps she shouldn't judge her too harshly. She might be boring, but Delia had her good points, top of the list being her fierce and unfailing loyalty. If anyone could be relied upon, it was her.

'So,' said Lena, leaning forward, 'are you going to tell me what's going on? What's so important that it couldn't wait until tomorrow?'

Delia put the mug down without taking a drink. Her lips parted as if she intended to reply, but no words emerged.

A couple of seconds passed. Lena felt the nerves fluttering in her stomach. She forced a smile. 'Come on, hon. Spit it out. It can't be that bad.'

'He ... he's back,' Delia finally managed to splutter.

'Who's back?'

'*Him.* Cato.'

Lena jumped at the name, the shock passing through the length of her body. 'What?' She could feel the blood draining from her face. 'He can't be. Have you seen him? Has he been here?'

Delia shook her head. 'No, I don't think so.'

'So what makes you—'

'The grave, Lucy Rivers's grave. He's got a girl tending it. I only found out this morning. Who else could it be but him?'

Lena sucked hard on the cigarette before releasing the smoke in a long, thin stream. Her hand was shaking slightly. 'It can't be. It has to be someone else.'

'Like who? No one's been near that grave for years.'

'An old friend, a member of the family, perhaps.'

'There is no family. And after thirty years, why should any old friend suddenly—'

'I don't know,' Lena snapped. 'Why do people do anything? Maybe one of them has a guilty conscience.' She leaped up out of the chair and started pacing. She knew that she was grasping at straws, but that was all she had left. 'How long has this been going on?'

'I'm not sure. A few weeks, a few months. I only found out today.'

Lena walked up and down, from one side of the office to the other, before stopping abruptly by Delia's chair. She waved her cigarette in the air. 'Who is this bloody girl, anyway?'

'Her name's Maddie Layne. She's one of the regular grave tenders, been here for about a year. She's local and cheap, so she gets a bit of work.'

'And how do you know that Cato employed her?'

'I don't, not for sure, but she didn't deny it.'

Lena stared at her, a look of incredulity on her face. 'What? You came straight out and asked her?'

Delia gazed back, her shoulders lifting slightly. 'Why not? How else was I going to find out? And anyway, there's nothing wrong with my asking. I work here. I've a right to know what's going on.'

Lena reckoned a more subtle approach might have been in order, but it was too late for that now. 'So what did she say, this Maddie girl?'

'Nothing much. She got all tight-lipped and defensive, said it wasn't her place to reveal her client's name.'

Lena started pacing again, up and down, up and down. 'Which means it must be him. Shit! Jesus!' She rubbed her face as sweat prickled her temples. 'But he's still inside. I'm sure of it.'

'Well, they've got phones in there, haven't they? It doesn't take much to organise a grave tender. Or maybe he got someone else to call her.'

'But why? Why is he doing this?'

'Why does Cato do anything?' Delia said. 'To wind you up, to get under your skin. He's crazy, Lena. You should call the police.'

Lena gave a snort. 'The filth? What the hell are they going to do about it? It's not against the law to put flowers on a grave.'

'It's harassment,' Delia said. 'It's ... it's ... I don't know, threatening behaviour or something.'

Lena took a last drag on her cigarette and looked around for somewhere to stub it out. 'Oh yeah? And how am I going to explain why that is, exactly? It's not going to help any of us if the truth comes out about Lucy Rivers.'

Delia visibly paled. 'You don't think he would? Tell, I mean?'

Lena went to the sink in the corner, ran the tap, doused the cigarette and dropped it in the bin. She sat down and stared at her old friend for a moment, seeing the worry etched on her face. 'No,' she said. 'No, that's not his way. He's just sending me a message, reminding me that he's still around. He knew I'd get to hear about the grave eventually.'

'Maybe that's why she did it,' Delia murmured.

'What?'

'The girl. Maddie Layne. She came to the office this morning, going on about some bloke lurking in the bushes. She made a point of telling me that it was near the Lucy Rivers grave. Maybe . . . maybe Cato told her to do that, to make sure I knew, to make sure I told you about it.'

Lena's hands, adorned with rings, wouldn't stay still. Her long, red fingernails tapped out a sharp, erratic beat on the top of the desk. 'How often does she come here?'

'It varies, but nearly always on a Wednesday. And early in the morning, about half eight.' Delia opened a drawer, took out a sheet of paper and passed it across. 'Here, this is a list of all our grave tenders. There's no address for her, but there is a phone number.'

Lena stared at the list, but all she could see was Jay Cato's dark, brooding eyes staring back at her. She clenched her jaw, a muscle twitching angrily at the corner of her mouth. What was he playing at? Some vile, devious game, no doubt. She might have known he wouldn't let it rest. Men like Cato never forgot . . . and they never forgave either.

'What are you going to do?' Delia asked.

Lena raised her eyes. 'Do?'

'You'll have to tell Tony.'

51

Lena's upper lip curled contemptuously. 'Tony? Are you kidding me? That idiot creates more problems than he ever solves.'

'But you can't deal with this on your own.'

'Deal with what? All Cato's done is arranged for some flowers to be put on a grave.'

Delia gave a quick anxious shake of her head. 'It's more than that, Lena – you know it is. The man's twisted. He's sick. God knows what he'll do next.'

'Well, we'll have to wait and see, won't we?' Lena threw out the retort with a casualness she didn't feel. Even in front of Delia – someone she had known for over forty years – she was unwilling to show any sign of weakness. 'If he thinks he can freak me out with a few damn flowers, he's got another think coming.'

Delia's eyes widened. 'But you know what he's capable of. He . . . he . . .'

'I know what he did, hon. You don't need to remind me.' Lena folded over the piece of paper, put it in her bag and rose to her feet.

'Where are you going?'

'Home,' Lena said. 'I've got plans for this evening.'

Delia jumped up too. 'But . . .'

'But what?' said Lena. 'I'm not going to waste my time worrying about it. That's exactly what he wants and I'll be buggered if I give him the satisfaction.'

Delia walked round the desk and laid her hand on Lena's arm. 'But you'll take care? Promise me you will.'

'I'm always careful, hon.' Lena bent and kissed her on the cheek. 'Thanks for letting me know. I'll call you, huh? I'll see you soon.'

She walked out with her shoulders back and her head held high. Her face was an impassive mask. She walked over to the car as if Cato was watching, as if his eyes were drinking in every facet of her face and every step she took. She walked with a swaying insouciance as if she didn't give a damn.

After climbing into the MG, Lena glanced across at the office. Through the window she could see that Delia was still standing by the desk. In that moment, her old friend looked as old and regretful as the grey stone angels that were scattered around the cemetery. She bent over the wheel, feeling a dull, dark pain in her chest.

Quickly she reached for her cigarettes. She lit one, sucked in the smoke, started the engine and drove off. Instead of doing a U-turn, she headed for the exit on the other side. Her gaze flicked in the direction of the Lucy Rivers grave, but it was out of sight, the path hidden by the group of weeping willows.

Once she was away from the office, Lena pulled the car into the side of the thoroughfare. She needed some time alone, time to think. She opened the window and stared out across the cemetery. Hadn't she always known that one day Cato would try to get his revenge? She imagined him in that prison cell, the minutes slowly ticking by, the walls gradually closing in. He'd had years to dwell on what she had done and now it was payback time. He had loved Lucy Rivers and Lena had destroyed her.

While she sat and smoked, she contemplated her next move. She had to stay calm. She had to try and still the fear that was gathering inside her. Although she didn't underestimate her enemy, the game was far from over yet. She was Lena Gissing and that meant something. She had power and she was going to use it. Reaching into her bag, she took out her mobile and dialled. It was answered after the first ring.

'It's me,' she said. 'I've got a job for you. Find out everything you can about a girl called Maddie Layne. That's L-A-Y-N-E.' She read out the phone number from the list that Delia had given her. 'She's local, lives somewhere in Kellston. And make it quick, huh? Get back to me as soon as you can.'

Lena dropped the phone back in her bag. She flicked the ash from her cigarette on to the grass that edged the path. The thick evening air stole into the car, hot and humid. She closed her eyes, feeling the heavy drag of memory. There was, she knew, no escape from the past. Like a dark assassin, it came creeping up when you least expected it.

5

It was after six thirty before Maddie left work and started to walk home. It had been a strange, discomfiting kind of day. The evening was warm and sticky, the air tainted by traffic fumes. Despite the heat, she kept up a brisk pace, not wanting to be late picking up Zac. Alisha and Winston would never complain – they loved their grandson and would do anything for him – but they weren't spring chickens and she didn't like to take advantage.

As she made her way along the High Street, her gaze took in her surroundings. Even at the height of summer, Kellston managed to retain a depressing greyness that seemed ingrained in the very bricks of the buildings, in the road and the litter-strewn pavement. On the horizon loomed the three tall concrete towers of the Mansfield estate, a constant reminder of the sister she had lost.

Maddie stared up at the towers. Even from a distance they could be seen to be crumbling, weather-beaten with rusting balconies and broken windows. Some of the flats were boarded up, unfit for human habitation. She quickly dropped her gaze again. Kellston was said to be up-and-coming, but from where she was standing there were no significant signs of it. Squashed between Bethnal Green and Shoreditch, the borough had none of the latter's fashionable edginess. There was high unemployment, poverty and way too much crime.

It was no place, Maddie thought, to be bringing up a child. What chance did any kid stand in a place like this? But she was stuck here and so was he. Although she longed to be on the move – she had inherited her mother's itchy feet – it would be unfair and probably damaging to take him away from his beloved grandparents.

That final image of Greta invaded her mind again. The past, it seemed, was intent on haunting her today. Her thoughts slipped back to the time, six years ago, when they were all trying to come to terms with the double murder. At first, everyone had rallied round to take care of Zac. How much of it had he understood? Two years old and deprived of both his mother and his father. It was cruel and tragic. But it was Bo's parents, Winston and Alisha, who had stepped up to the mark and taken him to live with them on a permanent basis. No one had argued about it. There had been no rows, no custody battles, no tug of war over the orphaned toddler.

'It's for the best,' her mother had said. 'He knows them better than anyone else. It'll be less of an ordeal for him.'

But Maddie had observed the relief in her eyes. Kim Layne was off the hook and she was glad of it. And, if she was being completely honest, Maddie had welcomed the decision too. To acknowledge this made her feel guilty, although she had barely known Zac back then. Since he'd been born, she had only seen him half-a-dozen times.

Winston's heart attack had come out of the blue, two months later. By then Kim Layne had decamped to Portugal and had no intention of coming back. Maddie had returned to work, a job on a London dig. She had only intended to stay on in Kellston until the dig had finished, but events had overtaken her.

At twenty-three, with her career just beginning, the last thing she had wanted or needed was the responsibility of a child, but she hadn't had a choice. Alisha couldn't cope with Zac and a sick husband. She'd needed help and there was only one person who could provide it. Maddie had taken temporary leave, but it had soon become apparent that she wouldn't be going back to her old job in a hurry. Even as Winston was on the road to recovery, it was obvious that taking care of Zac full-time would be too much for the Vales.

Maddie came to Violet Road and turned right, walking along the row of small terraced houses. She could vividly recall those early days, the panic and fear that rose up in her throat every time she looked at her nephew. She was terrified of doing things wrong, of being inadequate, of not being able to cope. The burden had felt like a great dark crow pecking away at her confidence. And, although it pained her to admit it, she had felt a simmering resentment too. It was as if the rug had been pulled from under her feet, with all her hopes and dreams tumbling into oblivion.

She wondered how she had managed to get through it. She had not realised then that all Zac really needed was love and care and stability. Now she couldn't imagine her life without him. Her maternal instinct might have been slow to kick in, but she'd got there in the end. He was the most important, the most precious person in her life and she couldn't envisage a time when that would ever change.

Until Greta's death, Maddie had barely known the Vales. She hadn't taken much of an interest in them. They were just the parents of her sister's boyfriend, a boyfriend who was big trouble. If she thought about them at all, it was only to wonder why they hadn't done a better job in managing to teach him right from wrong. Her attitude had changed a lot since then.

She was thinking about this as she walked straight past number 12 and had to turn round and retrace her steps. She strolled up the front path with its terracotta pots of pink and white geraniums, pressed the bell and waited.

Alisha answered the door almost immediately. She was a tall, stout woman in her late sixties with a smile bright enough to power the National Grid. Today she was dressed in a flowing red dress with yellow flowers splashed across the hem. 'Hello, love,' she said, beckoning her over the threshold. 'Come in, come in. How are you? Lord, it's a hot one today. I'll make a brew, shall I? You'll be needing a drink after that walk. The boys are out back.'

Maddie, following her through the house to the yard at the rear, found it hard to believe that she had ever disliked Alisha and Winston. Or perhaps not disliked them so much as *judged* them. After the murders, she had decided that they were to blame for how Bo had turned out. It had to be their fault. Who else's could it have been? She felt ashamed of herself now. How stupid! How naïve! She had come to understand that it didn't matter how hard you tried, there were no guarantees when it came to raising a child.

'Maddie, Maddie!' Zac called out, running over to her with his wide grin and infectious laugh. 'Hiya. Grandpa's teaching me how to bowl. Are you going to watch? Are you going to watch me?'

'Sure I am, sweetheart.'

A makeshift set of wickets had been set up in the back yard. Winston was standing at the far end wearing his baggy trousers and an old white vest. He gave her a wave with the cricket bat and she waved back. 'Hey, Winston. How are you doing?'

'Pretty good, thanks. Just giving our boy here some tips. He's coming along real good. I reckon he'll be a pro one day.'

'Good to hear it.'

Solomon, their elder son, was sitting on the back step. He glanced up at her and nodded. 'You okay, babe?' He shifted over to make room. 'Here, park yourself. You look tired. Tough day?'

'Oh, the usual.' She turned back to the kitchen and spoke to Alisha. 'You need a hand with anything?'

'No, no, you sit down. I'll be out in a minute.'

Maddie sat down on the step beside Solomon. 'When people say you look tired, what they really mean is that you look like something the cat's dragged in.'

Solomon gave her a sidelong glance. 'You don't look like nothin' my cat ever dragged in.'

'You don't have a cat.'

He gave a shrug. 'Hell, you're right. I was just trying to make you feel better.'

Maddie raised her brows and smiled. Despite getting to know him, even to like him, she still found Solomon Vale faintly intimidating. It was his size as much as anything else. At over six foot five, he dwarfed most people. And then there were the muscles. His bulging biceps strained at the white cotton of his T-shirt.

'Are you watching?' asked Zac, as he impatiently passed the ball from one hand to the other.

'We're watching,' she said. 'I promise.'

Zac, with his short, curly black hair, chestnut-brown eyes and coffee-coloured skin, had far more of Bo's physical genes in him than Greta's. He was a sweet, nice-natured boy, but that didn't stop Maddie from stressing over his future.

The two men in this small back yard were the primary male role models in his life. She wasn't worried about Winston – he was a decent, principled, honest man – but Solomon was a

59

different kettle of fish. She didn't doubt his affection for Zac, but she was concerned about what he did for a living. He worked for the Streets, and the Streets were the biggest villains in Kellston. What if Zac grew up wanting to be just like his uncle?

Maddie gave a yawn and stretched out her arms. She wasn't going to fret about that now. It was a beautiful evening and the scent of honeysuckle hung in the air. As she breathed it in, her thoughts drifted back to the morning and her strange altercation with Delia Shields.

'Sol?' she asked.

'Yeah?'

'Does the name Cato mean anything to you?'

He pondered on it for a moment, but then shook his head. 'Nah, can't say it rings any bells. Should it?'

'What about Lucy Rivers?'

Solomon splayed his palms on his wide thighs and gave her another sideways glance. 'You want to ask me a question I *do* know the answer to?'

'Mm, I may need a while to figure that one out.'

Solomon huffed out a breath. 'See you ain't lost any of your charm since I saw you last.'

'We aim to please.'

'So why the interest? Who are these people, anyhows?'

Maddie watched Zac bowl a few wide balls in the general direction of Winston. She leaned in towards Solomon, lowering her voice. 'Oh, just something a bit weird that happened down the cemetery this morning. This grave I'm tending – a girl called Lucy Rivers – well, I was asked to take care of it by a guy called Cato. It was over the phone. We've never actually met. But it seems this man, whoever he is, isn't too popular with a certain member of the office staff. I'm just curious, I guess. I wondered if you knew anything about him.'

'You want me to ask around?'

Maddie pulled a face. 'Best not,' she said. 'It's probably nothing. I don't want to stir up trouble.'

'I can do discreet. In the exalted circles I move in, I'm renowned for my tact and diplomacy.'

'Exalted, huh?'

'Don't be fooled by my ghetto reputation.'

'Ah, is that what you call it?'

'You want me to check out this Cato guy or not?'

Maddie hesitated, in two minds as to what to say next. She *was* curious – there was no denying it – but she was cautious too. 'I don't know. I suppose. I mean, can you do it without him finding out? I don't want to get his back up. He might decide to get rid of me if he gets wind of the fact that I'm checking up on him.'

'Don't worry, babe. I won't be shouting it from the rooftops.'

'That's reassuring.'

'So that's a yes?'

Maddie hesitated again. 'Well . . . '

'Always useful to know exactly who you're working for.'

And she couldn't argue with that. Hadn't Delia Shields been less than complimentary about Cato? 'Okay,' she said. 'Go for it. And thanks. I appreciate it.'

'No problem.'

Zac bounced over to them again. 'Why are you whispering? It's rude to whisper.' He frowned at Maddie. 'You told me that.'

Maddie smiled back at him. 'We're not whispering, love. We're just talking quietly so we don't put you off.'

'You're supposed to be watching.'

'We are watching.'

Zac narrowed his eyes. He seemed dubious, as if watching and talking were two quite separate acts and fundamentally incompatible.

'Go on, then,' she urged. 'Don't keep Grandpa waiting.'

As Zac returned to his bowling, Solomon said, 'Thought I'd take him to see the dinosaurs on Friday if that's okay with you.'

'At the museum?'

'Unless you know someplace else we can find 'em.'

Maddie grinned. 'Now who's asking the difficult questions?'

'And then get something to eat, and maybe watch a movie in the evening. He might as well stay over.'

'Are you sure? You want him for the evening too?'

'Sure. I like spending time with him. It's hard, you know, with the job and all, but I've got a few days off, so ... But if you'd rather I brought him home ...'

Maddie shook her head. 'No, no, that's fine. If you're up for it, I'm not complaining.' Solomon, who'd previously been living in Chigwell, had moved back to Kellston about six months ago and got himself a flat in Barley Road overlooking the green. It was only five minutes' walk from her house, close enough if any kind of emergency arose.

'You could go out,' he said.

'Or stay in, slouch on the sofa and watch exactly what I like on the TV.'

Solomon stared at her. 'Jesus, hon, you twenty-nine or fifty-nine? You don't want to be watching TV on a Friday night. Get out on the town, chill, have a few drinks.'

Maddie was surprised that Solomon knew how old she was. She wasn't sure of his exact age, only that he was about ten years older than Bo, which meant that he had to be knocking on forty. Not that he looked it, though. He had an ageless kind of face, and he kept himself in shape.

'Go out and see some mates,' he insisted. 'Make the most of it. I don't suppose you get much time to yourself.'

'Maybe I will,' she said, thinking of Rick Mallory's invitation. A night out at the Fox could be just what she needed.

'Good. I'll come over and pick him up at – what, about half nine?'

'Half nine,' she agreed. 'I'll see you then.'

Alisha came out with a tray of mugs, and Maddie and Solomon shuffled up to make room for her on the step. As she sat drinking her tea, Maddie's thoughts began to drift again. She hoped she'd done the right thing about Cato. Extra money was hard to come by and she couldn't afford to lose those monthly cheques. But then again, she didn't have a clue as to who he actually was. She reckoned that anyone who wanted such care taking over a grave couldn't, at heart, be a bad person – but what if she was wrong? The words of Delia Shields jumped back into her head. *That bastard! That bastard Cato!*

6

Maddie filled two glasses with orange juice, poured out a bowl of cornflakes and placed the bread in the toaster. The kitchen was warm and she opened the door to let in the air. The sky was a uniform blue without a cloud in sight. It was going to be another hot day. The heatwave had been going for over a week and there was no sign of it abating.

She folded her arms across her chest and gazed out at the small back garden. It was a meagre space compared to what she'd have liked, but at least it was something. She was growing mainly vegetables – potatoes, runner beans, onions, lettuce and carrots – with a display of roses off to the right. The vegetables were a way of saving money on the shopping. The roses were her luxury. She was trying to learn as much about them as possible in the hope that she'd eventually get a permanent position as a member of the gardening staff at Marigolds. If she did that, then she would finally be freed from the drudgery of garden furniture.

Maddie, hearing the ping of the toaster, turned back towards the kitchen. She was lucky, she knew, to even have this house. It belonged to the Kellston Housing Association and had been rented by her mother when she'd first come to London with Greta. The two-up two-down was in Morton Grove. It had a couple of advantages, one being the relatively cheap rent and the other that it was close to Violet Road, where the Vales lived.

Maddie had only stayed on after her mother's departure to Portugal because of the London dig. If it hadn't been for that, the keys would have been handed back. As it was, she'd been able, as Zac's main carer, to take over the tenancy and make it a permanent home. And although she wasn't the most domesticated person in the world, she tried her best. Keeping things tidy, however, wasn't always easy; living with Zac was like living with a human hurricane.

No sooner had she thought of him than he was sitting at the kitchen table, reaching for the milk and pouring it over his cornflakes. 'Maddie?'

'Yes?'

'Can we have a dog, please?'

She sat down opposite him, putting her elbows on the table. 'I don't think so, love. Not just at the moment.' She felt bad about saying no, but she had to be practical. Money was tight and she couldn't afford another mouth to feed, let alone any vet's bills that might come along.

'Kyle's got a dog.'

'I know.' Kyle Powers was Zac's best friend and his partner in crime. The two of them were virtually inseparable, attending the same school and spending most early evenings and weekends together. His mum, Shauna, lived at the end of the road, and although she was five years younger than Maddie, they'd become friendly too. It was a friendship of convenience more than anything else, but over the years they'd grown used to one another.

'So why can't we?'

Maddie didn't like to bang on about money and so she tried a different tack. 'Well, his mum's at home all day. Dogs don't like being on their own, sweetheart. They get lonely.'

Zac ate some of his cereal while he thought about this. 'I could stay home,' he said. 'Keep him company.'

Maddie grinned at him. 'Nice try, buster, but you have to go to school, and I have to go to work.'

'I bet Gran would take care of him. Just in the day, you know, until we got back.'

'I think Gran's got enough to do. It wouldn't really be fair.' Maddie saw the disappointment on his face and felt the familiar stab of guilt that she couldn't give him everything he wanted. Her only solution was to try and make him laugh. 'And anyway, if we got a dog, there'd be all that poo to pick up.'

Zac giggled, spluttering out a couple of milky cornflakes. 'You don't pick up poo!'

'Sure you do. If you didn't, the pile would just grow higher and higher until you couldn't see over the top.'

Zac's eyes widened a little, half in disgust, half in fascination. 'That big?'

'Yep, as big as a house. But you don't pick it up with your hands or anything – you have to use a plastic bag and put it in the bin.'

'And then where does it go?'

'It goes to the dump with all the other rubbish.'

Maddie knew that her mother would be horrified at the conversation – bodily functions, even of dogs, was hardly suitable for breakfast talk – but Kim Layne wasn't around to protest. She was too busy saving donkeys in Portugal. As such, Maddie had to find her own way of dealing with awkward situations.

Zac finished his cereal and pushed the bowl to one side. 'So what about the dinosaurs?'

66

Maddie, unsure as to what he meant, gazed patiently back at him. 'What about them?'

'Where did all their poo go?'

She laughed. 'Ah, now, there's a question. You'll have to ask your uncle Sol about that. He's the expert on dinosaurs.' Mentioning Solomon's name reminded her that he was going to try and find out about Cato and she wondered if he'd have any news for her tomorrow. It was probably too soon, but he may have discovered something. 'Come on, eat your toast or we'll be late picking up Kyle.'

Shauna Powers was still in her dressing gown when she answered the door. She was a small, skinny girl with an oval face, cropped peroxide hair and pale blue eyes. There were piercings in her upper lip and tongue, and large gold hoops in her ears. This morning, her eyes were rimmed with red, and the faint smell of alcohol drifted from her body.

'Kyle!' Shauna yelled, looking over her shoulder. 'Are you ready? Shift your arse. Zac's here.'

'Late night?' Maddie asked.

Shauna rubbed at her eyes. 'Had some mates round. You know what it's like. You have a few beers and before you can blink, it's two in the morning.'

Maddie, although she didn't exactly approve of being drunk in charge of an eight-year-old, wasn't about to criticise anyone else's parenting skills. Instead, she gave a sympathetic nod as if she knew exactly what she meant. The truth, however, was that Zac had a more lively social life than she did. It was time that she started changing that. 'I don't suppose you fancy the Fox tomorrow night? Sol's taking Zac, so I've got the evening free.'

'Tomorrow?' Shauna frowned, her thin brows coming together as she searched through the fuzzy data in her brain.

'Maybe. I dunno. I'll see if my mum can babysit. I'll give you a bell, yeah?'

'Okay, let me know.' Maddie didn't fancy going to the Fox unaccompanied. She was still unclear as to Rick Mallory's intentions and didn't want to make a fool of herself. What if she got there and found he was with his mates or a girlfriend or, even worse, a wife? It would seem odd her showing up alone. And then, of course, he might not be there at all and she had no desire to sit in a pub on her own.

Kyle appeared at the door, and after saying their goodbyes, the three of them set off for summer school, which was being run this year from Kellston Comprehensive. The secondary school was only ten minutes' walk to the south of the station and was, amazingly, still in possession of a playing field. This enabled the kids to play football, do athletics or just dash around and burn off some energy.

Maddie hadn't asked her friend how she'd managed to pay for it. Shauna was a single mum on benefits, and while the fees weren't exorbitant, they had still made a dent in Maddie's small income. Shauna, however, never seemed short of a few bob. Kyle always had the latest trainers and all the gadgets he could want, including a PlayStation, an iPad and a mobile phone.

Some of the stuff, Maddie suspected, had fallen off the back of a lorry. A lot of Shauna's mates lived on the Mansfield and could always get hold of dodgy gear. Cheap booze, fags, phones, laptops – you named it, they had it, or if they didn't, they knew someone who had. But as for hard cash, she had no idea where Shauna got it from. She didn't have a job, and Kyle's dad had done a runner years ago without ever paying a penny of child support.

Maddie looked at the two boys who were walking just in front of her, their heads bent together as they passed football cards to each other and chattered away. She was glad Zac had a best friend, something she'd missed out on when she was growing up. Moving from place to place wasn't conducive to building lasting friendships. She'd been close to Greta then, but that wasn't the same as having a friend her own age.

It was when they stopped on the corner that Maddie suddenly felt a weird prickling sensation on the back of her neck. She glanced over her shoulder – the street was busy with crowds of commuters going in and out of the station – but couldn't spot anyone looking at her. And yet she knew, in that odd instinctive way, that someone was watching.

As the traffic lights changed, Maddie chivvied the boys along. 'Come on, you two, or school's going to be over before we get there.'

She looked back over her shoulder again. Was it just her imagination? She hadn't slept well last night, waking over and over to the vivid, scary threads of nightmares, dreams about the cemetery, about being chased through the graves, about running in fear of her life as footsteps pounded behind her and malignant hands snatched at her hair.

Maddie gave a small shake of her head, trying to free her mind of the memories. What she needed to concentrate on was the here and now. As the three of them continued south along the High Street, she stayed close to the boys, alert to some imminent danger, although she couldn't have said precisely what that danger was.

Five minutes later, she dropped them off at the gates, said goodbye and waited until they passed safely through the main door. Shauna would pick the boys up this afternoon and drop Zac off at his grandparents'. Turning, Maddie gazed up and down the street. All she could see was women and children. Although there was no reason on earth why anyone should be following her, she still felt under scrutiny.

Maddie rubbed at her eyes. She was overtired, that was all.

There was nothing to worry about. But still she was anxious, fear niggling at the edges of her thoughts. Briefly, she raised her face to the wide blue sky. It was a warm morning, but the heat didn't penetrate her bones. All she felt was a peculiar coldness. The hairs on her arms stood on end and a shiver ran through her.

7

Delia Shields had perfected the art of keeping busy, but no amount of paperwork, of typing, copying and filing could completely erase the worry from her mind. As her fingers flew across the keyboard, she thought of Lena and wondered what she would do next. She would act quickly, that was for sure. Her old friend wasn't the sort to let the grass grow under her feet. If he was out there, she would track him down.

Delia hissed out the name in her head. *Cato.* She had prayed that he was gone for ever. She had even hoped, and the knowledge of this brought a red flush of shame to her cheeks, that he would die in prison. It had not been a Christian thought. Delia believed in goodness, in God and the Church, in forgiveness and redemption, but she had no mercy in her soul when it came to Jay Cato.

She stopped typing for a moment to wipe her hand across her brow. A thin sheen of perspiration had gathered on her skin. It was only ten o'clock, but already the August heat was seeping into the office. The fan was on, but the only effect of its whirring blades was to shift warm, muggy air around the office.

Across the room, Bob Cannon was on the phone. He was the seventh manager she'd worked for since becoming office secretary over thirty years ago. She could have applied for the manager's post herself – she was more than capable – but had no desire for the responsibility. In truth, she lacked ambition, but then she didn't see ambition as an altogether good thing. To be always wanting more, always striving for more, seemed an empty and futile way to live. Why couldn't people be content with what they'd got? Her salary was perfectly adequate for her needs, with enough left over to save for her retirement.

Bob put the receiver down, shuffled the papers on his desk and then picked the phone up again. As a manager, she thought, he was no better or worse than the ones who had preceded him. They came and they went, some more rapidly than others. Archie Moult had clung on for a good ten years, David Sanders for four, but Owen Vickery had cleared his desk after a mere ten months. No, the job wasn't for everyone.

Bob Cannon was in his early fifties, married with a couple of teenage kids. Although pleasant enough, he possessed – like most men of her acquaintance – a somewhat inflated sense of his own importance. Earlier, he had taken off his jacket and placed it over the back of his chair. Her nose wrinkled at the sight of two small circles of sweat staining the underarms of his white shirt.

As a whole, she was not a fan of the male species. They were lumbering and graceless, blind to their own imperfections and, more often than not, fuelled by testosterone. Even the clever men, the ones with wit and intellect had an unfortunate habit of storing their brains in their pants.

Delia had never slept with a man and had no desire to do so.

She was repelled by their very maleness, by their lingering musky smell and their misplaced belief in their own superiority. She despised their superficiality, the way they judged women purely on appearance, and she loathed their habit of spreading their legs on the Tube or bus, making it impossible to sit comfortably beside them. Yes, all in all they were tiresome creatures and she would be quite happy to live in a world without them.

Although Delia much preferred the company of women, she did not in any way, shape or form consider herself to be a lesbian. Indeed, the idea of having sex with a female was as repugnant to her as the thought of having sex with a man. Her love for Lena Bell – she still could not think of her as Gissing – was purely platonic, although not without passion. She had worshipped Lena since they were children, and the years had not dimmed that adoration. Knowing that Lena didn't feel the same way – that in fact she bored and disappointed her – was the heavy cross that Delia had to bear.

Bob Cannon finished his call, gave a sigh and looked across the office. 'Do you know if Eli's dealing with that damage?'

'I've told him about it.' Delia could not understand the mentality of people who desecrated graves. Sometimes it was graffiti; other times whole headstones were pushed over or smashed. It was not a regular occurrence, but whenever it happened, she felt the same sense of shock. It was the booze, she supposed, that cheap, nasty lager that the local yobs bought in the supermarkets. Once they had a few drinks inside them, they were capable of anything.

'Kids,' said Bob, shaking his head. 'That lot from the Mansfield, no doubt.'

Delia's gaze flicked over to the window, to the long rows of graves and the wide blue sky. She was hot and uncomfortable and had a sudden desire to be outside. 'Perhaps I should walk over and check. The Ransome burial's at twelve. It needs to be tidied up by then.'

'Would you mind?'

'Not at all.' Delia stood up and smoothed down her skirt. 'I won't be long.' But Bob Cannon was no longer listening; he'd picked up the phone and was busy dialling again.

As she stepped out of the office, Delia glanced towards the black wrought-iron gates. She almost expected to see Jay Cato walking in. In her head, he was still a young man, his shoulders straight, his dark hair slicked back from a lean, sculpted face. Of course, he would not look like that now. She didn't want to think what he would look like. She didn't want to think about him at all.

Delia set off along the main thoroughfare, heading towards the far side where the damaged graves lay. She tried to concentrate, to focus on the job in hand, but Cato refused to leave her alone. Like a snake, he coiled himself round her innermost thoughts, slowly squeezing out everything and everyone else. The breath caught in the back of her throat. But he couldn't have been released from prison. Not yet. The police would have told Lena, surely they would. She'd be entitled to know such a thing.

Delia wished that the past could be wiped clean, erased like the words on a whiteboard. She wished that she could turn back time. Would she have done things differently? 'Yes,' the rational part of her said, but in her heart she was not so certain. An ache passed through her jaw as she briefly clamped her teeth together. 'Leave us alone,' she muttered. 'Why can't you leave us alone?'

The cemetery was a large one, spread over twenty acres and it was another five minutes before she came across Eli and Rick Mallory. They both turned to look at her, their faces faintly hostile, as if suspecting that she might be checking up on them. Or perhaps it was just her imagination. Nothing was as it should be today.

'So how are we doing?' she asked, forcing a smile.

Eli gave a grunt, which was about as much as she ever got out of him. Rick, however, was more forthcoming.

'We've cleared the worst of it,' he said, gesturing over his shoulder with his thumb. 'But you'll need to get the mason in.'

Delia walked behind them and gazed solemnly down at the broken stones. They were old, nineteenth-century graves, but that didn't diminish her sense of outrage. Just because they were no longer tended didn't mean they were any less important. She felt anger and frustration well up in her chest. Evil, that's what it was. Wanton damage, just for the hell of it! No one gave a damn about anything these days.

'What is wrong with these people?'

'Kids,' said Rick in an echo of Bob Cannon.

'Then you need to keep a closer eye on them.' The sharpness in her voice reflected the rage she was feeling. 'It's not acceptable. It has to be stopped.'

Rick's eyebrows shifted up a fraction. 'We try, but we can't be everywhere at once. And anyway, the little sods sneak in at night. There's not a whole lot we can do about that.'

Delia didn't care for his tone – it had a somewhat disrespectful edge to it – but she knew that he was right. Although the gates at either end of the cemetery were locked every evening, the graveyard was surrounded by houses and any number of back gardens. For those who desired access, it wasn't too hard to find a wall to climb over.

Her mouth set into a tight, grim line as her eyes surveyed the damage. Three of the headstones had been smashed. The torso of a grey stone angel, her head decapitated, lay supine on the grass. There was something eerily disturbing about her, like a murder victim left out in the open for everyone to view.

'At least move that out of the way. The Ransome cortège will be passing by at twelve and that's the last thing they'll want to see.'

'Sure,' said Rick. 'No worries. We'll shift her over to the back.'

Delia felt Eli's gaze on her, but when she looked at him, his pale blue eyes slid away. Not, however, before she had seen the expression in them. Dislike? Contempt? She couldn't quite put her finger on it, and she wondered, not for the first time, just how much Eli knew. He was an odd, disconcerting man who rarely spoke, and then only with the bare minimum of words. How old was he now? In his early sixties, she thought. And he had been around back then, back when it had all happened.

Eli turned away from her and started picking up fragments of stone. He was small and wiry with a thin, gaunt face and a shock of white hair. The sharp bones in his cheeks seemed too close to the surface of his brown leathery skin. Like a starved man – or a dying one. She was wary of him, afraid of the knowledge he might possess. What if he said something? A sliver of ice slid down her spine. But it didn't matter, she quickly told herself. No one would take any notice of what Eli said. He wasn't right in the head, not all there. Anyone who could claim to hear the dead couldn't possibly count as a reliable witness.

Although she had no immediate desire to return to the office, Delia was even more reluctant to stay. She didn't want to spend any more time than she had to in the company of Eli Glass. Accordingly, she addressed her final orders to Rick. 'So you'll make sure it's cleared before twelve?'

'By twelve,' he repeated.

'Thank you.' Delia started to walk away, but then turned round again. There was something that she had to ask Rick before she left. Checking that Eli was out of earshot, she hesitated and then said, 'And that other business, over on the west side – no more problems there?'

'What?'

Delia frowned. 'The girl, yesterday? You know, the business about the man lurking in the bushes.'

'Oh, that. No, there's been no more trouble. I've been going over to check, but whoever it was hasn't come back.'

Delia tried to keep her voice as casual as possible. 'I don't suppose you know who she's working for?'

Rick Mallory gave a shrug. 'No idea. Sorry. Does it matter?'

'No, no, of course not. I was just curious.'

'I'll be getting on, then,' he said.

As he walked away to join Eli, Delia set off back along the path towards the office. She wished she hadn't asked now, but she couldn't bear the uncertainty. She *had* to know if Cato was responsible for the flowers on the grave. For some reason, she couldn't disconnect the decapitated stone angel from the long-dead Lucy Rivers. It was strange, she thought, how all the angels in the Bible were male and yet in graveyards they were often depicted as female. What was all that about? Some kind of pagan influence, perhaps. Maybe she'd ask the vicar about it when she went to church on Sunday.

Squinting into the sun, she wondered why she was even entertaining the thought. There were far more pressing, far more serious matters to be discussed with the Reverend Colin Jacobs. Not that she ever would discuss them. How could she admit to what she'd done? She was too afraid and too ashamed.

'What could I say?' she murmured. 'How could I say it?'

Her lips felt dry and she ran her tongue along them. She wondered what it would be like to be Catholic, to be able to step inside the confessional and admit to all one's wrongdoings. But was it that easy to slough off the burden of sin? She had lived it with it for so long that it now felt like a part of her. It was wrapped around her soul, attached to her heart like some dreadful cancer.

When she reached the weeping willows, she stopped and gazed along the narrow path that led off to the older part of the cemetery. She'd had no intention of going there and yet she felt a sudden urge to do so. She had to look. She had to see for herself.

Delia set off again at a brisk pace, frequently glancing over her shoulder like a furtive burglar afraid of being seen. And yet there was no reason why she *shouldn't* be going there. Maddie Layne claimed to have seen a man hanging around the graves yesterday. It was her duty, her responsibility, to make sure there were no dodgy characters skulking in the shrubbery. Not that she actually believed the girl. No, she was sure that she'd been lying.

As the path wound round and grew narrower, the long, dry grass brushed against Delia's legs. There were wild flowers, shrubs and red admiral butterflies dancing on the buddleia. She was aware of the prettiness of the scene, but took no joy in it. For years she had deliberately stayed away from this place, not wanting to be reminded of the past. But now the past was flooding over her, a great torrent of memories that couldn't be dammed.

Delia wrapped her arms around her chest as she tentatively approached the grave. There was no denying that Maddie Layne had done a good job. The weeds had all been cleared away, and the marble headstone was gleaming. It was, however, the deep red roses that affected her most profoundly. They were not like the ones you bought in the shops with the small tight buds that never opened properly; these were the old-fashioned type – big and blowsy and smelling of summer.

Men sent red roses as a symbol of love. Delia's hands clenched into two tight fists. *Cato.* The red against the white reminded her of blood. She stared long and hard at the grave. Deep down she had always known that one day the Lucy Rivers affair would come back to haunt her. How could it not? What went around came around, and the dead were unforgiving.

8

Lena usually looked forward to her visits to Chelsea – shopping on the King's Road and Sloane Street, followed by lunch at a fancy restaurant – but today her mood was a black one. She had more on her mind than designer clothes, Gucci handbags and Jimmy Choo shoes. It was bad enough having Cato messing with her head, but last night she'd found out that one of the girls was screwing her over too.

Driving along Chelsea Embankment, she barely glanced at the wide grey expanse of the Thames before veering left and making her way into Flood Street. Here, she pulled the MG into an empty parking bay outside the block of flats and stared up at the building. Of the six apartments inside, Lena owned three of them and rented the other three. She had learned from experience that when you were running a business like hers, it was sensible not to have any immediate neighbours.

Lena had other apartments scattered across London, but these were her favourite. Set in the heart of Chelsea, they were close to the money – and the money was big in South

Kensington. The streets here truly were paved with gold; the place was swimming in blue bloods and millionaires. But even this thought didn't lift her spirits. She couldn't stand being taken for a fool, and Louise Cole was doing just that. Well, the stupid bitch had made a big mistake – and she was damn well going to pay for it.

Lena got out of the car, slammed the door shut and locked it. She walked over to the entrance of the block and used her key to get in. Before she had even raised a hand to knock, the door to Flat 1 flew open and a smiling Maureen Dodds beckoned her across the threshold.

'Lena! Come on in, love, and sit yourself down. Hot out there, ain't it? How are you doing? I've been watching out for you. There's a brew on the go. You'll have a cup, won't you?'

'Ta – I could do with one.' Lena followed her through to the living room, sat down on the cream sofa and crossed her legs. This flat was the smallest of the six, but it was, as always, neat as a pin. Maureen was perfectly turned out too, dressed in a dusky-pink summer suit and kitten heels.

'I won't be a minute,' Maureen said. 'You just make yourself comfy.'

Lena lit a cigarette – there was no problem with smoking here – and then leaned across the coffee table and pulled the ashtray closer. She looked through the arch to where Maureen was pouring out the tea in the kitchen. It was hard to believe that this was the same woman she'd employed three years ago. Back then, Maureen had been knocking on fifty-five, eking out a living by working as a cleaner at the Fox and turning the odd trick in Albert Road whenever she could find a punter drunk enough or desperate enough to pay for the pleasure.

It had been a risk taking her on as a housekeeper, but the gamble had paid off. Yes, it had been a smart decision. By dragging her out of the gutter, Lena had gained her eternal loyalty.

Maureen not only ensured all the flats were immaculately clean, but also kept an eye on the girls. There wasn't anything that happened in this block that she didn't know about.

Maureen Dodds had, somewhat surprisingly, taken to Chelsea like a duck to water. Gone was the greasy, greying hair, replaced by soft blonde waves. Gone too were the cheap, tarty clothes. Now, as long as she didn't open her mouth, she could easily pass for a local. The old tom had embraced respectability, even if it was only on the surface.

'Ta,' said Lena, as her tea was delivered in a flowery china cup. She added a spoonful of sugar, stirred, took a sip and put the cup down again. Now it was time to get down to business. 'So, it's true, is it? That bloody Louise is fucking me over?'

Maureen gave a nod. 'It looks that way. Todd Greening? You remember him? He was here three times last week: Tuesday, Wednesday and Friday. I checked the appointment book and he wasn't in it. He showed up again last night and stayed for a couple of hours.'

Lena gave a snort. Greening was an ageing musician, the type who was rarely out of the gossip columns. He was a regular customer and had been using her girls for years. His career, however, was on the wane, which meant that his bank account would inevitably be waning too. If Louise had suggested cutting out the middle man, he'd have jumped at the opportunity of saving a few bob.

Maureen lifted a hand and gave her blonde waves a pat. 'I'd have told you sooner, love, but I wanted to be sure.'

Lena took a deep drag on her cigarette and expelled the smoke in a long, thin stream. 'So the little bitch is moonlighting.' It was an occupational hazard in this business, but it still made her angry, especially when her terms were more than fair. She took sixty per cent of the client's fee, but in return her girls got a decent place to live, regular health checks and the kind of customers who were carefully vetted and were never going to beat the shit out of them. Plus, they got to keep any tips that came their way.

'You want to see?'

Lena followed Maureen's gaze towards the computer screen in the corner. There were hidden cameras in the foyer and on both of the landings, providing constant coverage of everyone who came and went. She knew, though, that Maureen wouldn't have called her if she hadn't been certain. 'That's okay. I'll take your word for it.'

'So what are you going to do?'

'The only thing I can do. Get shot of the cheating cow. She can't carry on working here, not after this. If the other girls think she's got away with it, they'll all be at it.'

'Shame,' Maureen said. 'I know what you mean, but she's a looker and she's popular.'

But Lena had learned that there was no point in second chances. Once a girl had gone behind your back, she could never be trusted again. She stubbed her fag out, angrily twisting the butt in the ashtray and then rose to her feet. 'There's plenty more where she came from.'

'You off upstairs?'

'May as well get it over with. I take it she's in?'

'Yeah, she's in. Do you want me to come with you?'

'No, I'll deal with this myself. Thanks for the brew.' Lena glanced at her watch. 'Look, I have to be somewhere at twelve, so after this is done with, I'm not going to hang about. I'll give you a bell later, yeah?'

Maureen showed her to the door and, as Lena was leaving, placed a hand on her arm. 'You sure you're all right, love?'

'No, I'm not all right. I'm being taken for a bloody ride.'

'Apart from that,' Maureen said. 'Come on, you've dealt with far worse than this before. Sure you ain't got something else bothering you?'

Lena thought of Cato and Lucy Rivers and the grave in Kellston Cemetery. She had a fleeting impression of Jay standing in the dock, his dark eyes boring into her, and felt a tightening in her chest, a sudden breathlessness. Her hand fluttered involuntarily to her breast and she quickly forced it back to her side again. 'Nothing,' she said. 'It's just been one of those weeks.'

'Well, you know where I am if you want to talk.'

'Of course,' Lena said. She had, however, no intention of confiding in her. She might trust Maureen to take care of the girls, to be her spy in the House of Love, but she wasn't about to spill her secrets. A problem shared was a problem halved? Not in Lena's experience. It was her considered opinion that the more people knew about you, the more dangerous they became. 'I'll call you, hon. You take care, huh?'

'You too.'

Lena turned and headed for the staircase. She wasn't going to take the lift in case Louise heard it coming. With this kind of confrontation, it was always better to have the advantage of surprise. As she climbed up to the second floor, she tried to focus on what she would say to the treacherous bitch. She always took it personally when one of the girls betrayed her. It was an insult, a stab in the back, and the quicker it was sorted, the happier she'd be.

Although she tried to concentrate on Louise, her thoughts kept wandering. Cato was there like a shadow she couldn't shake off, glued to her heels, dark and heavy, sticky as treacle. For the last ten years she'd been able to sleep soundly, knowing that he was locked up, that he was safely behind bars, but now her dreams were not so peaceful.

'Fuck you,' she murmured, as her hand gripped the banister. 'I won't let you do this to me.'

On reaching the second landing, Lena took a moment to gather herself. She was never afraid to speak her mind, to take action when it was needed, but she resented even having to be here. As if she didn't have enough to deal with! She walked along the corridor and knocked lightly on the door. It was another thirty seconds before it was answered.

Louise Cole had the look of someone who has just been woken up. Wearing a silk ivory robe, her long black hair was mussed, and her wide brown eyes were full of sleep. Even in this tousled state, however, she remained an extremely striking woman: young and slim with curves in all the right places.

An expression of alarm passed over Louise's face. 'Mrs Gissing. What . . . what are you doing here?'

'I just dropped by for a chat.'

'A chat?'

'Yes, you know,' said Lena, 'one of those exchanges where I say something and then you say something back. It's quite simple once you get the hang of it. Aren't you going to invite me in?'

Louise was still holding on to the door. She glanced over her shoulder. 'Er . . . it's not very . . . I had a friend round last night and I haven't had time to tidy up.'

'I'm not here to check on the level of cleanliness.'

Louise stood her ground. Her voice was cool and slightly dismissive, her cut-glass accent an echo of a thousand other Chelsea girls who believed in their utter and absolute superiority. 'Perhaps, if you don't mind, you could come back later?'

'I do bloody mind,' Lena snarled. And before Louise knew what was happening, she had pushed her way into the flat and was gazing with disgust around the living room. The place was a tip, with discarded clothes lying on the sofa. Three empty wine bottles, a couple of dirty glasses, used plates, a cardboard pizza box and an overflowing ashtray were on the coffee table.

Mixed in with the debris was the telltale residue of white powder.

Louise sighed and shut the door. 'What is it, then? What's the problem?'

'Who said there was a problem?'

'Well, you don't usually ... I mean, I haven't seen you in ages.'

Lena glanced at the sofa and decided not to sit down. 'It'll be nice to have a catch-up, then, won't it?'

Louise didn't seem overjoyed at the prospect. She pushed her hair back from her face and wrinkled her nose. Finally, remembering her manners, she asked, 'You want a coffee or something?'

'No,' Lena said. 'What I want to know is why you've been seeing Todd Greening and it hasn't been going through the books.'

Louise assumed an expression of mock surprise. 'What? I haven't. I didn't. I don't know what—'

'He's been here. I know he has.'

Louise faltered for a second but quickly recovered. She made a *tsk* sound in the back of her throat. 'Oh, I get it. It's *her*, isn't it? That old cow downstairs. Well, whatever she's been saying, it's a heap of bullshit. She's just jealous of me. She's out to make trouble. And it's not my fault – I've tried my best to be nice, but she hasn't liked me since the day I moved in.'

Lena gave a small shake of her head. 'Don't lie to me, love. I don't like being lied to. I know that he's been here.'

'I'm not lying.' Louise put her hands on her shapely hips and stared Lena straight in the eye. 'I didn't say he hadn't been here. What I *mean* is that I haven't been seeing him as a client. He calls by sometimes, that's all. He's lonely and pathetic, surrounded by hangers-on who don't give a damn about him. Sometimes he drops in for a coffee. Am I supposed to charge him for that?'

'You know the rules,' said Lena sharply. 'Unless they're paying, you don't see them at all.'

'But what does that achieve? He'll just end up going to someone else. And yes, I know the rules and he knows them too. Nothing happens when he comes round, not unless he's gone through you first.' Her tone switched abruptly from aggressive to something more pleading. 'I swear that's the truth; it's the God's honest truth. You have to believe me. Do you really think I'd go behind your back, Mrs Gissing? I wouldn't. I really wouldn't. You have my word on it.'

Lena didn't believe a word she said. She'd heard it all before. Although Louise Cole was smart – she'd been to public school and to university, and even had a brief career in the City before finally becoming an escort – she wasn't smart enough. The words that dripped from her perfectly formed lips were about as convincing as a wasp selling honey. 'That's good to hear.'

Louise, thinking that she'd got away with it, allowed her mouth to slide into a wide, smug smile. 'I knew you'd understand.'

'Of course I understand,' Lena replied. She took a few steps forward until she was standing right in front of her. Her mouth widened into a smile as false as the one she was looking at. She was so close now that she could even smell the stale sleep breath of the girl. Leaning forward slightly, she hissed, 'I understand that you're a nasty, lying, conniving little bitch who thinks she can rip me off and get away with it!'

Louise flinched. She must have sensed what was about to happen next because she tried to dodge out of the way, but she wasn't fast enough. The hand was already flying towards her and the hard, angry slap caught her off balance and sent her reeling. Her eyes widened and a small, startled cry flew out of her mouth. She tottered for a moment and then fell back on to the sofa.

Lena loomed over, her face full of contempt. 'You're finished, you stupid little bitch!' She leaned down and slapped her again, this time with the back of her hand. The diamond ring caught the soft flesh of Louise's mouth and ripped it open. A trickle of blood ran down her chin. 'I want you out of here by tonight. You don't work for me any more. Do you understand? Is that clear enough for you?'

Louise touched her mouth, saw the blood on her fingers and winced. 'Look what you've done. Look what you've fucking done! I'll have you for assault. I'll call the fucking cops!'

'You do that, babe,' Lena scoffed. 'I'm sure they'll be more than happy to help, especially when they find out what you do for a living. Do you really want to go there? Do you really think they give a toss about dirty little toms like you?'

'Then I'll tell the press. I'll go to the papers and blow your whole bloody business out of the water!'

Lena stood up straight and gave a thin, caustic laugh. 'No, you won't, not if you know what's good for you. Don't even think about taking me on, love, because you won't win and you'll spend the rest of your life regretting that you ever tried. So just do the sensible thing, huh? Get out of my flat and find some stone to crawl under. You'll feel more at home there.'

Louise glared up at her. 'You'll pay for this. I'll make sure you bloody do!'

'I want you out by midnight. And I expect to find this place exactly as it was when you moved in. Anything missing, anything damaged and I'll make you pay for it. Do we understand each other?'

Louise opened her mouth, thought better of it and quickly closed it again.

'Good,' Lena said. 'And if I hear any rumours, even a whisper that you've been talking, I'll come looking for you. And I'll find you, hon. There won't be any place, not a place on earth that you can hide. I'll find you and I'll slice that pretty little face into shreds.'

Lena didn't wait for a response. She turned on her heel and stalked out of the flat. As she walked down the stairs, she gave a nod of satisfaction. Job done. If Louise Cole had any sense, she'd do the smart thing and keep shtum. It was a shame, though, that it had come to this. The girl had been a good earner, but she'd gone to the bad and no amount of money was worth the bother of a tom who couldn't be trusted.

Lena never asked her girls why they chose to sell their bodies. Sometimes, she knew, it was purely for money, but more often there were deeper psychological motives, problems with parents, bonding, bitterness and rejection. But none of that was her problem. She didn't want to hear their pathetic, whiny sob stories. In truth, she didn't give a damn about any of them. The only person she really cared about was Lena Gissing – and that was the way it was going to stay.

9

The first thing Lena did when she got out on the street was to light another cigarette. As she sucked in the smoke, she glanced towards the house, aware that Maureen would be watching from behind the blinds. In fact, she had probably been watching her for the last ten minutes, eyes pinned to the footage streaming from the camera on the landing in the hope of seeing some action. But Lena hadn't given her the satisfaction; she preferred to do business behind closed doors and without any witnesses.

She took her phone out of the red Louis Vuitton handbag, scrolled down the menu and pressed the name she wanted. It was answered after a couple of rings.

'Hello?'

'It's me,' Lena said. 'Are you there yet?'

'Yes, I just got here.'

'Good. I'll be five minutes. Order me a Bloody Mary.'

Lena needed a drink after her altercation with Louise Cole, something to take the edge off and help her to relax. Leaving the car parked where it was, she set off up Flood Street in the opposite direction from Chelsea Embankment. She walked with her head held high and her shoulders back, aware that posture was everything and that no one who slouched was ever taken seriously.

As Lena made her way towards her next appointment, her thoughts returned to Maureen Dodds and she wondered if the woman was getting just a bit too familiar. She'd need to be careful about that. It wasn't good to blur the boundaries; with familiarity came contempt, and with contempt came the temptation to take the piss.

Lena had employed housekeepers in the past who'd come to a private arrangement with the girls, overlooking their moonlighting activities in exchange for a cut. But no, she decided, she didn't need to worry. Maureen was sound. Maureen was grateful. And, perhaps most importantly, Maureen had no desire to return to some pit of a flat on the Mansfield estate.

At the top of Flood Street, she turned on to the King's Road, and shortly after, she was stepping through the door of the Jam Tree. It was only then, as she spotted Stephen Yeats sitting in the corner, that Cato automatically sprang into her head again. Her body stiffened as she made the short journey over to the table.

Yeats rose to his feet and extended a hand. 'Lena. Lovely to see you again.'

Lena braced herself. His palm was always clammy, his clasp a little more lingering than was strictly necessary. But she forced herself to shake his hand and to smile while she was doing it. 'How are you?'

'Good, very good.'

With the formalities over, Lena sat down and picked up her drink. 'Cheers,' she said, raising her glass before taking a few welcome gulps. The Bloody Mary went down smoothly, the kick of vodka taking the edge off her distaste for Yeats. There was something quite repulsive about the man, although that didn't stop her from hiring him. He was a private detective who got results and that was all that mattered. 'So what's the news?'

'Where would you like me to start?'

Lena did some more bracing. She took another sip of her drink. There was only one question on her lips and it was best to get it over with as quickly as possible. 'Jay Cato,' she said. 'Is he out of jail?'

Yeats gazed across the table at her. As if aware of the heavy thumping of her heart – and relishing the momentary power he had over her – he didn't immediately answer.

'Well?' asked Lena, unable to contain her impatience or her irritation. 'Is he or isn't he?'

Yeats paused for a further few seconds before eventually replying, 'No, not yet.'

The relief flowed through Lena. *Thank God. Thank bloody God.* Now, at least, she could stop worrying about seeing him every time she turned a corner. Knowing he was still banged up, still enclosed by four solid brick walls, made her spirits soar.

'But it might not be that long.'

'How long?'

Yeats pursed his lips. 'Hard to say exactly. Six months? Three? He's at Thornley Heath in Kent. He's going through the parole process, and from what I've heard, they're going to recommend his release.'

Lena didn't ask where he got his information. She knew he had contacts in the Prison Service, in legal departments and just about everywhere else. There probably wasn't a willing palm that he hadn't greased at one time or another. 'But not sooner? You're sure of that?'

'As sure as I can be. The wheels of the system grind slowly. It should be at least three months.'

Lena could cope with that. It gave her time to figure out a

plan of action, to sort out what to do next. Cato might think he had the upper hand, but there was only so much control you had from a prison cell. 'And the girl,' she asked, 'what about her?'

'Maddie Layne.' Yeats opened his briefcase, took out a slim blue file and passed it over to her. 'It's all here. She's local, like you thought. Morton Grove, number thirty-four. She lives there with a kid, Zac.'

Lena flipped open the file. Inside were several sheets of paper with details of Maddie Layne's work and home life, as well as a set of photographs. She stared hard at the pictures of the girl. Maddie was in her late twenties with long, dark brown hair and an attractive face. Not beautiful, Lena thought, but pretty enough. She didn't recognise her and was as sure as she could be that she'd never set eyes on her before.

'She works at the garden centre, Marigolds,' Yeats said. 'No criminal record, not even a parking ticket. She's squeaky clean on that front.'

'Has she been back to the cemetery?'

He shook his head. 'Not since I've been watching her.'

Lena looked thoughtful. 'So she's probably of no importance. Cato could have just employed her to tend the grave.'

'Maybe.'

Lena's gaze shot up from the photos. 'Maybe?'

'I think it could be more complicated than that.'

Lena stared at him. He was a short, balding man with a face that was utterly forgettable. Only his brown hooded eyes gave cause for alarm; there was something sly and cold about them. 'Meaning?'

'That she might not be as innocent as she appears on the surface.'

Lena leaned across the table. 'Explain.'

'Do you remember Bo Vale?'

93

Lena frowned. 'What, that little toerag from the Mansfield?'

'That's the one. Well, it seems our friend here,' he continued, nodding towards the photographs, 'has a connection to him. She's the sister of Greta Layne, and Greta was—'

'I know who Greta was,' Lena said sharply. 'I haven't lost my bloody memory.' She glared at him for a few seconds as she absorbed the information. Shit, this wasn't good news.

'So she's closer to Cato than we thought.'

'There's no proof as yet, but—'

'But nothing. He's using her to get to me. He has to be. And the vengeful little cow is more than happy to oblige.' Lena sat back again, wishing she could have a fag. She needed some nicotine to help her think it through. 'Greta Layne,' she murmured. It was a long time since she'd heard that name. Five, six years? They'd never found her body, but Bo's bloated corpse had been pulled out of the Thames. She'd hoped that was the end of it, but now it was all starting up again.

'You want me to carry on watching her?'

Lena's mind was elsewhere. 'Huh?'

'Do you want me to keep her under surveillance?'

Lena considered it for a moment, but then shook her head. 'No, not for now. I'll let you know.' If Maddie Layne was in contact with Cato, it was probably by phone. There was no point in her paying for Yeats to follow the girl to the garden centre every day. His fees were extortionate and she didn't like to waste money.

'There's one other thing,' he said. 'The kid that she's living with isn't hers. I checked out the birth certificate. He's her sister's boy. The father's Bo Vale.'

Lena raised her brows. 'Interesting.' She finished her drink and put the glass down on the table. It wouldn't have been difficult, she thought, for Cato to track down Ms Layne or to persuade her to help him out. Perhaps she had been to visit him at Thornley Heath. What had he told her? That they had a common enemy, perhaps. That Bo Vale had been doing business with Lena Gissing at the time of his death or that Greta had owed her money. Oh yes, Cato would have laid it on thick. And he would have been convincing too. He could always tell a good story.

'You want to nip it in the bud,' Yeats said. 'She could be trouble.'

Lena swept up the file and rose to her feet. 'She won't be, not after I've had a quiet word.'

'Be careful. You start threatening her and she could go to the cops.'

'Who said anything about threats?'

Yeats gave her a thin smile. 'All I'm saying is—'

'Yes, I know what you're saying. But the girl's not a problem. She'll soon back off once she knows the truth.'

'Your truth or Cato's?'

Lena gave him a long, hard stare. 'I'll see you around,' she said. 'Put the bill in the post.'

10

Maddie frowned at the bed and the heap of clothes that was growing larger by the minute. Jeans, trousers, dresses, tops were rapidly piling up on the duvet. She still couldn't decide what to wear. What was the matter with her? It wasn't as if this was a date or anything. A Friday-night drink with a mate, that's all it was. Nothing to get hot and bothered about. But still she couldn't decide. She didn't want to look too casual – as if she didn't care – but on the other hand, she didn't want to look as if she hadn't made much of an effort either.

'Just choose,' she muttered to herself. 'Stop behaving like a teenager.'

She pulled on a pair of cream linen trousers and a white shirt, and stood back to view the effect in the mirror. Well, the outfit was summery if nothing else. Her eyes raked the bed again, but she resisted the impulse to try on something else. After slipping her feet into a pair of heels, she headed for the bathroom to do her make-up.

Now, of course, she faced the same dilemma. Just how much

slap should she be putting on? Enough to hide the shadows under her eyes – she'd had another long day – but not so much as to make her look desperate. She smeared some BB cream across her skin and blended it in before setting to work on her eyes.

Five minutes later, with shadow, liner and mascara applied, she was starting to feel more confident. Those odd little butterflies were still dancing in her stomach, but at least she looked presentable. That was the great thing about make-up, she thought: it was like a mask you could hide behind. All your doubts and insecurities, all the cracks in your confidence were neatly concealed by a layer of paint.

As she carefully applied her lipstick, she wondered about the evening ahead. Rick Mallory was the first man she'd been interested in for years. There had been the occasional date, but nothing she'd wanted to take further. Having Zac in her life made everything more complicated. She couldn't just think of herself any more; if she was going to get involved, she had to consider the effect it would have on him.

But she was getting ahead of herself. She didn't even know if Rick fancied her or not. She suspected he did – she always seemed to be bumping into him at the cemetery – but that didn't mean that he was after anything serious. Plenty of men flirted just for the fun of it. The best thing was not to expect too much and that way she couldn't be disappointed.

It was six years now since her last serious relationship. Tom Bailey rarely entered her thoughts these days, and when he did, it was only with a tiny stab of regret as opposed to the aching, devastating pain she had felt when they'd first split up. He had been twelve years older than her, clever, handsome and witty, as well as a brilliant archaeologist. He'd been her mentor and her lover, and she'd firmly believed that it was going to last for ever.

'For ever,' she murmured, amazed now that she had ever been that naïve.

After Greta had died, Tom had been kind and supportive, a shoulder to cry on. But as the situation had changed with Zac, it had soon become clear that he had no intention of settling down and playing happy families. The relationship had staggered on for a few more months until Tom had agreed to run a dig in the north of Scotland, a year-long contract that had taken him about as far from London as he could get.

That, of course, had been the crunch point. There'd been lots of empty promises about travelling back to see her – she could hardly drag Zac up to Scotland – but over the following weeks his phone calls had gradually fizzled out until she was left with only silence. It had been down to a mutual friend to eventually break the news that Tom was seeing someone else.

She knew now that she'd had a lucky escape. Anyone who was so gutless that he couldn't tell her it was over didn't deserve to be loved. He didn't even deserve to be remembered. Not that she'd seen it like that at the time. His desertion had knocked her for six and it had taken a long time for her to recover.

Maddie ran a comb through her hair. Why was she even thinking about him? It was done, finished. It was – and she smiled at the pun – ancient history. Besides, she had more important things to worry about. Solomon's news was still spinning round in the back of her head. When he'd come to pick up Zac this morning, he had taken her aside in the kitchen, lowered his voice and told her what he'd managed to find out. The name Lucy Rivers hadn't rung a bell with anyone, but he'd managed to dig up some information on Cato.

'Jay Cato,' Solomon had said. 'That's J-A-Y. He's inside, babe. Living it up at Her Majesty's Pleasure.'

'What? He's in prison? What for?'

'Well, he's doing a fifteen-stretch, so I guess it's not for nicking a bottle of cider from the Co-op.'

Maddie's heart had leaped into her mouth. 'So you're saying that he ... that he ... ?' She glanced towards Zac, who was getting his things together in the living room. 'Just tell me what he did.'

Solomon's gaze followed hers and he kept his voice quiet. 'I ain't got the details, but yeah, I guess someone's not breathing any more.'

'Jesus,' Maddie said. She recalled Delia Shields in the cemetery, the look on her face, the accusation in her voice. *That bastard Cato!* For a few dreadful seconds she wondered if she'd been putting flowers on the grave of Cato's victim. The very thought of it made her blood run cold. 'But you don't know who? You don't know who he killed? Was it a man or a woman?'

Solomon shook his head. 'Sorry, babe. Like I said, I ain't got the finer details right now, but it can't be too hard to find out.'

And then Maddie realised that the victim couldn't possibly have been Lucy Rivers. What was she thinking? Lucy had been dead for over thirty years. But her relief was short-lived. When all was said and done, she was still taking money from a murderer every month. 'Maybe I should stop doing it, stop working for him.'

Solomon leaned back against the counter, put his hands in his pockets and stared at her. 'A man's got a right to put a few flowers on a grave even if he is banged up. Until you know for sure what he's done and why he did it, maybe you shouldn't be too quick to judge.'

'Who said anything about judging?' Maddie felt suddenly defensive, as if *she* was the one being judged. 'I just ... I just want to know who I'm working for.'

And that was where their conversation had come to a halt. Zac had appeared at the door, impatient to be off.

'Are you ready, Uncle Sol? Are you ready?'

'What's the rush, kid? Those dinosaurs ain't going nowhere.'

But Zac had hurried over and tugged at Solomon's sleeve. His eyes were bright, his face flushed with excitement. 'Come on, Uncle Sol. We don't want to be at the back of the queue.'

'Hey, no one mentioned nothing 'bout a queue. There weren't no queue last time we went.'

'Last time wasn't the school holidays,' Maddie said.

Solomon's upper lip curled a little. He was the sort of guy who kept queues in line, not the sort who stood in them. Pushing himself off the counter, he straightened up to his full height. 'Okay, okay, let's get this show on the road.' He turned to Maddie and said, 'We'll see you tomorrow, then. I'll bring him back in the morning. And that other thing we were talking about – don't worry about it, huh?'

Except, ten hours later, Maddie was still worrying. She took one last look in the mirror and then went through to the living room to wait for Shauna. As she sat on the sofa, she eyed her phone, wondering if she should try to contact Cato. She wasn't even sure now if the number she had, retained from when he'd first called her, was actually his.

It was not impossible that Jay Cato had a mobile. She'd heard about them being smuggled into prisons. And if this was the case, it was probably only turned on occasionally. Or maybe it wasn't his phone at all. But then where were the weekly photographs that she sent of the grave going? They must be delivered somewhere.

She picked up the phone and almost immediately put it down again. What would she say even if she did get through? *Hi. I was just wondering what your interest in Lucy Rivers was.* No, that was ridiculous. At best he would tell her to mind her own business, and at worst he might decide to fire her. Perhaps it was better to let things lie for now.

As soon as she had made the decision, Maddie's conscience began to niggle. Was she doing nothing because it was the right thing to do or because she didn't want to lose the monthly income? A bad feeling was starting to creep over her. Those extra pounds came in mighty useful, but if she was working for a murderer, then there could, eventually, be an even bigger price to pay.

11

The doorbell rang at seven forty and Maddie opened the door to find Shauna in her Friday finery: a red leather miniskirt, white stilettos, a skinny pink vest and enough gold bling to light up a room. Her white-blonde hair was gelled into tiny spikes, and her mouth was the same colour as her skirt.

'You ready, hon?' Shauna asked, shifting a wad of gum into her cheek.

Maddie glanced down at her own clothes, suspecting she'd been a bit too conservative, a bit too safe in her choice, but there was no time to change her mind now. She closed the door and stepped out into the front yard. 'Yes, I'm ready. Let's go.'

'Sorry I'm late. Our Kyle was playing up. I think he's got the hump 'cause Zac wasn't around today. Is he staying over at Sol's tonight, or do you need to get back?'

'Staying over,' Maddie said. 'He's bringing him home tomorrow morning.'

'You got the whole night, then. Best make the most of it. So what's the deal with Sol?'

'What do you mean? What deal?'

Shauna grinned. 'You know. Is he seeing anyone? Has he got a steady girlfriend or anything?'

'I haven't got a clue.' In truth, she knew very little about Solomon Vale's private life and wouldn't dream of asking him about it. 'If he has, I haven't met her. Anyway, what's with the interest? I thought you and Darren were an item these days.'

'Darren's an arse. I haven't seen him since last week. And not a call, not even a bleedin' text. Can you believe that? What a shit. No, hon, I'm keeping my options well and truly open.'

Shauna's boyfriends came and went with unerring regularity. Most of them were no-good losers who leeched off her for a month or two, using her house as a free hotel before disappearing into the sunset. 'I never realised you fancied Solomon.'

'What's not to fancy? Tall, dark and handsome, just the way I like 'em. Not to mention those muscles. He's hot, babe, *really* hot. Come on, don't tell me it's never crossed your mind.'

Maddie shook her head. 'It hasn't. I don't think of him like that.' She supposed he was good-looking in an overly large sort of way, but she thought of him more as family. He was Zac's uncle, Bo's older brother, Winston and Alisha's son. And even if he hadn't been any of those things, she still wouldn't be interested. Solomon worked for the Streets, and that, in her mind, made him a villain. Some women found bad boys exciting, but after what had happened to Greta, she didn't need that kind of excitement in her life.

'Well, just give him a shove in my direction, then.'

'Bit old for you, isn't he?'

'I don't mind that. Older guys know how to treat a woman. No, if he's ever at a loose end, send him over to my place. I wouldn't kick him out of bed.'

They walked to the corner and turned left on to the High Street. The air was close and humid, as if a thunderstorm might be brewing. The summer evening had drawn the crowds and there were a lot of people around, some of them going places, others simply hanging out. Lads sprawled on the pavement, swigging cheap cans of lager with their backs against the wall. Girls strolled past trying to impress them. Kids played their games, dodging between the parked cars, whirling around on the pavement, their young voices rising and falling.

'Bo was pretty fit too,' Shauna said. 'But right cocky with it. He really rated himself, that one.'

Maddie flinched at the name. Sometimes she forgot that Shauna had once lived on the Mansfield estate and had known Bo Vale. She'd been friendly with Greta too. 'Do you think she was happy?' she suddenly found herself asking. 'Greta, I mean. I didn't see much of her before . . . We didn't get the chance . . . Do you think she was?'

Shauna looked at her. 'Are you okay, hon? Has something happened?'

'No. I don't know. I've just been thinking about her recently. I only met Bo a few times and we never really talked. They were together for over three years and I barely knew the man. And Greta never . . . Well, she never said much about him.'

Shauna was quiet for a few seconds as if she was thinking of how to respond. 'Oh, Bo was all right. Sure, he was cocky, but you have to be like that to live on the Mansfield. If you don't play the part, you get pushed around, walked all over. That place is a fuckin' jungle. I wouldn't live there again if you paid me.' She paused again before adding, 'But Greta was fine. She could deal with Bo. She never did anything she didn't want to do.'

Maddie heard an edge to her voice and wasn't sure what it meant. She looked at her for a moment, but Shauna wouldn't meet her gaze. When it came to Greta, Shauna rarely had much to say. Maddie had originally put it down to grief, to the loss of a friend, but now she wondered if there was more to it. Perhaps there were things she didn't know. Before she could ask any more questions, Shauna quickly moved on.

'So what about this Rick guy? What's he like? Is he fit? Tell me everything.'

Maddie threw her another glance, trying to read her face but failing. Had she deliberately changed the subject, or was it just her paranoia? 'There's not much to tell. Yeah, he's not bad. He seems nice enough, but he might not even show. It was only a casual sort of arrangement, not really an arrangement at all. He probably won't be there.'

'Course he will, hon. He wouldn't have said it otherwise, would he?'

'Men say all sorts of things.'

Shauna gave a snort. 'True enough. Lying bastards, most of them. Still, it's not the end of the world if he doesn't turn up. Plenty of fit blokes down the Fox. I'll fix you up with someone.'

'Don't even think about it.' Maddie sent up a silent prayer that Rick would put in an appearance and she'd be saved from Shauna's dubious matchmaking. 'I don't want fixing up, thanks very much.'

'You've been on your own for ages.'

'Maybe I like it that way.'

'Or maybe you've just got used to it. C'mon, Maddie, it's time you had a bit of fun. When was the last time you even went out with a bloke?'

'I don't know. It was so traumatic that I've wiped it from my memory.'

Shauna laughed as they stopped at the traffic lights and waited for them to change. Then they crossed the road to the Fox. There was a group of people standing outside, chatting and drinking as they made the most of the warm summer evening. Others were seated on the wooden benches to the side. Maddie quickly checked out the faces, but Rick's wasn't among them.

It was busy inside, the way it always was on a Friday. The Fox, with its real ale, good food and friendly atmosphere, was the most popular pub in Kellston. The clientele were a mixed bunch, everyone from businessmen, cops and students through to villains and the local toms. Everyone was welcome at Maggie McConnell's pub as long as they behaved themselves. The rules, displayed on a sign on the wall, were simple: no fighting, no soliciting, no thieving and no drugs.

As they forged a path towards the counter, Maddie made what she hoped was a casual survey of the room. She still couldn't spot him. It was so crowded, though, that she couldn't be sure he wasn't there. And there were other rooms at the back, other places he could be sitting. Or maybe he hadn't arrived yet. Or maybe he wasn't coming at all.

They reached the bar and stood waiting to be served. Maddie fought against the temptation to take another look round. She didn't want to appear too eager – or too desperate, come to that. If he came, he came, she decided. If he didn't, it wasn't the end of the world.

12

There was a five-minute wait while the bar staff dealt with the queue of customers. When she finally got served, Maddie ordered a pint of lager for Shauna and a dry white wine for herself. She was taking her change when she felt a tap on her shoulder and turned to see Rick Mallory standing behind her.

'Oh, hello,' she said, as if it was a complete surprise to see him there. With one quick glance her gaze took in his sun-streaked hair, his tanned face and lean, muscular body. He was wearing chinos and a light blue shirt that matched the colour of his eyes. 'How are you?'

'Good, thanks. You managed to get a babysitter, then?'

'Yes, he's staying over at his uncle's tonight.' And then, as soon as she'd said it, she wondered if he'd take it the wrong way, that he'd see it as some kind of come-on, that he'd think she was letting him know that she was free for the *whole* night. She felt a flush of embarrassment burn across her cheeks. 'Er . . . not that I'm planning on staying out too late. Zac's always up at the crack of dawn. You know what kids are like. As soon as the sun rises, he reckons it's time to get up. So I probably won't stay that long, just a few drinks and then ...' Oh God, now she was starting to ramble. What was wrong with her? She was back to behaving like a gauche teenager. With an effort, she tried to pull herself together. 'Sorry, would you like a drink? I've just bought a round.'

'I'm good, thanks. I managed to bag a table in the other room, the one at the back. Unless you'd rather go outside and breathe in the exhaust fumes? I could take a butcher's, see if there are any free benches.'

'The table sounds fine.'

'Ain't you going to introduce us, then?' Shauna asked, nudging Maddie's elbow.

'Yes, sorry, of course. Rick, this is my friend Shauna. Shauna, this is Rick.'

'Hey, Rick,' said Shauna, blatantly looking him up and down. 'Nice to meet you, babe.'

'You too.'

As the three of them wound their way towards the back, Shauna asked him, 'Is this where you usually drink?'

'Yeah,' Rick said. 'Why?'

'It's just that I've been coming here for years and I ain't never seen you before.'

'That's me,' he said. 'Mr Memorable.'

'Oh, I'd have remembered you, hon. I'm sure of it. You local, then? You don't sound like you're from London.'

'I only moved here ... three, four months ago.'

'Really?' Maddie said. 'I never realised that. Where were you living before?'

'Kent, Surrey, Devon, Essex. I've moved around a fair bit in the past few years.'

Maddie felt a tiny stab of disappointment. She processed this information as meaning that he probably wouldn't be staying in

Kellston for long. She knew what it meant to have itchy feet, to be forever moving on. It was easy when you didn't have any responsibilities.

They finally reached the corner table, which he'd managed to reserve by draping his jacket over the back of a chair, and the three of them sat down. Rick still had three-quarters of a pint, and when they were settled, he lifted his glass and said, 'Cheers, then!'

'Cheers,' echoed Maddie, taking a sip of her wine.

It was pleasantly cool and crisp. Just enjoy the evening for what it is, she told herself. Although her hopes had been dashed – there was no point in starting anything with a man who wasn't going to hang around – she refused to let it dampen her spirits. She would simply enjoy the company and have a good night out.

'Where are you living, then?' Shauna asked. 'You got a place in Kellston?'

Rick gave a nod. 'A two-minute walk away. Silverstone Road.'

'Not the Heights?'

He laughed. 'I'm a gravedigger. You ever met a gravedigger who can afford to live in the Heights?'

'I ain't never met a gravedigger before,' Shauna said. 'It's a first for me.' She sat back and stared at him. 'What's that like, then? Must be sort of . . . '

'Sort of . . . ?'

Shauna shrugged. 'I dunno. Weird? Ain't it weird being surrounded by dead people all day?'

'It's quiet,' he said. 'I like it that way. Helps me to think.'

'Yeah? Think about what?'

'Oh, you know, *stuff.*'

Shauna pulled a face and glanced at Maddie. 'He's a thinker, hon. He's one of those deep ones.'

But Maddie understood what he meant, even if he wasn't

being entirely serious. There was something about a cemetery that concentrated the mind. Perhaps it was the way it put things into perspective. Surrounded by the dead, you could see the unimportant things for what they really were. 'And by "stuff" he doesn't mean birds or football,' she said.

Rick grinned at her. 'You remembered.'

Shauna looked from one to the other, aware that she was missing out on a private joke, and then said, 'Maddie here used to do some digging too, didn't you, love?'

'Digging?' asked Rick, looking bemused.

'I trained as an archaeologist,' Maddie explained. 'It's been a while since I worked as one, though.'

He leaned forward, placing his elbows on the table. 'Really? That's interesting. How come you're not doing that any more?'

'Oh, you know.' Maddie lifted her shoulders in a light shrug. 'Long hours, inconvenient places, low pay. Sometimes you can't be sure where you'll be working from one month to the next, which isn't great when you've got a kid to look after. When Zac's older, I might go back.'

Shauna took a slurp of lager and put the glass back on the table. 'When you think about it, you two have a lot in common. I mean, one of you buries people, and the other one used to dig them up.'

Rick caught Maddie's eye and grinned again. 'There you go,' he said. 'That's us sorted.'

Twenty minutes later, Shauna got to her feet and said she was off to chat to some mates who had just shown up. She winked at Maddie. 'Catch you later, huh?' Then she looked at Rick. 'Nice to meet you, love. See you around sometime.'

'Bound to,' he said.

'Okay, cool. Have a good night, you two.'

'Subtle,' said Rick, as he watched her battle towards the bar, her distinctive blonde head bobbing up and down in the crowd.

'As a brick.'

'So do you mind being left alone with me?'

'Horrified,' Maddie said.

'Hey, don't hold back on my account. Just tell it like it is.'

Maddie kept a straight face. '*Utterly* horrified.'

'Ah, now you're starting to dent my confidence. And, I might add, if I'd known you were bringing a wingman, I'd have asked Eli along.'

'Eli?'

'Yeah. You don't think Shauna and Eli would have hit it off?'

Maddie laughed. 'Mm, can't say I'm convinced. I'm not sure if Shauna's altogether keen on the strong, silent type. Although she did mention earlier that she wouldn't mind an older man.'

'Great, that's settled, then. Next time I'll invite him.'

'Who says there's going to be a next time?'

He looked at her over the rim of his glass, his eyes bright with amusement. 'Sorry, am I being presumptuous?'

'Just a little.'

'Sorry,' he said again, smiling. He drained his pint and put the glass down on the table. 'So, would you like another drink while you think it over?'

'Be rude not to,' she said.

As soon as Rick had gone to the bar, Shauna scooted over and sat down beside her. 'How's it going, hon? What do you think?'

Maddie gave another shrug. 'He's okay,' she said.

'He's more than okay.' Shauna's eyes flicked towards the bar. 'Look at the guy! He's hot. He's a catch if ever I saw one. If you're not interested, I'll be more than happy to take him off your hands. Just give me five minutes and—'

'Hey, who said I wasn't interested?'

Shauna grinned from ear to ear. 'Ha, so you do fancy him? I knew you did.'

Maddie, admitting defeat, smiled back at her. 'All right, so maybe I do. A little bit. But you heard what he said. He's always moving around. He could be gone again in a month or two.'

'And?'

'And so what's the point?'

Shauna raised her eyes to the ceiling. 'The point, hon, is to enjoy yourself while you can. You never know what's gonna happen. Life's too short for stressing about tomorrow. Stop worrying about maybes and the rest, and just get out there and grab what's on offer.'

A part of Maddie thought she was right, but the other part – the careful, cautious part – was less than willing to volunteer for another dose of heartache. 'You reckon?'

'It's up to you, babe, but if you don't grab him, someone else will.' Shauna put a hand on her arm. 'Anyway, look, we're off up West. We're going to hit a club or two. I'll give you a bell in the morning, yeah?'

'Okay, have a good time.'

'I always have a good time, babe.'

Maddie watched her as she left, wondering what it would be like to throw caution to the wind. She hadn't always been so staid and boring, but then she hadn't always been a surrogate mum. It was hard to be reckless when someone else relied on you. And then she started thinking about Greta again, about what Shauna had said: *She never did anything she didn't want to do.*

'Penny for them?' asked Rick, as he came back with a pint and a glass of wine.

'Huh?'

'You looked miles away, or were you just planning the best escape route?'

'Oh, I've already worked that out. There's a window in the ladies' takes you straight out into the car park.'

'Handy,' he said. 'I'll try not to get too paranoid.'

'Sounds like a plan. Thanks for the drink.'

He sat down opposite her, took a swig of his pint and put the glass back on the table. 'So, Maddie Layne,' he said, gazing directly into her eyes, 'tell me about yourself. You got family here in Kellston?'

She shook her head, overly aware of his scrutiny. 'No, not here. My mum lives in Portugal, and my dad ... well, he lives wherever the fancy takes him. He's in the States quite a lot, California mostly. That's where he comes from. To tell the truth, he's a bit of a hippy.'

'What, all long hair, beard, love, peace and Bob Dylan?'

'Ah, you've met him.'

Rick laughed. 'I know the type.'

'Yeah, well, he turns up from time to time, but he's not what you'd call the reliable sort.' She paused and then added, 'But I've got Zac's grandparents, Winston and Alisha. They're great. I couldn't manage without them.'

'And Zac's father? He's not on the scene?'

Maddie hesitated before answering. She didn't want to go into it all, not right now. The murder of her sister was an emotional subject and she didn't want to explain until she got to know him better. 'It's a long story.'

'Sorry,' he said. 'I didn't mean to pry.'

'You're not. It's fine. Maybe another time, huh?'

Rick sat back and put his hands behind his head. 'So you're saying there *is* going to be another time?'

'I think the word I used was "maybe".'

'Still,' he said, giving her a wide smile, 'sounds like progress to me.'

Maddie raised her eyebrows. 'Good to know you're the optimistic sort.' She picked up her glass and took a sip of wine. 'Anyway, enough about me. Tell me about your family.'

'It's not very interesting.' He gave a dismissive flap of his hand. 'I wouldn't want to bore you.'

'I'll take the chance. But if I start to yawn, you'll know it's all going horribly wrong.'

Rick laughed and gazed at her for a moment. 'Well, there's not a whole lot to tell. My parents live in Kent, in Canterbury. Dad's a cabbie, and Mum works a part-time job at the local deli. I've got two brothers, younger than me, one married, one not, but both equally annoying. And that's about it, really.' He laid his hands on the table, his palms facing up. 'My family in a nutshell.'

'There, I didn't fall asleep once. Are you close to them? Do you get on? I mean, apart from the brother thing.'

'We get by,' he said. 'You know what families are like. We have our ups and downs, but nothing too dramatic.'

Maddie forced a tentative smile. Drama was her family's middle name. She wondered how he'd react if she ever told him the truth. And then, before he could return to the subject of the Laynes, she quickly shifted the focus off family matters. 'So have you always worked in cemeteries, or is this your first time?'

'No, I've worked in a few. I like them. I'd rather be outdoors than stuck in an office – or a cab, come to that. Although I probably won't be quite so happy when I'm freezing my bits off in the middle of January.' He grinned at her. 'That's the downside, but I reckon there are more positives than negatives. And I'm pretty much my own boss. I don't have anyone breathing down my neck all day. Although that reminds me ... ' He paused to take a drink before continuing. 'Delia Shields was asking about you yesterday.'

Maddie's brow furrowed. 'Me? Why?'

'She wanted to know who was paying you to tend that grave over on the west side.'

'You're kidding? And what did you say?'

'I said I didn't have a clue. She didn't seem best pleased about it, though. I mean, she was trying to act all casual, but I could see she was desperate to find out.'

'She asked me too,' Maddie said.

'And you wouldn't tell her? Why's that?'

Maddie took hold of the stem of the glass, twisting it round between her forefinger and thumb. 'I wasn't sure that it was any of her business.' She stared at the glass for a while before raising her eyes to him again. 'Although, I probably would have if she hadn't got all antsy about it. There was just something about her attitude. She was saying that the family wanted to know, but if the family was that concerned, why have they neglected the grave for so long? It all felt odd, a bit wrong somehow. That's why I didn't tell her.'

Rick's mouth slid into an amused smile. 'The secret of Kellston Cemetery.'

'Oh, it's not much of a secret. She already knows who employed me – or she's taken a pretty good guess. She just wanted me to come out and say it.'

'Really? God, this gets more intriguing by the minute.'

'You haven't heard the half of it.'

'And?'

Maddie tilted her head to one side. 'And what?'

'Don't give me that,' he said, shuffling closer to her and nudging her elbow. 'You can't tell half the story and not the rest. Are you going to spill or not?'

'Well,' she said, 'I still have to figure out whether you're the kind of guy who can be trusted.'

'I am. I'm the most trustworthy guy you could ever hope to meet.'

'And I should believe that because . . . ?'

Rick's voice took on a mock-wheedling edge. 'Because you're a great judge of character. Because you know that really, deep down, you want to tell. Because your secret's safe with me.'

'As I said, it's not exactly a secret.'

'What if I crossed my heart and hoped to die?'

'That tends to work better for eight-year-olds.'

Rick sat back, folded his arms and gave a sigh. 'Well, I'm done. I've given you all my best lines, but it appears that tonight the famed Mallory powers of persuasion are failing to persuade.'

'Famed, huh?'

'Well, I don't like to blow my own trumpet, but . . .'

'Your modesty is most becoming.'

Rick gave a small bow. 'Thank you. Although I would like to add that allegedly a problem shared is a problem halved.'

'Do I have a problem?'

'Delia seems to think so, judging by the expression on her face yesterday.'

'Mm, you could have a point.'

And so, finally, Maddie told him what had happened with Delia and what she'd later found out from Solomon. By the time she'd finished, Rick was looking pensive.

'So what do you think?' she asked.

'It sounds kind of . . .'

'Kind of what?'

He paused for a few seconds before replying. 'Like someone else's argument. Are you sure you want to get caught in the middle of it?'

'Not especially,' she said. 'But until I know what it's all about, I can't really make a decision one way or the other.'

'Maybe you should talk to Delia again.'

Maddie wrinkled her nose. 'Or maybe not. I don't think I'm her favourite person at the moment.'

'You want me to have a word?'

'No, I don't want you getting dragged into this. I'll wait for a while, see if Solomon comes up with anything else.'

'If in doubt, do nothing.'

Maddie gave him a look. 'You think I'm wrong to wait?'

'It just … it just sounds like something you shouldn't get involved in. This guy's in jail and he's in for murder. I don't mean to be judgemental, but is that really someone you want to be working for?'

Maddie put her elbows on the table and placed her chin in her hands. His view, she noted, was the polar opposite to Solomon's. 'And how pleased is Cato going to be if I tell him I'm not going to tend the grave any more?'

'You worried about that?'

'Of course I'm worried. Like you said, the guy's inside for murder. He's hardly the sort of man you want to get on the wrong side of.' But in truth that wasn't the only reason for her reluctance to terminate the contract. She'd developed an attachment to Lucy Rivers's grave, one that was not perhaps entirely healthy but which she didn't yet feel ready to give up. It was the place she went to think about Greta.

Rick picked up a beer mat and tapped it against the side of his glass. His face had become thoughtful again. 'It's too quiet on the west side. If I was you, I wouldn't spend more time there than I had to. I mean, there was that bloke the other day …'

Maddie was reminded of the drifting smell of cigarette smoke, of the feeling of being watched. She remembered with a jolt the rush of fear, of adrenalin, and her overwhelming urge to run. Fight or flight? She had chosen the latter. Now, even though Rick knew nothing of her sprint down the path, she felt the need to play down the incident. 'I'm sure it was nothing. I've never had any trouble there before. Anyway, I can take care of myself.'

Rick looked at her, concern gathering in fine lines at the corners of his eyes. Then his lips parted and a smile appeared. 'Yeah, but you're not the one I'm worried about, babe. It's the poor bloke who tries to creep up on you. There are enough corpses in that cemetery already.'

117

Maddie laughed. 'Is that what they call a back-handed compliment?'

'That's what they call a plea from an overworked gravedigger.'

'I'll watch my back. I'll even keep an eye out for those zombies you're always banging on about.'

'Ah,' he said, shaking his head, 'in my experience it's not the living dead you need to watch out for; it's the living, breathing buggers who cause all the trouble.'

'I can believe it.'

'And so?'

Maddie met his gaze again, their eyes locking. 'And so?'

'You'll be careful, right?'

'Course I will.' But even as she said the words, Maddie felt an odd feeling run through her. It was as if she was having some kind of premonition. It was like someone had walked over her grave.

13

Eli Glass unlocked the heavy wrought-iron gates at eight o'clock precisely. 'Easy does it,' he murmured as he carefully drew them back. Every weekend, for almost fifty years, he had carried out the same procedure. First he opened the gates at the main entrance before walking through the cemetery to the second set. During the week Bob Cannon or Delia Shields did the honours, but on Saturday and Sunday the job was his.

Back in the day, his father had done the very same thing. It was a Glass tradition, but once Eli was gone, there would be no one left to carry it on. He had no children. He hadn't even got a wife. A thin, mirthless laugh escaped from his lips. As if any woman would marry a man like him! Everyone knew that Eli Glass was crazy.

He set off down the main thoroughfare, sniffing at the morning air. It always smelled nicer in the cemetery, fresher and cleaner than on the street. Like the countryside, he thought, although he couldn't actually remember the last time he'd been there. Back when he was a nipper, he reckoned. Anyway, you didn't need the country when it was all right here on your doorstep, the trees, plants and flowers, the squirrels, birds and foxes. There were plenty of parts you could walk and not meet another human being – leastways, not one who was above ground.

He'd been a nipper too when he'd first set foot in the grave-yard, keeping close to his dad, although he hadn't been afraid. No, not afraid, only wary. And it was smart to be wary with all the dead folks wanting to be heard. His father, though, never listened to a word they said; he kept his ears firmly closed to the clamour.

'There ain't nothin' to hear, son,' he'd insist. 'At least, nothin' that's any of our business.'

But Eli hadn't been able to blank out the voices; they'd washed over and around him like waves battering on the shore. It had taken a while before he'd been able to separate one from the other, to make out individuals, to gradually come to recog-nise the men and women who surrounded him.

'He's got the gift,' his mother had said.

But talk like that made his father angry. 'It ain't no gift. Don't you go encouraging the lad.'

His dad had been small and wiry, but strong with it. You had to be strong back in those days with graves to dig by hand and no heavy machinery to do the hard graft for you. It took a pickaxe in the winter to break the ice on the ground. Things were easier now, but Eli still missed the old ways. He liked the connection to the soil, the hard slog, the feeling of achievement when the job was done. There was something . . . well, imper-sonal, about getting a chunk of steel to dig a final resting place.

Eli reached the second set of gates and went through the same procedure as the first. These gates, although solid, weren't as grand as the ones at the front. He drew them back and dropped the bolts into the holes in the ground. How many times had he done this before? Too many to count. The action was automatic now, second nature to him. After the gates were secured, he glanced up and down the street, saw nothing to interest him and retreated into the cemetery.

Fifteen, he'd been, when he'd first come to work here on a proper legal basis, but he'd been coming with his dad for years before that, learning the trade and getting his hands dirty. There was none of that health and safety lark in the sixties, at least none that was taken seriously. And boys could leave school before they'd started to shave. Glad he'd been, bleedin' overjoyed, to leave that place behind.

'You don't want to take no heed of them boys,' his mother used to say, as she brushed the dirt off his blazer. 'Ignorant, that's what they are. You know the problem? People are scared, Eli. They're scared of anyone who's different to themselves. They want everyone to be the same, and by that I mean the same as *them*. And what kind of a world would that be, eh? A world full of idiots.'

Eli's shoulders tightened as he turned off the main thoroughfare on to one of the narrower paths. He'd had no desire to be different, to be anything other than ordinary. For a long time he'd stopped speaking about the voices, but now he no longer cared what others thought of him. If he was still not entirely comfortable in his own skin, he had at least grown accustomed to it.

He came to Lizzie Street's grave – once the most powerful woman in the East End – and stopped for a moment to gaze at the plot. A bunch of yellow chrysanthemums was turning brown in the urn. Not a loving gesture from her husband or from her son either. Neither of them gave a damn. When it came to family, the only legacy Lizzie had left was one of bitterness and resentment. A faint muttering came from the

121

ground, but Eli didn't hang about. He had learned long ago not to get involved in other people's arguments.

Lowering his head, he pushed on until he came in view of the old chapel. A sight for sore eyes it had been back when he'd first come here, with its beautiful white stone, tall steeple and rose-stained windows. Like a fairy-tale castle. They'd held funerals in it then, but not any more. It had been closed to the public for years. The roof was leaking, and vandals had broken most of the glass.

Eli stood and stared at the building. Sometimes, when no one else was around, he would go inside and sit on one of the ornately carved pews. The lower part of the building was boarded up, but he still had a key to the heavy metal door. No one had thought to ask for it back. It was still and peaceful inside, with pure pale light, like rays from heaven, slanting in through the upper windows.

A thin sigh escaped from his lips as he resumed his walk. Nothing was like it had been. Time passed, the world changed, and everything became altered. The shattered windows of the church saddened and disgusted him. There was no respect now for God or religion. Eli wasn't overly fond of God – the two of them had parted company long ago – but he still believed in a deity's right to have his house protected from mindless yobs.

'Animals,' he muttered under his breath.

The creatures crept in at night, bringing their lager and their foil and their pipes, leaving all the shit behind for Eli to clear up in the morning: empty cans, needles and used johnnies. As if he didn't have better things to do than pick up all their crap. There was other stuff went on too, bad stuff that he didn't like to dwell on. You messed with the Devil, he thought, and the Devil would mess with you.

In summer, the cemetery closed at six o'clock. Fifteen minutes before, Eli would get into the truck and make a circuit of the grounds, checking that everyone was gone before he locked the gates again. There were, however, some who chose not to leave, who hid in the bushes or the old crumbling crypts. For a few of the Kellston homeless, sleeping with the dead was a more agreeable prospect than taking their chances on the street. Eli knew they were there but never threw them out. As well as the things he pretended not to hear were the things he pretended not to see.

Delia Shields didn't approve. Her thin lips would purse into a moue of distaste, as if the cemetery was her property and she didn't want it littered with unfortunates.

'Do try and move them on, Eli,' she'd say. 'This really isn't the place for them.'

Missing the point, he thought, that the reason they were here was because they didn't have a place. But then people like Delia had no sympathy for those who had fallen on hard times. She didn't believe in bad luck, couldn't grasp how despair could bring a person to their knees.

Eli knew that Delia didn't like him. It was the kind of dislike that sprang from suspicion and fear. He was odd; he was different; he scared and repulsed her. But it was more than that. She feared him because he *knew* things. She saw her secrets reflected in his eyes. That was why she couldn't meet his gaze, why she could barely stand to be in his company. More than once she had suggested retirement, eager to see the back of him.

'You've worked hard for all these years. Why not take a rest? You deserve it.'

'And do what?' he'd asked.

'Oh, you know. Put your feet up, enjoy yourself, have a nice holiday.'

'I don't care for holidays. Can't see the reason in 'em. Come to that, I don't care much for sitting on my arse all day neither.'

Delia's face had hardened into irritation and impatience. 'Everyone has to retire eventually.'

'And I'll do it when I'm good and ready.' He was still strong and active, still capable of doing his duties, and they'd have a fight on their hands if they tried to get shot of him. No, he intended to keep going for as long as he could. He'd seen the old geezers in the pub, their eyes blank and empty, with nothing more to look forward to than the next pint being passed across the bar.

Eli was approaching the west side now, with its overgrown tangle of grass and weeds. 'You'll not get rid of me that easy,' he muttered. He headed down the narrow, twisting path, his strides long and steady. His boots made a dull thump against the dry earth. Above him, the sky was a clear sheet of blue without a cloud in it. The sun's rays warmed his shoulders and the top of his head. From beyond the walls he could hear the sound of traffic, but it was no more than a distant buzz. Here, in the place of the dead, the external world was of no consequence.

When he came to the grave, he stopped and stood gazing at it. 'Lucy,' he murmured. He did not expect a response and did not receive one. It had been a long time since she'd last spoken to him. His eyes narrowed a little as he stared at the polished headstone. He'd preferred it when the plot was overgrown and hidden, before the girl with the long brown hair had come and cleared away the blanket of ivy. Even with the sun shining down, the ground now seemed cold and exposed.

Eli took a pouch of tobacco from his pocket and slowly, carefully rolled a cigarette. He placed the skinny fag between his lips, struck a match and lit it. While he smoked, he thought about the past, about those long-gone summer days when Lucy would come to the cemetery. A vision, that's what she'd been, the most beautiful woman he had ever set eyes on.

He could have told her – although she wouldn't have listened – that no man was worth it. Broken hearts could be healed, could be glued back together. Hope could be found with the passing of time. His own heart began to thump as he thought about the day he'd found her lying in the silvery water. Shallow, it had been, barely deep enough to drown a child. Her fair hair spread out like a fan. Her eyes still partly open. Her white dress wrapped around her like a shroud.

For a moment he could feel again the tug on his shoulders as he'd half pulled, half dragged her out. Already knowing that it was too late. That had been the first, the only time he had touched her. Her skin smooth and pale and icy. Her mouth slightly open, her curved lips parted as if waiting to be kissed.

He had studied that mouth for longer than he should. And although no sound had come from it, he had heard the whispers on the breeze. Grief had played out its notes on the still summer air. A terrible accident, that's what they said later. But he knew hopelessness when he saw it. He knew desperation and despair.

Eli shifted from one foot to the other. His sunken cheeks hollowed into caverns as he pulled hard on the cigarette. His chest tightened as he held and then expelled the smoke. It drifted for a while, a thin, aimless cloud, before dissolving into nothingness. His gaze slid down to the dark roses, their colour red as blood.

'Lucy,' he murmured again.

It was only then that he stepped forward and laid his hand on top of the stone. Eli believed in justice. Not in courts and police and barristers and judges, but in a natural law, a law that righted wrongs no matter how old they were. What goes around comes around – and that bastard had, eventually, got what he deserved.

So what was happening now? There was a stirring, a shifting, as if Lucy Rivers was slowly waking from a long and dreamless sleep. Over and over she drew him back to her grave, but then presented him with silence. The breath caught in the back of his throat. Something was unfinished. That was what he sensed. The past was catching up and loose ends were starting to unravel.

14

Lena Gissing took the two mugs of tea out on to the roof terrace and put one on the small circular table beside her husband. It was Saturday morning, twenty past nine, and the temperature was rising by the minute. She sat down on the sun lounger and looked out across London. Usually the panoramic view would be enough to put her in a good mood – queen of all she surveyed – but today it did nothing to lift her spirits.

'What?' asked Tony.

She frowned. 'What do you mean, what?'

'What's the matter?'

'Nothing's the matter.' She stretched out her long, smooth legs and examined her scarlet toenails. 'Why should anything be the matter?'

'Because you've got a face like a wet weekend.'

'Yeah? Well, you've got a face like the backside of a bus, but you don't hear me whining about it.'

Tony gave a snort and went back to reading the football news in his paper.

After the trouble with Louise, it had been Lena's intention to check the books and make sure that none of the other girls was taking liberties. But her files, all carefully coded, remained unopened on the table beside her. It wasn't hard to suss out when someone was moonlighting. If the housekeeper didn't pick up on it, then a quick look through the takings would be enough to show if a girl's income had suddenly gone down. It was important to keep on top of things, to not let anyone take the piss, but this morning she couldn't concentrate.

Instead, she gazed out over the rooftops of the houses, the tiles bathed in golden light. In the distance, she could make out the dome of St Paul's. She watched as the cars travelled along the streets, a stream of bright little boxes with glinting windscreens. Kellston was already busy, the market in full swing, and from up here the people looked as small as ants. She flexed her toes and ran her fingers through her hair. She blew across the top of her tea and sipped it absent-mindedly.

A minute passed, and then two. Lena sighed and glanced at Tony. 'I heard a rumour,' she said.

'Huh?'

'About Jay Cato.'

Tony Gissing lifted his eyes from the newspaper and looked at her. 'What about him?'

'He's coming out soon. A few months, six maybe.'

'And?'

'And nothing. Thought you might like to know, that's all.'

Tony shifted on the lounger. He had his shirt unbuttoned and his dome of a stomach, covered in dark hair, protruded into the air like some great abnormal growth. 'Why should I give a toss about that piece of shit?'

'Why do you think?' she snapped back at him. 'He's spent ten years banged up. He ain't going to be happy about it.'

'And he ain't going to do nothin' about it neither. He'll be on licence, won't he? If he comes anywhere near you, they'll haul him straight back to the slammer.'

Lena shrugged and smoothed down her hair. Last night, she'd dreamed about Jay Cato and he was still inside her head. 'He's crazy. Who's to say what he might do?'

'What you heard, then?'

'Not much,' she said quickly. 'Only that he's coming out. It might not even be true.' She wasn't going to tell him about the Lucy Rivers grave. He wouldn't understand why it got under her skin, why it made her flesh creep. Anyway, that was something she was going to sort herself. She didn't want Tony getting in the middle of it, making trouble where it wasn't needed.

'No problem, then, is there?'

'No.' Lena's mouth tightened as she pressed her lips together. She wasn't even sure why she'd mentioned it. Except that she'd wanted to say his name out loud. *Jay Cato. Jay Cato.* As if the more she said it, the easier it would become. She'd spent the past ten years pretending that he didn't exist, blocking him from her thoughts, but now he was back, taunting her with those bloody flowers and ...

'Unless there's something you're not telling me.'

Lena gazed at him from behind her shades. 'Like what, for instance?'

'If I knew that, I wouldn't be asking.'

From beyond the glass doors that led out on to the terrace came the sound of the kettle boiling and the rattling of plates.

'Don't say anything,' she said. 'Don't tell Adam.'

'He'll find out soon enough.'

'Not now,' she said with a warning note in her voice. 'Not today.'

Tony gave her another of his looks. 'He won't thank you for keeping it from him.'

'I'm not keeping anything from him. I don't know yet, do I?

129

Not for certain.' She glanced over her shoulder towards the kitchen. 'What's the point of stirring up . . . ? I'd rather wait, wait until we're sure.'

'It's your call. I ain't going to interfere. All I'm saying is—'

'Yeah, I hear what you're saying.' Lena knew from his tone that he thought she was making a mistake, but Adam was her son, not his, and it was up to her to make the final decision. Adam was twenty-four now, fully grown, but there was still no good way and no good time to reveal the news that the man who'd murdered his father was coming out of jail. 'I'll deal with it.'

Tony took a slurp of tea, put his mug down on the table and went back to reading his paper.

Lena lit a fag and went back to gazing at the view. Except now she wasn't seeing the rooftops or the cars or the little scurrying people – all she could see was Cato's face as he stared up at her from the dock. She was sitting in the gallery of the Old Bailey, watching his eyes as the verdict came in. *Guilty.* And that was justice, wasn't it? That was only fair. If you did wrong, there was always a price to pay.

Five minutes later, Adam came out on the terrace with a plate of toast and a large white mug. 'Mornin',' he said, slumping down beside Lena.

She gave him a nod. 'Good sleep?'

Adam glanced at his fancy Rolex watch as if she was passing judgement on the time he'd got up. 'It's not late,' he snarled defensively. 'I didn't get in till after one.'

'I only asked if you slept well.' The smell of coffee floated over to her and made her feel slightly sick. Or maybe it wasn't the coffee. Sometimes when she looked at her son, all she could see was Brendan Vasser: the same tawny-brown hair, the same cold eyes, the same sneer that played around his lips. 'No need to bite me head off.'

Adam shrugged, shoved the toast into his mouth and started chewing noisily.

Sometimes Lena felt like nature had played a trick on her. It was as if, while her son was in the womb, all her DNA had been discarded, leaving only Brendan's. Everything about Adam, from his physical appearance to the very core of his personality, had Vasser written all over it. Yeah, he was his father's son all right, and that certainly wasn't a compliment. She loved him – she was obliged to do that much – but she didn't actually like him. He was clever and cruel and manipulative.

'We'll need to get them motors sorted soon, Tone,' Adam said, speaking across Lena as if she wasn't there. 'Can't hang about. Boat sails on Thursday.'

'Tuesday,' Tony said. 'We'll have all the chassis numbers changed by then.'

It was Lena who had set up the whole business – nicking luxury cars and shipping them out to Eastern Europe – but she had passed the running of it on to Adam. Now he had a carefully chosen gang of thieves targeting the well-heeled residents of the Home Counties. Tony had dealt in stolen motors for years, but hadn't had the nous to go upmarket. It was Lena who had put it all together, who'd stepped it up a gear. In her view, cars were no different to the girls she employed – not worth the bother unless they were high end, classy and could bring you in a hefty profit.

While her husband and Adam talked business, Lena returned to studying her son. Even his gestures, she noted, were Vasser's: the way he ate and drank, the way he moved his hands, the way he spoke. It was like having Brendan sitting right beside her. As if she could never really be free of him, as if he continued to haunt her even after all these years. The thought of that sent a shudder down her spine.

It had been the best day of her life when she'd heard that

Brendan Vasser was dead. She could still remember that feeling now, the rush of elation, the joy, the knowledge that she was finally free. She had been the merriest widow in the East End. Watching the coffin slide back behind the blue velvet curtain had come a close second. Consigned to the flames, he could no longer hurt her. His power was gone. He was finished, done with, on his way to hell.

There had, however, still been the ashes to deal with. If it hadn't been for Adam, she'd have flushed his sorry remains down the nearest toilet, sent him swirling into the sewers and the shit, but instead she'd taken the container to the cemetery and scattered the contents over the Vasser family grave. Adam had been with her, his face pinched and solemn. She supposed he had the right to say a decent goodbye to his father, even if that father hadn't been worth pissing on in a fire.

'Boys are coming over later,' Tony said to Adam. 'Might nip over to the Fox. You gonna come and have a pint?'

'Sure,' Adam said. 'Why not?'

Adam had his own flat but still stayed over at the Heights two or three times a week. And it wasn't for the company, she thought. It wasn't 'cause he missed his dear old mum. No, he only did it to keep his finger on the pulse, to make sure he wasn't missing out on anything. Keeping an eye on her like Brendan had always done. And keeping his stepfather sweet too, even though he couldn't stand the man or his idiot sons.

Ryan and Luke Gissing were slightly younger than Adam, twenty and twenty-one. They still lived with their mother over in Chigwell. And there was no reason why they shouldn't. The house was plenty big enough for the three of them. She should know. It was her hard-earned cash that had helped pay for it. Still, it had been worth the expense to shut the bitch up and get the divorce pushed through quickly.

Like their father, the boys were both short and squat and

132

ugly. Hardly a brain cell between them either. What was it with small men? It was as if they always had something to prove, that they learned from an early age to overcompensate for their lack of height. Still, Ryan and Luke were easier to deal with than Adam. She knew how to flatter men, how to manage them, and they were both too stupid to realise what she was doing.

'Yeah,' Adam said. 'Be good to catch up.'

Lena threw him a glance. Adam had nothing but contempt for the Gissing boys, but he was smart enough to hide it. In the criminal world, it was always useful to have some mindless muscle, someone to do your dirty work for you. That way, when the law came sniffing around, you could present a clean pair of hands and there was sod all they could pin on you.

'You heard about Terry Street?' Adam said. 'He's been in the Fox again, looking for Joe Quinn.'

Tony gave a grunt. 'Geezer's losing his marbles. Joe's been brown bread for … Jesus, must be forty years or thereabouts. Back in the seventies, I reckon.' He scratched his chin where the morning growth was starting to prickle. 'Yeah, '74, '75, something like that.'

'Makes you think, though, don't it?'

Tony, to whom the concept of thinking was alien, failed to get the drift. 'Eh?'

Adam's mouth slid into a thin, patient smile. 'Gonna be a gap in the market soon, ain't there? Terry's away with the fairies, and his two boys … well, Danny's doing a stretch, and Chris ain't got the heart for it. Writing's on the wall, Tone. Kellston's up for grabs and someone's going to muscle in before long.'

Lena gave an incredulous shake of her head. 'You want to go to war with the Streets? Is that what you're saying?'

'I didn't say nothin' about a war. There ain't gonna be no war. Terry … well, he don't know what day of the week it is, and that only leaves Chris. Right now he's running the whole show

on his own, and there's only so much any man can do. He's jug-
gling, see, and one by one he's gonna start dropping them balls.
Why shouldn't we be there to pick them up?'

'I don't care how many bleedin' balls he drops. We stay out of
it, right?'

'Nah, hold on a sec,' Tony said. 'The lad could have a point.'

Lena gave another exasperated shake of her head. The Streets
and the Gissings had a history going way back, a history where
the Gissings had always come off second best. 'Shall I tell you
what the real point is? The minute you start moving in, you're
going to have Old Bill crawling all over us. Is that what you
want – the law poking their noses into every business we run,
every deal we make? They'll be breathing down our necks
twenty-four seven.'

Tony shifted in his seat again. 'Still,' he said, clearly tempted
by the carrot that Adam had dangled under his nose, 'there
could be a way.'

'Sure,' agreed Adam slyly. 'There's always a way.'

Lena glared at him. 'Yeah, and we'll all end up in the same
place as Danny Street. Is that what you want, to spend the next
ten years of your life in the slammer?' Men just didn't get it
when it came to keeping a low profile. They needed to strut and
brag and flaunt their success. *Respect.* That was the stupid word
they bandied around, taking offence at every slight, real or per-
ceived, and responding more often than not with their fists.

'No need to get the hump, Mum. I was only stating the obvious. And if I can see it, everyone else can too.'

'So leave it to everyone else. Let *them* fight it out with the
Streets. We've got a good thing going here, plenty of cash and
no bother from the law. And that's the way I want to keep it.
Right?'

'Sure,' Adam said. 'I hear you.'

'Tony?'

Tony raised his arms as if in surrender. 'Loud and clear, love. Loud and clear.'

But she noticed the two men exchanging a glance, a quick look of understanding. They'd shut up for the time being – anything to placate her – but later, over a few pints, they'd undoubtedly return to the subject. The trouble was that Ryan and Luke were dim enough to fall for Adam's patter. He'd have them wrapped round his little finger in five minutes flat.

And Tony wasn't much better. Some people, no matter how much they had, always wanted more.

Lena leaned back and closed her eyes. All this talk about Terry had reminded her of Lizzie Street. Lord, she still missed her, still grieved for the friend she had lost. It was Lizzie who'd taught her about business and how to take care of herself. Back in the eighties, Terry had been a real name in the East End, top of the pile, Mr Big, but the marriage hadn't been a happy one. Lena had understood what that was like.

The two women had forged a strong bond, broken only by Lizzie's death a few years ago. Not a day went by when Lena didn't think of her. It was Lizzie who had supported and consoled, guided and encouraged. It was Lizzie who had given her the gun and showed her how to use it.

'It ain't difficult,' she'd said. 'Next time Brendan has a go, just point it at the bastard's bollocks and shoot.'

And Lena would have done too, if someone else hadn't done the job for her. There was no one now she could trust absolutely. Well, apart from Delia, but Delia didn't count. You couldn't have a proper friendship with an uptight spinster who'd never even shagged a man. What did they have in common? Nothing – other than a past that refused to go away, a past Lena would rather forget about.

Cato's face rose before her, mocking and accusing. She gave a jolt and blinked open her eyes. Why couldn't he leave her alone?

135

The man was crazy, sick in the head. She took the files off the table and put them in her lap. Quickly she found the one from Yeats, dug out the pictures of Maddie Layne and stared hard at the girl.

'Who's that?' Adam asked.

'No one,' Lena said.

'She's a fit no one. What's her name?' He reached out a hand. 'Here, pass it over. Let's have a look.'

But Lena held on to the file. 'Just one of the tarts,' she said dismissively. 'Just a sad, pathetic little tart.' Except that this tart was in league with Jay Cato. And that made her the enemy. She could feel the anger welling in her chest. Well, if she couldn't take out her frustration on Cato, she'd do the next best thing. She stared hard at the pictures, memorising the girl's features. It wouldn't be long now before the two of them came face to face.

15

Zac didn't stop talking for the first five minutes after he got back, an endless flow of excited chatter about the museum and his day with Uncle Sol. He paused only to take a sip of the glass of milk that Maddie had poured for him.

'And last night, we watched *Jurassic Park.*'

'Wow,' Maddie said, 'a whole day of dinosaurs. That must have been fabulous.' She grinned at Solomon. 'The two of you must be experts on the subject by now.'

Solomon was slumped at the kitchen table. He was wearing the dazed expression of a man who had gone ten rounds with a stegosaurus and lost. 'Yeah, I ever see one of them lumps walkin' down the street, I'll be sure to know it's a dino.'

Zac tugged at his uncle's sleeve. 'You can't see them now, Uncle Sol, not in Kellston. They've all gone extinct. They don't live here any more.'

'You sure, kiddo? 'Cause I reckon I saw one hiding behind the bushes when we were walking over the green just now.'

Zac giggled. 'Nah.'

'Maybe there's just one left. Like that Loch Ness Monster.'

'They're too big to hide. They're even bigger than you, Uncle Sol.' Zac looked at Maddie. 'Oh, and we had pizza too.'

'Healthy pizza,' Solomon said. 'Had tomatoes on it.'

'And a Coke,' Zac said. 'I had a Coke too.'

'Hey,' Solomon said, throwing him a glance. 'What are you doing, pal? You're not supposed to give away the secrets of a boys' night in.'

Zac stifled a laugh and put his hand over his mouth.

'Yeah, that's it. Keep it zipped or everyone'll want a piece of the action. What happens at Sol's place stays at Sol's place.' He looked at Maddie. 'How about you, babe? You get out last night?'

'Just down the Fox. I went for a drink with Shauna.'

'You have a good time?'

Maddie gave a nod, trying to act casual about it. 'Yes, it was nice, thanks.' In truth, the night had gone much better than she'd expected. Rick had walked her home after the pub had closed, and although she hadn't invited him in – she was too wary to jump headlong into a new relationship – they had arranged to meet again on Saturday. This time he was taking her for dinner at the local Italian, Adriano's. 'And thanks for having Zac.'

'Made a change to get out, huh?' Solomon gave her a long, scrutinising look. 'You should do it more often.'

'Maybe I will.'

Zac finished his milk and put the glass in the sink. 'Maddie? Please can I play on my Nintendo?'

'I suppose. But only for an hour, right?'

'Thanks.' He picked the gadget off the table and zoomed off into the garden.

'Guess the novelty of my company's starting to wear off,' Solomon said.

Maddie gazed through the window, watching as Zac made his way past the vegetable patch and then sat down cross-legged in the small central square of lawn. 'I wouldn't take it personally. You'd have to be Tyrannosaurus rex to compete with that gizmo.'

She turned back to Solomon. 'You look worn out. Is it just my imagination or are you in desperate need of a Red Bull?'

Solomon's eyes lit up. 'You got Red Bull?'

'No, but I've got coffee.'

'Coffee it is, then.' He stretched up his muscular arms and yawned. 'I've never been so knackered in my whole life. That kid never stops.'

'Only when he sleeps.' Maddie put the kettle on and waited for it to boil. 'So how come you weren't working last night? Aren't Fridays busy at Belles?'

'I just fancied a few days off. And it's always busy. Man never tires of the beauty of the female form.'

Maddie leaned against the counter and instinctively folded her arms across her chest. Belles was a lap-dancing club in Shoreditch, a popular haunt of the slick City boys looking for somewhere to squander their bonuses. It was owned by the Streets, the family of villains that Solomon worked for. 'Maybe man should learn a little self-restraint.'

'Ah, Lord, you ain't gonna give me a lecture on the evils of lap dancing, are you? Have some pity, babe. I'm not sure I can take it after enduring all those dinosaurs. Might break down and run screaming from the room.'

'Well, I'd hate to have that on my conscience.' She paused for a moment and then added, 'But it might not stop me.'

'Girls earn good money. Guys get an eyeful. What's the big deal? Everybody goes home happy.'

'You don't believe that for a second.'

Solomon heaved out a breath. 'There's worse things happening out there, babe. Bit of baby oil and a few bare tits ain't nothing compared to some of the shit going down. Worse stuff happening every day; that's the way I look at it. Talking of which, I've got more news on your Mr Cato.'

'Really?'

'Make me that coffee and I'll fill you in.'

'I can listen and make coffee at the same time.'

Solomon grinned. 'Sure you can, hon, but it's hard to talk when your throat's this dry.'

Maddie quickly made the drinks and took them over. She put the two mugs down, pulled out a chair and sat opposite him. 'Okay? Now, what have you found out?'

Solomon took a gulp from his mug and frowned. 'You put sugar in this?'

'Two,' she said. She passed him a teaspoon. 'Here, give it a stir.' She waited impatiently while Solomon stirred, sipped, stirred and sipped again.

'Yeah, that's better.' He put his elbows on the table and looked at her. 'Right, back to Cato. Seems he wasted a geezer by the name of Brendan Vasser. You heard of him?'

'No. Should I have done?'

'Not really. He was a face for a while, but more around the West End than here. Did a bit of business with Terry Street, though. That was back when Terry had interests up West. We're talking years ago, before my time. Vasser had more or less retired when Cato put a bullet in him, and from what I've heard, no one did a whole lot of grieving.'

'Do you know why he did it?'

'Vasser was a shit, apparently. Reason enough for some people.'

Maddie thought about this for a moment. 'So this Cato, was he a "face" too? Was it a gangland killing?'

Solomon shook his head. 'More personal than business. Ain't sure of all the ins and outs, but one thing's for certain – there was a woman in the middle of it.'

'Lucy Rivers,' she said with confidence.

But Solomon gave another shake of his head. 'Nah, it wasn't Lucy Rivers. This war was over Lena Gissing, or Lena Vasser as she was then.'

Maddie, who had thought she was beginning to understand, now found herself back at square one. She picked up her mug and frowned at Solomon over the rim. 'Lena Gissing?'

'Don't tell me,' he said, grinning, 'you ain't never heard of the Gissings neither.'

'Sorry.'

'You need to brush up on your villains, girl. Can't live in the East End and not know who's who.'

She raised her brows a fraction. 'Lucky I've got you to educate me, huh?'

'It's a mercy,' he agreed. 'Now, you think you can remember all this, or do you want to take notes?'

'Just get on with it.'

'Okay, here we go. Well, the Gissings have been around since Noah – family going back generations. And all of them on the wrong side of the law. Nothing big time, just petty thieves, dodgy scrap merchants and the like. But they got a history of trying to muscle in on the major firms.'

'Ambition,' she said dryly. 'That's always good to see.'

'All well and good having ambition if you've got the nous to go with it. Trouble is, the Gissings ain't got nada up here.' Solomon tapped his forehead with his index finger. 'Tossers, the lot of them. Type that give stupidity a bad name. Don't stop 'em trying, though. Got to give 'em credit for blind optimism, if nothing else.'

'And what about Lena?' asked Maddie, keen to find out more about the woman at the centre of it all.

'Hang on – I'm getting there. Seems Cato had the hots for her back when she was married to Vasser. Depending on whose story you believe, he was either trying to save her from a vicious thug or just eliminating the competition.'

'So they were having an affair? Cato and Lena, I mean.'

Solomon picked up the teaspoon and began to tap out a rhythm on the table. 'Not according to her. She reckoned she barely knew him.'

Maddie frowned again, confused. 'What?'

'Yeah, reckoned he was one of those stalker types, that he'd got this obsession with her, wouldn't leave her alone. Didn't do nothing about it, 'cause she figured he'd get bored before too long, move on to someone else.'

'And was she telling the truth?'

Solomon threw back his head and laughed. 'Man, that Lena Gissing wouldn't know the truth if the Angel Gabriel came down to earth and delivered it in person.' He took a moment to recover himself and then added, 'Nah, she was probably screwing the poor bastard. Maybe got him to do her dirty work for her too. Least, that's what most folks suspect. Not the jury, mind – they swallowed the grieving widow routine hook, line and sinker.'

'So Cato went down for murder and she—'

'Got away with it. Yeah. That's how it looks. A year or so later, she went on to marry Tony Gissing.'

'Lena certainly likes her villains.'

'Don't she just. But second time round, she was careful to marry one who wasn't smarter than her. Tony struts around like he owns the neighbourhood, but she's the one calling the shots. Everyone knows that. Doing a damn fine job of it too: fancy apartment in the Heights, couple of tasty motors, nice holidays in the sun every year. Yeah, Tony landed on his feet there.' He put the spoon down and leaned back. 'Anyway, that's the story, hon. Got any questions?'

'Yes,' Maddie said. 'What's Cato's connection to Lucy Rivers?'

Solomon gave a shrug of his mighty shoulders. 'Sorry, babe, can't help you there. No one I spoke to has ever heard of her.'

'Still a mystery, then.'

'Could be she was just a friend or an old girlfriend, someone he was thinking about. You do a lot of thinking inside. You've got plenty of time for it.'

Maddie had the feeling he was speaking from experience. Had Solomon been to jail? She didn't know and didn't like to ask. 'Maybe,' she said softly, although she thought there was more to it. The cleaning of the grave, the weekly flowers, all spoke of some grand gesture – but did that gesture spring from love or guilt?

Solomon glanced at his watch before rising to his feet. 'I'd best be off. Promised the old man I'd take a look at that clapped-out motor of his. Thanks for the coffee, hon.'

'Thanks for the info.'

He went to the garden, waved and shouted out to Zac, 'Hey, pal! I'm off. See you soon, yeah?'

Zac waved back. 'See you, Uncle Sol. Thanks for taking me to the museum. Can we go again?'

'Sure we can.' He walked to the front door with Maddie. 'You reckon he'll grow out of these dinosaurs soon?'

'Probably,' she said. 'In a year or so.'

Solomon's face took on a pained expression. 'Lord, a man could suffer a lot in a year.'

Maddie grinned, said goodbye and went back to the kitchen. She washed the mugs and left them on the drainer to dry. Then she stood by the window watching Zac while she mulled over what she'd learned about Cato. It was a relief, she supposed, to find out that his victim had been a less-than-pleasant character. But Cato was still a murderer. Had he killed to protect Lena Gissing or to get her for himself? Either way, Maddie didn't want anything more to do with him.

Opening the drawer beside the sink, she reached into the back, rummaging behind the tea towels until she found the gold wedding band. She held it up to the light for a second and then drew it closer to her eyes. She studied the engraving on the inner rim. *For ever.*

Maddie felt a coldness wash over her. She thought of Lucy Rivers, dead and buried for over thirty years. When she'd first found the ring, she'd wondered if it was the symbol of some great romance, a tragic love affair, but now she had her doubts. What if there was something more sinister about it? If Solomon was right, then Jay Cato was a man of extreme obsessions. It was better, she decided, to sever whatever limited ties she had with him.

She gave a nod, the decision made. On Wednesday, she would tidy the grave for the last time, put the ring back where she had found it and then send a text message to Cato's phone informing him that she could no longer tend the plot. And that, all things being well, would be the end of it.

16

Adam Vasser's face took on a hard, resentful edge as he pushed through the early evening crowd and walked out of the Fox. One day, people would make an effort to get out of his way instead of blocking his path like he was a bleedin' nobody. One day, people would show some respect. He could imagine that moment – the crowd parting like he was Moses doing his trick with the Red Sea – and the prospect made him feel marginally better.

'Shitheads,' he muttered.

Had his father still been alive, everything would be different. Brendan Vasser had been a somebody, a name, a man with a reputation. Adam could have been working beside him now instead of being tied to his mother's apron strings, still reliant on her for weekly handouts. The business bored him – motors coming in, motors going out – and it wasn't as if he was really the boss. She was always looking over his shoulder, checking up on everything he did.

Four pints of beer were sloshing about in his bloodstream,

but he still felt stone-cold sober. As he headed across the road and back towards Silverstone Heights, his list of grievances grew longer. Close behind the way his mother treated him was the fact that he was related – albeit only by marriage – to the ridiculous Gissing clan. The whole family was a waste of space and despised by everyone who mattered. They were wankers, idiots, a bunch of losers. His stepfather, Tony, had only managed to avoid the slammer by attaching himself to the Black Widow. Yeah, that name suited his mother down to the ground. She was a poisonous spider spinning her web round everyone she knew.

Well, he wasn't going to be another of her victims. He was a Vasser, not a Gissing, and he had big plans. He looked along the High Street, lifting his gaze to scan the three tall concrete towers of the Mansfield estate. To be a somebody, you needed turf, a base, a place to rule from, and he intended to have Kellston. Terry Street was on the way out and Adam intended to step into his shoes.

The future was in drugs, in crack, cocaine, cannabis and all that other shit. For the past few months he'd been sussing out the dealers on the Mansfield. They were mainly Street men, but in this world loyalty didn't count for much. Money speaks, and for those who couldn't be bribed to come and work for him, there were more physical means of persuasion.

This was where the extended Gissing family would finally come in useful. Tony's two brothers were banged up, but there were enough sons, nephews, cousins and second cousins to form a small army. Adam wasn't planning on a war – wars were too bloody, too protracted – but rather a few quick strikes that would take the Streets by surprise and knock them off their perch for ever.

Yeah, if you ran the drug supply, you ran the area. He'd already got a stash hidden away from the prying eyes of his mother, but he needed more – and he knew how he was going to get it. Soon the Streets would get a delivery from their Colombian friend Mendez, and Adam planned to snatch it from them.

For the past year he'd been staking out Chris Street, studying his movements, his comings and goings. This wasn't so easy when it came to Belles or the Lincoln Pool Hall, but spying on the house itself – where both Chris and Terry lived – was a doddle. Once he'd discovered there was a clear view of Walpole Close from his mother's penthouse apartment, he'd been able to do his surveillance in comfort. All he'd needed was a pair of good-quality binoculars and enough coffee to keep him awake through the early hours.

Eventually, he'd built up a picture of how the system worked. Once a month, Chris would leave the house at five in the morning, pick up Solomon Vale and then drive down to the lock-ups near the old railway arches. The Colombians would arrive at half past five, always in a white van. The van would drive into the open lock-up, the steel shutters would come down, and the exchange would be made. The whole procedure never took more than ten minutes.

'Lazy,' Adam murmured smugly. It was a mistake never to change the routine. But that was the Streets all over. Believing in their own infallibility, they'd grown overconfident and careless. Or maybe Chris Street was too preoccupied by his old man's slide into madness to give any proper attention to the business.

The Street family had ruled for too long. It was a tired regime, past its sell-by date. What Kellston needed was fresh blood, young eyes, a new perspective, and he was just the guy to provide it. He didn't care what his mother thought; he felt nothing but contempt for her lack of vision. Safety first, that was always her motto, but you never got anywhere by playing it safe.

He went back to thinking about the lock-up. There were

security cameras there, but that was the least of his problems. The tricky part would be actually getting into it. Even from a distance he could tell that the shutters were reinforced and that it would probably take dynamite to blow a hole in them. He quite liked the idea of blowing the doors off – there was nothing like making a statement – but what if all the contents went up in smoke too? No, he might have to consider a more subtle approach.

He was still pondering on this when his phone started ringing. 'Yeah?'

'It's me. Where are you?'

'I'm on my way.'

'You said that last time I called. I've been sitting on this bloody doorstep for hours. I bet you're still in the pub. Are you? What are you doing? Are you coming or not?'

Adam raised his eyes to the heavens. What was it with women that they always felt the need to nag? The bitch should be grateful that he'd offered her a bed for the night, a roof over her head, but instead she was intent on giving him an earful. 'Keep your hair on. Two minutes. I'm two minutes away.'

He hung up before she had the chance to say anything else and was tempted to take the scenic route home. It was bad enough having his mother on his back without her joining in too. If it hadn't been for the fact that he was in desperate need of a slash, he might have walked around for another half-hour just to teach her a lesson.

As Adam turned the corner into Cherry Street, he could see the lovely Louise sitting on the top step, flicking through a magazine. She had a half-angry, half-sulky look on her face and was puffing on a cigarette with the same impatience as she was turning the pages. He was already regretting that he'd invited her to stay. In truth, he'd only done it to spite his mother. He frowned. No, that wasn't the only reason. He reckoned Louise

Cole could be useful, although he hadn't quite figured out how. Still, he'd think of something. A girl like her would never go to waste.

Irritated by her presence, he lifted his gaze to take in the house. The building, a three-storey Victorian conversion, was leaning towards the shabby, but the rooms inside were large and airy. He rented the first floor, a two-bedroom flat that suited him nicely. He could have lived on the Heights, but had no desire to do so. The place was all walls and locks and cameras, like some bloody prison, except it was designed to keep the lowlifes out of the compound rather than in.

Adam was almost at the gate before she clocked him.

'Jesus, where have you been?' she said, jumping to her feet. 'I've been here for hours.'

Adam's lip curled. 'Haven't we already had this conversation? Shit, I'm doing you a favour here. A "thank you" wouldn't go amiss.'

Her eyes flashed as if she was about to have another go at him, but then she thought better of it. When she spoke again, her tone was more peevish than accusatory. 'I'm just tired, that's all. I've been lugging this case around for ever.'

He put his hands on his hips and stared at her. It was only a couple of days since his mother had chucked her out of the Chelsea apartment and already she'd exhausted all her other options. Sometimes you didn't have as many friends as you thought. 'I had a bit of business. I told you.' He glanced up at the clear blue sky. 'Anyway, it's not as though it's pissing down. Come on, let's go inside.'

Adam walked along the short path and up the steps, put the key in the lock and opened the door. He entered the shared lobby hallway, went over to the table and checked through the mail. Nothing for him. When he turned round, she was still standing on the doorstep. 'What now?'

Louise glanced down towards her large brown Louis Vuitton suitcase. 'You going to help me with this, babe?'

Adam walked back to the door. The case had wheels, but Louise was the type of woman who expected a man to do everything for her. He grabbed hold of the handle and rolled it into the hallway. 'First floor,' he said, gesturing with his free hand. 'You go on. I'll follow you.'

As she started climbing the stairs, he picked up the case by its handle. It weighed a ton. He was tempted to put it down again and jolt it up on its wheels but decided this might make him look less than masculine. 'Fuck, what have you got in here – bloody bricks?'

'Just stuff.'

Adam's arm was aching by the time he reached the top. It took a concerted effort not to wince in front of her. He unlocked the door and yanked the case into the flat. 'I need a slash,' he said, heading for the bathroom. 'Kitchen's through there if you fancy a coffee or anything.'

When he got back, Louise was roaming around the living room, picking things up and putting them down. She had the critical look of a prospective tenant examining the fixtures and fittings. After the luxury of her Chelsea apartment, the prospect of kipping down in the backstreets of Kellston was clearly less than appealing. Still, beggars couldn't be choosers. She was lucky that he'd said yes.

Anyway, there was nothing wrong with the flat. It was clean and tidy, everything in its place and a place for everything. He liked things organised. He couldn't stand mess. In fact, just the presence of Louise seemed to make the spacious room feel cluttered.

'What are you doing? Why don't you sit down?'

Louise lowered herself on to one of the black leather sofas and crossed her long, tanned legs. She flicked back her hair and looked at him. 'It'll only be for a few nights, until I get myself sorted.'

'No problem,' he said. But girls like her, girls with a habit, didn't get themselves sorted – at least not until they reached rock bottom. Then she would go running home to Mummy and Daddy, to the house in the country and the month in rehab. But not yet. She hadn't reached that point yet. She was on a downward spiral – losing her job, losing her home – but was still blindly oblivious to the darkness that was coming.

Louise gave him a thin, slightly pleading smile. 'So, er . . . did you get it?'

'Course,' he said, digging into his pocket and pulling out the sachets. He threw them on the sofa. 'Help yourself.'

She snatched them up, her eyes glinting. 'Ta.'

Adam went over to the cabinet, reached into the back and took out a tortoiseshell box. He placed it on the low table in front of her, flipping open the lid. Inside was an oblong mirror, a small pile of razor blades and a pack of plastic straws. He watched as she leaned over and quickly, impatiently, poured the powder on to the mirror before nudging it with a blade into long, fat lines. Some of the coke spilled out over the coffee table, leaving an untidy trail of dust across the shiny polished glass. He instinctively flinched, fighting the urge to bend down and clear away the mess.

'Careful!' he snapped. 'Doesn't grow on bleedin' trees, you know.'

She glanced up at him, hearing the hard edge to his voice. 'Sorry, hon.' But the apology was a cursory one and she immediately switched her attention back to the coke.

'You want a beer?' he asked.

She didn't answer.

'Louise?'

She looked up at him again. 'Huh?'

'Beer,' he repeated. 'Do you want a beer?'

'Oh, okay. Cool.'

Adam walked through to the kitchen, grabbed a couple of bottles from the fridge and flipped off the caps. He went back to the living room and sat down at right angles to her on the other smaller sofa. He took a long pull of beer, watching as Louise picked up the straw and bent over the mirror. She was wearing a scoop-necked black and white dress and he could see straight down the front of it. Her breasts were a honey-brown colour, large and smooth. Her white bra had a ruffle of lace round the edges.

He stared at her cleavage, feeling nothing but indifference. Although he occasionally slept with girls, it was only for appearance. He felt no real lust for them, no desire. The trouble with women was that ... Well, the trouble was that they weren't men. He disliked the softness of their flesh, their smell, even the way they moved.

In the company of blokes like the Gissings, Adam was careful to keep these feelings to himself. It might be the twenty-first century, but in certain circles it was still unacceptable to be gay. Once he had power and influence, he could do as he liked, be who he liked, but until then he would conduct his liaisons away from prying eyes and away from Kellston.

Louise snorted a couple of lines, sat back and sniffed loudly. 'Go on, hon,' she said, nodding towards the mirror. 'There's plenty to go round. Fill your boots.'

Adam shook his head. 'Nah, I'm not in the mood.'

'That's the point, babe,' she said, giggling. 'It's to get you in the mood.'

But Adam rarely touched the stuff. Sure, he had all the paraphernalia, but that was only for when he had visitors. He had seen what addiction did to people, how it pulled them down into the abyss. It was a weakness, and he despised weakness.

'You know something?' she said. 'Your mother's a bitch.'

'Get your facts right.' Adam took another swig from the bottle and grinned at her. 'My mother's a *rich* bitch.'

'You're not wrong there. Can you believe it, just chucking me out like that? What a cow! And I'm the one who's been doing all the damn work, lining her pockets while she swans around like Lady Muck. Did I tell you what she said to me? She just turns up out of the blue and ...'

As Louise embarked on a tale he'd already heard over the phone, Adam's thoughts drifted back to the morning and to the file that his mother had been reading. The fact that she hadn't wanted him to see it had made him all the more determined to do so. He couldn't stand the way she hid things from him, the way she treated him like a kid.

' ... and if she thinks she's going to get away with it, she's got another think coming. I mean, it's not bloody fair, is it? It's not right. And you can't just throw someone out on the street like that. It's not as though ...'

The early evening sun was slanting through the windows, casting a lemony glow over the moss-green carpet. Louise continued her tirade. Adam raised a hand to his mouth and chewed on a nail. He'd finally got a chance to see the file when his mother had received a phone call and disappeared into the apartment. A part of him wished he hadn't read it now.

The report was from that slimeball Yeats and was all about a girl called Maddie Layne. The face in the photographs had seemed vaguely familiar to him. One of his mother's tarts? That was what she'd said, but he hadn't believed her. Something had told him otherwise. He had skimmed through the written contents – age, address, where she worked, who she saw – none of which was particularly interesting.

It had taken a minute or two for the penny to drop, for him to suddenly realise. The shock had been like a low, painful thump to his guts. Maddie *Layne*. There had to be a connection. An unwelcome image of Greta had risen into his mind. Jesus! Yes, of course, this girl must be her sister – the same slim build, the same eyes, the same hair – but why the hell was his mother having her followed?

Adam's fingers tightened around the bottle. Louise yattered on, her voice like an irritating buzz in his ear. He would have liked to smash the bottle in her face, to shut her up for good. He needed to think. He needed to figure out what he was going to do next. One thing was for certain: he should never have got involved with Bo Vale. That had been a big mistake. He had thought it was all over, done with, but now he wasn't so sure. Getting away with murder wasn't always as easy as it seemed.

17

The days passed by in a blur of work, school runs, cooking, cleaning and washing. Before Maddie knew it, it was Wednesday morning again and she was on her way to the cemetery. This time, in addition to her final visit to Lucy Rivers, she also had two other graves to tend. Zac had been dropped off at his grandparents' – Alisha would pick up Kyle and take the boys to summer school – and she had two clear hours before her shift started at Marigolds.

Now that she had made the decision to sever her ties with Jay Cato, she felt a mixture of relief and guilt. She would be glad to be free of her involvement with a murderer, but felt bad about abandoning Lucy. A part of her felt, irrationally, as if she was turning her back on Greta too. Not that the plot would be neglected: Cato would simply employ someone else to tend it. And if he didn't . . . well, there was nothing to stop her visiting the grave from time to time.

The rucksack, heavier than usual, bounced against her back. As well as her tools, her cloths and water, it also contained bags of potatoes, carrots and beans. She had a detour to make before passing through those cemetery gates. Turning left along Lester Road, she kept on walking until she reached a small terraced house that, on the outside, was almost identical to her own. The inside, however, couldn't have been more different.

Agnes Reach must have been watching out for her because she had the door open before Maddie had even reached for the bell. 'Hello, dear. Come in, come in. It's lovely to see you again.'

'And you. How have you been?'

'Oh, very well, thank you. Isn't it a marvellous day? They say the weather might break at the weekend, so we'd better make the most of it.'

Agnes was eighty-two years old, a tiny, bird-like woman who, despite her physical fragility, still had an active mind and a keen interest in everything that went on in the world. She had lived in the house for over sixty years and the interior, with its patterned carpets and tasselled lamps, still had a fifties feel to it. The only nod to modernity was a small flat-screened TV nestled in the corner of the living room.

Maddie followed her through to the kitchen, where a teapot with a pink knitted cover was already sitting on the table along with two china cups and saucers. She heaved the rucksack off her shoulder, put it down on the floor and opened it.

'I've brought some veg. I hope you can use it. We've had a bumper crop this year, much more than we can eat ourselves.'

'Are you sure?' Agnes asked, as she peered inside the brown paper bags.

'It'll only go to waste otherwise.'

'Well, if you're sure. Thank you, dear. That's very kind.'

Agnes had been Maddie's first client and over time the two of them had become friends. Her husband, Alfie Reach, had been dead for seven years. With her dodgy hip and her painful arthritis, Agnes couldn't walk far and had needed someone to tend the grave and put flowers on once a month.

Maddie didn't like taking her money – she knew that Agnes lived on a meagre pension – but her offer of doing it for free had been flatly refused. Agnes was a proud woman and wouldn't take charity. By bringing regular supplies of 'unwanted' vegetables, Maddie was able to still her own conscience and everyone was happy.

'You'll stay for a cuppa?' Agnes asked. 'It's all brewed and ready.'

Although she had work to do, Maddie knew that Agnes didn't get many visitors and looked forward to having someone to talk to. 'Thanks. I'd love one.'

She pulled out a chair and sat down at the table. As Agnes poured the tea, her gnarled hands shook a little. Maddie bent down over the rucksack, pretending not to notice. 'Oh, I almost forgot. I brought you roses too,' she said, pulling out one of the stiff cardboard containers that protected the flowers. Inside were half-a-dozen blooms with long arching stems, the outer petals blush-pink, the inner ones a deeper shade. 'They're called Gentle Hermione. I've got some for Alfie as well.'

'Well, aren't they beautiful,' Agnes said. 'They'll cheer up the place no end.' She put down the teapot and picked up one of the roses, bringing it close to her face so that she could breathe in the fragrance. 'And what a smell! They're like the ones my mother used to grow.'

Maddie stood up. 'Here, I'll put them in the sink and you can find a vase for them later.'

'You're a darling. Thanks. So how's it going at the cemetery? Got any new customers yet?'

'Sadly not.' Maddie put the plug in and ran some cold water. She didn't mention that as of today she was about to be one customer down.

'I'm sure things will improve come winter. People don't want to be out in all weathers.'

'I hope so,' said Maddie, joining Agnes at the table again. Losing that monthly cheque from Cato was going to put a hole in her finances. 'Perhaps I'll place another ad in the paper, see if I can drum up some trade. Or try and get more shifts at Marigolds.' She took a sip of tea and placed the cup back on the saucer. 'Actually, there was something I meant to ask you. Did you ever come across a girl called Lucy Rivers? I'm going way back here, about thirty years or so.'

'Lucy Rivers,' Agnes repeated. She gave a light sigh. 'Now, I haven't heard that name in a long time.'

Maddie leaned forward, her eyes flashing with interest. Before she'd retired, Agnes had worked at the post office, where she'd come into contact with most of the local population at one time or another. 'You knew her?'

'She was a nice girl, a lovely girl. Such a shame about what happened.'

Maddie waited, hoping she'd go on, but Agnes simply sighed again, inclined her head and gazed off into the middle distance. For a while there was no sound in the kitchen other than the loud ticking of the clock on the wall. Eventually, having learned that these silences could go on indefinitely unless interrupted, Maddie gave her a prompt. 'So ... er ... what did happen to her?'

Agnes gave a tiny jump as if she'd been startled. 'Sorry, dear?'

'Lucy Rivers.'

Agnes frowned as if the name meant nothing to her, but then her brow suddenly cleared. 'Oh yes, poor Lucy. I remember now. She drowned, you know. It was a such a tragedy.'

Maddie started, reminded of Greta's terrible death. 'Drowned?'

'Yes, dear. In the cemetery of all places. There used to be a pond there, round the back of the old chapel. It's gone now, of course: they drained it after ... And it wasn't very deep, a few feet at the most. They said it was an accident, but ...'

Maddie felt a chill run through her. 'You don't think it was?'

'Well, there was a man involved.' Agnes gave a wry smile. 'Isn't there always? She'd got attached to some undesirable sort and—'

'You think he murdered her?'

Agnes's eyes widened in surprise. 'Murdered her? Heavens, no! Whatever makes you think that?'

Maddie shook her head, confused. 'But I thought you said ...'

'Oh, I didn't mean that he killed her. Although perhaps in a roundabout way he did. He was married, led her on, the usual story. Nothing but empty promises. Never had any intention of leaving his wife. A bounder through and through.' She paused. 'Although I don't suppose you call them "bounders" these days. It's an old-fashioned sort of word. Anyway, after he'd got what he wanted, that was that. And the poor girl was heartbroken. Everyone with eyes could see she was distraught, but no one imagined that she'd ... Well, I can't be sure. Maybe it was an accident. But it was a warm day, a summer's day, and the ground was dry. Even if she had fallen in, she could have easily got out again.'

Maddie sat very still, taking it all in. Her mind, though, was whirring away. Had Jay Cato been the man who'd betrayed Lucy Rivers all those years ago? Perhaps it was playing on his conscience. Perhaps, as Solomon had suggested, he had time on his hands and was dwelling on the past.

'It was Eli Glass who discovered her,' Agnes continued. 'Must have been a terrible shock, finding her dead in the water like that. And there were some who pointed the finger, said that Eli was crazy, that he probably killed her. Luckily for him, he'd been digging graves all morning and hadn't been alone. Didn't stop the gossip, though. People can be cruel, very cruel.'

'They can,' Maddie agreed. But it was hardly surprising that Eli had been a suspect. He was different, and people didn't like difference. It made them uneasy. And there was something disturbing about all his talk of ghosts and voices. She shifted a little in her seat, uncomfortably aware that she wasn't entirely innocent of passing judgement on him either.

'What makes you ask? About Lucy Rivers, I mean. It was all such a long time ago.'

'I've been tending the grave,' Maddie said. 'She was so young and . . . I suppose I'm just curious about her.' She hesitated, took a breath and then asked the question that had been on her lips for the past few minutes. 'I don't suppose you remember the name of the man, do you, the one that Lucy was seeing?'

Agnes thought about it for a bit, the wrinkles growing deeper on her temples, but then shook her head. 'No, sorry, I can't say I do. I'm not good on names these days. Faces, yes, I can still recall those, but names escape me.'

'It wasn't Cato, was it? Jay Cato?'

'No, no, it definitely wasn't that. That's a rather unusual name, isn't it? I'm sure I would have . . . No, I'm sure I've never heard that before.'

Maddie sat back, swallowing her disappointment. Another theory shot to bits. She was still no closer to unearthing Cato's connection to Lucy Rivers. Just for a moment she'd been convinced that he must have been her lover, her seducer, the man who'd driven her to suicide, but unless Agnes was mistaken, he couldn't have been.

'Sorry, dear. I'm not being much help, am I?'

Maddie smiled and rose to her feet. 'Not to worry. It doesn't matter, really it doesn't. Thanks for the tea. I'm sorry to rush off, but I've got to be at work by ten and I have to call by the cemetery first.'

Agnes accompanied her to the front door, said goodbye and then just as Maddie was strolling down the path, called out, 'Do you know, I could be wrong, but I think it might have begun with a "V". Varley, Venables, something like that.'

Another name instantly jumped into Maddie's head. 'Vasser?' she suggested.

Agnes lifted and dropped her thin shoulders. 'Maybe. It could have been.'

'Okay, thanks. I'll see you soon.' Maddie gave a wave and set off down the street. She repeated the name to herself as she walked: *Vasser, Brendan Vasser.* Now she was even more confused. He was the man who Cato had murdered, the man who'd been married to Lena Gissing. So what did that mean? What was the connection between them all? She went over what she knew in her head, but still couldn't make any sense of it.

Maddie continued to ponder on the mystery. With Vasser entering the equation, things had taken an unexpected turn. But why was she even thinking about it? In a few hours, after the grave had been cleaned and the gold ring returned, her part in it all would be finished. She shifted the rucksack on to her other shoulder and quickened her pace.

18

Maddie gave a fast sideways look towards the low-slung build-ing as she passed through the cemetery gates. The office didn't open until nine, but Delia Shields was already at her desk. Had she seen her? She must have. Maddie hurried up the main thoroughfare, hoping that the woman wouldn't come out to harass her again.

At the willow trees, she stopped and glanced over her shoul-der. The office door was still firmly closed. Maddie let out a breath, not even realising that she'd been holding it. Whatever Delia's problem – and it was clearly connected to Cato – she didn't want to get involved in another altercation. Up until last week, she'd viewed the cemetery as a peaceful place, some-where she could come and think, but the row had changed all that.

A few people passed by her, commuters taking a short cut to the station. They walked quickly with the same intent expression on their faces. Office workers, she thought, with their smart suits and shiny shoes and briefcases. Well, she didn't envy them. She'd rather flog garden furniture than be trapped within four walls on a day like this. And it wasn't much fun being stuck on a hot packed train either.

Aware of the time ticking away, she carried quickly on up the thoroughfare. She would do Alfie Reach first, then Annie Patterson before going on to Lucy Rivers. The cemetery work truck was parked up to the side, the rear full of soil, and she scanned the surrounding area but couldn't see any sign of Rick. Since their drink on Friday, he'd been sending her texts, funny messages, and she'd been wondering if she'd bump into him today. Not that she particularly wanted to see him or anything. Still, it might be nice to say hello.

At the water butt, Maddie turned right and walked up the shallow slope to Alfie's grave. As she cleaned and polished the black marble headstone, she pondered on the fact that he and Agnes had been married for over fifty years. How had they done that? The longest relationship she'd managed to sustain was for two years, and that had ended in heartache. Well, heartache for her at least. Tom Bailey had moved on faster than a greyhound chasing a rabbit.

'You did good, Alfie,' she said, sitting back on her heels. 'What's the secret, huh?'

In another ten years, she thought, Zac would be eighteen. He might leave home, go to college or find a job somewhere else. It was hard to imagine life without him being around every day. She had always intended to return to archaeology, but wondered now if that would ever happen. Perhaps the nearest she would get to exploring the past was tending graves in Kellston Cemetery.

Maddie gave an impatient shake of her head. She was always telling Zac that if he put his mind to it, he could do whatever he wanted. The trick was to stay positive, to make the most of what you'd got. Fate had thrown up some surprises, but she was still standing. That, she decided, was an achievement in itself.

After sorting Alfie, she moved on to Annie Patterson. Working quickly, she had everything finished in fifteen minutes. It was easy in the summer, when her only enemies were dust and weeds. There was much more to do in autumn, when the leaves floated down from the trees, blew across the ground and gathered in great sodden piles on the graves.

She stood back to view the effect and then moved forward again, bending down to rearrange the flowers slightly. Once she was sure that it all looked perfect, she took a photo on her phone and sent it straight through to Annie's son, Michael. Now, with the first two jobs completed, there was only one left to do. She picked up her rucksack and started walking towards the old part of the cemetery.

As she approached the grave of Lucy Rivers, Maddie felt a spurt of anxiety. Usually, she looked forward to spending time here, but today she was jumpy and ill at ease. Half of that was down to what had happened last time she'd come – the stranger lurking in the bushes – and the other half to what she had learned about Cato.

Cautiously, she advanced towards the grave and touched the top of the headstone with the tips of her fingers. 'Hi, Lucy.' The white marble was smooth and cool. 'Last day today, but don't worry – I'll keep an eye on you. I'll still drop by from time to time.' Even as she spoke, she had the feeling that she wasn't alone. She looked around, peering into the undergrowth, her ears straining to hear any sound. But everything was still and quiet. No, it was just her imagination. There was nothing to be worried about. She laid the rucksack down on the grass and took out the things she needed.

Maddie poured water on to a cloth, kneeled down and started cleaning. But she'd only been working for a couple of minutes when she got that uncomfortable prickling sensation on the back of her neck. She jumped to her feet again, her heart starting to thump. With the cloth still in her hand, she moved away from the grave, hesitated and then walked a little way along the narrow path that led down to the Belvedere mausoleum.

'Who's there?' she said sharply, trying to sound braver than she felt.

Silence.

'Hello?' Maddie took a tentative step forward. With nothing more than a cloth in her hand, she felt singularly unprepared to face an attacker. Perhaps she should go back and fetch the trowel. It wasn't exactly her weapon of choice, but it was better than nothing. 'Hello?'

And then, out of nowhere, there was a sudden flapping of wings and a black crow rose from the ground into the trees. She started back, a cry catching in the back of her throat before she heaved out her breath in a sigh of relief. A bird! It was only a damn bird! And then, as if to mock her, the crow settled in the branches above and let out a series of loud shrieking caws.

Maddie waited until her heart rate slowed before continuing along the path. There was nothing to be afraid of. She would go as far as the mausoleum, have a quick look round and then return to the grave. That way, she would know for sure that nobody was there. Pushing her way past the buddleia, she moved quietly, her feet making barely a sound on the hard, dry earth.

The light grew dimmer as she advanced, the canopy of trees closing over her head so only a few rays of sunshine cut through the leaves, dappling the earth with a pale yellow glow. She stopped in front of the small brick building, more like a tiny windowless house, she thought, than a burial place.

Remembering the cigarette ends she had found, she scanned the ground, but found no new evidence of the mystery smoker.

She turned her attention back to the tomb, reading through the inscriptions. The last person to be buried was Margaret Jane, wife of Henry James Belvedere and mother of Harold. That was in 1937. Harold James Belvedere had been interred at the age of twenty-two, a victim of the Great War. She moved away the ivy so that she could read the rest of the inscription. *Wounded at the Somme. Died 24 December 1916.* The fact that he had died on Christmas Eve added an extra poignancy to his death. There had been, or so it seemed, no other children. With Harold's tragic demise, the line had come to an end.

Maddie's gaze switched to the arched metal door, dusty and covered in cobwebs. She thought of the coffins inside, of the generations lying together in the darkness. But then, as she made a closer study of the ornate metalwork, of the panels and scrolls and winding flowers, she noticed something odd: the webs had all been torn apart along the hinge as if the door had been opened recently. She frowned, taking a closer look. Yes, they'd definitely been disturbed. From the top of the door to the bottom, there wasn't a single one intact. And the handle was clean too, not a speck of dust on it. That could be down to Rick – last week, he'd checked to make sure the mausoleum was locked – but that didn't account for the broken webs. Someone had been inside.

She reached out her hand, folding her fingers around the heavy metal ring. But then she hesitated, in two minds as to whether to turn it or not. She could imagine the low creak, the sound as the door swung slowly open. What if there was someone inside, someone *living*, someone who would leap out at her and—

She didn't get a chance to finish the thought. From behind, from the direction of Lucy Rivers's grave, came the heavy tread of footsteps along the path. For a second she froze, but then jumped back, unsure of what she was more bothered by – being caught trying to enter a family's resting place or coming face to face with some weirdo who got his kicks from hiding in bushes and spying on women. Should she run or stay put? Paralysed by indecision, she remained rooted to the spot.

The next few seconds felt like a lifetime. She heard the crack of twigs, the rustle as he brushed by the buddleia. Any moment now. He was almost on her, so close she could hear his breathing. Or maybe it was her own breathing. Her lungs had started to pump heavily, and her pulse was racing. Her body stiffened as a figure came into view, but then instantly relaxed again. The face was familiar; the face was friendly. Thank God! It was only Rick.

'Jesus! What are you doing here?' She put her hand on her heart. 'You half scared me to death!'

'I work here,' he said, laughing. 'What's your excuse?'

'Hey, I work here too. Kind of.'

'I saw your rucksack, figured you must be about somewhere. Are you okay? Our peeping Tom hasn't come back, has he?'

'No, I just ... er ... wanted to stretch my legs.'

Rick's brows shifted up a fraction. He gazed at her for a while and then said, 'Ah, sorry. I get it.'

Maddie stared back at him. 'Get what?'

'That's another way of saying that you needed a pee, right?'

She put her hands on her hips and then, realising that she was still holding the cloth, quickly moved them back down to her sides. 'Do I look like the kind of girl who goes around peeing in graveyards?'

Rick grinned. 'When you've gotta go, you've gotta go. Can't argue with nature.'

Maddie pulled a face. 'Anyway, while I *wasn't* having a pee, I noticed something odd. Come and have a look at this.' She stepped towards the mausoleum and pointed at the hinge.

Rick peered over her shoulder. 'What am I looking at exactly?'

'Don't you see?' She ran a finger down the side. 'All the webs have been broken. The door must have been opened recently.'

He bent his head, looking sceptical. 'You reckon?'

'For sure. And the last time anyone was buried here . . . well, not buried exactly, but you know what I mean . . . was in 1937. Don't you think that's strange?'

Rick moved to the side of her and rattled the handle. 'Door's still locked. Could have been Eli,' he said. 'He checks these places out from time to time, makes sure there's no leaks or anything.'

'Oh,' said Maddie, feeling faintly disappointed. Her incredible skills of detection were apparently not so amazing after all. 'I didn't realise that.'

'I can't see anyone dossing down in here.' He pressed his hand against the heavy iron door and pushed. 'No, there's no way. This thing's rock solid – must be a couple of inches thick. You couldn't get in without a key.'

'I guess not.'

He turned and grinned at her. 'And I don't think you need to worry about the folks inside. They only come out when there's a full moon.'

'Ha, ha.'

'You think I'm joking? Hey, never mock the powers of darkness, babe.'

Maddie, who was overly aware of the closeness of his body,

gazed up into his eyes. 'The powers of darkness, huh? If you're trying to spook me, Rick Mallory, you're doing a God-awful job of it.'

'Damn,' he said, looking rueful. 'And here was me hoping that you'd fall into my arms and beg me to protect you.'

'Maybe I will,' she said, moving away from him and back on to the path. 'When there's a full moon. But in the meantime you can escort me back to the grave if that'll help with your machismo levels.'

'Better than nothing, I suppose. I'll go first – face the danger head on.'

'I'm feeling safer already.'

As they strolled back up the narrow path in single file, Rick glanced over his shoulder. 'You still good for Saturday?'

'I'll let you know if I change my mind.'

'You won't be able to.'

'I won't? Why's that?'

''Cause I'm going to turn off my phone and go sit in the restaurant until you show up.'

'I like that in a man,' she said, 'blind optimism.'

'And you know what I like in a woman?'

'Surprise me.'

'Punctuality,' he said. 'I've always seen that as a great virtue.'

'Really? I wouldn't have thought it was top of the list.'

'And what would you have thought?'

'Oh, I don't know – an understanding of the subtleties of the offside rule, a sense of humour, nakedness?'

He glanced back at her again, grinning. 'Well, yeah, those too, of course, although not necessarily in that order.'

They reached the grave of Lucy Rivers and stopped. Maddie looked up at him and smiled. 'Thanks again for coming to my rescue. I don't know what I'd have done without you.'

'Had a pee in private, perhaps?'

'I was *not* having a pee.'

'Whatever you say. Anyway, I'd better get back to work before Delia fires me for fraternising with the local grave tender.' He gave her a wave and started walking off. 'I'll see you on Saturday. Don't be late.'

19

Maddie kneeled by the grave, moving the cloth across the surface of the headstone in a series of small circular motions. Her gaze, however, was fixed firmly on the departing figure of Rick Mallory. She started from the bottom up: work boots, long legs in blue jeans, a neat butt, dark red shirt, tanned muscular arms, a powerful set of shoulders and dark blond silky hair. It was only when he went round the corner and disappeared from view that she turned her attention back to Lucy.

'Well, what's not to like?' she murmured. 'A dubious sense of humour, perhaps, but I can live with that.'

As she cleaned and polished, her thoughts shifted back to what Agnes had told her. Wasn't there something odd, coincidental, about the fact that Lucy had drowned just like Greta? And at the same age too. Except she didn't know for sure that Greta had drowned. Bo had been dead before he'd even hit the water and maybe her sister had been too. She hoped that this was the case. The thought of a slow watery death, of a struggle, of a panicked gasping for breath was too much to bear.

She pulled the slim cardboard box out of her rucksack, took out the roses and laid them gently on the white quartz stones. Would this be the last time she'd ever do this? Perhaps the next time she called by, there would be different flowers sitting here: carnations, lilies or chrysanthemums. She hoped that whoever took her place would feel something more than duty.

Maddie took the old blooms, wilted and drooping now, out of the urn and dropped them on the grass. She threw away the water and replaced it with fresh. The roses she had chosen were called Lady of Shalott. The cups of incurved petals were soft salmon-pink on the upper side and warm orange-gold on the reverse. They had a beautiful, pungent smell.

As she arranged the stems, she thought of the famous John William Waterhouse painting she had once seen at the Tate Gallery: the Lady of Shalott drifting along the river in a boat, yearning with unrequited love for the knight Sir Lancelot. Poor Lucy had known all about unrequited love, and Maddie wasn't exactly a stranger to it either.

'Men,' she said, making a clicking noise with her tongue. Had Brendan Vasser been Lucy's Lancelot? From what she'd heard, it seemed unlikely, but there was no accounting for why one person loved another. If Agnes was right, Lucy had been so full of despair that she'd preferred to end her own life rather than to go on living without him.

Maddie sat back, viewed the display and then reached into her pocket for the gold wedding band. She didn't immediately bury it under the stones again, but laid it instead on the shelf in front of the headstone. She wanted a few minutes to think – about Greta, about Lucy – before she returned the ring to the place where she had found it.

She wrapped her arms around her knees and gazed solemnly at the grave. Doubts crept into her mind as to whether she was making a mistake in giving up the job. Hadn't it always felt right to come here, to *be* here, to do for Lucy what she couldn't do for Greta? But on the other hand, there was Cato to think about. Now there was a man who provoked strong emotions. His connection to Lucy was still a mystery to her, and perhaps it always would be. She didn't want any more trouble in her life. Yes, the sensible thing to do was to walk away, to sever all ties. So why did she feel so bad about it?

Maddie closed her eyes, leaned back her head and let the morning sun fall across her face. She would sit here for a while and drink in the peace. Above her, high in the trees, she could hear the cooing of a wood pigeon. There was the soft buzz of bees and a rustling of leaves in the light breeze. And then another sound infiltrated her ears. It was faint at first, distant footsteps, but gradually they grew louder.

She blinked open her eyes and looked to her right. A tall, striking blonde was approaching from the direction of the thoroughfare. The woman was in her thirties, slender and elegant, with her long hair swept up and gathered at the nape of her neck. She was wearing a pale grey dress with matching high heels and handbag. The attire, although stylish, seemed out of place in this wilder, dustier part of the cemetery.

Maddie watched, expecting her to turn off the path at any moment and make her way across the grass towards one of the other graves. It was rare to see anyone else round here; in fact, the only other person she had come across before was Rick Mallory. But the woman didn't change course. She kept on walking in a straight line until twenty seconds later she was standing right in front of her.

Maddie unwrapped her arms from around her legs, looked up and smiled. 'Hello,' she said.

There was no return greeting and not even the semblance of a smile. The blonde looked down, her gaze cold and imperious. 'What do you think you're doing?'

Maddie frowned, the curt question taking her by surprise. 'I'm sorry?'

'You heard.'

Maddie didn't like the hard edge of her tone or the way that the blonde was staring at her. Usually, even when provoked, she would try and maintain a veneer of politeness, but she sensed that on this occasion it would only be seen as weakness. Instead, she gestured with a loose flap of her hand towards the headstone and the flowers. 'Isn't it obvious?'

'Don't play games with me, sweetheart. I'm not in the mood.'

'No one's playing games.'

The woman gave a snort. 'I know all about you and Cato. And I know what you're trying to do. But it stops right now. Do you understand me?'

Maddie, feeling herself at a disadvantage down on the ground, quickly scrambled to her feet. She was still a few inches smaller than the woman, but at least they were on more of a level footing. 'Look,' she said, 'I don't know what you think is going on, but I'm paid to tend this grave, nothing else.'

'Well, you would say that, wouldn't you? You probably think you can trust him, but believe me, you can't. The man's a compulsive liar. He's also a murderer, in case you'd forgotten. I don't know what he promised you, but—'

'He didn't *promise* me anything.'

'Sure he did. You wouldn't be here otherwise. But he's only using you, Maddie. You do realise that, don't you? You're not so stupid that you actually think he'll stick to his side of the bargain?'

Maddie frowned, utterly bemused by the exchange – and by the fact the woman knew her name. 'I'm sorry,' she said, 'but I don't have a clue what you're talking about. I don't even know who you are.'

The woman's eyes narrowed as if she'd been deliberately

insulted. 'I'm Lena Gissing,' she hissed. 'Who the fuck do you think I am?'

Maddie, remembering what Solomon had told her, felt her stomach sink. So this was Brendan Vasser's widow, the woman for whom Cato had allegedly killed. 'Oh,' she said.

'Oh? Is that all you've got to say? You must have been expecting me. It can't be that big a surprise. I mean, isn't that why you're doing all this – to get my attention?'

Maddie stared back at her. 'And why should I want to do that?'

But Lena Gissing ignored the question. 'It's pathetic. *You're* pathetic. And this ridiculous farce – it's over, right? You tell him that from me. And you stay away from this grave. It has nothing to do with you, nothing at all. You come near it again and you'll be sorry.'

'Is that a threat?'

Lena blatantly looked her up and down, her nose wrinkling with distaste, as if Maddie was something nasty she'd picked up on the bottom of her shoe. 'Call it what you like. Just don't mess with me, darlin'. I've had enough of Cato, and I've had enough of you.'

Maddie gave a small shake of her head. The whole conversation was both scary and surreal, as if she was inside one of those senseless dreams from which she couldn't wake. 'I think there's been some kind of misunderstanding,' she said. Lena had got her back up – no one liked being bullied – but she tried to keep her voice calm and collected. 'Like I said, I'm only paid to come here and tend the grave. Whatever your argument with Jay Cato, it's nothing to do with me.'

Lena gave a snarl, her eyes flicking towards the headstone. It was then that her expression suddenly changed, her mouth opening slightly, her face visibly paling. 'What?' she murmured.

Maddie, following her gaze, turned to see what she was

looking at. At first, she thought it was the roses, but then quickly realised that it was the gold wedding band, still lying on the ledge where she had put it earlier.

Before she could stop her, Lena swooped down and snatched up the ring. She held it between her finger and thumb, reading the words that had been engraved on the inner rim. Her whole body seemed to tighten. She glanced from the ring to Maddie, her face contorting in a grimace of rage. 'You bitch! You vile little bitch!'

Maddie jumped back in alarm. If she'd been afraid of the woman before, she was positively terrified of her now. She opened her mouth to speak, but no words came out. Lena raised her arm and for a second Maddie thought she was about to hit her. Instinctively, she lifted her hands to protect her face. But that wasn't Lena's plan. Instead, she hurled the ring with all her force and it arced through the air, landing in the long grass down by the Belvedere mausoleum.

Then she leaned in to Maddie and said, 'You ever interfere in my business again, I'll cut your fuckin' throat and feed you to the pigs.'

Maddie, even if she could have spoken, was too shocked to do so. She stood and watched as Lena Gissing strode off towards the main path. And that might have been that if the woman hadn't stopped suddenly and glanced over her shoulder. 'You're just the same as your bloody sister – and if you're not careful, Maddie Layne, you'll end up in the same place too.'

20

It took a moment for the words to sink in, but as they did, a cold jolt ran the length of Maddie's spine. For a few seconds, immobilised by shock, she remained rooted to the spot, and then before she could think about the wisdom of what she was doing, she dashed along the path, caught up with Lena Gissing and grabbed hold of her arm.

'What do you mean? What do you mean about my sister?'

Lena stared down at the hand. 'Get your filthy mitt off my arm.'

But Maddie only tightened her hold. 'Not until you tell me. What do you know about Greta?'

'Only that she's dead,' said Lena. 'And if she was anything like you, she probably got that way by poking her nose into someone else's business.'

'No,' Maddie insisted. 'You know something else. You know what happened, don't you?' She glared into the other woman's eyes, her fear subdued now by anger. 'You can't just say that stuff and walk away.'

Lena prised Maddie's fingers from her arm. 'Watch me.'

But Maddie wasn't giving up. She jumped in front of her, blocking her path. 'You're not going anywhere until you tell me. I've a right to know. I'm her goddamn sister.'

'Yes, you're that all right.' Lena looked her up and down again. 'You've got the same pea-sized brain. And just like her, you don't know when to stop. You don't know when to keep your big mouth shut.'

'And what the hell does that mean?'

'It means you should stay away from me. Didn't Cato warn you? Oh, I'm sure he did. I'm sure he's been whispering all sorts in your ear.'

Maddie didn't deny it. She wasn't about to reveal that all she knew of Cato came from a two-minute phone conversation and a few basic facts that Solomon Vale had passed on. 'Are you saying he's a liar?'

'What do you think? He's a murderer, love.'

'And you're whiter than white?'

'I'm not the one who's spent the last ten years banged up.'

Maddie could feel her frustration growing. She wanted to grab the woman again, take her by the shoulders and shake the truth out of her. 'All I want is to find out what happened to Greta.'

'Then go to the law. I've heard that's their job.' Lena gave a taunting kind of smirk. 'Although they don't seem very good at it.'

Five minutes ago, Maddie had been arranging flowers on Lucy Rivers's grave, hoping that she'd made the right decision about severing the ties to Cato. Five minutes ago, she'd never even met Lena Gissing. But now everything had changed. Her stomach was churning, her thoughts spinning so fast she could barely contain them. It was as if she had been passed the end of a piece of string and if she tugged hard enough, the truth about

Greta would start to unravel. 'Maybe I will. Maybe they'll be interested to hear that you're withholding information about her death.'

Lena barked out a laugh. 'You do that, sweetheart. As it happens, I have a few contacts at Cowan Road myself. Maybe I'll pop in and have a word. And you know what I'll tell them? That you're doing Cato's dirty work for him, that he's paying you to harass me. Old Bill take a dim view of that kind of thing.' She paused before adding, 'And then there are social services to consider. Once that lot get their claws into you, they never let go. I mean, what kind of mother gets involved with a murderer? Although, of course, you're not *actually* his mother, are you? Just his guardian . . . for now.'

Maddie felt a wave of fear sweep over her. How did she know about Zac? Jesus, how did she know about anything? And the answer came to her with startling clarity – because she'd made it her business to know. 'You can't . . . '

But Lena was already walking away. 'Think on – that's all I'm saying.'

This time Maddie didn't try to stop her. She stood very still, with her heart thumping in her chest. Despite the warmth of the sun, she felt cold and shivery. And suddenly she realised that Jay Cato hadn't chosen her by accident, hadn't plucked her from a list of grave tenders by chance. No, this had all been carefully planned. He was using her as a way to get at Lena Gissing. The man had deliberately pulled her into a war and placed her directly in the line of fire.

Abruptly she turned and ran back towards the grave. She crouched down and rummaged in her rucksack for her phone. Snatching it up, she jabbed clumsily at the buttons until she found Cato's number. It went directly to voicemail, but this time she didn't hesitate in leaving a message. 'It's Maddie Layne. It's urgent. You have to call me. We need to talk.'

Even after the line was disconnected, Maddie continued to grip the phone. Her breathing was fast and shallow as she gulped in the morning air. She was scared and angry and confused, but from deep within a tiny flower of hope blossomed too. Was it possible that after all this time she might finally find out why Greta had been killed? The truth was out there somewhere. That much was obvious. But how much would it cost her to find out what it was?

Quickly Maddie packed up the rucksack and jumped to her feet. If she didn't leave soon, she'd be late for work. And then she considered ringing in sick. Maybe, instead of going to the garden centre, she should call Lena's bluff, head down to Cowan Road and talk to the police about what had been said. But she knew, even as the thought crossed her mind, that she wouldn't do it. She had no solid facts, no real evidence. Lena could easily deny it all. And what if the woman did have friends in high places? Rich, powerful people usually did. No, she'd better stay clear of the cops. She was in enough trouble already without adding to it.

Maddie felt sick. It was scary, terrifying, that she'd somehow become embroiled in a private war between two such dangerous characters. The smart thing, the wise thing, would be to keep away from both of them. But if she did that, she had no chance at all of uncovering the truth about her sister's fate. And she owed her that much, didn't she? Greta had been denied a decent burial, a grave, a place to rest in peace. The least she could do was to try and find out why.

As she started to walk towards the main path, Maddie remembered the ring. There wasn't time to go and look for it; it would have to stay where it was for now. She recalled the look on Lena's face as she'd read the inscription on the inside rim. *For ever.* Those words had meant something to her. The ring had meant something. What was the link between Lena and Lucy Rivers? She still couldn't figure it out. But Cato knew. Cato knew everything. And now she only had to wait until he picked up that phone and called her back.

21

Adam Vasser was sitting in Connolly's, drinking his second mug of tea while he tried to figure out what was going on. Last night, unwilling to spend the evening watching Louise shove yet another pile of shit up her nose, he'd retreated to the Heights. It was at breakfast, an hour ago, that his mother had received the call. She'd snatched up the phone as quickly as a nervy teenager hoping for a date.

'Delia?' A pause. 'Is she? . . . Good. Okay, I'll be right there.'

'Where's the fire?' he'd asked, as she grabbed her bag and car keys and made for the door.

'No fire. Just a bit of business.'

'Since when did you do business with Delia Shields?'

'Do I poke my nose into everything you do?'

'Yes.'

His mother had given him one of her looks. 'See you later. And clear up those plates before you leave.'

But Adam's mind had been focused less on the washing-up and more on his mother's sudden departure. What was Delia doing ringing at this time of the morning? Something was up and he wanted to know what. He'd waited two minutes and then followed her down in the lift. By the time he reached the foyer, the red MG had already disappeared. But that hadn't mattered, because he knew where she was going. Delia Shields worked at the cemetery, and come rain or shine, that was where she'd be on a weekday morning.

The traffic was heavy and it had been another ten minutes before Adam had arrived at the main entrance. He'd pulled up by the gates but hadn't driven in. His mother's car – empty – was parked up twenty yards to the right on the main thoroughfare. He had let the BMW idle for a while as he checked out the office – Delia was there, but no sign of his mother.

Not wanting to be spotted, he'd swung back into the traffic and circled round to the other entrance on the far side of the cemetery. He'd pulled the car in just inside these gates, where he had a clear view of the length of the thoroughfare and of the red MG. He hoped he'd be far enough away for her not to clock him when she came back.

Adam had opened the window, sat back and waited. What the fuck was she doing here? Had she found out something? No, she couldn't have. That was impossible. But she sure as hell wasn't paying respects to his father; she hadn't been near the grave for years. The bitch was up to something, and it was something she didn't want him to know about.

The minutes had ticked by, long, slow minutes that seemed to go on for ever. Eli Glass had wandered past, throwing him a dirty look, as if he didn't have the right to be there. Adam had glared back at him. The man was nuts, creepy. Rumour had it that he'd killed a girl and got away with it.

When his mother had finally appeared, it had given him a shock to see the direction she was coming from. The path led to the old, neglected part of the cemetery, and she was stomping along it with a face like thunder. He'd ducked down, although he needn't have bothered. She was clearly in a rage and the only thing she was seeing was red.

Thirty seconds later, she was gone, the car roaring off down the thoroughfare and out through the gates. He had driven to the willow trees, parked again and got out. By this point his anxiety had reached monumental proportions. She had to be on to him. She must. Why else would she be here? He had half walked, half run along the path until he'd reached the even narrower one that was flanked by long grass and weeds. By now he was convinced that somehow the bitch had sniffed out his stash.

'Fuck it! Fuck it!'

And he'd been so caught up in his own thoughts, his own rage, that he'd almost run straight into the girl. She'd been crouching down by one of the graves with her back to him, rapidly gathering up stuff and shoving it into a rucksack. Quickly he'd turned away, veering across the grass and ducking down behind one of the old grey headstones.

She hadn't seen him, he was sure of that. But he'd managed to get a good look at her as she'd walked off. And been able to guess that the meeting with his mother hadn't been an amiable one. The girl was pale, her expression one of shock and fear. He'd recognised her instantly – she was the girl in the photographs, the girl in the file. She was Greta's sister, Maddie Layne.

He'd stayed hidden for a couple of minutes until he was sure that she wasn't coming back and then ventured over to the grave. *Lucy Rivers.* The name didn't mean anything to him. Some old relative, he presumed. The headstone had been polished, and there were fresh flowers in the urn. But none of that explained what his mother had been doing here. What the hell was she playing at?

Still, he'd been relieved about one thing. At least this was nothing to do with his stash. He'd taken a good look round, making sure nobody was in the vicinity before striding down to the Belvedere tomb. He'd checked the door, made sure it was locked and looked for signs of anyone trying to force an entry. Nothing. Good. But still he'd felt uneasy. His mother had been too close for comfort. Maybe he should move the gear, put it somewhere else. But where was better than here? The last place the law would look was in a brick box full of dead people.

Adam raised the mug to his lips and drank some more of his tea. Connolly's was still busy, the staff dealing with the tail end of the breakfast trade. The smell of fried bacon, of eggs and coffee hung in the air. In the small hours of the morning, the whores would gather here, taking a break and exchanging gossip, but for now it was occupied by a different kind of worker. They were office sorts mainly, men dressed in the boring uniform of suit and tie. There were a few cops too from the Cowan Road police station. All in plain clothes, but you could smell them a mile off.

He gazed surreptitiously at the young black man behind the counter. The lad had a look of Bo Vale about him, the same build, the same high cheekbones, but he lacked the charisma. Bo had been special, one of a kind. Even after six years, Adam still thought about him more often than he liked.

There was a stirring in his guts as the past slithered into his mind again. *You always hurt the one you love.* That was a song, wasn't it? But he couldn't remember who it was by. His hand tightened around the mug. Bo would still be alive now if it wasn't for him; he'd still be strutting around in that cocksure way of his, grinning from ear to ear, knowing that he had that special something, that God-given something that made him irresistible.

You always hurt the one you love. Except Adam didn't believe in love. It made people weak and vulnerable. It was like an infection that got into your bloodstream, disabling your reason,

185

making the muscles of your heart contract. And sometimes, in order to be well again, the only thing you could do was to cut away the badness, to get rid of it once and for all.

He didn't want to think about Bo Vale. He'd been sure it was over, finished with, but now it was all being stirred up again. Greta's sister. It had to be. Some people just couldn't let things lie. His eyes narrowed with anger. No one could be trusted. Even his bitch of a mother was sneaking around behind his back, keeping secrets like she always did.

He looked at his watch, scowled and picked up his phone. It took seven rings before Louise finally deigned to answer.

'Yeah?'

'You're late. Where the fuck are you?'

'I'm coming. Five minutes. I'll be there in five minutes.'

'Two minutes,' he said. 'Shift your bloody arse or you can find somewhere else to live.' He hung up and threw the phone back on the table. Why should he have to wait around for that stupid cow? It was about time she started earning her keep, and he had just the job for her.

22

The morning dragged by at Marigolds, every minute feeling like an hour. Although Maddie had the phone in her back pocket, set to vibrate, she still feared missing that vital call. Occasionally, when the manager wasn't around, she pulled it out, staring at the blank screen as if she could make it ring with the sheer force of her will.

Today, thankfully, she was on the plant section rather than garden furniture. The centre was quiet, but that only added to the sense of time creeping by. At least when it was busy, there was less time to think. And she was doing a lot of that as she marked down the prices on the roses, placing 'Summer Sale' stickers across the previous prices.

The exchange with Lena Gissing kept spinning round in her head as she reviewed every word, every nuance of every word. Why hadn't she just told her that she wouldn't be tending the grave any more? Because she didn't like being pushed around, that's why. Powerful women like Lena thought they could walk all over you, that they only had to snap their fingers and you'd do whatever they demanded.

But Maddie knew that wasn't the only reason. Once Greta had been mentioned, everything had changed. It was no longer about whether she should be working for a convicted murderer or not. Now it was personal. If there was a chance, any chance at all of finding out what had happened, then she couldn't back away from it. This wasn't to say that the prospect didn't frighten her; she'd already heard from Solomon how the Gissings conducted their business and the knowledge wasn't conducive to a good night's sleep.

Maddie slapped another sticker on a pot. As she withdrew her hand, a thorn pierced the skin, drawing blood. 'Damn!' she exclaimed, quickly lifting her thumb to her mouth. As she sucked on the wound, she wondered just how much worse things could get. A touch of blood poisoning would round the morning off nicely.

She glared down at the rose as if it had deliberately injured her. Now, of course, she was simply feeling sorry for herself, and that was never a good thing. What she needed was to talk to someone, to get some advice, to get a different perspective. She ran through the options, trying to decide on the best person for the job.

The first to be dismissed was the cops. She was too scared to go to them after what Lena had said. Shauna was out too – she had a gob the size of the Blackwell Tunnel and couldn't keep anything to herself for more than five minutes. And definitely not Alisha and Winston. Although she could chat to them about most things, she couldn't burden them with this. She set aside her mum and dad too: having already lost one child, they'd be none too keen on the other one going to war with the apparently infamous Gissings.

Having exhausted most of the obvious choices, Maddie was

left with only two: Rick or Solomon. But Rick was a big no-no. She barely knew the man. He'd probably run a mile – and understandably so – if she offloaded all her problems on to him. So, by a matter of elimination, she was left with Solomon.

This, however, didn't appeal that much either. Although she wasn't sure exactly what Solomon's job was, she knew that he worked for the Streets and that meant being on the wrong side of the law. What if he decided to take matters into his own hands and go after Lena Gissing? After all, this wasn't just about Greta's death; it was about Bo's too. Even though she was sure that Solomon was more than capable of taking care of himself, there wasn't much any man could do when a bullet was careering towards his brain. With this unpleasant thought in mind, she decided that, on balance, it might be better if she just kept quiet for a while.

Maddie took her thumb away from her mouth and examined the tiny puncture wound. Amazing how something so small could be so painful. She was still contemplating this when her phone started vibrating. She had a quick look round to make sure the manager wasn't in sight and then pulled the mobile out of her pocket. The name Cato had flashed up on the screen.

She took a deep breath before pressing the button. 'Hello?'

But the voice on the other end of the line wasn't male. 'Oh, hello. This is Hayley Whittaker.'

Maddie moved behind a tall palm and frowned. 'I'm sorry?'

'You left a message for me earlier? You are Maddie Layne, aren't you?'

'Yes.'

'Sorry it's taken me so long to get back. I've been in court all morning. So, how can I help you?'

Maddie rubbed at her forehead with her free hand. 'Er . . .

189

I'm not sure if you can. I was actually trying to get in touch with Jay Cato.'

'Ah,' Hayley said. 'I see.'

'You do know him, then?'

'Yes, I'm his solicitor. You're the lady who tends the grave, aren't you? The photos come through to my phone and I show them to him when I go on visits.'

Maddie heaved out a sigh. So this wasn't his number at all. He must have borrowed Hayley's mobile on that one occasion when he'd rung her. 'Right. Only the thing is, I really need to speak to him.'

'You are aware that he's in jail?'

'Yes, I know. But they have phones in there, don't they? Is there any way you could get him to ring me?'

'Well, I can try. I can't promise it'll be today, though. I'll leave a message with the staff, but there's no telling when they'll pass it on. Are you sure there's nothing I can help you with?'

'No,' Maddie said. 'Thanks, but it's kind of personal.'

'Okay. Well, if that's all . . . '

'Actually, there is one other thing before you go. I was just . . . I was wondering if you knew what Mr Cato's connection was to Lucy Rivers.'

There was a short silence. 'Sorry, I can't help you with that.'

'You don't know, or you can't tell me?'

'If you have any questions, I think it would be better if you asked him yourself.'

'All right. I'll do that.' Maddie said goodbye and hung up. A wave of frustration flowed over her. Just for a second, when she'd seen Cato's name appear, she'd imagined herself closer to getting some answers. But now she was back to playing the waiting game.

As she went to return the phone to her pocket, she noticed

that her hand had started to bleed again. A thin stream of red slid down her thumb, pooling briefly at her wrist before dripping on to the ground. She gave an involuntary shiver. The tiny drops of crimson seemed like a warning, a portent, a chilling sign of things to come.

23

By the time Maddie finished work, she still hadn't heard from Jay Cato. Impatience snapped at her heels as she strode down the High Street. How long was she going to have to wait? The suspense was killing her. You've waited six years, she told herself, a few hours isn't going to make any difference. But still she couldn't contain her frustration.

With Winston at the hospital for one of his check-ups, Shauna was looking after Zac. All Maddie wanted to do was to pick him up and take him home. She had the kind of tiredness that comes from going over the same things over and over again without reaching any new conclusions. A dull headache hammered at her temples.

She quickened her pace, took a right turn into Morton Grove and a minute later came to number 62. Shauna answered the door dressed in denim shorts, a white skinny vest and a pair of flip-flops. There was a heavy gold link chain round her neck and two big gold hoops in her ears. The faint smell of suntan lotion drifted from her skin.

'Hi there.'

'Hi,' Maddie said. 'Everything okay?'

'Sure it is. Why wouldn't it be?'

But the reasons were so manifold that Maddie wouldn't have known where to start even if she had been prepared to share them. 'Oh, I don't know. I've just had one of those days. Is Zac ready? I won't hang about. Thanks for taking care of him.'

'Zac!' Shauna yelled. 'Shift yourself. Maddie's here.'

Zac came running to the door, his eyes pleading. 'Hi, Maddie. Can I just stay and watch the end? Please can I?'

'SpongeBob,' Shauna explained, her eyebrows shifting up as if she'd had enough of the character's maritime adventures to last her a lifetime.

Maddie hesitated. All she wanted was to go home, make dinner and put her feet up. 'How long is it going to be?'

'Five minutes, that's all.' Zac jumped up and down, tugging on Maddie's arm. 'Can I? Please can I?'

'Why don't you come in?' Shauna said. 'Come and have a drink. I haven't seen you properly since Friday.'

'Okay.' Maddie looked at Zac. 'But only five minutes, right? Then we have to go.'

'Thank you! Thank you!' And he went rushing back to join Kyle.

Maddie followed Shauna through the living room, where the two boys were curled up on the sofa glued to the TV, and on into the kitchen.

'You want a Coke?' Shauna went to the fridge and took out a can. 'It's a cold one.'

'Ta.'

They sat down at the kitchen table. 'So?' Shauna asked. 'How's the big romance going? How was the date? Are you seeing him again?'

'I might.'

'Which means you are. Come on, spill. I want all the juicy gossip!'

Maddie took a swig of Coke and put the can back on the table. 'There's nothing to tell, not really. Early days and all that. But we're going for dinner on Saturday.'

'Where's he taking you?'

'Adriano's.'

'Cool,' Shauna said. She put her chin on her hands and stared at Maddie. 'And?'

'And what?'

'Well, you don't seem all that excited. Was he a bit of a let-down . . . you know . . . in the bedroom department?'

Maddie widened her eyes in mock astonishment. 'Excuse me, but we haven't been anywhere *near* that department.' A kiss on the cheek was the closest they'd come to any kind of carnality, and even that had been a somewhat awkward affair, with their faces veering off in different directions. 'I don't want to rush into anything. He's nice, but . . .'

'But?'

'I just want to get to know him better first. If he's only going to hang around for five minutes, then what's the point? I don't need some unreliable drifter in my life – even for a bit of fun.'

'Maybe he'll stick around.'

'And maybe he won't.' Maddie drank some more Coke, not sure if it was helping her headache or making it worse. She rubbed at her temples with the tips of her fingers. 'I don't know, perhaps it's not the right time for me to get involved with some-one.'

Shauna pulled a face. 'God, if you wait for the right time, you'll be drawing your bleedin' pension. Sometimes, girl, you've just got to go for it.'

Maddie, though, had more important things than romance on her mind. She glanced towards the living room, lowering her voice even though the boys couldn't hear her above the sound of the TV. 'Can I ask you something? You've heard of the Gissings, haven't you?'

'Yeah. Why?'

'How did Greta know Lena Gissing?'

Shauna was clearly surprised, even shocked by the question. She hesitated before answering, her gaze roaming around the kitchen before eventually coming back to rest on Maddie. Her voice had a sudden sharpness to it. 'What makes you think she knew her? Who told you that?'

Maddie, picking up on her agitation, wondered what was at the root of it. 'You don't think she did?'

Shauna gave a shrug. 'How would I know? She might have done.' She paused again before adding, 'She and Bo used to hang out with Adam sometimes.'

'Adam?'

'Adam Vasser, Lena's son.'

And now it was Maddie's turn to be surprised. There was that name again – *Vasser*. She took a moment to let it sink in, wondering what it meant, if anything. 'So she was friendly with this Adam?'

Shauna barked out a laugh. 'I wouldn't say that exactly. She couldn't stand the guy, thought he was a creep. Well, he is a creep, and nasty with it. Twisted, if you know what I mean.'

'So why did she—'

Shauna interrupted before she got the chance to finish. 'The same reason Greta did anything – because there was something in it for her.' She'd spoken in haste, without thinking, and now she quickly flapped a hand. 'Oh, sorry, I didn't mean ... I liked Greta, honestly I did. She was a laugh. I suppose she just wanted to keep the guy sweet. Bo did some work for him, and it was good money, so ...'

'I thought Bo worked for the Streets?'

'Yeah, he did. He was on the door at Belles and the Lincoln. But I reckon he only did that as a cover for what he was really up to.'

'Which was?'

Shauna screwed up her face again. She put her elbow on the table and her hand over her mouth as if she'd already said too much.

'Shauna, he's dead. What difference does it make if you tell me or not?'

There was a brief silence before Shauna removed her hand. 'Why are you asking about all this stuff? What's going on? I don't get it. It's been years.'

'Six,' Maddie said. 'And no one's any closer to finding out what happened. So please, if you do know anything . . . '

'I don't. I swear. Not about that.'

'But you do know what Bo was doing?'

Shauna worried on her lower lip for a few seconds, still in two minds as to whether she should tell. 'Okay, but this didn't come from me, right? Because if it gets back to—'

'It won't. I promise.'

Shauna hesitated again, clearly weighing up her fear of the Gissings against her friendship with Maddie. Eventually, she came to a decision. 'He was nicking motors, okay. Luxury numbers, high end. He and Greta used to drive out to Surrey, Sussex, them sorts of places and check out the smart houses.'

Maddie, astonished, took a quick, sharp breath. 'What, Greta went with him?'

'Course. Had to, didn't she? Bo needed a way of getting his own motor home after he'd nicked someone else's. You'd be surprised how many people just leave them on the drive. And Bo could get into any car in twenty seconds flat.'

Although Maddie had known that her sister was no angel, she hadn't expected this. But she didn't have time to dwell on the revelation now. 'And they were working for Adam Vasser?'

Shauna gave a nod. 'But like I said, that man's fuckin' evil. You don't want to get on the wrong side of him or ...'

'Or?' Maddie prompted.

Shauna looked away.

Maddie stared at her. 'Or you might end up in the Thames with a bullet in your head?'

'I didn't say that. No, Adam liked Bo. He was always round their place. He wouldn't have ... No, I'm sure he wouldn't. Why would he?'

'Maybe they fell out, had a row over money. Do the police know that Bo was working for Vasser?'

Shauna gave another of her shrugs. 'Dunno.'

And then Maddie had another thought. The Streets wouldn't have been too happy if they'd found out that one of their firm was working with the Gissings. Weren't they old enemies? Although Adam Vasser wasn't strictly a Gissing, he was Lena's son, which made him pretty much a member of the family.

'What are you going to do?' Shauna asked. She sounded jumpy and anxious, as if Maddie was about to drag her into the kind of trouble she really didn't need.

'I don't know. Keep digging, I suppose.' Maddie was still pondering on the Streets. But they wouldn't have killed Bo, would they? Bo was Solomon's brother, and Solomon was close to Chris. But how much did friendship count for when it came to betrayal? 'Don't worry, I won't tell anyone what you told me.'

'You can't,' said Shauna.

'I won't. Look, do you know anything about Lena Gissing?'

'No,' said Shauna tightly. 'Only that she's not the sort of woman you mess with.'

Maddie had already gathered that much. 'You never saw her with Greta?'

'No, never.'

'And Greta never talked about her?'

'No,' Shauna repeated. She rose to her feet, effectively ending the conversation. 'Kyle,' she called out. 'Turn that TV off. It's time for tea.'

Maddie, taking the hint, stood up too and went through into the living room. 'Come on, Zac. You ready?'

Shauna saw them to the door, hustling them out before she had to answer any more awkward questions. 'Bye, then. See you tomorrow.'

'Bye.'

As they walked along the road, Zac gave Maddie a rundown of his day along with a summary of SpongeBob's latest exploits. She only listened with half an ear. Most of her mind was focused on what she'd just learned, turning it over in her head and trying to figure out what it all meant. She was pretty sure that Shauna hadn't told her everything, but it was enough to bolster her suspicions about Lena Gissing being involved in Greta's death.

Maddie was also trying to come to terms with what her sister had been involved in. Up until now she'd put all the blame squarely on Bo, but Greta had clearly played a part in his criminal activities. And then there was Adam Vasser to consider. Perhaps it was Lena's crazy son who'd committed the murders.

Zac ran in front of her, did a few dipping circles with his arms out like an aeroplane and then rushed back. 'Maddie, Maddie, what do you call a snail on a ship?'

'I don't know, hon. What do you call it?'

'A snailer!' Zac roared at his own joke, jumping up and down. 'A snailer – do you get it?'

Maddie smiled at him. 'That's the worst one all week.'

'It's the best. It is. It's the best one of all.' Zac ran on ahead again, still laughing. He turned into the gateway of number 34 and rushed up the path. A few seconds later, he was back with a small parcel held up above his head. 'Look, you've got a present. Someone's sent you a present.'

Maddie took the parcel from him and looked at it. It was about six inches wide, a box wrapped in brown paper with her name and address scrawled on the front. There were no stamps or any postmark, so it must have been delivered by a courier. She flipped it over, but there wasn't a return address on the back.

'What is it?' Zac asked.

'I don't know, hon. I won't know until I open it.' She got out her keys, walked up the path and unlocked the door. Inside, she went through to the kitchen. After putting the parcel on the counter and switching on the kettle, she took a bottle of aspirin out of the top cupboard and swallowed two capsules with a glass of water. Then she went to the fridge to see what delights she could conjure up for dinner.

'We'll have chicken, shall we? Be a love and get me some spuds from the garden.'

But Zac remained standing by the counter, gazing curiously at the package. 'Aren't you going to open it?'

'I'm sure it's nothing very interesting.'

'It might be.'

'Okay, let's take a look.' Maddie ripped the brown paper off to reveal a small cardboard box. She picked at the sellotape until she could free the flap and flip it open. And then ... It took a second for her brain to absorb what she was seeing. The breath caught in the back of her throat as she stifled a cry. For a moment she froze, her eyes widening with horror, the blood draining from her face. And then, before Zac could see the contents properly, she slammed the lid shut again.

'What is it?' he asked, leaning forward. 'Is it a toy?'

'N-no,' she managed to stammer. 'It's not ... it's not for us.'

She shoved the box along the counter, away from his curious hands. 'It's a mistake. It's come to the wrong address. Now, why don't you get those spuds for me?'

Zac gave her a curious look, his gaze flitting between her and the box. He pointed towards the ripped brown paper. 'But it's got your name on it.'

'I know, but ... but someone's got it wrong.' Quickly she turned away from him and went over to the sink. Her stomach was heaving. She thought she was going to be sick. She thought she was going to pass out. Her hands gripped the cool metal while she tried to steady herself. Then, aware that Zac was watching her, she glanced over her shoulder. 'Go on,' she said, her voice sounding odd and croaky. 'Hurry up! Get those spuds or we won't be eating till midnight.'

Reluctantly, Zac moved away from the counter and went out of the back door. She watched from the window, waiting until he'd picked up a trowel from the garden box and started digging in the soil. Only then did she release her grip, walk back across the room and stare at the box. Her chest felt tight. Her heart was racing. Slowly, very slowly she lifted the lid again. A thin groan escaped from her lips and her stomach gave another lurch. A tiny sparrow, its dead body pierced by a nail, was impaled on a piece of gold card. And written on the card were the words *RIP, Maddie Layne.*

24

Maddie, unable to bear the sight of the poor dead creature, quickly shut the lid again. Her hands were shaking as she placed the box on the highest shelf in the cupboard, out of Zac's line of vision and out of his reach. But out of sight wasn't out of mind and she had to decide what to do next. Call the cops – wasn't that the right thing to do? This was a threat, a blatant threat, and she didn't have much doubt where it had come from. Lena Gissing had made her feelings crystal clear when they'd clashed earlier in the day.

Maddie pulled her phone out of her rucksack and began to dial. But no sooner had she started than she had second thoughts. What would she tell Zac when the police came round? How would she explain? She didn't want him scared, but he was bound to be. No, maybe it would be better if she went down to Cowan Road. But then she'd need to get some-one to sit with Zac. Not Shauna – she reckoned she'd exhausted any outstanding goodwill there – which meant that it would have to be Alisha.

Maddie put the phone down while she thought about it some more. If she asked Alisha, then she'd either have to tell her the truth or make up a damn good excuse as to why she had to leave the house for an hour. Neither of these prospects was especially appealing; she didn't want to lie, and she didn't want to stress her out either. There was no nice way, no good way, to explain the horror of a threat like this. Maybe it was better to wait until morning, when she could go to the police station after taking the boys to summer school.

Suddenly, Maddie was hit by a wave of panic. She dashed to the front door, opened it, ran down the path and stared up and down the street. But whoever had left the parcel was long gone. Of course they were. It could have been dumped on the doorstep hours ago. She tried to remember if they'd passed anyone when they were walking back from Shauna's, but she'd been too distracted to be paying much attention.

Quickly she ran back inside, locked the door and pulled across the bolts. She leaned against it for a while, her heart pumping. Maybe she should call Solomon, but he'd be at work, and anyway, what could he do? What could anyone do? Her hands clenched into two tight fists. This was all Cato's fault. Damn him! He'd dragged her into his war with Lena Gissing and placed her directly in the line of fire. While he was sitting safely in his cell, she was the one taking all the flak.

When her breathing had slowed, Maddie pushed herself off the door and walked through to the back. Try and act normally, she told herself. For Zac's sake, she had to pretend that nothing untoward had happened. None too easy, she thought, when there was a dead sparrow lying in a box in the kitchen cupboard. Not to mention that chilling message: *RIP, Maddie Layne.*

For the next couple of hours, she went through the motions, making dinner, chatting, doing the dishes, watching TV – all the time trying to keep the strain out of her voice and off her face. It felt like for ever before Zac was showered and in his pyjamas and finally in bed. Only then, when she was alone, did she fully give in to the fear she was feeling.

Curled up on the sofa, Maddie clutched a cushion to her chest. Now that it was dark outside, she was beginning to wish that she had called the cops. She had checked three times that all the doors and windows were locked, but she still didn't feel safe. What if someone tried to break in? Her hand reached for the phone and she stared down at the keypad. It was all very well trying to protect Zac, but what if she was putting him in even more danger by doing nothing? But still she hesitated, remembering what Lena had said about having contacts at Cowan Road.

She turned the phone around in her hand. Still no call from Cato. Maybe she'd never hear from him again. Maybe, so far as he was concerned, her usefulness was over. She'd done the job he'd paid her for and that was that. He probably didn't give a damn about the fallout.

Maddie went back to watching the TV. Although she was looking at the screen, she wasn't taking anything in. Scenes changed, characters came and went, but her mind was somewhere else. She thought of Lena Gissing's face as she'd raised her arm to hurl the ring across the graveyard. Pure rage. And that was something else that had been down to Cato. He must have arranged for the ring to be left there, knowing she would find it. What he couldn't have known, however, was that Lena would come along just as she was about to bury it again.

She still couldn't figure out the triangle. Lena Gissing, Jay Cato and Lucy Rivers. What connected the three of them? What was it that fuelled such bitter and angry emotions? Was it Brendan Vasser? She understood the Lena–Cato conflict, but the rest remained a mystery to her. And now the death of her sister had become entwined in it all. She looked down at her phone again. If only Cato would call. She had to find out what he knew.

It was another half-hour before her mobile finally sprang into life. She snatched it up, checking out the caller. Number unavailable. Could that be a prison payphone? She had no idea of the times that inmates were allowed to use them.

'Hello?'

She waited, but there was only a thin crackling at the other end of the line.

'Hello?' she said again.

Still nothing. Maddie waited a few seconds and then hung up. Had that been Cato trying to get through? If so, then hopefully he would keep on trying. She kept the phone in her hand, willing it to ring again.

It was another five long minutes before she got her wish. 'Hello?' she repeated for the third time. But again she was greeted with silence. Except it wasn't quite silence. It took a moment for her to realise that someone was actually there. That sound . . . breathing . . . deliberate heavy breathing.

'Who is it?' she asked sharply, a thin shiver of fear running through her. When there was no reply, she jabbed at the button to end the call. But still the sound echoed in her ears, soft and cruel and malicious. Someone trying to scare her to death. And it was working. First the sparrow and now this.

Two minutes later, the phone began to ring again. The same unavailable number. Well, she just wouldn't answer it. Let them breathe into her voicemail if they wanted to. But then she wondered if this time it might actually be Cato. Could she take the chance of missing him? It could be ages before he tried again.

Reluctantly she answered the call. 'Yes?'

But of course it wasn't Cato. Just that dark, threatening breathing again. In and out, in and out. Steady, monotonous, nasty. She hung up and threw the phone away from her, towards the far corner of the sofa. Wrapping her arms around her chest, she rocked back and forth. 'Leave me alone,' she muttered.

And then, as if to defy her, the phone began its menacing ringing again. She put her hands over her ears. No, she'd had enough. She couldn't take any more. But the phone kept on ringing until something snapped inside her. Leaning forward, she grabbed it and in an explosion of anger yelled down the line, 'Listen, I don't know what your bloody game is, but I've had enough. It stops, right? It stops right now.'

This time she heard a different sound, an intake of breath that was more surprised than intimidating. And then a voice that she recognised. 'Maddie? Is that you? Are you okay?'

It was Rick Mallory. She had snatched up the phone in such a hurry that this time she hadn't even checked who the caller was. She was instantly hit by a mixture of relief and embarrassment. 'Oh God, sorry, I didn't realise . . . '

'What's going on?'

'Sorry, I've been . . . been getting crank calls. The whole heavy-breathing bit. I thought you were . . . And it's not just that. There's been other stuff too.' She could hear her voice starting to break and quickly tried to pull herself together. 'I thought . . . '

'You want me to come round?'

Maddie hesitated. She swallowed hard, still trying to get some control of her voice. 'I don't know.'

'I'll be there in five minutes,' he said firmly.

She didn't argue with him. 'Okay, thanks. But don't ring the bell or it'll wake up Zac. I'll watch out for you.'

'Five minutes,' he said again. 'Don't worry.'

Maddie immediately turned off the phone. If she missed Cato's call, she missed it. She'd rather that than have to listen to the breathing again. She went out into the hall, climbed the stairs and looked in on Zac. He was fast asleep, his eyelids flickering, his right arm flung across the duvet. Carefully she closed the door and went into her own bedroom. It was at the front and overlooked the street. From here, she'd be able to see Rick when he arrived.

As she stared anxiously along Morton Grove, she wondered if her sick caller was out there somewhere. Her eyes raked the parked cars, searching for one that might be occupied, but in the thin orangey light from the street lamps she could only see shadows. She lifted a hand to her mouth and chewed on a fingernail. Had she done the right thing in asking Rick to come? Well, she hadn't actually asked, he'd volunteered, but she'd said yes and so it amounted to pretty much the same thing. It wasn't in her nature to go running to a man for help – she dealt with most things on her own – but this, she decided, wasn't most things. Anyway, that was just her pride talking. Sometimes the wise thing, the smart thing to do was gratefully to accept the help that was offered.

It was only a couple of minutes before she saw Rick jogging along the street. There was something touching about his sense of urgency. She ran down the stairs as quietly as she could, pulled across the bolts and opened the door. A moment later, they were face to face.

'Hi,' he said softly. 'Are you okay?'

The relief at seeing him was almost too much to bear. She felt the tears prick her eyes and tried to wipe them away. Even as her hands rose, she was aware of him moving forward and of the gentle, reassuring tone of his voice. She wasn't quite sure how it happened, but suddenly, somehow his arms were around her holding her tight, and for the first time all day she felt safe.

25

Rick leaned forward with his elbows on the counter, gazing down at the dead bird. It was half an hour since he'd arrived, time that Maddie had spent explaining the whole sorry story. Now he knew everything. He knew about Greta and Bo, Cato, Lena Gissing and the mystery surrounding Lucy Rivers.

He gave her a sidelong glance. 'And you haven't called the cops because . . . ?'

Maddie was trying to avoid looking at the tiny corpse. Instead, she kept her eyes fixed firmly on Rick. 'I thought about it. I almost rang them. I don't know. I didn't want them to come while Zac was here. And I was hoping that Cato would call.' She folded her arms across her chest. 'And then there was what Lena said, about having friends at Cowan Road. If I report it, I might make things even worse. What do you think? Do you reckon she might have that kind of influence?'

'Hard to know, but she could have contacts. Her sort usually do.'

'Her sort?'

'Gangsters, criminals, whatever you want to call them. I'm sure she's bribed a few officers in her time. If nothing else, she might get to hear that you'd been to the station.'

Despite the warmth of the kitchen, Maddie gave a shiver. 'That's what I'm worried about. And I can't prove that she did this.' Although she didn't want to look, her gaze automatically slid down to the dead bird. It was the long silver nail that made it so much worse, the nail that pierced the centre of the body. It reminded her of a crucifixion. 'It's sick. What kind of person ...?'

'The kind of person who's worried about what you might know – or say.'

'Which is ironic, seeing as I hardly know anything at all. And I still don't get why Delia Shields had a go at me. Where does she figure in all this?'

'She's a friend of Lena Gissing.'

Maddie frowned, surprised by the revelation. 'What? Delia? Delia and Lena? How do you know that?'

'Because I've seen them together. And because Eli says they go way back, went to school together apparently. Maybe you should ask him about Lucy Rivers.'

'Or you could,' she said, not relishing a conversation with the strange Eli Glass. 'He's more likely to talk to you.' She turned her back to the counter so she couldn't see the bird. 'I'm still trying to get my head around Delia and Lena Gissing. I mean, Delia always seems so ... prim and proper. It's hard to imagine the two of them being friends.'

'Although it accounts for how Lena knew where to find you this morning. Delia must have called her as soon as you got there.'

'That's true.' She rubbed her face, exhausted by the day's events. 'God, what am I going to do? What do you think I should do?'

'It's your call, babe.'

'Would you go to the cops? If you were in my shoes?'

'I'm not sure. I suppose you have to weigh up the pros and cons. If you report it, then they'll probably go and talk to Lena Gissing. But of course you can't prove anything, and she's bound to deny it, so . . .'

'So it'll be a waste of time.'

'Well, I know you don't want her to get away with it, but once she sees that you haven't gone to the cops, she might back off and leave you alone. And if you're not tending the grave any more, then she's got no reason to keep hassling you.'

'Except she thinks I'm in league with Cato.'

'Like I said, it's your choice. You have to do whatever feels right.'

Maddie ran her fingers through her hair and released her breath in a long, low sigh. 'I wish I knew what felt right. *Nothing* feels right.'

'Maybe you should wait and see if Cato gets in touch.'

'And what about . . . ?' She gestured with her head towards the box. 'What do I do with him?'

Rick leaned in closer to the bird, examining the body. 'Looks like its neck got broken. It was probably a cat. Wrong place, wrong time and all that.'

'Yeah, but the cat didn't skewer the poor thing to a piece of card, put it in a box and leave it on my doorstep.'

'Seems unlikely,' he agreed. 'You want me to bury it, or are you going to keep it as evidence? Doubt there's any fingerprints lying around. They wouldn't have been that careless.'

Maddie sighed again. She had pretty much decided that she wasn't going to the police, at least not for the moment. What would it achieve? They could hardly offer her twenty-four-hour protection. In fact, the only thing they probably would offer was a promise to 'look into it'. And in the meantime, Lena

Gissing would find out that she'd been to talk to them. 'Would you mind? And would you, you know, take the nail out before . . . ?'

'Sure,' he said.

Maddie went to the living room while he was carrying out the procedure. She pulled a handful of tissues from the box and took them back to Rick. 'Here,' she said. 'You can wrap him in these.'

They went out into the yard, where there was just enough light from the kitchen for them to see what they were doing. Maddie got a spade from the garden box and passed it to him. Then she found a nice spot near the roses where the bird could be buried.

While Rick was digging, she kept glancing up towards Zac's bedroom window. She prayed that he was still asleep, that he wouldn't hear the soft sound of the spade cutting through the earth. She wondered if she was making a mistake, burying the evidence like this. But she didn't want Zac finding the bird. And anyway, unless she put it in the freezer, there was a limit on the time she could keep it before the body started to rot.

It didn't take long for Rick to complete the job. He bent down, laid the tiny parcel in the hole and glanced at her. 'You want to say a few words?'

Maddie looked at him. 'Like what?' she whispered. 'It's not a funeral.'

He grinned back at her. 'Well, it is, kind of.'

'Just cover it over.'

Rick filled in the hole and patted down the soil. 'There. All done.'

'Thank you. Thanks. I appreciate it.'

They went back inside, where Maddie closed the door and bolted it. There was no direct access to the back of the house, but she wasn't taking any chances. 'God, you must be regretting the day you ever met me.'

'Why do you say that?'

'All this,' she said, nodding towards the box that was still sitting on the counter. 'And everything else. It's not exactly normal, is it?'

'And is any of it your fault?'

Maddie gave a shrug. 'That's not the point.'

Rick bent down and kissed her on the top of her head. 'Course it's the point. Now, have you got anything stronger than coffee in this house? I don't know about you, but I could do with a real drink.'

Maddie went to the fridge and opened it. 'There's only wine,' she said. 'No beer, I'm afraid.'

'Wine will do fine.'

She took the bottle and a couple of glasses through to the living room and they sat down at either end of the sofa. Although the poor bird had been disposed of, the threat still loomed large in her mind. She poured the wine, passed him a glass and then pulled up her knees and wrapped her arms around her legs. 'Thank you,' she said again, 'for coming round and everything. Thanks for dealing with the ...'

'No need to thank me. It was a tricky burial, but fortunately I'm a highly trained gravedigger.'

'I picked the right guy for the job, then.'

'You picked the right guy full stop.'

Maddie smiled. 'You think?'

'Who could doubt it?' Rick sat back and sipped on his wine. There was a short but not uncomfortable silence. 'So you and Greta,' he asked. 'Were you close?'

'When we were kids, but not so much as we grew older. And I think that was my fault. I was so wrapped up in my own life, my own career that I didn't really make time for her any more.

By the time she died . . . was murdered . . . we were almost like strangers to each other. And now I'm finding out this stuff and . . .' She stopped. 'But you don't want to hear about all that. You've had enough of my life story for one night.'

'Not true,' he said. 'I'm interested. So did the cops find any link to the Gissings back then?'

Maddie shook her head. 'Not as far as I know, but then they didn't tell us much. I think they pretty much wrote it off as some kind of gangland killing. Bo worked for the Streets, but I've heard he was close to Adam Vasser too.'

'Vasser?' Rick said, his eyebrows shooting up. 'Jesus, he certainly picked his company.'

Maddie reached for her glass and drank a little wine. She'd have liked to drink a lot of it, to drown her fears and sorrows in alcohol, but was aware of having to get up early in the morning to take Zac to summer school. 'How long did you say you've lived in Kellston?'

'A few months,' he said. 'Why?'

'Because I've lived here for six years and I'd never heard of him. I'd never heard of Lena Gissing either.'

Rick laughed. 'Ah, well, there's a good reason for that. You don't waste your time sitting around in the Fox, listening to the local gossip. It's amazing what you hear in that pub.'

'And what have you heard about Vasser?'

'That he's a nasty bit of work, but then that goes with the job description. And being Lena's flesh and blood can't do much for the personality. Rumour has it that she runs a high-class escort service – beautiful girls for men with large bank accounts.'

'Really?'

'That's what they say.'

'But if you know that, then why don't the police?'

'Maybe they do,' Rick said. 'Maybe they just don't want to go there. You start turning over stones in that kind of business and you never know what's going to crawl out – or rather, *who* is going to crawl out. And a scandal is the last thing they want, especially if it involves some of their own.'

Maddie took another sip of wine while she thought about this. 'So it's okay to break the law so long as you're dealing with the rich and the powerful?'

'Hasn't it always been that way?'

'Doesn't make it right.'

'No,' he agreed. 'It doesn't. But that's how it is. And it's what gives her protection. So long as she's discreet, she won't get any bother.'

Maddie was sure now that she'd made the right choice in not going to the law. 'And what if she did have something to do with Greta's murder? What happens then?'

'It gets complicated.'

'It's already complicated.' She leaned her head back against the sofa. 'I wish Cato had called. He must know something. He has to or he wouldn't have gone to all the bother of hiring me.'

'Give him time. It's only been a day. It's not always easy to get on the phone in those places.'

Maddie threw him a look. She hardly knew anything about his past; perhaps he had some dark secrets of his own. 'Is that from personal experience?'

'If you're asking if I've ever done time, then no. But I've had mates who've been in for the odd short stretch. Never fancied it myself, so I try and keep out of trouble.'

'You've come to the wrong place, then.'

'Ah, but this is a righteous sort of trouble. Not the same thing at all.'

'Seriously, though, I don't expect you … don't *want* you to get involved in all this. It's not fair. It's my problem, not yours.'

'Now you're just being selfish.' He leaned forward, took hold of the bottle and topped up both their glasses. 'Didn't your mother ever teach you about sharing?'

'All my mother ever taught me was how to pack a suitcase. I'm exceptionally good at that.'

'Lots of practice, huh?'

'Lots.'

'But getting back to the point, it's too late to dismiss me now – I'm already involved.'

Maddie peered at him over the rim of her glass. 'Digging a hole in the ground doesn't count as being involved.'

'I'm shocked,' he said, placing a hand on his heart. 'That wasn't just any old hole. It was a highly professional piece of digging.'

'For which I'm very grateful, but it doesn't mean that you're obliged to do anything else.'

'What, not even moral support?'

Maddie hesitated. 'I suppose there wouldn't be much harm in that.'

'Good, that's settled, then. Now, about all this packing you did as a kid . . . '

An hour later, when the past had been shared, the wine finished and a cup of coffee drunk, Rick glanced at his watch. 'I'd better make a move. Will you be okay?'

'I'll be fine.' Maddie forced a smile. She hadn't been looking forward to the time when he'd leave and she'd be on her own again. 'Really I will. Thanks for coming round. It was good of you.'

He stood up. 'No problem.'

She rose to her feet too, trying to appear perfectly calm about him going.

'Unless . . . ' he said.

She gazed up at him, her eyes locking on to his. 'Unless . . . ?'

'I could stay if you want.'

His words hung in the air and for a moment Maddie was tempted, but she knew she'd be doing it for all the wrong reasons. Fear and gratitude weren't good motives for going to bed with a man, no matter how attractive he was. She made a vague flapping motion with her hand. 'Er ... I don't think ... you know, with Zac and everything. I do like you, of course I do, but it's probably not a good idea.'

He put his hands on his hips and stared at her. 'Hey, I wasn't ... I was just offering to kip on the sofa if you'd feel safer having someone around.'

'Oh, right.' Maddie, feeling foolish, glanced away and then back at him. 'Well, this isn't awkward or anything.'

'You think I'm the kind of guy who'd try and take advantage?'

She studied him closely, watching the corners of his mouth twitch. 'Now you're just trying to make me feel bad.'

'Is it working?'

'Yeah, pretty much.'

Rick grinned. 'So, what do you reckon? To be honest, you'd be doing me a favour. It'll save me the walk home. And I'll make myself scarce before Zac gets up – he won't even know I've been here.'

Maddie didn't need much persuading. With Rick in the house, at least she'd get some sleep and not be lying awake listening for the slightest noise. She pretended to think about it some more even though her mind was already made up. Then she gave a light shrug as if she was the one bestowing the favour rather than the other way round. 'Okay, I'll get you some blankets.'

26

Adam Vasser watched from the bed while the boy stood up, tucked in his shirt and did up his flies. Already he was regretting the encounter. With his desire now sated, he was filled with that familiar self-loathing, the sense of disgust that always overwhelmed him at these times. He had met the boy in a bar in Brewer Street. What was his name? Already he'd forgotten. Lewis or Leo, something like that.

Earlier, he had found the guy attractive. Slim build, dark hair flopping over his forehead, a full mouth, a tattoo of a snake wrapped round the well-toned bicep of his right arm. He had an Italian look about him, although that illusion was shattered as soon as he opened his mouth. Pure Essex. And now Adam saw him for what he really was – just a dirty little rent boy.

He rose to his feet, rage starting to blossom in his chest. His hands curled into two tight fists. He'd only gone into the bar for a drink, a few whiskies to help him wind down. He'd had no intention of . . . No, it had been the guy who'd approached him, started chatting, eyeing him up in the way they always did. Predators, the whole fuckin' lot of them.

He glanced around the room, a shabby Soho dive where the boy conducted his business. Brown furniture, brown carpet, a layer of dust over everything. Dirty. Filthy. He scratched the back of his neck. God knows what diseases were lurking in the place. And he was expected to pay for the privilege of being here. It was a joke, a bleeding joke.

'You ready?' the boy asked, wanting to get rid of him. His tone was cool and dismissive. He pushed back the hair from his forehead, a gesture that Adam had found sensuous an hour ago but now only filled him with revulsion.

'No,' Adam said. 'We're not finished yet.'

'You got what you paid for, man. Now it's time to go.'

But no one told Adam Vasser what to do or when to do it. He quickly stepped forward, taking his victim by surprise. As his fist made contact with his jaw, there was a satisfying cracking sound. The boy staggered back, knocking over a lamp before his knees crumpled and he fell to the ground.

Adam could have left it at that, but he wanted more, needed more. A punch in the face – even if it had broken his jaw – wasn't enough. The boy had taken advantage and he was going to pay for it. Drawing back his foot, he kicked him hard in the groin, in the ribs, in the stomach.

The boy instinctively tried to curl up, attempting to protect himself. Adam launched himself on top, straightening and straddling the boy's body, his eyes burning with uncontrollable rage. 'Bastard!' he spat. 'Fuckin' whore!' Pinned to the carpet, his victim had no hope of escape. The universe had shrunk to the dimensions of these four shabby walls; there was nothing in the world now but the two of them. He punched over and over, only stopping when the face had been reduced to a bloody pulp.

Adam, heaving from the exertion, sat back and viewed his handiwork. Already he was feeling better, a sense of euphoria flowing over him. The boy had deserved it, *asked* for it. He was a filthy, shitty crackhead, a punk, a pervert. Slowly he rose to his feet and stood staring down at the smashed-up features. 'Not so pretty now,' he murmured.

The boy wasn't moving at all. He looked like a corpse. Adam nudged his chest with the toe of his shoe. A low groan slipped from between the bloodied lips.

'Not dead, then.'

There was no reply. The boy's eyes fluttered but remained closed. The room was quiet, very quiet. Adam listened, but heard nothing. Even the groaning had stopped. He prodded the boy in the chest again. Then he sniffed and wrinkled his nose. There was a bad smell in the room, a repellent stench of shit and piss and blood. Glancing down at his clothes, he saw that his shirt was stained with red. He put on his jacket, buttoned it and walked out of the door. On the landing, he paused, making sure that no one was around, before he jogged down the stairs and out on to the street.

The air that had been warm earlier had turned chilly now. A spatter of rain fell against the pavement. He walked with his head down, mingling with the crowd. Soho was always busy, its streets awash with tourists, with tarts and punters, pimps and dips. The fancy restaurants and the slick bars sat side by side with the strip joints and the sex shops. It was more respectable than it once had been, but only on the surface. Underneath it was still pure filth, the rancid underbelly of London.

It was years now since Brendan Vasser had made his mark on this enclave of the West End. Once, he'd owned three clubs here, a casino and a string of porno outlets. He'd had power and influence, controlling the drugs trade and the girls. He'd been a major player, and that's what Adam wanted to be. It was in his genes, his DNA. Soho was his rightful inheritance and one day he'd take it back.

By the time he reached Shaftesbury Avenue, the rain was coming down hard. He stepped out into the road, hailed a cab and jumped in the back. 'Kellston, please, mate. The High Street.'

'Filthy evening, huh? Still, I ain't complaining. It's good for trade.'

'Yeah.' As soon as the driver set off, Adam slid the glass screen across, making it clear that he didn't want to talk any more. He had stuff to think about and he didn't need an opinionated cabbie giving him earache for the next twenty minutes.

As they headed towards the East End, he raised his right hand to his mouth and sucked on his bruised knuckles. A dull throb was spreading through his fingers. Still, it had been worth it. Had he killed the stinking bastard? He didn't know and didn't care.

Adam leaned into the corner of the cab, gazing out at the passing streets. It was time for a change, time for him to step up to the mark. No more loitering in the shadows waiting for his life to begin. He was sick of the motors, sick of his mother being forever on his case. And when she wasn't interfering, she was sneaking around behind his back.

He could have confronted her about this whole Maddie Layne business, but he knew there was no point. She'd only lie to him like she always did. It was a worry, though, a fly in the ointment. What if the law decided to reopen the case? Was there some new evidence that he didn't know about? There had to be something or the bitch wouldn't have paid Yeats to go snooping. She wouldn't pay out good money unless she thought Maddie Layne was a serious threat.

A small smile tugged at the corners of his lips. Greta's sister would have found his gift by now. He hoped she appreciated it.

A God-given gift, as he'd found the bird lying dead in the gutter when he'd left the house this morning. It had been too good an opportunity to pass up. She had probably gone crying to the pigs, but this didn't bother him. She'd soon learn that no one, no one in the entire wide world could protect her from Adam Vasser.

27

When Maddie went downstairs at seven thirty in the morning, Rick had already gone. In the living room, the blankets were neatly folded on the sofa, and in the kitchen, the wine glasses had been washed and left on the drainer. She also found a note lying on the counter: *See you Saturday. Don't be late. Call me if you need me.*

She smiled, feeling better about things today. Although the fear still niggled in the back of her mind, it had receded enough for her to be able to cope. The dead bird seemed more like a bad dream than something that had actually happened. Having Rick on her side – someone to talk to, to rely on – made everything seem less bleak.

As she organised breakfast, she went over the evening's long conversation. It had been an age since she'd spoken to anyone in that way, opening up about her childhood, about Greta, about her worries that the murderer would never be brought to justice. Perhaps it had been a mixture of the wine and the shock of the parcel that had loosened her tongue to such an extent. Or perhaps Rick was just an easy person to chat to.

When Zac came down, Maddie searched his face, wondering if he'd been aware of Rick's presence last night. She put the toast on the table and sat at the table with her mug of tea.

'Sleep well?' she asked.

'I dreamed about Mrs Forsyth,' he said. 'She was chasing me down the corridor.'

Mrs Forsyth was his form mistress at Kellston Primary. 'Why? Had you done something bad?'

'No,' he said firmly. 'But she thought I had. She thought I'd taken her parcel. I think it was the parcel that was here yesterday.' He looked around the kitchen, peering at all the surfaces as if it might still be lurking somewhere. 'She said it was hers. She said I had to give it back.'

'Well, it wasn't hers, so you don't need to worry about it.' Maddie glanced towards the window, eager to change the subject. Outside, the sky was low and grey, and the rain was coming down steadily. 'You'd better take a jumper today as well as your coat. I don't think we'll be seeing much sunshine.'

Zac gave her a steady look. 'What did you do with it?'

'With what, hon?'

'With the parcel. You said it was a mistake, so what did you do with it?'

Maddie sipped her tea, trying not to appear as shifty as she felt. 'It's gone. I got rid of it. It was nothing interesting.'

Zac poured some cereal into a bowl. 'But if it wasn't for you, why did you get rid of it – and why did it have your name on the front?'

She racked her brains, trying to think of something feasible. 'It was sent by somebody who thought I might be interested, but I'm not. It was just ... er ... some old books, boring books.'

'Oh,' he said. He poured some cereal into a bowl. 'Maddie?'

'Yes?' She waited for another question about the mystery parcel.

'Kyle has chocolate cornflakes. Can we get some?'

'No, hon,' she said with relief. 'They're not very good for you. Don't you like the ordinary ones?'

'They're okay.'

There was a clatter from the letterbox and the thud of mail landing on the carpet. Maddie got up and went through to the hall. She bent down to pick up the small pile: two bills, some advertising bumf and a handwritten letter. She didn't recognise the writing. She flipped over the envelope, but there was nothing on the reverse. Returning to the kitchen, she sat down again, dumped the bills on the corner of the table – no point in depressing herself before she had to – and tore open the letter.

Maddie gave a gasp, surprised by the contents. It was a visiting order from Cato for HMP Thornley Heath. There was no covering note, just the single slip of paper. At best she'd been expecting a call, but now she was suddenly faced with the prospect of meeting him in person. How did she feel about that? On the one hand, she wanted to find out what he knew about Greta; on the other, she had serious reservations about coming face to face with a murderer.

She quickly read through the instructions. Unless she took a day off work, the only time she'd be able to visit was Saturday or Sunday. Saturday would be better, as Alisha had already agreed to have Zac overnight. Hopefully, she wouldn't mind taking him for the afternoon too. The visit ran from two to four, which should give her enough time to get back for her date with Rick in the evening.

So she was really going to go to the prison? She frowned down at the piece of paper. If Lena Gissing got to hear of it, all her suspicions would be confirmed. But Maddie couldn't pass over the opportunity. She might never get another chance to find out the truth.

'What's that?' Zac asked.

'Just a work thing,' she said, quickly stuffing the order back into the envelope.

'Remember you're staying over at Gran and Grandpa's on Saturday, so don't go making any arrangements with Kyle.'

'That's not till the night.'

'Change of plan, sweetheart. I've … I've got to work for a few hours in the afternoon, so we'll be going round after lunch. You don't mind, do you?'

'Course not. Do you think Grandpa will give me more bowling lessons?'

'I'm sure he will if you ask him nicely.' She was glad that Zac was still of an age where he enjoyed his grandparents' company. The difficult teenage years were yet to come. She gazed at him, hoping that he wouldn't change too much.

Zac buttered his toast, took a bite, chewed and swallowed. 'Maddie?'

'Yes?'

'Are you going to a party on Saturday night?'

'No, it's not a party, just a meal with a friend.'

'Is it Shauna?'

Maddie shook her head. 'No, not Shauna.' She hesitated, but then decided to tell him the truth. 'A different friend. He's called Rick. We're going to Adriano's, the Italian place on the High Street.'

'Is he your boyfriend?'

'Just a friend. He works at the cemetery.'

Zac thought about this while he ate some more toast. 'Is he going to move in with us?'

'God, no!' Maddie's mouth dropped open. 'Why would he do that?'

He gave a shrug. 'Shauna's boyfriends are always moving in. Kyle says they smell.'

'Does he?' She hid a smile behind her hand. 'Well, Rick isn't moving in here. This is our house, yours and mine. There isn't room for anyone else.'

Zac seemed satisfied with the answer. He was quiet for a while and then he said, 'I'm sure Uncle Sol would take you for a meal.'

Maddie looked across the table. Was he trying to fix her up with her brother-in-law, or was it a completely innocent comment? 'I'm sure he'd take us both, love, but he's a busy man and he's got work to do. Now come on and finish your breakfast or we'll be late.'

Fifteen minutes later, they were at Shauna's door picking up Kyle. Maddie thought there was a certain coolness about her friend today – she hardly said more than a couple of words – but it might just have been her imagination. Shauna was never at her best first thing in the morning.

As Maddie walked along the High Street with the boys, her mind was preoccupied by the forthcoming visit. She wondered if she should call Rick and tell him about it. But what if he tried to persuade her not to go? There were good reasons why she shouldn't, top of the list being the fact that Jay Cato was a convicted killer. Closely followed by what Lena Gissing would do if she found out. Neither of these was an attractive prospect, but they were both better than the regrets she would feel if she passed over the opportunity.

On balance, she decided that the best thing to do was keep quiet. That way, she couldn't be swayed. And anyway, she didn't want to go running to him every five minutes. What if she came across as one of those clingy, needy women who always looked to a man for protection? The very thought made her wince. No, she would tell Rick when she saw him on Saturday night. By then she might have a clearer picture of what had happened to Greta.

They reached the gates of the school and she watched as Zac

225

and Kyle dashed down the path sloshing through the puddles. At the door, Zac turned round and waved. She waved back. Once they were safely inside, she set off towards Marigolds. She'd be early for her shift, but that didn't matter. Before she started work, she had a call to make to HMP Thornley Heath.

28

Lena Gissing gazed at her husband as she ate her breakfast. It wasn't a pretty sight. Every day he became a little uglier, a little more repulsive. And that was some going, she thought, for a man who hadn't had much to recommend him in the first place. She studied the mauve shadow on his unshaven face, the heavy jowls, the huge paunch that pressed against the edge of the table. It was enough to put anyone off their food. She dropped what was left of her toast, pushed the plate away and lit up a fag.

'What's he up to?' she asked.

'Huh?'

'Adam. I know he's up to something.'

Tony shovelled the bacon and eggs into his mouth. He was still chewing when he answered her. 'How would I know? He's your fuckin' son.'

'And it's your fuckin' sons that are going to pay the price if he drags them into a war with the Streets.'

'There's not going to be a war.'

'What, you think they're just going to sit back and take it? Let him move in on their manor? It's not going to happen. He's going to end up with his head blown off. And your boys too. Is that what you want? Is it?'

Tony raised his eyes to the ceiling. 'It ain't going to happen.'

'Oh, because you say so?' She pulled hard on the cigarette, exhaling the smoke in a long, angry stream. 'Jesus, you're all so bloody stupid! You think because Terry ain't got all his marbles, he's going to be a pushover.'

Tony glared at her. 'For fuck's sake, can't a man even eat his breakfast in peace? I've told you I don't know nothin'. Why do you keep going on about it?'

'Because you're a liar,' she said. 'And a shit one at that.'

'Whatever.'

Lena leaned across the table, eyeballing him. If she hadn't been so wound up, she might have kept quiet, but her back was up and the words were out before she could stop them. 'We've got enough problems as it is.'

This time Tony finally took some notice of what she was saying. He put down his knife and fork, his forehead puckering into a frown. 'And what problems are those, then?'

Lena hesitated, unsure as to how much to tell him. His solution to most trouble was to act like a bull in a china shop. Act first and think later. That's if he ever got round to thinking at all. But she had to find a way to stop Adam in his tracks. If he carried on with his attempts to oust the Streets, he'd end up with his brains spattered across the pavement.

'What problems?' Tony asked again. 'What are you talking about?'

Lena was still turning over how much she should divulge. If she was being honest, it wasn't only Adam she was worried about. Her concerns were a lot more selfish. By keeping a low profile, she was able to conduct her escort business without any interference from the law, but if Adam made a bid to take over Kellston, all that would change. Word would get out and her clients would take fright. None of them would want any dealings with a business connected to gang warfare. That level of violence meant news, press coverage and a whole pile of grief. She had to put a stop to it before it all got out of hand.

'Remember Bo Vale?'

'Who?'

'Bo Vale,' she repeated. 'The one who was ... He worked for Adam, on the cars. God, it's not that long ago. Don't pretend you can't remember.'

Tony pulled a face. 'Long enough. It was years back. Shit, that's all dead and buried. Why are you going on about it?'

'Because it might not be as dead and buried as you think. Someone's sniffing around. I think they might be trying to get the case reopened.'

'What?'

'Her name's Maddie Layne. She's the sister of Bo's girlfriend. Greta – you remember her, don't you?' She sat back and folded her arms. 'Course you do. You always remember the pretty girls. Anyway, this bitch, this Maddie woman, she's stirring things.'

'Since when?'

'Since recently.'

'How recent?'

Lena took a couple more puffs on her fag. 'A while. A few weeks.'

'So she's stirring. So what? She can't know anything for sure. If she did, she'd have gone to the filth.'

'Maybe she will. Maybe she already has. I don't know.' Lena released an exasperated sigh. 'But don't you see, the last thing Adam needs at the moment is to be drawing attention to himself. If they start looking into the case again ...'

'They'll find nothin',' Tony said. 'Because there's nothin' to find.'

'You sure about that?'

Tony stared across the table at her with his small, piggy eyes. 'You telling me something different?'

'I'm just saying we need to be careful, that's all.' Lena didn't tell him about Cato. He'd have laughed out loud, thought it was hilarious that she was being spooked by a girl putting flowers on a grave.

'Anyway, what are you bending my ear for? It's Adam that needs a word.'

'And since when has he ever listened to me? You need to tell your boys to back off, to not get involved. Adam can't take on the Streets without them behind him.'

'They're old enough to make up their own minds.'

'And stupid enough to do exactly what they shouldn't.'

Tony's lip curled. 'If we're talking stupid, your Adam ain't got much to recommend him. If it hadn't been for—'

'Yeah, yeah, you think I don't know that?' She stubbed out her cigarette in the ashtray. 'There's nothing we can do about that now. But let's not make it even worse, huh?'

Tony gave a shrug and went back to eating his breakfast. 'You want me to have a word with this Maddie Layne?'

'No, I'm dealing with it. You just sort your boys out.' She pushed back her chair and stood up. 'I mean it, Tony. This is serious. Get your finger out or we're all going to end up in the shit.'

29

Eli Glass stared down at the decapitated angel. The stonemason was supposed to have come and picked her up, but he'd caught a dose of summer flu. It would be a while yet before she was removed. Lying next to her body was her head, her face gazing up at the grey sky with a look of stolid forbearance.

Although it wasn't cold, the rain was coming down steadily. Eli turned up the collar on his jacket as the rain slid down the back of his neck. Last week, he and Rick had managed to move the angel up against the wall where she was less visible to people passing by on the thoroughfare. She'd been a dead weight, mind, and his shoulders had ached for a few days after.

The cemetery had lots of angels like these. Mainly old. Most of them going way back. People weren't so keen on them these days, or maybe they just didn't have the cash. One of her wings was damaged, the tip snapped off. A small pool of water was gathering in the curve. The rain pocked the surface, creating tiny circles. He gazed at the broken statue for a while longer before pushing his hands deep into his pockets, turning round and heading for the office. It was getting on for eleven. Time for a brew.

On his way there, he saw Terry Street standing by the grave of his wife. The man was often here now, staring hard at the headstone as if he was trying to figure out something. Even though he was ten yards away, Eli could still hear her strident complaints. Lizzie Street didn't know the meaning of resting in peace. The fading yellow chrysanthemums, left by Lena Gissing, had been pulled out of the urn and chucked on the grass. But they hadn't been replaced by any fresh flowers.

Eli didn't speak. Sometimes, occasionally, they'd exchange a nod, but usually Terry looked straight through him as if he wasn't even there. And anyway, what was there to say? Every man had his own demons and Terry Street had more than most. It was ironic that the old gangster couldn't remember what he'd done yesterday, but that the sins of the past were always with him.

Thinking of Lena Gissing reminded Eli of what he'd witnessed yesterday. He'd seen the red sports car pull up on the thoroughfare and watched as she got out and walked not to the office as he'd expected, but across the cemetery towards Lucy's grave. Curiosity had made him follow her. He'd kept his distance, though, not wanting to be spotted.

The girl with the long brown hair had been tending the grave. He'd seen her stand up, watched as the two of them exchanged words. He was too far away to hear the row, but that hadn't mattered. He'd known why Lena was there, why she had to be, why she couldn't stay away. Like Terry, her past was coming back to haunt her.

What Eli didn't know was what she'd thrown. He'd seen her bend down, pick something up and shout at the girl. He'd seen her arm swing back, seen her throw that something – with force, with speed – in the general direction of the Belvederes. What had it been? He would have gone to look, but after Lena had left, her son had arrived. Had he been following her? He must have been.

Eli had waited long enough to be sure the girl was safe before making himself scarce. Adam Vasser wasn't just bad; he was shot full of evil. To be close to him, to be anywhere near him was to risk contagion. The man danced with the Devil.

Eli quickened his pace, trying to push all thoughts of Vasser from his mind. He veered off the main thoroughfare and on to one of the smaller paths. By the time he got to Lucy's grave, the ankles of his trousers were soaked through from the long, wet grass. He reached out and touched the marble headstone. He gazed down at the roses; the peach-coloured blooms were just opening, the petals glistening with raindrops.

'It's me,' he murmured. 'It's only me.'

He waited, hoping she might speak to him, but there was nothing, only the steady patter of the rain against the earth. With a heavy heart he walked on, brushing past the sodden buddleia, scouring the ground as he went. He searched to the left and the right, and was almost at the mausoleum before he eventually found it.

Crouching down, he moved aside the dock leaves to reveal the gold wedding band. Carefully, he picked it up and weighed it in his palm. What did he feel? A faint tingling against his skin. An odd, confusing emotion, but no words. Nothing he could really grasp. He concentrated hard, briefly closing his eyes. The ring was as silent as Lucy Rivers. He held it for a while longer and then slipped it into his pocket.

Eli trudged back across the cemetery, his shoulders hunched against the rain. Five minutes later, he was standing outside the office. There was a small room at the back of the building where the workers could eat their lunch or have a brew. It had a separate door, so they didn't need to tramp through the main reception area.

He paused for a moment, trying to decide which door to head for. He was desperate for a brew, but the ring was burning a hole in his pocket. If pushed, he wouldn't have been able to explain why he felt the need to get rid of it. It was a gut instinct, a feeling that he couldn't ignore.

Delia Shields was alone in the office. She looked up, frowning, as he opened the door.

He knew better than to take his muddy boots inside. Instead, he waited for her to come to him. She didn't rush. She walked slowly across the room as if he was the very last person she wanted to talk to.

'Yes, Eli?'

'I found something,' he said, holding out the ring.

She stared at it, keeping her hands by her sides as if reluctant to touch it. 'Where?'

'Over on the west side. It was in the grass.' He didn't mention Lena Gissing or what he had witnessed with the girl. Delia might think he'd been spying. It would give her another excuse to try and get rid of him. 'Must have been dropped by someone.'

'No one's reported it as lost.'

'You want it or not?' he asked, thrusting it closer to her.

Delia flinched as if the ring was some kind of weapon. Her face had grown flushed, a red stain that spread across her cheeks and down her neck. Finally, reluctantly, she took the gold band from him. 'I'll keep it for a few days, see if anyone claims it. If not, I'll hand it in at the police station.'

Eli gave a nod. She knew who'd thrown the ring. Of course she did. He could tell that from her reaction. And she knew who it had once belonged to.

'Was there anything else?'

'No.'

Without another word, she turned, went back to her desk,

opened the drawer and dropped the ring into it. Then she looked over at him again. It was a searing glance, accusing, as if what he'd just done was a deliberate act of malice. 'Thank you, Eli,' she said stiffly. 'I'm sure you want to get on.'

Eli closed the door and left.

30

On Saturday morning, Maddie woke to find her stomach full of butterflies. The prison visit loomed ahead, along with all the hours she would have to wait before she finally came face to face with Cato. Now that she had made the decision, she wanted to get it over and done with as soon as possible.

Over breakfast, Zac was unusually grumpy. Was he picking up on her anxiety, or had he just got out of the wrong side of the bed? She made an effort to be cheerful, trying to cajole him into a smile.

'So, are you looking forward to your bowling lesson with Grandpa?'

'It's raining,' he said sulkily. 'We can't go outside in the rain.'

'It might have stopped by then.' However, as she gazed out of the window, that prospect seemed unlikely. The sky was dark and thunderous, the grey clouds lying low over the rooftops. 'Well, I'm sure you'll find something fun to do.'

'Will Uncle Sol be there?'

'I don't know, hon. Maybe he'll pop in.' She felt guilty about withholding information from Solomon. Her visit to see Cato wasn't just about Greta's death but about Bo's too. Didn't he have a right to know? But know what? She had no firm facts, nothing solid, nothing that could really be described as evidence. It was better, surely, to hang on until the picture became clearer.

'Can I go and watch TV?' Zac asked.

'You haven't finished your breakfast.'

'I'm not hungry.'

Maddie wasn't a fan of leaving kids in front of the television for hours, but with no chance of him playing outside and with her mind so distracted by the forthcoming visit, she gave in to the easy option. 'All right. Just for a while. But take your toast with you – and don't get crumbs all over the sofa.'

He grabbed his plate, jumped up and fled to the living room. Seconds later, she heard the jingly sound of the cartoons he loved so much. Maddie guiltily sipped her tea, feeling that she should have made more of an effort to find a way of entertaining him: drawing or painting, something more creative than just staring at a screen. But this morning she was too preoccupied. Did that make her the worst mother in the world? Probably.

After clearing up the breakfast things, Maddie went upstairs and studied her wardrobe. She had no idea what you wore to meet a murderer. Black seemed a little dramatic. White too . . . Too what? She wasn't sure. Too innocent perhaps. Jeans? Too casual. A suit? Too smart. A dress? Too much leg on show. Trousers, then. Trousers and a top.

She dug out a pair of cream trousers and a pale green cotton top with buttons down the front. Sitting down on the bed, she glanced at her watch for the twentieth time. She leaned forward, placing her elbows on her knees and her chin in her hands. What was she going to say to Cato? She ought to figure it out before she got there. A slow, sneaky fear was creeping up on her – a fear that this might all be a waste of time. Greta and Bo had been killed six years ago. Jay Cato had been inside for the last ten years. How could he know anything?

Quickly Maddie rose to her feet again. If she thought about it too much, she'd end up changing her mind and bottling out. No, the visit was booked and she was going to go through with it. She'd figure out her questions on the way there. And then she wondered if she should ask Winston if she could borrow his old Ford. It would make the journey easier – unless the car broke down again. Solomon's skills as a mechanic left a lot to be desired.

In the end, she decided to stick with public transport. Thornley Heath wasn't that far away, although she'd need to take two trains and a bus. If she left at midday, she'd have a couple of hours, which should be more than enough.

At half eleven, Maddie dragged a complaining Zac off the sofa, got him into his jacket and passed him the little rucksack containing all he needed for an overnight stay.

'Now, you'll be good for your gran, won't you?'

Zac lifted his shoulders slightly.

'Was that a yes?'

'Yes,' he repeated, although in a somewhat dispirited tone.

Maddie looked at him. 'What's the matter? I thought you liked being with Gran and Grandpa.'

He gave another shrug, glanced away and shifted from one foot to the other. It was a few seconds before he met her gaze again. 'Are you going to come back?'

'What do you mean? Of course I'm coming back.'

'When?'

'I'll see you tomorrow morning, won't I?' Concerned, she leaned down and took hold of his arms. 'Why wouldn't I come back?'

Zac squirmed a little. 'Kyle says that when Shauna leaves him with his gran, she doesn't always ... Sometimes she stays away all weekend. Sometimes even longer.'

'And when have I ever done that?' she asked, silently cursing Shauna. 'That's never going to happen. I promise, okay?'

'Swear to God and hope to die?'

'Swear to God and hope to die.'

Zac finally managed a semblance of a smile. 'You can call me at Gran's this evening.'

'I'll do that. I'll call you at seven. So, are we okay now? Are we ready to go?'

'Ready,' he said. 'Ready, steady, go.'

Walking along the street towards Rose Avenue, Maddie wondered if Zac's fears were purely down to Kyle's tales of abandonment or if they were more deep-rooted. He'd lost both his mum and his dad at an early age. It had to leave scars. Did he worry that she'd leave him too, or was she overcomplicating things? Maybe he had simply picked up on her anxiety about the visit. It was impossible to know what went on in a child's head.

As they approached Alisha and Winston's house, she considered changing her plans and cancelling the date with Rick. Perhaps Zac needed her more this evening. Or was that the entirely wrong thing to do? Would that be giving in to his fears, confirming that there was something to worry about after all? No, she was better leaving things as they were. She'd call him at seven and see how he sounded.

With time to spare, Maddie accepted Alisha's invitation to stay for a cup of tea. While Zac went to raid the biscuit tin in the kitchen, she sat down with Winston in the living room. She asked how he was. He said he was fine. He asked how she was. She said she was good.

He gave her a long, steady look. 'You got something on your mind, hon? Something bothering you?'

'No,' she said too quickly. And then, because he could read her like a book, she added, 'Well, nothing more than the usual.'

'If it's money worries, you only have to ask. We don't have much, but—'

'No, it isn't that. Honestly.' She hesitated, glancing towards the kitchen. 'But I don't think Zac's too happy about my date this evening.'

'He's worried about losing you to another man.'

'Oh, it isn't anything serious,' she insisted. 'Just a meal. I mean, it's not ...'

Winston leaned forward, putting his hands on his knees. 'You go out and enjoy yourself, girl. He'll be fine. We'll take good care of him.'

'I know you will. You always do.' It crossed her mind, suddenly, to tell him about Jay Cato, to admit where she was really going this afternoon. But she resisted the temptation. What was the point of raising his hopes when they could so easily be dashed again? Although they rarely talked about Bo and Greta these days, she knew that Winston and Alisha craved the truth just as she did – and that closure couldn't come until the killer had been caught. Would Cato provide the information they needed? It wouldn't be long before she found out.

31

From the moment she left Rose Avenue, Maddie kept her eyes peeled for anyone who might be following her. The trouble was that after a while everyone began to look suspicious: the man standing on the corner, the middle-aged woman with the shopping bags, even the group of lads loitering by the entrance to the station. She went to the office, bought a return ticket to Chingford and walked down the steps on to the platform.

While she waited for the train, she continued to scrutinise the people around her. Was anyone watching, paying too much attention? She exercised her peripheral vision, her gaze sliding sideways. The last thing she wanted was to antagonise Lena Gissing, and that was exactly what would happen if the woman found out she was visiting Jay Cato. It would be like a red rag to a bull.

Maddie took the train to Liverpool Street, where she had to change. There was a fifteen-minute wait for the connection to Chingford and she went for a browse in the shops. By now, however, the paranoia was really starting to kick in and she spent more time staring at the other customers than at the goods on display.

By the time she got to Chingford and caught a bus to Thornley Heath, her stress levels were going through the roof. She gazed out of the rain-spattered window, questioning yet again the wisdom of what she was doing. Cato wasn't a man who could be trusted. She had to be careful. She had to watch her step. Standing in the crossfire between him and Lena Gissing was not a safe place to be.

Maddie had checked the bus route on her laptop and knew that the prison wasn't far off. Quickly she looked through her bag, making sure she had all the ID she needed. To be sure, she had brought her passport and her driving licence, even though the visiting order only specified one or the other. She had come this far and had no intention of being turned away at the gates on a technicality.

A couple of girls got off at the same stop as her. They were young, in their early twenties, with long straight blonde hair. The two of them wore tight blue jeans, stilettos, skinny vests and, despite the weather, matching Prada sunglasses. As this area was hardly the social hub of London, Maddie could guess where they were heading.

She fell in behind them and after a while found herself walking adjacent to a high grey stone wall. A minute later, she was standing in the queue waiting to book in. The reception area was crowded and noisy, the general babble of conversation interspersed by shrieks from crying babies. The room, which was too small to fit everyone comfortably, smelled of wet coats and perfume.

Eventually, Maddie got to the counter and passed over the VO and her driving licence. The prison officer typed something into his computer. 'First time?' he asked.

'Yes.'

He looked at her, looked down at the passport and glanced back up again. 'You can't take your bag into the visiting hall,' he said. 'Only a purse. Do you want a locker?'

'Yes, please.'

'It's a pound deposit. You'll get it back when you hand the key in at the end of the visit.'

Maddie dug out a coin and slipped it under the grille.

The officer handed her back the passport along with a piece of card with the number 31 printed on it and a key tagged with the number 26. 'They'll start calling at two,' he said.

'Thank you.'

Maddie forced a path through the crowd to the back of the room, where there was a bank of old metal lockers. She scanned the row until she found the right one, unlocked it and put her coat, umbrella and bag inside. It was only as she closed the door that she remembered about the purse. Quickly she opened it again, removing the purse from her bag.

She looked at her watch. What now? It was ten to two. Not much longer before the visit began. Clutching her purse to her chest, she let her gaze roam around the room. It was women mainly, women and kids. There were only a few guys. She wondered what it would be like to be visiting someone you really loved in a place like this. Soul-destroying, she decided.

The minutes ticked by slowly. She realised as she stood there that she didn't even know what Jay Cato looked like. How was she going to recognise him? Something else to add to the stress that was already washing over her. Maybe she should get her phone out of the locker and give Hayley Whittaker a ring. Should she? Did she have time? But even as she was contemplating it, the doors behind her opened and the first numbers were called.

Maddie waited impatiently while the other visitors went through for their visits. She was torn between hope and anxiety.

Please, God, she silently prayed, let me get some answers.

It was getting on for twenty minutes before she finally got to go through the first set of doors into the search area. There were three prison officers and a dog there. One of the officers took her purse to check through it. She passed successfully under the metal-detecting arch and was made to stand briefly in front of the chocolate Labrador. It sniffed suspiciously around her legs and groin, its nose searching out any trace of drugs. She resisted the urge to pat its head, fearing that this might be viewed as an attempt at bribery.

After the dog had done its job, she was passed on to a female officer, who asked her to spread her arms. A quick search followed, the woman's hands racing expertly over her body, along her arms, down her legs. It was no worse than the kind of routine search that might take place at an airport and yet Maddie felt curiously violated. Although she wasn't carrying anything illicit, she was starting to feel guilty, as if she'd already been judged and found wanting.

After the purse was returned to her, she was ordered to wait in a small holding area at the rear of the room. Four other women were already there, including the two blondes she'd seen on the bus. When their number was up to six, they were escorted across a grey courtyard and into another building.

This, finally, was the visiting hall. It had the look of a works canteen, with long rows of square Formica-topped tables. The room was busy – already many of the inmates had come out to meet their wives and girlfriends, their mothers and their mates – and there was a low, steady hum of conversation. An officer asked her name. She gave it to him and was directed to table 40.

Maddie made her way to her designated position and sat down. Her chest felt tight. Her stomach twisted and turned. While she waited, she examined the room. The walls were a dull magnolia, with the paint peeling off in places. The windows were high up, and the area was lit by tubes of bright fluorescent light. To her left, across the far side, was a counter from where teas and coffees were being served. Behind her was a raised stage where five officers sat behind a wide desk looking down on their charges. It was an uncomfortable feeling being under surveillance, although not as daunting as the thought of the encounter she was about to have.

At regular intervals, a door at the rear of the room opened and an inmate came out. Every time it happened, Maddie felt her heart leap, wondering if it was him. Her mouth had grown dry. She ran her tongue across her lips. How old was he? Probably around the same age as or slightly older than Lena Gissing. Now, instead of looking around, she kept her gaze fixed firmly on that door. Soon, it would happen soon. Jay Cato would come and everything would change.

32

It was another five minutes before Cato eventually appeared. Maddie had only a second's doubt before she knew for sure. He was a tall, handsome man with a chiselled face and dark hair streaked with silver. From the way he hesitated, from the way his eyes quickly raked the room, it was clear that he was searching for a stranger. She was one of the few people left sitting alone and his gaze finally settled on her.

Maddie gave a thin smile as he walked towards her. Her heart had started a heavy hammering, a beat so intense that she thought she could hear it. She tried to breathe deeply, breathe slowly, to get her nerves under control. She had come this far; she couldn't afford to blow it now. Think of Greta, she told herself. Think of Zac.

'You must be Maddie,' he said, looming over her.

She gave a nod but didn't stand up, unsure as to whether her trembling legs would take the weight of her body. Should she shake hands with him? She didn't know. There were no written rules of etiquette for the first time you met a murderer. 'Yes, I'm Maddie Layne.'

Cato pulled out the chair opposite to hers, sat down and put his elbows on the table. 'Pleased to meet you,' he said. 'Jay Cato. Nice of you to drop by.'

His voice was deep with a gravelly tone. A slight London accent perhaps, but the edges had been smoothed off. *Nice of you to drop by?* She wasn't sure if he was aiming for humour or sarcasm. 'I thought we should talk. I thought—'

He smiled, showing a row of straight white teeth. 'I take it that the lovely Lena Gissing has been giving you grief?'

'Yes,' she said. 'But that's what you wanted, isn't it?' Maddie drew a quick breath and carried on before she lost her nerve. 'You wanted her to think I was in league with you, that we were working together. Well, that's what she thinks all right. And now . . . now I'm top of her list of least favourite people. And you know what? That doesn't make me sleep easy at night.'

'Oh, not the very top of the list,' he said. 'I'm pretty sure that position's reserved solely for me.'

Maddie took a moment to study him more closely. What did a killer look like? No different, she concluded, to anybody else. Had she passed him on the street, she'd have had no idea of his history. The only clue was in his eyes. They were an unusually deep shade of grey but had a peculiar blankness about them too – as if he felt nothing, as if he'd withdrawn into himself. 'I've been getting threats, nasty ones.'

'Empty,' he insisted. 'You don't need to worry. Lena's just throwing her weight around.'

Maddie thought of the dead sparrow skewered to the piece of card. 'And what makes you so sure of that?'

'Because I know Lena.'

'You knew her ten years ago,' she snapped. 'That doesn't mean you know her now.'

'I can see you've done your homework.'

Again that edge to his voice, as if this whole scenario amused him. 'Just like you did,' she retorted. 'You used me. You used me to get to her.'

Cato gave a shrug. 'You got paid, didn't you?'

'To tend a grave, not to wind up Lena Gissing.'

'I think I was more than generous.'

Maddie ignored the comment. 'You chose me because of Greta and Bo Vale, didn't you?' She leaned forward, lowering her voice. 'You wanted her to think that . . . that I knew something about the murders, something connected to her.'

Cato said nothing. His face remained expressionless.

'You have to tell me,' she continued. 'If there is . . . I need to know. You understand that, don't you? Please, it's been six years and the cops haven't even got a lead. They're as much in the dark as they were when it happened.'

'And if I do know something, what then? Are you really prepared to take on Lena and her family?'

Maddie hesitated, but only for a moment. 'If that's what it takes.'

Jay Cato gave her a long, hard look. 'I could do with a coffee,' he said. 'Would you go and get me one? I'm not allowed to go to the counter. Black, no sugar.'

She stared back at him, steadily holding his gaze without looking away. Then, with a sigh, she picked up her purse and got to her feet. As she walked towards the refreshments area, she wondered if he was just playing with her, some cat-and-mouse game to help pass the time.

After she joined the short queue, she took the opportunity to sneak a few more glances in his direction while she waited to be served. He was dressed in the regulation blue-and-white-striped shirt with jeans. His face was strong, memorable, with classically handsome features: a firm chin, a wide sensual mouth, the shadow of a beard. But there was a kind of nonchalance about him, a carelessness that might have been a natural part of his character or just the result of spending ten years behind bars. She hadn't sussed him out yet and wasn't sure if she ever would.

After shuffling to the front of the queue, she ordered two coffees, one black and one white.

There was snack food for sale too and she wondered if she should buy something to eat. Crisps? A Mars bar? He hadn't asked for anything, but she wanted to get on the right side of him. That's if he even had a right side.

The woman serving put two plastic cups on the counter and held out her hand. 'That'll be one pound ten, please.'

Maddie grabbed a couple of KitKats, paid, put the chocolate in her pocket and carried the cups over to the table. Putting the drinks down, she pulled out the KitKats. 'I got you these too. In case you were hungry.'

Cato's dark eyebrows shifted up a notch as if unimpressed by her feeble attempt at bribery. Confectionery clearly wasn't his weak spot. He lifted the cup to his lips and drank some coffee. 'So what now?' he asked.

Maddie sat down again. 'So now you tell me what you know about Lena Gissing's involvement in my sister's death.'

'Who says I know anything?'

She frowned at him, suddenly afraid that this would all be a waste of time. 'Please don't play games. That's why I'm here, isn't it?'

'I didn't ask to see you. You were the one who wanted to talk.' He inclined his head, studying her. There was a short silence and then he said, 'If I do help you, what do I get in return?'

'You've already had it. Six months of tending Lucy Rivers's grave.'

'Like I already said, you were paid for that.'

'This isn't about money. You know it isn't.' While she was speaking, a couple of prison officers were patrolling the aisles, up and down, up and down, their eyes peeled for anything suspicious. It put her on edge, even more on edge than she already was. Every time the men walked by, she stopped talking, waiting until they'd passed before resuming the exchange with Cato. 'You put me in the firing line without me knowing it, without giving me a choice.'

Cato sat back for a moment as if he was thinking this over. Then he shifted forward again and said softly, 'Sometimes it's more dangerous to know things than not to know them.'

Maddie narrowed her eyes. Her heart was beginning to thump again. 'I'll take the chance.'

'It isn't a chance. It's a sure thing.' Cato paused, rubbing the stubble on his chin. Then, as if he'd made up his mind, he gave her a nod. 'How much do you know about what Bo was doing before he was killed?'

'A bit,' she said, recalling what Shauna had told her. 'Some work for the Streets, on the door at Belles or the Lincoln. And . . . ' She hesitated, in two minds as to whether to mention the rest. But she'd come this far – there was no point in holding back now. 'And he was stealing cars for Adam Vasser.'

He seemed surprised. 'You know about that?'

'I only found out recently.'

'And the rest?'

She gave a small shake of the head. 'Enlighten me.'

'He had another lucrative sideline.' Cato scratched at his chin again. 'Blackmail.'

'What?'

'Yeah, it's true. Apparently Vasser prefers the company of men to women, but he'd rather it wasn't public knowledge. The old denial syndrome. Plus the fact that in some circles – especially the ones that he moves in – being gay still isn't acceptable. Seems he developed an attachment to Bo Vale, probably made a move on him at some point, and Bo saw a golden opportunity.'

Maddie pulled a face. She hadn't been overly impressed when she'd found out that Bo was nicking motors, but there was something truly sordid about blackmailing a man over his sexuality. 'How do you know all this?'

'Because Bo didn't have the sense to keep his big mouth shut. He went bragging to his mates, telling them all about the money he was screwing out of Vasser. One of those mates ended up in here a year ago. He's a Kellston boy just like me. We got talking and he told me about it.'

'Doesn't mean it's true,' she said.

'Why would he lie? There's nothing in it for him.'

Maddie considered this for a moment. 'So this guy, did he tell the police about the blackmail when Bo was murdered?'

'No.'

'Would he give a statement now?'

'No.'

'Why not?'

'Because he doesn't want to end up like Bo Vale.'

She gave another sigh, feeling her frustration rising. 'So how does any of this help me?'

'It gives you a motive,' Cato said. 'It provides a reason for Adam Vasser to commit murder. Or for Lena to arrange it for him.'

'But there isn't any solid evidence.'

'That's for you to find.'

Maddie gulped down some coffee. It was weak and watery and slightly bitter. 'And what about Greta? Where does she figure in all this?'

'From what I've heard, they were in it together. I imagine she didn't take too kindly to Vasser making a move on her man.'

Maddie didn't want to believe it, but was gradually coming to realise just how little she had known about her sister. Yet still she continued to clutch at straws. 'But there wasn't any cash in either of their bank accounts. Well, nothing substantial. A couple of hundred quid between them. That's hardly blackmail money, is it?'

'No one with any nous would put blackmail money into an account. It's a cash transaction. That way, it's untraceable.'

'But there wasn't any money in the flat either.' She thought back to that day when she and Solomon had gone over to the Mansfield to clear out Bo and Greta's home. The place had been untidy, stuff lying around everywhere, but she hadn't been sure whether that was down to the cops – they'd made a search of the rooms after Bo's body was found – or if it was the norm. Greta had never been the tidiest of people. A large widescreen TV had been the most expensive item there, along with some music equipment.

'Perhaps they stashed it somewhere else. Or maybe someone got there before you did.'

It crossed Maddie's mind that the money could have been taken by a police officer. Was that possible? Nothing was impossible these days. But perhaps the more likely explanation was that the place was turned over before the police even got there. The Mansfield was crawling with lowlifes; any one of them could have got into the flat. Or then again, maybe there had never been any cash to start with. 'How do I even know that you're telling the truth? You've got every reason to hate Lena Gissing and her family.'

He gave a wry smile. 'I can't deny that. She got me banged up for ten years, so yes, I'd be happy to see some justice fly her way.'

Maddie heard the restrained anger in his voice. She looked at him, trying to read his face. Once, he had loved Lena Gissing enough to kill for her, but those feelings must have long since died. Ten years of incarceration had seen to that.

'I know what you're thinking,' he said. 'If I was you, I'd be the same. That I deserve to be in here? That I was convicted of murder and I should just shut up and do my time?'

'It's none of my business,' she said.

'Maybe it is, though. If you're going to take on Lena Gissing, you'll need all the ammunition you can get.'

Maddie lifted her shoulders a little. 'Did I say I was going to take her on?'

'Or you could just let her get away with it. I guess it's up to you. She's got away with plenty else. Why should this be any different?'

'What else are you talking about?'

He put his hands behind his head, linking them before quickly dropping them again. 'I'm just one of her victims, but at least I'm still breathing. I should be grateful for that small mercy.' He glanced around the room, at the other men hunched over the tables, before returning his gaze to her. 'Half the guys in here claim to be innocent. By the law of averages, a few of them probably are.'

'And you're one of them?' she asked sceptically, convinced he was about to spin her a line.

'Depends how you look at it.'

'I don't understand.'

'Guilt,' he said. 'It's a relative thing. Am I guilty of killing Brendan Vasser? As it happens, no. But what I am guilty of is helping to turn Lena into the woman she is today. I guess I have to take some responsibility for that.' He paused, his mouth sliding into a sardonic smile. 'I was set up, but I don't suppose you'll believe that for a second.'

'Does it matter what I believe?'

'I've got no reason to lie to you.'

'Sure you have,' she said. 'You want me on side. You want me to help you get revenge on Lena Gissing. That's reason enough, isn't it? Maybe you think I'll be more likely to believe an innocent man than a guilty one.'

253

Cato smiled again, this time with obvious amusement. 'It's a point of view. I guess you'll just have to make up your own mind.'

'So what's the story?'

'I'll give you the edited version. I wouldn't want to bore you.' He hesitated as if gathering the words in his mind. 'Eleven years ago, I fell in love with Lena Gissing and she fell in love with me. She was married to Vasser, a man for whom the word "bastard" was probably invented. He was violent, crazy, the sort of man who has no conscience. She wanted to be free of him – anybody would – but he wasn't the type to let go.

'My answer to this problem was for us to quit London, to quit the country, to get as far away as possible. But Lena wasn't having any of it. She reckoned wherever we went, Vasser would find us eventually. He'd hunt us down and kill us both. Plus, she wouldn't leave the kid behind and he was too old to be forced into leaving. And so she came up with a more drastic solution.'

'You decided to kill him?'

'Lena decided to kill him. Well, not personally, of course – she'd be top of the list of suspects when it came to the law – but for *someone* to do it.'

'Someone like you?'

Cato nodded. 'Nobody knew we were seeing each other and so, theoretically, I had no motive. One small pull on that trigger and all our problems were over.' His eyes briefly roamed around the room again. He looked down at the table and back up at her. 'I'd be a liar if I said I didn't think about it. I did, long and hard. And I came up with plenty of good reasons why wiping Vasser from the face of the earth would be an entirely justifiable thing to do.'

'But?'

'But it wasn't really my style. Or maybe I just didn't have the bottle. Either way, I told her I couldn't. I wouldn't. She wasn't happy. She saw it as . . . as an act of betrayal. We had what you might call an open and frank exchange of views. We split up for a while, but then got back together again. It was never the same, though. Once she'd asked me to do that, it was out there and couldn't be taken back. And what I didn't know was that all the time she was secretly making her plans. If I wouldn't kill Vasser, then she'd get someone else to do it.'

He rubbed at his forehead with the tips of his fingers. 'She must have already started seeing Tony Gissing. I was a fool. I didn't figure it out until it was too late. I knew too much, you see. If she was getting rid of Vasser, she also had to get rid of me. She couldn't take the chance that one day I might talk.'

Maddie sat and listened. The story was plausible, but she wasn't sure if it was true. 'So why not kill you too?'

'Because they needed a fall guy, a scapegoat to keep the spotlight off Lena. I was the perfect patsy, a man who was allegedly obsessed with her, who'd go to any lengths to have her for myself. And so she stitched me up, hid the gun in my flat, made sure there was enough evidence to make me look guilty as sin. That way, no matter what I told the law, they weren't going to believe me.'

'They weren't interested in your side of the story?'

'What do you think? They had a motive and a murder weapon, and I had no alibi for the night in question. No, I can't say they were interested.'

'But Lena must have known that one day you'd be coming out. They weren't going to keep you locked up for ever.'

'Even if it does feel like it sometimes.' He played with the plastic cup, turning it round in his fingers. There was sharpness in his voice that hadn't been there before. 'After ten years, why should she care? She knows I haven't got the heart for murder. What does she have to worry about?'

'Except she clearly is worried, or what's with all the fuss at the cemetery?'

'She's not concerned about the murder of Vasser. She knows I can't do anything about that now. But the fact that I'm apparently working with you has put the wind up her. She's put two and two together and come to the conclusion that something must be going on, something connected to the deaths of your sister and Bo Vale.'

'Although it's nothing we can prove.'

'Except she doesn't know that. And just the fact that she tried to scare you off shows that she has got something to hide.'

Maddie couldn't argue with his reasoning, but she resented the way she'd been used. Why couldn't he have been honest with her from the start? Cato wanted revenge and he was trying to get it through her. She'd been like the tethered goat put out in the field, unaware of the tiger hiding in the bushes. 'So what do I do now?'

'That's your call. But people can get jumpy when they think their dirty little secrets are about to come out. Lena and Adam don't have the best of relationships.'

'Meaning?'

'Meaning that they don't trust each other. You can use that to your advantage, play one off against the other. Adam would sell his mother down the river if he thought it would save him from a jail sentence. If they think you know more than you do, then—'

'Then they'll both want to get rid of *me*,' she interrupted testily. 'Is that the plan? I go out there and provoke the Gissings, see what happens next? Somehow I don't see that as being entirely good for my health.'

Cato smiled at her. 'Then you'll have to be smart about it.'

'Easy for you to say.'

'It depends how much you want it. Life's full of risks, chances, things you might have done.'

Maddie found herself wondering if he wished he had killed

Brendan Vasser. And then she smartly pulled herself up, realising that she still didn't know for sure that he hadn't. But there was a part of her that believed his story. She couldn't have said why exactly; it was just a feeling, a gut instinct. 'How can you bear it,' she suddenly blurted out, 'being locked up in here?'

A thin smile appeared on his lips. 'You can get used to anything . . . eventually.'

Maddie stared at him. She noticed the fine lines that fanned out from the corners of his eyes. She thought of all the years he'd spent behind bars, wasted years that he would never get back. And all because he had fallen in love with the wrong woman.

'What?' he asked as she continued to look at him. 'What is it?'

'Oh, nothing.' She shook her head. 'I was just wondering how you even got to hear about me.'

'I asked around. I still know people out there.' He gestured towards the door she'd originally come through as if it symbolised the outside world. 'After I was told about Bo, about the blackmail, I figured it wasn't a coincidence that he'd ended up dead. I thought there might be some family, so I asked a mate to check it out. He told me about Bo's parents and his brother.'

'Solomon,' she said.

'That's who I was going to talk to until I found out about you. And then when I heard that you worked at the cemetery . . .'

'I still don't get that,' she said. 'What is it about that grave? What's the connection between Lena and Lucy Rivers?'

Cato shook his head. 'Old history. It doesn't matter. I knew it would get her attention and it did.'

And now, she thought, he was being deliberately evasive. 'Is it something to do with Vasser?'

He wouldn't be drawn. 'Really, it's not important. A means to an end, that's all.'

She could see that he wasn't going to tell, but still she persisted. 'You could have just asked me to come and see you right from the start. You could have told me about the blackmail, about Adam Vasser. Why bother with all the grave business?'

'I could,' he agreed. 'But I wanted to see how Lena would react. I reckoned it would spook her and it has. She doesn't know what's going on and it freaks her out. Lena likes to be in control.'

'Don't we all,' she said caustically. 'It's none too great being left in the dark.'

'For which I apologise. But by doing it this way, you got to see at first hand what Lena's really like rather than me just telling you.'

'Yes, well, I've certainly done that.'

'Five minutes, please,' one of the prison officers proclaimed from the stage. 'The visits will be ending in five minutes.'

'Time's almost up,' Cato said. He pushed the uneaten KitKats back across the table. 'You'll have to take these with you. I'm not allowed to take stuff back.'

'Not a chocolate fan, then?'

'I seem to have lost my appetite these days.'

Maddie became aware of a change in the atmosphere of the room, a shifting, a sighing, a scraping back of chairs. People were beginning to stand up and say their goodbyes. If she had anything left to ask, she'd better do it quickly. 'But what do I do? How can I prove anything about this blackmail?'

'Start talking to Bo's friends,' he said. 'And Greta's. If I know about it, then others do too. Stir things up and see what happens.'

'Just promise me one thing,' she said, rising to her feet.

'What's that?'

'If I meet the same fate as Lena's other enemies, you'll employ someone to put roses on my grave every week.'

He stood up too, smiling. 'Goes without saying.'

There was an odd, awkward moment when neither of them seemed to know what to do next. Around them, others were kissing, embracing, saying their final farewells. She put out her hand. 'Goodbye, then.'

He took her hand and shook it. His fingers were cool and dry. 'Goodbye, Maddie.'

It was only as she was walking away that she remembered about the gold wedding ring. Who had put it on the grave? Why had Lena hurled it into the weeds? She turned, but already it was too late. He had disappeared back through the door through which he had come.

33

Adam Vasser stood on the roof terrace and gazed down over Kellston. The rain had stopped, but the air was still and heavy and full of thunder. He had that edgy, restless feeling that he always got when a storm was brewing. And it wasn't just the weather that was rumbling towards him. Being summoned by his mother was never a good sign.

'Be at the Heights in half an hour,' she'd ordered when she phoned him.

No explanation, nothing. She just clicked her fingers and he was supposed to come running. He flexed his own fingers, feeling the ache in his knuckles. He'd watched the local news, but there had been nothing on it about the boy in Soho. Maybe he hadn't been found yet. Or maybe he wasn't even dead. Was that what his mother wanted to talk about? Had the bitch found out? Maybe she'd had Yeats following him around too.

He looked at his watch. Where was she? Typical that she got him to come rushing round and then couldn't be arsed to turn up herself. Or maybe she just wanted to keep him waiting.

Yeah, that was probably it. Leave him here kicking his heels while she went shopping for shoes or handbags.

He moved closer to the rail and gazed out in the direction of the lock-ups. It was coming up to the end of August and he'd have to make a decision soon. In the early hours of 1 September, the Colombians would make their delivery. Should he strike then or wait another month? If he went too soon, he might not be properly prepared, but if he waited, he took the risk of them changing their routine.

In his head, he had two separate plans. The first was to go in there all guns blazing as soon as the Colombians had left. There was a tiny window of opportunity then, a chance to take Chris Street and Solomon Vale by surprise as they were locking up. Although, when he said all guns blazing, they would actually have to have silencers fitted. The lock-up wasn't close to any houses, but sound travelled and he didn't want the filth turning up as they were clearing out the gear.

He played through this plan in his head like he was watching a movie, imagining the surprise of the two men, seeing their blood-spattered bodies crumple backwards and fall to the ground. Once Chris Street was eliminated, the firm was finished. With a huge stash of drugs, Adam could easily move in and take over Kellston.

He liked this plan, liked its dramatic qualities, but it also had a downside. The pigs would be crawling all over the place. Two murders, even if they were just local gangsters, would create a stir. Did he really want that kind of attention? It could make it difficult to operate, cause problems where they weren't really needed.

Maybe, after all, he should go with Plan B. This was less fun but more practical. He'd noticed on the last delivery that it was Solomon Vale who'd done the locking up, who was carrying the keys. And this was where Louise came in. Once she'd inveigled her way into Vale's bed, it shouldn't be too hard to get a copy of those keys. He'd already provided her with a mould; now all she needed was the opportunity. Knowing Louise, it wouldn't take her long. She was adept in the art of seduction, in getting any straight man to fall for her charms.

Plan B involved going into the lock-up in the middle of the night and snatching the gear before it had been distributed. There would be alarms – he was sure of it – but that didn't matter. They could be in and out in a matter of minutes. By the time Chris Street arrived on the scene, it would all be too late. And then, with no goods to supply, he'd find himself out in the cold. The clients didn't care who they bought their gear off. There was no loyalty in the drugs world.

There would be a backlash, though. There was little doubt about it. Chris Street would come after him, but how far would he go? From what he'd heard, Street didn't have the heart for full-on gang warfare; he preferred the quiet life. And Terry Street wasn't fit to organise a piss-up in a brewery. So long as Adam got his own firm established quickly enough, *violently* enough, the manor would be his for the taking.

He was still contemplating this when he heard the sound of the front door opening and closing, followed by his mother's clicking footsteps on the hard wooden floor. His insides clenched the way they always did when a confrontation was in the offing. He knew from the tone of her voice on the phone that she hadn't summoned him for a friendly chat. No, she was here to have a go at him over one thing or another.

'Oh, you're here,' she said, looking towards the open French windows.

Adam moved back inside the living room. 'I've been here for twenty minutes. I've been waiting for you.'

She gave a small shrug as if his waiting was neither here nor there to her. 'Close those doors, will you? It's about to piss down. I don't want the curtains drenched.'

He did as she asked, aware of the sour look on her face. 'So what do you want?' he asked, eager to get it over and done with as soon as possible. 'I'm busy. I've got things to do.'

'We've all got things to do. You think I want to be running around after you?'

Adam gave a snort. If anyone was doing the running, it was him. Wasn't he the one who'd had to leave the garage and come over here? Wasn't he the one who'd been hanging around until she deigned to join him? But he didn't say any of it. There wasn't any point. So far as his mother was concerned, she was always in the right.

Lena sat down on the plush leather sofa, crossed her long legs and lit a cigarette. She took a few puffs before she raised her eyes to him again. 'I know what you've been up to,' she said.

Adam flinched, his hands instinctively curling into two tight fists. Shit, so she did know about the boy! 'What's that supposed to mean?'

'Don't give me that. You think I was born yesterday?'

'I don't have a clue what you're talking about.' His default position, whenever he was confronted by his mother, was to deny everything. 'What are you going on about? What the fuck is this?'

'Sit down,' she said wearily.

He slouched down into an armchair and glared at her. The bitch was always on his case, never letting him alone. 'So? What is it this time?'

'Don't give me that crap. You bloody well know what it is.'

There was a silence, which Adam didn't fill. It was best, he found, to always keep his mouth shut until he was sure what she had got on him.

'Well?' she asked after a few seconds had ticked by. His mother wasn't the patient sort.

'Well what?'

263

She couldn't contain herself any longer. 'I know what you're planning, and you must be bloody delusional if you think the Streets are going to let you do it. What's the matter with you? Have you got a screw loose? Are you stark, raving mad?'

Adam felt relief that this wasn't about the boy. After the incident with Bo, she'd sworn that she'd kick him into touch if it ever happened again. And he believed her. The bitch was more than capable, and he didn't need that kind of grief with everything else that was going on. At the moment, he relied on her for every penny he earned, and so until he had the drugs, until he had the *power*, he'd better keep her sweet. 'Ah,' he said, flapping a hand dismissively. 'Jesus, that was just talk. Who said I was planning anything?'

'Don't lie to me.'

'I'm not lying,' he said, deliberately looking her straight in the eye. 'I'm not the one who goes sneaking around behind other people's backs.'

She pulled hard on the cigarette, her lips pursing. 'And what's that supposed to mean?'

'Maddie Layne?' he said, hurling the name at her. He could see that she was startled, but she quickly composed herself again.

'What about her?'

'You've had Yeats following her. I saw it in that report. *She's* the one who's up to something, and you haven't even bothered to tell me about it.'

Lena raised her eyes to the ceiling. 'And you're accusing me of sneaking around. Christ, is nothing private in this place?'

'If you don't want anyone to look, you shouldn't leave your stuff lying about. And anyway, that's not the point. I've a right to know what's going on. Has she gone to the law? Has she found out something? I need to know if the pigs are likely to turn up on my doorstep anytime in the near future.'

'Probably,' she snapped back, 'if you carry on the way you're going. You try and muscle in on the Streets and all hell's going to break loose. You'll have the filth crawling all over you – all over *us*.'

'Jesus, not this again. I've already told you, there's nothing going on. But I need to know about the girl. What else are you keeping from me? There must be something or you wouldn't be paying Yeats to keep an eye on her.'

'She's just . . .'

'Just what?'

'Trying to stir things up again. It's not important. No one's taking any notice of her. Why should they?'

Adam could always tell when his mother was holding back – which was, as it happened, most of the time. 'Oh, I don't know,' he said sarcastically, 'perhaps because we're talking about a double murder here.'

'Six years ago.'

He glared at her. 'What aren't you telling me?'

'If there was anything to tell, I would.'

'Why do you always do this?' he said, jumping to his feet and starting to pace restlessly around the room. 'I'm not a kid any more. You don't need to protect me. I've got a right to know if someone's gunning for me. I've got a bloody right.'

'Why?' she answered curtly. 'So you can go and do something stupid like you usually do? I've got it under control, okay? Don't start interfering.'

'Interfering? You're the one who bloody interferes in every-thing.'

'Just stay away from her. You'll only make it worse.'

As he walked back and forth, Adam raked his fingers through his hair. 'Worse? I thought you said there wasn't a problem and now—'

'There won't be a goddamn problem if you just leave it

alone.' Lena stubbed out her cigarette and gave a sigh. 'I've had enough of sorting out your mistakes. You fuck up again and you're on your own.'

He stopped dead in the centre of the room, knowing exactly what she was referring to. The blood rushed to his cheeks. 'And did I ever ask you? Did I? You're the one who—'

'Who what?'

There was a sharp, nasty silence while the two of them glared at each other. Adam felt his stomach lurch, the bile rising into his mouth. Whenever he thought about Bo Vale, he felt sick inside. 'You know what. It was only money, for fuck's sake. It wasn't worth killing for.'

'My money,' Lena said coldly. 'Anyway, it's done with. Let's not go over it again.' She rose to her feet, smoothing out her skirt.

'Where are you going?'

'I promised Delia I'd pop round.'

Adam's lip curled. Delia Shields – someone else he couldn't stand. A prissy, uptight spinster who always looked down her nose at him. As if she was anything special. He didn't understand why his mother kept in contact with the stupid cow. 'And that's more important than this, is it?'

'There's nothing left to say, Adam. I think we've covered all the bases, haven't we?'

'You might have, but I'm just getting started.'

'Well, would you mind saving it for another day?' She glanced deliberately at her watch. 'I don't want to be late.'

'Don't let me keep you, then,' he said resentfully.

'I won't.'

Adam watched as she swept out of the room in her usual haughty fashion, like some catwalk model past her sell-by date. Seconds later, he heard the front door close. 'Fuck you,' he muttered, making a hissing noise through his teeth.

He went through to the hallway and waited until he heard the smooth swish of the lift going down before returning to the living room. And then he started searching for the Yeats file. He wanted to take another look at it. Perhaps there was something that he'd missed first time round.

It wasn't on the table or in the bureau. He checked the kitchen drawers, but there was nothing there except cutlery and tea towels and loose bits of string. Shit, perhaps she had put it in the safe. He went back into the living room and stared at the landscape on the wall. There was no point in even swinging the picture back – he didn't have a clue what the combination was.

He was going to give up, but on a whim wandered through to her bedroom. His nose wrinkled at the pungent smell of perfume. The room was opulent, the walls painted in dark cream and gold, the curtains a heavy brocade. Like a tart's boudoir, he thought. The bedding was a rich shade of red. A fancy chandelier with teardrop crystals hung from the ceiling.

He went over to the dressing table and pulled out the top drawer, full of knickers and bras and silk negligees. Tentatively, he prodded at them with his fingers. There was something faintly disgusting about touching his mother's underwear. It made him wince, his insides curling up.

Suddenly, he thought of Bo and his perfect brown skin. He remembered being in the flat on the Mansfield estate. He remembered with a sharp stab to his heart the first time he'd ever kissed him, ever really touched him, running his hands across the planes of his stomach, the feel of his lips, the whispered words, the gentle caresses.

Pain and anger swelled up in his chest. He flinched as if hearing the door flung open again, as if seeing Greta's face full of fury. He saw her look of shock and disgust, her eyes taking in everything, forgiving nothing. And from the second she walked in on them, there was no way back.

Unless . . .

She would keep quiet, Bo said, so long as they paid her. If they didn't, she would let the whole of Kellston know about it. If they didn't, she would take his kid away and never let him see the boy again. That's what she was like – cruel and vengeful, the bitch from hell. But money, a few quid, a few thousand, would shut her up. Bo had begged, pleaded with him. How could he refuse? And anyway, he hadn't wanted his private business broadcast to the world.

Blackmail – that's what his mother had called it. Well, he'd had to get the cash from somewhere and she'd quickly figured out who'd been thieving from her. It hadn't taken her long to get the truth out of him either. Her face loomed into his mind, her eyes flashing, her disgust and contempt as overwhelming as Greta's. Only, his mother didn't give a damn about his sexuality; she was just bothered about the money and the damage to her reputation if anyone found out.

'No one blackmails this family. *No* one. You sort it out, you hear me? It stops right now. And you're paying back every bloody penny.'

Except in the end she had been the one who had sorted it. Brutally. Finally. She had been the one to make sure that Bo and Greta never spoke of the incident again. Adam closed his eyes as he thought of Bo floating in the Thames, his face blown off, the breath extinguished from his beautiful body. He would never forgive her for that. She had killed the only man he had ever really loved.

Adam blinked open his eyes and slammed shut the drawer. He'd lost interest in the file now. What did it matter? He knew enough. Already he loathed and despised Maddie Layne. She reminded him too much of Greta, with her long dark hair and her wide eyes. Another woman who wanted to hurt him, to cause him damage. He was sick of the whole damn lot of them.

Needing some air, he went back to the living room, opened the French windows and stepped out on to the roof terrace. The rain was pelting down now, flying against the concrete in long, fast arrows. A rumble of thunder rolled through the air. He lifted his face to the sky and let the rain wash over it.

What was his mother doing at this very moment? She was probably discussing the Maddie Layne business with Delia Shields. That dried-up old spinster knew more about what was going on than he did. And how was that right? He thumped his fist against his thigh. It was time to find out the bloody truth – one way or another.

34

Delia Shields couldn't sit still. She got up from the sofa again and began tidying things that didn't need tidying. Her little two-up two-down house was a modest affair – nothing like Lena's fancy apartment, with its panoramic views – but she was still proud of it. She wanted it to look its best for when her friend arrived.

She glanced at the clock. Ten past six. Lena was ten minutes late already. Perhaps she wasn't coming. Her heart sank at the thought. She'd been looking forward to the visit all day. Over the years the amount of time they spent together had grown increasingly smaller but, to her at least, increasingly precious. Every word, every gesture was stored up in her mind to be taken out later and examined at length.

As she ran her hand along the smooth surface of the mantelpiece, her eyes alighted on the wedding ring. She reached out intending to touch it, but didn't complete the action. She felt suddenly afraid, as if the gold might burn the flesh from her fingertips. The ring was a symbol of death and despair. She cursed Eli Glass for having found it, for having brought it back to her.

Delia, hearing the sound of a car, went over to the window and pulled aside the net curtain. Yes, finally, it was her. Quickly she dropped the curtain, not wanting Lena to think that she'd been watching out for her. It was important to maintain the little dignity she had left in the relationship. What she usually got from Lena Bell – Lena Gissing – were scraps, hurried coffees, meetings often cut short by important phone calls, but perhaps today would be different.

There was the sharp click of footsteps coming up the path, followed by the light ding-dong of the bell. Delia made herself count to ten before she went to the hall and opened the door. She hated looking too keen, too eager. It made her feel as desperate as she had been as a schoolgirl to bask in Lena's glory.

'Hello. Come in. It's good to see you again.'

'Sorry I'm late,' Lena said, closing and shaking her umbrella. 'Family problems. I never seem to get a minute to myself these days.'

Delia took the wet brolly – the rain was bucketing down now – and led her through to the kitchen, where the coffee had already percolated and was ready to drink. She opened the umbrella again and left it to dry in the corner of the room.

'Isn't that bad luck?' Lena asked. 'That's what my mum always used to say.'

Delia smiled. 'I hope not. We've had enough of that recently.' She poured the coffee into two china cups and placed them on the tray alongside a plate of chocolate biscuits, two smaller side plates, a bowl of sugar, a jug of milk and a couple of silver teaspoons. 'Let's go through to the living room, shall we? It's more comfortable there.'

Lena sat down on the green cord sofa and gave a cursory glance around the room before settling her gaze on Delia again.

She watched as milk and sugar were added to the cups. 'It's ages since I was last here. How long is it? Must be about a year.'

Delia could have told her that it was getting on for two, but didn't want her to think she was counting. 'Well, you're welcome anytime.' She passed a cup over. 'So, nothing too disastrous, I hope?'

'Sorry?'

'You said there were family problems.'

Lena pulled a face. 'Oh, that. Yeah, just Adam giving me grief again. He's got wind of this whole grave thing and won't leave it alone. He's like a dog with a bone, yapping away in my ear all the time.'

Privately, Delia believed that Adam Vasser was as psychopathic as his father. She'd disliked and distrusted him even when he'd been a child, and now, as an adult, he was a thousand times more dangerous. 'Does he know about Cato coming out of jail?'

'Not yet. Maybe he won't have to.'

'And if he comes back to Kellston?'

Lena drank some of her coffee. 'Why would he do that? He'd have to have a death wish.'

'But Adam knows about Maddie Layne, about the flowers on the grave? What if he talks to her? What if—'

'Then I'll cross that bridge when I come to it.' Lena looked around the room again. 'Where is the damn ring, anyway? It's like a bloody boomerang. Just when I think I've got rid of it . . .'

Delia stood up and fetched the gold band from the mantelpiece. 'Here,' she said, quickly passing it over. 'What are you going to do with it?'

Lena held the ring in her hand, her face looking weary suddenly. 'Find a bin to throw it in, or the bottom of a river. Someplace, anyway, where I won't have to set eyes on it again.' She prodded it, nudging it across her palm. 'The trouble with

Jay Cato is that he never lets things drop. Even after all these years . . .'

'He was crazy then and he's crazy now.'

Lena dropped the ring into the back pocket of her handbag. 'Probably.'

'So how's Tony?' asked Delia, not the slightest bit interested but wanting to get the subject off Jay Cato.

'Same as always: fat, stupid, lazy. But I suppose I'm stuck with him.'

Delia had never figured out why, when she could have had her pick of men, Lena had chosen Tony Gissing. He was an ugly brute, a villain without a single redeeming feature. It had been the shock, perhaps, of Brendan Vasser's murder. And then the subsequent conviction of Cato for the killing. Had she turned to someone who could protect her, who could keep her safe?

Lena leaned her head back against the sofa and gave a sigh.

Delia frowned. 'Is everything all right?'

'Not really,' said Lena, sitting upright again. 'He sent me a letter, you know, a year or so after he got sent down. Cato, I mean.'

'You never said. Is he allowed to do that, write to you? I'd have thought—'

'He didn't send it from the jail. He got someone who was being released to post it for him.'

'Still protesting his innocence, I suppose? Was that it? Was that what he wanted to say?'

'No, not exactly.'

Delia had a bad feeling in the pit of her stomach. 'What, then?'

Lena fixed her blue eyes on her, her gaze oddly cool. 'He said he'd worked it out, who it must have been. He said he was sure.'

'The murderer?'

'No,' Lena said. 'Not that. The letter wasn't about that.'

'Oh?'

'He said it was your fault, that you'd done it. That you were the reason it had all gone wrong.'

Startled, Delia shifted forward, the cup clattering against the saucer in her lap. 'What? I-I don't understand,' she stammered. 'What did he mean? How could ...? It wasn't anything to do with me. He was the one who—'

'I didn't believe him, of course. He's a liar. Everyone knows that. Always has been, always will be.'

Delia's lips had gone dry, and she could feel the colour rising into her cheeks, a hot flush making her face burn. 'Why would I ...? I wouldn't ...' But her throat had grown tight and she could barely squeeze out the words.

'Of course you wouldn't. Why would you want to hurt me like that?'

Delia glanced away, unable to bear Lena's piercing gaze. It was as though she was staring right into her soul. And suddenly, as if the burden she had been carrying around for so many years was too much to bear, she felt a desperate need to confess. It was welling up inside, a surging volcano about to erupt. 'He was never good enough for you,' she blurted out. 'I did you a favour.'

Lena's voice was low and incredulous. 'A favour? A fuckin' favour? Is that what you call it?'

'He was a murderer! That's the kind of man he was. He killed your husband.'

'You know nothing,' Lena hissed. 'Nothing at all.' Her hands, clenched into two fists, lay on her thighs. Her knuckles were white. '*You!*' she spat out as if she could still barely believe it.

Delia hadn't wanted it to come out like this. She shouldn't have said anything. It had been a mistake. She should have kept her mouth shut. But maybe that nugget of doubt had been in Lena's mind for a long time, ever since she'd received the letter from Cato. And now that it was out, there was no point in holding back. 'Someone had to stop you. Can't you see? He was no good. It was never going to work.'

Lena pulled in her breath in an audible gasp. 'And the alternative was better?'

Delia opened her mouth and smartly shut it again. She could see the expression on Lena's face, a hard, cold rage that sent a shiver through her.

'Well?' Lena pressed.

Delia gave a small shake of her head.

Lena glared at her for a few seconds more before snatching up her bag, getting to her feet and walking out of the room.

Delia hurried after her. 'What are you doing? Where are you going? We need to talk, Lena. You can't just leave like this.'

Lena flung open the front door and stepped out on to the path. She turned and said, 'Leave me alone. I have nothing to say to you, nothing at all.'

'Lena!'

But already she was through the gate and getting into the car. Delia might have run after her if she hadn't noticed Mrs Kent peering out of the window from the house opposite. She hesitated and in that moment the chance was lost. The MG roared into life and disappeared down the road.

Delia's heart was hammering as she went back inside the house and closed the door. What had she done? Lena would never forgive her. There was no going back from here. If only she had been able to explain properly. Maybe when Lena calmed down, when she ... But already she knew that it was hopeless.

Automatically, she gathered up the cups and took them through to the kitchen. She ran the hot water and half filled the bowl. As she washed up, her regrets were pierced by a feeling of resentment. How come it was always about Lena? Everything was about Lena Bell, Lena Vasser, Lena Gissing. When had Lena ever stopped for one single second and thought about *her*?

Delia slammed a cup down on the draining board, hitting it with such force that the fine porcelain shattered in her hands. She felt the tears rise to her eyes. It had been one of her mother's cups, part of a set that she'd kept intact for the past twenty years. And now ... now suddenly everything felt broken. Leaning against the sink, she gripped the cool, smooth metal and gulped down the sobs.

35

Maddie was eating pasta with a creamy mushroom sauce, but she could have been chewing on cardboard for all the notice she was taking of it. Her thoughts were elsewhere, her mind still on the visit with Cato. What he had told her continued to spin round in her head. And even now, hours later, she wasn't sure how much of it was true.

'You should have called me,' Rick said. 'I'd have taken you over to Thornley Heath.'

'You've done enough. I'm sure you've got better things to do with your Saturdays than play chauffeur. Anyway, it's not that hard to get to.'

Rick twisted the long strands of spaghetti expertly round his fork. He raised the fork to his lips but paused before putting the food into his mouth. 'So what do you think? You reckon he could be right about this blackmail scam?'

'Hard to tell. He seemed convincing enough. The story's credible, but ...'

'But?'

Maddie toyed with the pasta, shifting it around in the bowl. Slowly she raised her eyes to him again. 'I suppose I just don't want to believe it about Greta. That she could have done something like that.'

'Even if the guy is a vicious thug?'

'Does that make it okay?'

'Is it okay for some geezer to try and get into your boyfriend's pants?'

Maddie gave a faint smile. 'Well, it's hardly polite, but there are better ways of dealing with it.'

'Perhaps if you live on the Mansfield, you grab what you can when you can. Your prospects aren't too great in a place like that. And your moral compass probably shifts a little when you're stuck in a concrete tower all day with a kid to raise, bills to pay and no money for the meter.'

'You're defending her?'

He gave a shrug. 'Just playing devil's advocate.'

'She didn't have to live on the Mansfield. She and Zac could have moved in with my mum. There's enough room in the house.'

'And what about Bo?'

Maddie knew that her mother hadn't been keen on Bo Vale. Kim Layne would put up with most things – she was as liberal as they came – but she drew the line when it came to dealing drugs. It was doubtful if any invitation for Greta to come and live in Morton Grove would have extended to her boyfriend. Everyone knew that Bo sold dope on the estate. 'Greta could have still seen him.'

'Maybe she didn't want to go running back to her mum. It's not always easy to admit you're in trouble.'

Maddie speared a slice of mushroom, dipped it in the sauce and popped it in her mouth.

'How's the pasta?' he asked.

'Oh, lovely,' she replied guiltily, realising how little notice she'd been taking of it. 'Really nice. How's yours?'

'Mm, good.'

And Maddie was suddenly aware that it wasn't just the pasta she was taking for granted. Here she was in a swanky restaurant with a funny, good-looking guy and all she was talking about were her own problems. She let her eyes roam over him for a moment, taking in his handsome face, his solid shoulders and the smart dark blue suit he was wearing. His shirt was white, and he had even put on a tie. 'Sorry,' she said. 'I've been droning on, haven't I? Tell me what you've been doing today.'

'Nothing as interesting as you. It's been seriously dull in comparison. And if you're suggesting that you're boring me, you're not. I want to hear about it, really I do.'

'I think I've just about covered everything.'

'It's fascinating, though, isn't it? Something that happened all that time ago and—' He stopped abruptly, his mouth twisting.

'What's the matter?'

'I didn't intend that to come out, so . . . Sorry, I didn't mean to sound callous. I know this is about your sister and what happened to her.'

'You didn't. I know what you meant.' Maddie found that she liked him even more for considering her feelings. 'The whole Cato thing *is* fascinating. Although it's scary to think that he could be innocent. Imagine spending all that time in jail, being convicted of something that you didn't do.'

'Not a happy thought.'

Maddie gazed around the restaurant, which was somehow smart and rustic at the same time. It was ages since she'd been here. She thought it must have been when her father had last visited, back in 2012. The place was packed, with every table taken. 'It's busy,' she said.

'That's because it's the place to be on a Saturday night in Kellston.'

'Come here a lot, then, do you?'

His eyes glinted with amusement as he looked at her. 'Are you probing, Maddie Layne? Are you trying to discover if I often wine and dine beautiful young women in these pleasant surroundings?'

'And do you?' she asked, keeping her voice as light as his.

'No,' he said.

'Well, I'm flattered.'

He picked up his glass, took a drink and grinned. 'Although I haven't lived here for long.'

'Not that flattered, then.'

'Hey, we gravediggers like to try and retain at least a modicum of mystery.'

'It's not working,' she said.

He placed his hand on his chest. 'Now you're shattering my ego.'

'Eat your spaghetti,' she said. 'You'll get over it.'

A waitress walked past holding a plate in each hand and one balanced on her arm. Maddie followed her progress as the woman glided effortlessly across the room. It was only as she shifted her gaze a little that she noticed Solomon Vale sitting at a table near the window. He was sharing a candlelit supper with a very attractive black-haired girl. Was she his girlfriend? Maddie, curious, peered between the heads, trying to get a better look.

Rick glanced over his shoulder and back at her. 'Should I be worried?'

'Sorry?' she said, focusing on him again.

'You've been staring at that guy for the last thirty seconds. If I was the insecure type, I might start to get a complex.'

'Ah, how sweet. Are you feeling threatened?'

'What, just because the guy's a little bigger than me?'

'Yes.'

Rick grinned again. 'Come on, then. Who is he?'

'That,' she said, 'is Bo's older brother, Solomon.'

'Really?' He turned to look again. 'Not the kind of guy you'd want to get on the wrong side of.'

'Best not get on his wrong side, then.'

Solomon, as if instinctively aware of eyes being on him, tensed and quickly glanced around the room. He saw Maddie, relaxed and raised his hand. She waved back. The girl he was with gave her a long, hard stare as if assessing the possible competition. Maddie smiled. The girl didn't smile back.

'Who's the woman?' Rick asked.

'No idea. It's the first time I've ever seen her. Pretty, though, don't you think?'

'Ha!' he said, shaking his head. 'I'm not falling for that one. I learned a long time ago never to say anything complimentary about another woman.'

'Someone trained you well.'

'I trained myself. I'm a very fast learner.'

Maddie looked towards the table again. 'I wonder who she is.'

'New girlfriend?'

Maddie hoped not. There was something about the girl, about the way she'd stared, that she didn't like. She thought about the conversation she would need to have with Solomon at some point. It wasn't a talk that she was looking forward to. Would he simply dismiss what Cato had told her, or would he confront Adam Vasser? That could mean trouble and she didn't want to be the cause of it.

'So,' Rick said, 'you fancy a sweet?'

Maddie's thoughts were still with Solomon. 'Huh? Sorry?'

'A sweet,' he said. 'Or coffee?'

'Yes, a coffee. That would be nice. Thanks.'

'Or . . . ' he said.

'Or?'

'You could invite me back to your place for one.'

Maddie inclined her head, studying his face. She waited a moment before replying. 'Well, I could, but then you might get the wrong idea.',

'If I was that kind of guy,' he said. 'But of course I'm not.'

'Aren't all guys that kind of guy?'

'Isn't that a sweeping generalisation?'

'Yes,' she said. 'Doesn't mean it's not true, though.'

'And here was me thinking I was the perfect gentleman.'

Maddie had to admit that he hadn't tried to take advantage on what she had come to think of as the Day of the Box. The image of the dead impaled sparrow jumped into her head again. Perhaps it wouldn't be such a bad thing to invite him back. With Zac staying at his grandparents', she would be alone overnight and it would be reassuring to have some company for an hour or two.

'All right,' she said. 'But *just* a coffee, okay?'

'What, no biscuits?'

'I'll think about it.'

Rick asked for the bill, and when it arrived, Maddie went through the obligatory motions of reaching for her bag and offering to pay half. She was relieved when he refused; she couldn't really afford it. Adriano's, although not extortionate, wasn't the cheapest place to eat.

'No, this is on me. I invited you, didn't I?'

'Are you sure?'

'Absolutely sure.'

'Well, thank you,' she said. 'It was lovely. I've enjoyed it.'

As they left the restaurant, she waved goodbye to Solomon. This time the girl, who by now must have discovered who she was, gave her a thin but in no way friendly smile. Maddie found herself hoping that it wasn't anything serious between the two of them.

Outside, the air was heavy. They had barely got a hundred yards down the road when they heard the first roll of thunder, quickly followed by a bright lightning flash. Maddie glanced up at the dark sky, regretting that she had left her umbrella at home. After returning from Thornley Heath, she had left it to dry in the kitchen and forgotten all about it.

At first, it was just a few big drops splattering on the pavement. And then, gradually, the rain gathered pace. Suddenly, the heavens opened. They began to run even though it was pointless. The rain was fast and torrential, a deluge that was impossible to escape. As if a tap had been turned on, it fell from the sky like a waterfall.

By the time they reached Morton Grove, they were both drenched. Stepping into the hallway, they shook themselves like wet dogs, laughing at the sight of each other soaked to the skin. Maddie rushed through to the kitchen, flicking on the lights as she went.

'Coffee,' she said. 'We need hot coffee.'

'You know what I think?' he said, coming up to her as she switched on the kettle and started reaching for mugs.

She turned to face him. 'And what's that, Mr Mallory?'

He came very close to her and placed his arms round her waist. 'I think the first thing we should do is get out of these wet clothes.'

'I bet you do,' she said, gazing up at him.

He pushed a sodden strand of hair behind her ear. 'Purely on health and safety grounds, you understand.'

She smiled, about to wriggle out of his hold, when she suddenly had second thoughts. Perhaps it was time to stop running away from things, to take a risk, to grab a little happiness.

For Greta, all those opportunities had gone. Her life, all her hopes and dreams, had been snatched away from her. Sometimes there were no second chances.

'Maybe you're right,' she murmured. 'I mean, we wouldn't want to go breaking the law.'

'No,' he agreed. 'That's the last thing we'd want to do.'

As he bent his head, she closed her eyes and felt his lips brush hers. Light kisses at first, slow and thoughtful, tender and coaxing, until he felt her respond, until he felt her need growing as forcefully as his. And then his hands began to roam over her abdomen, exploring her back, her thighs, her breasts, searing a path along every plane and curve of her body. With her senses reeling, with her breath no more than a moan, she gave in to desire and pulled him closer.

36

Adam Vasser prowled the backstreets of Kellston, keeping to the shadows. He didn't want to go home, not yet. First, he needed to walk off the rage that was surging through his veins. And he needed to think. Yes, he had a lot of thinking to do. It was pissing down with rain, but that was a good thing. No one looked at you when it was raining; people kept their heads down or sheltered under umbrellas. And the fact that it was raining like this, wasn't it proof that God was on his side, that He was taking care of him, protecting him?

His hoodie was up, but somehow the cold still leaked down the back of his neck. He needed a shower. He needed to get rid of the clothes he was wearing. Where could he dump them? In a bin, perhaps, in one of the alleyways. It was too wet to light a fire, and anyway, burning them was too risky. All it would take was one nosy neighbour peering out of a window and he'd be done for. Maybe the best thing would be to take a cab and dump them somewhere else.

He hissed out a breath. All of this was *her* fault, his bloody mother's. If she'd told him, if she'd been honest, then none of this would have happened. Secrets and lies – that's what it was all about – secrets and bloody lies. His gloved hands curled up in his pockets. He had a right to know that the bastard who'd killed his father was coming out of jail, but had anyone told him? No, of course they fuckin' hadn't. He'd had to find out like this. So who could blame him for getting mad? It was enough to try the patience of a saint.

'Cato,' he murmured, with his voice full of hate. What was ten years? Nothing. A drop in the bloody ocean. That shithead was still breathing, still existing, while his father was ... his father was nothing more than grey, gritty ash. He recalled the feel of it running between his fingers in the graveyard. Flesh and blood turned to dust.

Why was everyone against him? What he couldn't bear was people talking behind his back, laughing at him, sniggering. It wasn't right. It wasn't respectful. He'd only done what he had to, what his father would have done. The bitch deserved it. She'd had it coming. The way she looked at him, the things she said. Although, he still didn't get why she'd been gabbling on about a ring. It hadn't made any sense.

As he breathed in the dank wet air, a sudden shiver of alarm ran through his body. What if she'd already been found? The filth could be knocking on his door right now. He'd be buggered. He wouldn't have time to get rid of the evidence. Her blood was on him, soaked into the white cotton of his shirt. Shit, what if ... ?

'Calm down,' he muttered to himself. Only fools panicked. He was smart. He was sly and invincible. He was shot through with brilliance. No one had seen him, and even if they had, they couldn't have recognised him. It was dark and he'd had his hood up covering his face. No, nothing was going to go wrong. He would get away with it like he got away with everything else.

Adam slunk along Rose Avenue and cut through a side alley until he came out in Morton Grove. He stopped across from number 34 and stared at the house. There was a light on in the hall. Was she home, or was it just some pathetic attempt to deter burglars? He could imagine himself walking across the road, making his way up the short path and ringing the bell.

Maybe she was in bed. Maybe she'd forgotten about the light.

But not tonight. It wasn't safe. You could only push your luck so far. There was no hurry, no rush. He pushed his hands deeper into his pockets, a smile catching the corners of his lips. 'You're next, Maddie Layne,' he whispered. 'You're next.'

37

Maddie couldn't stop smiling as she headed towards Violet Road. Her head was still full of the night before, her limbs aching with a deep, sensual pleasure. She recalled the smell of him, the touch of him, the sweet, easy rhythm as their bodies moved together. His kisses, as if imprinted on her lips, still lingered. Everything had been *so* right. She had slept in his arms and had never felt so wanted, so safe or so damn lucky.

Even the morning had been perfect. He had got up, raided the fridge and made scrambled eggs on toast. They had eaten it in bed, scattering crumbs in the crumpled sheets. They had drunk their mugs of tea and talked. And then they had made love again. Nothing so perfect, she reflected, could ever be wrong.

She had not wanted it to end, but time had eventually caught up with them. With Zac due to be picked up from his grandparents, the goodbyes had to be said. One day soon, she thought, the two of them would need to be introduced. Would Zac like him? Would he like Zac? Or was she getting ahead of herself? It was early days yet. Best to live in the moment and make the most of it.

'I'll see you soon?' he'd asked, standing on the doorstep.

'I'll call you.'

'Will you?'

'I just said I would.'

'I'm feeling insecure.'

She had stood on her toes and kissed him on the mouth. 'No you're not.'

'Less than I was.' He'd kissed her back, holding her face in his hands. 'But don't keep me waiting.'

'Patience is a virtue.'

'I don't want to be virtuous.'

'Me neither,' she whispered, but quickly pushed him away before she succumbed to temptation again. 'I'll call. I promise. Now go.'

Maddie had watched as he'd walked off down the street, wanting to run after him and drag him back. It had taken every ounce of self-restraint to close the door and go inside. Even then she had almost changed her mind, thinking of how she could ring Alisha and tell her she'd be round later. It was only the thought of Zac that stopped her. He'd been none too happy about her date with Rick in the first place. If she failed to turn up on time, she would only make matters worse.

She was strolling past Shauna's house when she remembered what Cato had told her about the blackmail. Would Shauna know about it? She might. If she'd heard about the stolen cars, she could have heard about that too. Maddie looked at her watch. She wasn't due until midday and it was barely a quarter to. She could spare five minutes. Turning round, she retraced her steps and walked up the path.

The doorbell was answered by a sleepy-looking Shauna, still wearing her pyjamas. 'Oh,' she said. 'It's you.'

Maddie had had nicer welcomes, but she didn't let it put her off. 'Hi. Have you got a minute? I just wanted a quick word.'

Shauna, obviously suffering from one of her hangovers, pulled the sort of face that suggested she'd rather walk over red-hot coals. 'Now?'

'Unless you're busy.'

Shauna wrinkled her brow as if trying to think of something she might be busy doing while still wearing her pyjamas. The effort was clearly too much for her. With a grunt, she stood back and waved her over the threshold. 'You'd better come in, then.'

Maddie followed her through to the living room, as untidy as always but unusually quiet. The huge widescreen TV was blank. 'No Kyle?' she asked.

'He's at my mum's.' Shauna slumped down on the sofa and stared at her. 'You want a brew?'

'No, it's okay. I'm not stopping. It's just . . .' Maddie sat down, trying to think of the right way of putting it. 'Someone told me something and I wondered if you knew anything about it.'

'What's that, then?'

'About Bo and Greta.'

'If this is about the motors, then I don't know nothin' else,' Shauna snapped. 'I've told you everything. That's it.'

'It's not about the motors.'

'Oh.'

Maddie, short on time, decided there was no point in beating about the bush. She may as well come right out and say it. 'I've been told that they were blackmailing Adam Vasser. Is it true?'

'What?' As if she'd been slapped, Shauna flinched and her face went pale. 'Who told you . . . ? Why would . . . ? What?'

Maddie stared at her. Shauna was more than flustered. There was a sense of panic about her. Her eyes darted around the room as if searching for an escape route. 'So it is true. Why didn't you tell me?'

Shauna shook her head furiously. 'I don't know nothin' about any blackmail.' Her hands did a manic dance in her lap, rising and falling and twisting round each other. 'I don't. Why would I? Why are you asking me?'

'Oh, come on, Shauna. I can see by your face . . . and I'm not blaming you for anything. It's not your fault.' It was patently obvious that the blackmail story was true. Maddie felt a tiny stab of disappointment. A part of her had still been hoping that Cato had made it up, some tall story to get him off the hook and shift suspicion on to someone else. 'I just want to know what you know. We're mates, aren't we? I need your help if I'm ever going to find out who killed Greta.'

Shauna seemed to relax a little, as if this wasn't what she'd expected her to say. She thought about it a bit and then gave a shrug. 'I won't talk to the filth, though,' she said sulkily. 'Whatever I tell you, I ain't repeating it to them.'

'No one's asking you to.' Maddie leaned forward, her hands on her thighs. 'Just tell me. That's all you need to do. I won't ever say it came from you. I promise.'

Shauna stared at the carpet for a while before lifting her gaze again. 'Okay,' she shrugged. 'I did hear something. But not much. Only that Adam Vasser had tried it on with Bo. You know, he'd—'

'What? Made some kind of pass?'

'Yeah, and Greta was well pissed off about it. The guy had been coming round, all friendly like, drinking her coffee, drinking her beer, and all the time he'd had his eye on her feller. So she wanted to make him pay, didn't she? Wanted some compo from him. She figured that was only fair.'

Maddie found herself thinking, yet again, how little she had known her sister. 'And did he pay?'

Shauna shrugged. 'I think so. Some, anyway, before … I'm not sure how much. She never said exactly. But she was well pleased about it. Reckoned she was sorted, that she could screw him for thousands.'

Maddie felt a wave of anger wash over her. What was wrong with Shauna? She'd known all this, must have realised that Vasser was a prime suspect, but hadn't said a bloody word about it to the cops. All this time and … She bit down on her tongue, knowing that she had to keep calm if she was going to find out the rest. This wasn't the moment to be losing her rag. She tried to keep her voice calm, without accusation, as she asked her next question. 'But didn't you wonder if Vasser had done it, if he'd killed them?'

Shauna grew antsy again, her eyes flashing. 'How would I know? Bo and Greta were into all kinds of stuff. It could have been anyone. Maybe they nicked the wrong car. Maybe they ripped the wrong person off. I couldn't be sure it was him, could I? I'm not going to go grassing him up to the pigs. You think I wanted to end up like Greta? That guy's a fuckin' psycho.'

And Greta was your friend, Maddie felt like hurling back. She swallowed down the retort and took a few deep breaths. 'I understand,' she said, trying to make her tone sympathetic. And actually a part of her did understand. When you lived on an estate like the Mansfield, it didn't do to be branded a grass, no matter what the circumstances. Not to mention the fact that Adam Vasser would scare the hell out of anyone. The price for loyalty could sometimes be too high. 'I really do.'

Shauna raised her hand to her mouth and chewed on her fingernails. 'It might not have been him,' she said, as if the more she repeated it, the more likely it was to be true.

'What I don't get, though, is why we didn't find any money when we cleared out the flat. There was hardly anything in their bank accounts either. What happened to it all?'

Maddie had only been thinking aloud, but Shauna's reaction was telling. She jumped up off the sofa with her hands curled into two tight fists. Her face was bright red, and her chest was heaving.

'What are you saying? That I took it? Are you calling me a fuckin' thief?'

'No,' Maddie said, staring at her. She hadn't thought that at all . . . until now. 'No, of course not.'

'Well, it sounds like it to me. It was your bloody sister who was the thief. I wasn't the one nicking motors or screwing Vasser for cash.'

'Did I say you were?'

'I want you to go. I've had enough. Just leave me alone. I've got a fuckin' headache and you're making it ten times worse.'

Maddie slowly rose to her feet. 'You took the money, didn't you?'

'I didn't! I didn't!' Shauna stamped her foot like a five-year-old. Her cheeks were bright red and she was starting to sweat. 'It wasn't me.' And then, as she gradually realised that the game was up, her mouth twisted into a snarl. 'You can't prove it,' she hissed. 'You can't prove anything.'

Maddie took a step forward, bringing her face close to Shauna's. 'You think I give a damn about the cash? This isn't about that. It's about two people who are dead. Remember them? Bo and Greta. It's about finding out the truth.'

Shauna continued to glare for a moment, but then the rage seemed to drain out of her. Her shoulders fell and she slumped back on to the sofa. There was a short silence before she finally began to talk.

'It went on for a couple of months. Greta was constantly banging on about it, saying she was set for life, that she had Vasser over a barrel. He was queer, an arse bandit and all that . . . and the guy was terrified of anyone finding out. Liked to pass himself off as a Jack the Lad, one of the boys. She bought a load of new stuff with the money, clothes and bags, a fancy TV, things for Zac.'

Maddie remained on her feet, looking down at Shauna, saying nothing.

'A mate called me on the night that they found Bo. He said they'd found the body in the Thames. Greta was still missing, though, and they didn't know what had happened to her.'

Shauna paused, her gaze fixed firmly on the carpet again. 'I reckoned it wouldn't be long before the law came round to search their flat. And then ... well, they'd find all the cash, wouldn't they? And they'd know it was dodgy, bound to. Anyway, I had a spare key – Greta was always locking herself out – so I figured I'd nip along the landing, grab the money and keep it at my place until ... ' She glanced up at Maddie. 'I never meant to keep it. I swear. I was just keeping it safe until Greta came back.'

'Except she didn't.'

Shauna gave a gulp, although whether it was from grief or guilt, it was hard to tell. 'No,' she murmured. 'And then later I thought, Why not? Why not keep it? What else could I do with it, anyway? I could hardly give it back to Vasser, and I didn't see why the pigs should have it.' Her voice suddenly grew indignant. 'I wanted to get me and Kyle out of that place, off the estate, but the council wouldn't shift us. And I didn't have the deposit for a private rental unless ... and so that's what I used the cash for, moving here. That and some stuff for Kyle. Why shouldn't he have nice things for a change? Why should he have to go without when he don't need to?'

'How much was it?' Maddie asked. 'The money in the flat, I mean. The money you took.'

Shauna gave a shrug. 'I dunno exactly. A few thousand?'

Maddie didn't believe for a second that she hadn't counted every penny. 'Is that all?'

'Five or six, maybe.'

It wasn't really the taking of the cash that made Maddie so angry. It was all the lies and deceit from someone she had viewed as a friend. It was the fact that she'd withheld the information about the blackmail from the police and let Adam Vasser get away with it. The money was the evidence, and Shauna had removed it. 'Five or six,' she repeated softly. 'Doesn't seem that much, considering the risk they were taking.'

'That was just the latest instalment. They'd spent the rest. They got loads out of him.'

'Until he decided he'd had enough.'

'You don't know that,' Shauna said.

'No, but the odds are pretty good, don't you think?'

'I can't give it back,' Shauna said. 'I ain't got it any more.' She looked up, her eyes faintly pleading. 'What you gonna do?'

Maddie gave her a contemptuous glance. 'What do you think I'm going to do? I'm going to nail the bastard who murdered my sister.'

38

By the time she left Shauna's house, Maddie's good mood had evaporated. Even the thought of Rick, of the night they had spent together, couldn't restore her earlier spirits. All she had in her head now was how Greta had been as a child: kind, sweet-natured and generous, always laughing. What had happened to that girl? Bo Vale had happened to her, she thought bitterly, but then wondered if that was strictly true.

If she was dishing out blame, there were others who should take their share. Like their parents, for example, with their careless, selfish way of living. And Maddie knew that she was not above reproach herself. How much time had she actually spent with Greta in the final years? Hardly any. She'd been too wrapped up in her own life, her own career, to wonder how her sister was coping. If only she'd made the effort to talk to her more, to try and understand what she was feeling.

'Adam Vasser,' she murmured. It seemed likely, after everything she'd learned, that he was responsible for killing Greta. Unless he'd got someone else to do his dirty work for him.

And Lena Gissing definitely knew about it. Why else would she have said those things in the cemetery? She'd been trying to warn her off, and you didn't do that unless you had something to hide.

Maddie tramped along the road, avoiding the puddles that had been left by last night's storm. A thin, watery sun peeked out from between the clouds. Summer was almost over and before long Zac would be back at school. She had things to buy for him before the new term started, new shoes and shirts and trousers. Mentally, she juggled her finances in her head, wondering how she would cope. The cheques from Cato wouldn't be coming any more – the job he'd wanted doing had been completed – so she'd have to find another way to plug the gap.

As she turned into Violet Road, she saw Zac and Solomon bent over the open bonnet of Winston's old Ford Escort. They were so absorbed they didn't even notice her approaching.

'Hi, there,' she said. 'What are you up to?'

'Hiya, Maddie.' Zac grinned and pointed at the engine. 'Guess what? We're fixing Grandpa's car.'

'Ah,' she said, glancing at Solomon and giving him a nod. 'Only from a distance there, it looked like the two of you were just staring at the engine.'

Solomon stood up straight and put his hands on his hips. 'Are you dissing the workers, missy? I'll have you know we wasn't doing no staring – we was musing. Tell her, Zac. Tell her we was musing.'

'Yeah, we was . . . we were.'

'Sounds like hard work.' She leaned over to look at the tangle of metal. 'You come to any conclusions at the end of all this musing of yours?'

'Sure have,' Solomon said. 'We reckon it's broke.'

'Now you're going all technical on me.' She smiled at Zac.

'You ready to go, hon? Why don't you go and say goodbye to Gran and Grandpa. And don't forget your bag.'

Zac's face fell. 'Aw, do we have to go already? I want to finish the car.'

Solomon pulled down the bonnet. 'Ain't nothing more we can do here, pal. Not today. Soon as I get the spares, you can help me to fit them.'

'Can I? Do you promise?'

'Sure. Couldn't do it without you.'

Mollified, Zac headed off inside.

'Thanks,' Maddie said. 'Has he been okay?'

'Yeah, he's cool.'

'Only he wasn't too happy about me going out last night. I think he thought I might not come back.'

'He ain't said nothin'. He'll be fine. You can't stay home the rest of your life, hon. That the new squeeze I saw you with last night?'

'Rick Mallory,' she said. 'And who was the divine creature you were wining and dining?'

'That's the lovely Louise.'

'Where did you meet her?'

'Around,' he said.

'Around?'

'What's wrong with around? Where'd you meet this Rick?'

'In the cemetery.'

Solomon wiped his oily hands on his overalls. 'Jeez, never realised that place was such a hotbed of romance.'

Maddie noticed Winston and Alisha coming out and said hurriedly, 'Look, can we have a chat later? Not here. I need to talk to you about something.'

'Sure. I'll walk back with you.'

Five minutes later, after the goodbyes had been said, they set off for Morton Grove. Maddie always felt minuscule when

298

she was beside Solomon, like she was walking with a giant. Every time she looked up at him, she had to lean her head back. While Zac was with them, they kept the conversation neutral, but as soon as he had run on ahead, Solomon said, 'So, I'm only guessing here, but I'm thinking you're after some boyfriend advice.'

Maddie laughed. 'Yeah, right. And when was your last long-term relationship, exactly?'

'It's not the length, babe – it's the quality. Didn't no one ever tell you that?'

'I'll take your word for it.'

'Okay, so if it's not man trouble, this about that Cato business?'

'You could say that. Yesterday, I went to—'

Zac chose that moment to come running back. 'Can I go and see Kyle, Maddie? Can I? Please?'

'Sorry, love, but he's at his gran's today.' They were passing his house at that very moment and she hoped that Kyle didn't suddenly appear. She had no idea whether he was there or not, but she wanted to avoid an awkward meeting with Shauna. Tomorrow, on the way to school, she'd have no choice, but until then she preferred to keep her distance. 'We'll be having lunch soon, anyway.'

Zac stared longingly towards the front door, as if by sheer force of will he could conjure up his playmate. 'He might be back later.'

'You'll see him tomorrow,' she said firmly.

Zac opened his mouth as if about to protest, but then saw the expression on her face. He could always tell when she wasn't going to change her mind. He gave a sigh and jogged off towards home.

'Can you come in?' Maddie asked Solomon. 'I don't really want to talk out here.'

'Sounds serious.'

'It is.' Maddie wished she could say otherwise. By telling Solomon, she was about to prise the lid off a whole can of worms. Once the information was out there, it couldn't be taken back. Was she doing the right thing? Winston and Alisha would never get over the death of their son, but they'd had some time to come to terms with it. Now she was about to stir it all up again, to open old wounds and create fresh ones.

Once inside, she went to the kitchen, poured Zac some orange juice and banished him to the living room.

'Why?' he asked, standing on one leg.

'Because I need to talk to Uncle Sol.'

'What about?'

'Stuff,' she said. 'Private stuff. We won't be long. You can watch the TV if you like.'

Zac gave her a long look as if weighing up the pros and cons – the TV versus missing out on something interesting – but then gave a shrug, took the glass of orange and went to find some cartoons to watch.

Maddie made two mugs of tea and sat down at the table with Solomon. She waited until she heard the sound of the TV before she started, and even then she kept her voice deliberately low. 'I went to see Jay Cato. He told me . . . he told me something about Bo and Greta.'

'Oh yeah?'

'Yes.' Maddie placed her hands around the mug, looked down at the table and then let the story spill out in one continuous stream without pausing to let Solomon interrupt. She told him about the dead bird, the stolen cars and the blackmail. The only part she missed out was about Shauna taking the money. When she'd finally finished, she raised her eyes to look at him again. 'That's it. That's everything.'

'You should have called me when you got that box. It's sick, man, leaving something like that. Why didn't you call?'

Maddie gave a shrug. 'I don't know. I suppose I thought you'd be at work. Anyway, Rick dealt with it. He buried it in the back garden.'

Solomon was quiet for a moment as if mulling it all over. His forehead creased into a frown. 'Just 'cause this Cato says all this don't mean it's true.'

'I know that, but I've asked around and had it confirmed. A friend of Bo and Greta, they said they'd heard the same thing.'

'Who's the friend?'

'They won't talk to you,' she said, being careful not to specify the sex. She didn't approve of what Shauna had done, but she didn't want Solomon going round and shouting the odds either. Maddie reckoned she'd learned all there was to learn and it was best to leave it at that. 'They won't talk to anyone else.'

Solomon huffed out a breath. 'So Bo was nicking cars for Vasser.'

'You never suspected?'

'Nah. Bo always did his own thing. Sometimes I didn't see him from one week to the next. I got him some work on the doors, but he was never really into it.' He shook his head in exasperation. 'Vasser, though. Why the fuck was he messing with that psycho?'

'For the money, I presume.'

'There's other ways to make dough.'

'Did you know that Vasser was gay?'

Solomon shrugged his massive shoulders. 'Heard a few rumours, nothin' solid. His brothers sure as hell wouldn't have been happy about it.'

'I didn't know he had any.'

'Stepbrothers, then. Tony's boys. The Gissing lot. They ain't

301

too keen on gays, view them as a threat to their raging masculinity.'

'Which is probably why he paid up. And Lena must have known about the blackmail, because why else would she have said what she did at the cemetery? She obviously hated Greta.'

Solomon's face had grown dark. 'Blackmail,' he said, almost spitting the word out as if it left a bad taste in his mouth. 'Sounds like one of Greta's lousy scams.'

Maddie scowled at him. 'Oh, and Bo was entirely innocent, was he?'

'Did I say that?'

'As good as.'

The two of them glared at each other for a few seconds in a futile attempt at defending their siblings. Solomon was the first to break the stare. 'Aw, hell,' he said, sitting back and placing his hands behind his head. 'This is crazy. You realise what's happening here, babe?'

'And what's that?'

'We're having our first row.'

Despite herself, Maddie had to smile. 'I guess it had to happen one day.'

He leaned forward again, putting his burly arms on the table. 'How about we agree that they were both as fuckin' stupid as each other?'

'Sounds like a plan.' She rubbed at her eyes, feeling a wave of tiredness wash over her. 'Sometimes I feel like I didn't know Greta at all. The more I find out, the less I understand. I should have tried harder, tried to talk to her.'

'You gonna start blaming yourself now? You never made her do nothin'. She made her own choices, hon. They both did.'

But Maddie still felt partly responsible. It was impossible just to wash her hands of the past. 'So what do we do now?

We can't prove anything. All we've got is hearsay and rumours.'

'More than one way to skin a cat,' he said.

She looked at him. 'Meaning?'

A hard expression had entered Solomon's eyes. 'Meaning that I'll sort it.'

'Which doesn't make me feel any better. Oh God, please tell me you're not going to do anything stupid. Think about your mum and dad, Sol. It's not going to help if you end up in jail ... or worse. We don't even know for sure that it was Vasser.'

'Just a coincidence, then, that Bo and Greta happened to be blackmailing him and suddenly turn up dead? Or that you've had a skewered bird land on your doorstep? Strikes me that someone's mighty worried, babe. Don't you think?'

Maddie knew he was right, but she didn't want him taking the law into his own hands. 'Yes, and he's probably worried enough to try and silence anyone who might be on to him.'

'I'm not scared of Vasser.'

'Nor was Bo, nor was Greta, but look what happened to them. You've said it yourself – he's a psycho.'

'Best get him off the streets, then.'

Solomon got to his feet and Maddie jumped up too. She took hold of his arm and looked up at him. 'Promise me you won't do anything rash. *Please*. I wouldn't have told you if ... I don't want you ending up in the mortuary too.'

He smiled thinly down at her. 'You know what your problem is, hon?'

'Yes. I'm terrified of what's going to happen next.'

'You worry too much. Have a little faith.'

Maddie released her grip on his arm and gave a sigh. 'Is that supposed to reassure me? Only it doesn't. It doesn't at all.'

'You take care, huh? Call me if there's any trouble.'

She watched as he walked out of the kitchen. Her heart had started to hammer in her chest. The trouble, she suspected, was about to get a damn sight worse.

39

DI Valerie Middleton took a moment to prepare, to gather her thoughts, as she walked up the path of the small terraced house in Clover Road. The outside of the building was neat and tidy with clean windows, smart paintwork and a hanging basket filled with multi-coloured petunias. The inside ... well, she already knew what she was going to find there.

She breathed deeply before slipping on the plastic shoes and stepping over the threshold. From the door, she could see through the tiny hallway to the activity in the living room. The SOCO team was already busy, an army of white swarming over the house. Although she had dealt with numerous murder victims in her time, every death still had an impact. It wasn't true that you got used to it; you simply found a way of dealing with it.

DS Kieran Swann appeared from the sea of faces and approached her. 'Morning, gov. Just what we need first thing on a Monday, huh?'

'I'm sure our victim feels a damn sight more inconvenienced than we do,' she replied dryly. 'So what have we got?'

Swann led her through to the living room. 'Delia Shields. Forty-eight and lives alone. No partner that we know of. Beaten to death by the looks of it. A series of blows to the back of the head and some bruising on the neck and arms. No sign of any sexual assault. Pathologist reckons she's been dead for about thirty-six hours.'

'Saturday night, then.'

Valerie gave a nod to a couple of officers as they stood back to let her see the victim. Delia Shields was curled on her side, her glazed eyes partly open, her mouth twisted in the rictus of death. She was an ordinary-looking woman, middle-aged and conservatively dressed in a cream shirt, beige knee-length skirt and a pair of brown sandals. The back of her skull had been caved in, exposing a pulpy mass of bone, congealed blood and tissue.

'Was it a robbery?' she asked.

Swann shook his head. 'Nothing missing so far as we can tell. Her bag's still here and her purse is in it. None of the cards has been taken, and there's a small amount of cash. No sign of anything disturbed upstairs either.'

'Not one of the local junkies, then.' Valerie glanced around the room. Apart from the mess caused by the attack, it had an air of neatness about it, everything in its place and a place for everything. It was a tidy but uninspiring living space, with chintzy wallpaper and rather dull furnishings. A couple of seascapes hung on the wall, and there was a row of porcelain figures on the mantelpiece. A small teardrop chandelier hung from the centre of the ceiling, the candle-shaped bulbs giving off a faint glow. 'Was the light on when you got here?'

'Yeah,' Swann said. 'And the curtains were drawn too, which suggests her visitor arrived after dark.'

Valerie gave a nod, glancing back towards the body on the floor. 'She doesn't look to me like the type of woman who'd answer the door to a stranger at night. More likely that she knew her attacker, don't you think?'

'Maybe it's a domestic, a row with the boyfriend. Just 'cause we don't know about any regular partner doesn't mean there wasn't one.' He gestured with his head towards a large plastic bag leaning against the wall. 'And we've got the murder weapon.'

'An umbrella?' Valerie said, surprised. She went over to take a closer look. The fabric of the brolly was grey and black, and the heavy, ornate silver-coloured handle was stained with dried blood. Judging from the contents of the room and the clothing she was wearing, the umbrella didn't seem to fit with Delia's taste. It was too fancy, too showy, although it was always possible that someone might have bought it for her as a gift. 'Perhaps it belongs to the perp. It was raining on Saturday, wasn't it?'

'Off and on. Be kind of careless to leave it behind, though. It's pretty distinctive. I've never seen one like it before.'

'So maybe they panicked and took off in a hurry. Maybe they didn't come with the intention of killing her, but got into an argument and just picked up the nearest object to hand. What else do we know about her?'

'Not much. Only that she worked at the cemetery, been there for over thirty years. That's how she was discovered. The manager, Bob Cannon, started to worry when she didn't turn up and wasn't answering her phone. She's the reliable sort, apparently. He came round to the house, noticed the curtains were still pulled across, and when she didn't answer the door, he called us.'

Valerie's eyes were drawn back towards the body and the dreadful wound on Delia's skull. 'Someone was angry. You can't inflict damage like that without major force. Any prints on the brolly?'

'Some partials. We'll have to see what the lab can salvage. Oh, and there is one other thing: the victim had a visitor in the early evening, a woman.'

Valerie gave him a cool look. 'And you're only just telling me this? You didn't think it was important?'

'She came and went, and the victim was still alive at that point. Neighbour from across the road saw her leave, saw Delia Shields too. She was still breathing then.'

'So what about this woman?'

'Tall, blonde, late thirties, well dressed.' He smirked, looking Valerie up and down. 'Hope you've got an alibi for Saturday night.'

'Yes,' she replied, 'because I'm the only tall blonde living in Kellston, right?'

Sometimes, often, Swann infuriated her with his references to her height. He was only a few inches shorter than her, but had a major complex about it. Size, for him, definitely mattered. 'So what else do we know about this woman?'

Swann put his finger in his ear and probed its depths for a second. He grinned at Valerie. 'She drives a red sports car.'

Valerie lifted her brows. 'Really?'

'Straight up. And the neighbour, Mrs Elizabeth Kent, reckons she's local. Says she's seen her around Kellston, although she doesn't know her name.'

'And you're thinking . . .'

'I'm thinking the same as you, gov. Sounds suspiciously like Lena Gissing.'

'She can't be the only blonde in the area with a red sports car.'

Swann glanced towards the corpse. 'The only one likely to be involved in something like this. Although, Mrs Kent is sure that Delia was alive when our mystery blonde left the house. Says she saw Delia at the door. But she also reckons that there'd been a row, that neither of them looked too happy. Maybe Lena had a think about it and came back later.'

'We don't know it was her. I mean, how were they even con-nected?' Her eyes roamed around the room again, trying to picture how Lena Gissing could fit into the scene. 'And Lena's not late thirties. She's knocking on fifty.'

'Hard to tell from a distance, though.'

'I don't suppose the neighbour got the registration number?'

'No.'

'And she didn't see the blonde returning at any time?'

'No.'

'How about Bob Cannon. Is he still around?'

'He had to go back to work. There's a funeral at eleven.'

Valerie, aware that there was nothing more she could do at the house, decided to get out of the way of the Forensics team. 'Okay, let's go and see the neighbour first and then we'll head over to the cemetery.'

Elizabeth Kent was plump and elderly with steel-grey hair and a pair of sharp dark eyes. She'd been standing at the window as they walked up the drive and had the door open in five seconds flat. The woman was a bundle of nervous excitement, her arms flapping by her sides, her gaze rapidly switching between the two officers and the activity going on across the road.

Valerie showed her ID and made the introductions. 'I'm DI Valerie Middleton, and this is DS Kieran Swann.'

'I can't believe it,' she said, as she led them through to her living room. 'Murdered. The poor thing. It's terrible, terrible. Who'd want to do a thing like that? You're not safe in your own home these days. Do you know yet? Do you know who did it?'

Valerie gazed patiently back at her. 'We were hoping you could help with our enquiries.'

'Sit down, please,' Mrs Kent said. 'Would you like tea? It won't take me a minute.'

'No, thanks.' Valerie lowered herself on to the blue sofa, and

Swann sat down beside her. 'It's very kind of you, but we're fine.' She waited until Mrs Kent had settled into an easy chair before continuing. 'Did you know Delia Shields well?'

'Oh, I wouldn't say well. She was the private sort, you know, not one for chit-chat. But she's lived across the road for years – must be almost twenty – so ... we'd say hello to each other, that kind of thing.'

Valerie got the feeling that she hadn't especially liked Delia. 'So you weren't close?'

'Just neighbours. To be honest, she was a bit ...' Mrs Kent stopped suddenly and pulled a face, her teeth drawing in her lower lip.

'A bit?' Valerie prompted.

Mrs Kent gave a somewhat exaggerated shudder. 'I don't like to speak ill of the dead.'

Although she was going to, Valerie thought, with a little more encouragement. 'Please. Anything you can tell us could be useful. I know it's not easy, but the truth is always best in these circumstances.'

'Well,' Mrs Kent said, gazing down at her lap for a moment before looking up at Valerie again, 'she could be a bit standoffish. Not very friendly, if you know what I mean. I asked her round for coffee once, but she said she was too busy. Didn't even say it in a nice way, just looked down her nose at me and ...' She stopped again, aware that she was letting her mouth run away with her. 'I suppose she just wasn't the type for company.'

'But she had a visitor yesterday,' Swann said.

'Yes, I told the young lady, the PC who came round earlier. The nice girl with the red hair.'

'Perhaps if we could go over it again. Did you recognise the woman?'

'Oh yes – I've seen her around. I don't know her name,

though. But she has been here before. Not recently, mind. It's been a while now.' Mrs Kent wrinkled her brow as if trying to remember the last time she saw the blonde. 'Must be over a year. Maybe even longer.'

'What time did she arrive?' Swann asked.

'It must have been about six, perhaps a bit after. I was watching TV and I noticed the car pull up – you can't really miss it, can you? – and then this woman got out. She put up her umbrella even though it was only a hop and a skip to the front door. Didn't want to spoil her hair, I suppose.'

'Could you describe her for me?'

Mrs Kent inclined her head a little. 'Let me see. Late thirties? She was tall, attractive, fair-haired – it was tied up in one of those knots at the nape of her neck – and very stylish. She was wearing a long white raincoat. Expensive by the looks of it.'

'Do you recall the colour of the umbrella?'

Mrs Kent looked surprised at the question. 'The colour?'

'Yes.'

As if Swann was trying to catch her out in some way, she gave him a suspicious look. 'What difference does the colour make?'

'You don't remember?'

Mrs Kent lifted her shoulders a fraction. 'Er . . . I'm not sure. Black, maybe? Or grey? She didn't have it up for long.'

'And was she carrying it when she left?'

'I don't . . . What's this got to do with anything?'

'If you could just try and remember,' Swann urged.

'I don't know. Like I said, she left in a hurry. It wasn't up, but . . . ' Mrs Kent gave a small shake of her head. 'No, I don't recall if she was carrying it or not.'

Valerie moved the interview along. 'And how long was she inside for?'

'Not more than fifteen minutes,' Mrs Kent replied, her voice growing firmer now that she was on safer ground. 'I saw the door open again and the woman came out. Delia was behind her. I could see her quite clearly.' She took a small breath, leaving a dramatic pause before making her next pronouncement. 'I'm pretty sure they'd been arguing.'

'And what gave you that impression?'

'The face on her, that's what! The blonde woman, I mean. She stormed along that path and into her car, took off like a bat out of hell. I'm surprised she didn't kill someone.' And then, suddenly realising what she'd said, she gave a tiny gasp and raised her hand to her mouth. 'Oh, I didn't ...'

'It's all right,' Valerie said softly. 'Don't worry about it. What about Delia? How did she seem?'

Mrs Kent took a moment to think about it. 'Sort of shocked. And upset. Yes, definitely upset.'

'And you could see this from where you were sitting?'

Elizabeth Kent had the grace to blush, a pink tinge colouring her cheeks. 'Well, no, I was standing at the window. It was grey outside, still raining, and I was thinking of pulling the curtains.'

It was obvious that she'd been snooping, but Valerie gave her a reassuring nod as if it was perfectly normal to be closing curtains at six fifteen on an August evening. 'And that's the last time you saw Delia Shields?'

Mrs Kent's head bobbed up and down. 'Yes. I thought ... I thought she was going to run after the woman, but then I think she saw me and changed her mind. She just went back inside.'

'Okay,' Valerie said. 'And you didn't see this blonde woman come back at any point?'

'No.'

'Or did anyone else call at the house?' Swann asked.

'No, I didn't see anyone else.' Mrs Kent's hands fluttered up to her face as if the realisation of what had happened was just starting to sink in. 'Why would anyone ...? It's just too awful. I don't understand it.'

Valerie rose to her feet, sure that they had exhausted the sum of Mrs Kent's information on the matter. 'Thank you. You've been very helpful. Are you all right? Would you like us to call someone for you?'

'No, no, my daughter's coming round. I'll be fine. She doesn't live far away.'

'Well, thank you again.'

Valerie waited until they were out of earshot of the house before speaking to Swann. 'So if the mystery visitor was Lena Gissing, what the hell did those two have to argue about?'

'Well, whatever it was, we both know who won.'

Valerie got into her car and fastened the seatbelt. 'Lena may be a lot of things, but she's not stupid. She came round here in daylight. She must have realised that she could have been spotted. Especially with that car of hers. It hardly blends into the background, does it?'

'Except, if all those rumours are true, she never does her own dirty work. I bet she's got a watertight alibi for the time of death.'

'True, but why take the risk? She'd know that if she was seen, she'd automatically be a suspect. Why not wait a few days, a week before killing the woman?'

'Maybe it couldn't wait. Maybe, for one reason or another, Delia Shields had to be got rid of.'

'Except it doesn't look or smell like a professional hit. They used an umbrella, for God's sake! It's hardly a weapon of choice, is it? No, this feels more . . . impulsive, spur of the moment, like someone got mad and picked up the nearest thing to hand.'

While he was thinking, Swann began excavating his ear again.

'Do you have to?' she asked.

'What?'

'That.' Valerie wrinkled her nose. 'Whatever horrors are lurking in there, can you kindly leave them in situ, at least until you're out of my car?'

Swann gave a smirk. 'Sorry, gov.'

But he wasn't sorry, not in the slightest. Valerie knew that he took pleasure in annoying her. It was one of his delightful little quirks, like the way he always strained his neck to look up at her face as if she were a twenty-foot giant. 'Let's go see what Bob Cannon can tell us.'

Valerie had just pulled into a parking space in front of the cemetery office when her phone started ringing. She dug it out of her bag and glanced at the screen. 'The station,' she said, pressing the button and raising the mobile to her ear. 'Hello. Valerie Middleton.' She listened to the voice on the other end of the line. 'Yes, gov, we're there now. We've just arrived.'

Valerie's eyes scanned the graveyard as she absorbed what she was being told, her gaze taking in the rows of headstones, the neatly mown grass and the flashes of colour from the flowers that had been left. 'Okay, I understand. Yes, yes, of course.'

'Problem?' Swann asked as she hung up.

'You could say that. Seems we've got a complication.'

'What kind of complication?'

'The type that means we're going to have to tread carefully.'

40

The interview with Bob Cannon had proved to be an informative one, confirming their suspicions that Lena Gissing was indeed acquainted with Delia Shields and that he'd seen them together on a couple of occasions. The man, unsurprisingly, had been decidedly shaken up about the murder. He had stared at Valerie and Swann with fear and confusion in his eyes.

'You don't think it's to do with . . . with this other business?'

Valerie had been the one to answer in what she hoped was a reassuring tone. 'We're not entirely sure, but there's nothing to suggest it, not at the moment.'

Superintendent Saul Redding's call had meant that discretion was called for. Normally, they'd have interviewed the other members of the cemetery staff there and then, but under the circumstances it had been decided to defer it until later. The last thing they wanted was to scare anyone off. And, as they already had a major suspect, their statements would probably be irrelevant anyway.

'What was Delia Shields like?' Swann had asked.

Bob Cannon had struggled with the question. Hesitating, he had picked up a pen and tapped it against his desk. 'She was very ... er ... efficient. She'd been here for years, knew the place inside out.'

It hadn't been much of a eulogy, Valerie thought, considering they'd shared the same office space for the last four years. No mention of being kind or generous or funny. She'd got the impression that Cannon, like Mrs Kent, had not been overly fond of the victim.

Valerie switched her thoughts away from the earlier interview and back to the here and now. The room – interview room 3 – was small, overly warm and somewhat claustrophobic. There was lino on the floor, and the pale brown walls were scuffed. The single window, set high up, had a set of bars across it, and the main light source came from a bright fluorescent tube in the centre of the ceiling. She was sitting beside DS Swann, across the table from Lena Gissing and her solicitor, Michael Brookes.

Valerie stared hard at Lena Gissing, taking in every look, every gesture, every facial tic, anything that could provide some evidence of the woman's guilt. But unless she was an exceptionally good actress, Lena seemed genuinely shocked that Delia Shields was dead. She wasn't making any attempt to deny that she had seen her on Saturday either.

'But she was fine,' Lena said. 'I can't ... I don't ... Christ, who'd do a thing like that?'

Valerie noted the paleness of her face, the tightness around the eyes. 'So how, exactly, did you and Delia Shields know each other?'

'We went to school together. We've been friends for years.'

'And why did you go to see her on Saturday?'

'No reason in particular. Just for a coffee, a catch-up.' Aware that she was under scrutiny, Lena stared back at Valerie. 'That's what friends do, isn't it? It's not against the law.'

Valerie gave a thin smile. 'And how did she seem?'

'Seem?'

'In herself. Was she happy, sad, anxious? Was she upset about anything?'

Valerie thought she saw something flicker in Lena's face, but it was there and gone in a second.

'No. She was just ... Delia. There was nothing out of the ordinary. We had a coffee, a chat and then I left. I don't think I was there for more than twenty minutes.'

'That was a short visit, wasn't it? Not much time for catching up.'

'There was a gala in the evening, a charity do in the West End. I had to go home and get changed.'

Valerie felt Kieran Swann shift beside her as if reminding her of their earlier conversation about the alibi. There it was already, dropped neatly in at the first opportunity. But then that would be second nature to a woman like Lena Gissing. She knew how the law worked, knew how to cover her back. 'We have a witness who claims that you seemed upset when you left.'

'Me?' Lena said. 'Why on earth should I have been upset?'

'And that you left in a hurry.'

Lena's hands fluttered up from the table and dropped back down again. 'I did leave in a hurry. Like I just told you, I had somewhere to be and I was running late.'

'This witness, they claim that Delia was upset too.'

Lena released a thin hiss of breath. 'Then your witness was wrong. Delia might have been a little ... well, irritated by the fact I was leaving so soon, but she certainly wasn't upset. I turned up a bit late, you see, and then had to rush off again. She wasn't very happy about it, and I can't say I blame her. If I'd known what was going to happen ...' She stopped, her eyes raking the walls before coming back to settle on Valerie again. 'I still can't believe that she's dead.'

Valerie allowed a short silence to settle over the room before continuing. 'Do you own a grey and black umbrella with a silver-coloured handle?'

Lena seemed as startled as Mrs Kent at the question. 'What's that got to do with it?'

'If you could just answer the question, please.'

'Yes, yes, I do.'

'And is that umbrella currently in your possession?'

'No, I left it at Delia's. By the time I went, it had stopped raining and I forgot all about it. But why are you asking about—' She broke off suddenly as if a light bulb had gone on in her head. 'No, you can't mean . . . You can't . . . You don't . . . '

'Yes,' Valerie said. 'It would appear so.'

Lena shook her head. She swallowed hard, her mouth twisting. 'But . . . Jesus, my umbrella?'

Valerie might almost have felt sorry for her, but she knew too much about Lena Gissing to waste her sympathy. The woman was a madam, everyone knew that, albeit a high-class one. She pimped out girls to the highest bidder. And she wasn't above a spot of murder either. The jury might have believed her when it came to the death of her first husband, but the police and the CPS remained convinced of her guilt. 'As you were the last person to see Delia Shields alive—'

'Not quite the last,' Michael Brookes interrupted tartly. 'I think you'll find that was the murderer.'

Lena's eyes grew cold and hard. 'Don't think you're pinning this on me. I had nothing to do with it. Nothing! I want to take a break,' she said, glancing at her solicitor and dabbing at her eyes with a tissue. 'My best friend has just been killed and – ' she gave a rather histrionic gulp '– it's all a dreadful shock.'

'Any objections, Inspector?' Michael Brookes asked.

'No,' Valerie said, reaching for the button on the recorder, and relaying the information out loud. Even as she spoke, she knew that Lena's penthouse apartment at Silverstone Heights was being searched. Would they find anything useful? It was doubtful, but still worth a try. Even professionals like Lena could make mistakes.

Outside in the corridor, she looked at Swann. 'What do you think?'

'She's lying about Delia Shields. Reckon the two of them had a major falling-out.'

'Yes, me too. She's never going to admit it, though.'

They walked along the corridor, pushed through the swing doors into the busy incident room and made a beeline for the coffee machine. While Valerie sipped on the insipid brown liquid, she tried to sort out her approach for the rest of the interview. She was sure that Lena's alibi for later on in the night would stand up, but that didn't mean she hadn't got someone else to do her dirty work for her. If they could only get to the bottom of what the row had been about, then they might be able to make sense of the murder.

A young DC gave her a wave from across the room. 'Call for you, gov. It's Jenny. She's at the Heights.'

Valerie went over to the desk and picked up the phone. As she listened to what PC Jenny Allen had to relay, a smile spread slowly across her face. 'Good. That's excellent. Get it over to the lab as quickly as you can.' She put down the receiver and walked back to Swann, still grinning like a Cheshire cat.

'Good news, gov?'

'The best. You won't believe what they found in Lena's washing machine.'

'I'm not even going to guess.'

'A man's white shirt,' Valerie said triumphantly. 'One white shirt heavily spattered with blood.'

'You're kidding? Before or after it had been through the wash?'

'Before. Thankfully, Lena hadn't got round to doing the laundry yet. Bit careless of her, huh?'

Swann's face took on its thinking expression, his heavy eyebrows coming together. 'Tony Gissing, then? We still don't know the exact time of death. He could have paid Delia a visit after this gala thing was over.'

Valerie shook her head. 'No, the shirt's too small to be Tony's, or either of his sons'. Which leaves us with?'

'Adam Vasser,' Swann said.

'Exactly. Got it in one. Let's pull the bastard in.'

41

Adam Vasser lay supine on the thin uncomfortable mattress, staring up at the cracks in the ceiling. The cell was warm and stank of piss and bleach. Across the way, a drunk was cursing and hammering on the door, a noise that had been going on for most of the night and which showed no sign of abating.

'Just shut the fuck up!' he yelled.

'You shut the fuck up!' came the prompt reply.

Resigned to sleeplessness, Adam found himself reliving snippets of his two-hour interrogation at the hands of DI Valerie Middleton and her sidekick. The bitch already had him in the frame for murder, but she was about to get a nasty surprise. When the report came back from the lab, it would show that, just as he'd claimed, the blood on his white shirt didn't belong to Delia Shields at all.

'So you're saying that this blood came from a fight you were in?'

'Yeah,' he'd said, sitting back and folding his arms. 'Last week. I don't know, Tuesday, Wednesday night? I was walking home minding my own business – about midnight, I think – when a couple of geezers jumped me. Druggies, I reckon, after some cash or my phone. So we had a bit of a scuffle and then they ran off.'

'You beat off two of them?' DS Swann had asked, not even bothering to hide the incredulity in his tone. 'That's some going.'

'What can I say? Used to do a bit of boxing when I was younger. I like to keep myself fit. Plus, to be honest, I reckon they were off their heads and didn't actually expect me to fight back.' He had stretched out his right hand across the table, palm down. 'See,' he'd said, showing them his still-bruised knuckles. 'That's what I got for my trouble.'

Adam smiled as he thought about his actual victim, the filthy rent boy in Soho. He felt again the thrill of bringing his fist down into the boy's face, of the cracking of bone against bone, of the splitting of flesh. But no one knew about the whore; no one knew and no one cared. It had been careless, though, leaving the bloodied shirt at the Heights – and typical of his slattern of a mother to leave the dirty washing sitting there for days. But at least he'd got rid of the clothes he'd been wearing when he'd battered Delia Shields to death. He'd put them in a black plastic bag, caught a bus to Bethnal Green and wandered around the backstreets until he found a bin to dump them in.

'Let's go back to Saturday,' Middleton had said.

'Haven't we already covered that?'

'Let's go over it again.'

Oh, he'd known their game all right, making him repeat the story over and over in the hope that he'd eventually trip himself up. But he hadn't been born yesterday. Keep it simple, that was the trick. Never embellish. Never provide unnecessary detail. 'I was at the garage for most of the afternoon, and then at about half five I went over to the Heights. I'd left my watch there, in my mum's apartment, and wanted to pick it up. We had coffee together and then she went out to see Delia Shields. About ten minutes later, I went home to Cherry Street, and that's where I stayed for the rest of the night.'

'On a Saturday?' Middleton had asked. 'You stayed home on a Saturday night?'

'I wasn't in the mood to go out. Just fancied a quiet night in, bit of music, a few beers. Nothing wrong with that, is there?'

'And no one else was there with you?'

'All on my lonesome.'

'You didn't leave the flat at any time?'

'No.'

They had asked a lot of stuff about Delia and he'd kept his answers simple. 'I didn't really know her that well. I mean, she's been around since for ever, but my mother didn't see her that often.'

'Did you like her?'

He had given a shrug. 'Never thought much about it. To be honest, I can't even remember the last time I saw her.'

Adam's gaze slipped down from the ceiling and focused on the graffiti-covered walls of the cell. The light, a dim bulb, cast deep shadows over the room. He suddenly recalled that afternoon a year or so ago when he and his mother had been on their way back from the West End and she'd decided to call in at the cemetery. He'd been desperate for a slash and so had gone with her into the office. Delia had pointed him towards a short corridor leading off from the back.

'It's just down there, Adam. Go to the end and it's on your right.'

As he was heading towards the bog, he'd passed a small side room with its door open. He'd glanced casually inside and seen the rows of hooks on the wall with heavy metal keys hanging down from them. Attached to each key was a label with a name and plot number. It was only while he was relieving himself that the idea sprang into his head. The keys, he realised, were for the old brick mausoleums scattered around the graveyard. On his way back, he had slipped into the room and picked a key at random, figuring that no one would even notice it was missing.

Adam stretched out his arms, smiled and yawned. 'God bless the Belvederes,' he murmured. And he'd chosen well too, the coffin house being situated well off the beaten track and away from prying eyes. It had been the perfect place to hide his stash. Drugs, guns, knives – over the past twelve months he'd accumulated everything he'd need for when the time came.

It was another two hours before Adam finally heard the heavy tread of shoes on the lino outside. The door was unlocked and swung open. A uniformed officer looked at him with nothing but contempt in his eyes.

'Okay, shift yourself. You're being released.'

'About time,' he said, swinging his legs off the bed and standing up. The report from the lab must be in. He was in the clear. Blondie wouldn't be pleased. He could imagine the look on her face as she'd read through the results, the words destroying all hope of an easy conviction.

His mother, with a face like thunder, was already being booked out at the counter. Her clothes were crumpled, and her usually immaculate make-up was smeared. There were dark circles under her eyes. She glanced at him, her mouth a thin, tight line. He was going to get a bollocking, but she wouldn't do it in front of the filth.

Ten minutes later, after Adam had retrieved his watch, his wallet, his phone and his keys, the two of them left the station.

'Swear to me you didn't do it,' she said as they walked together along Cowan Road.

'They've just released me. Doesn't that tell you something?'

Lena gave a snort. 'Only that they haven't got enough to charge you with.'

'Why would I want to kill Delia?'

'Why do you do anything?'

An antagonistic silence fell between them, lasting all the way to the corner of Cherry Street. 'See you, then,' he said.

Lena glared at him. 'So that's it, is it? I spend the night in the slammer and you're just going to piss off home without so much as an explanation.'

'There's nothing to explain. They found the shirt, put two and two together, and came up with five. How is that my fault?'

'If you're lying to me . . .'

'What?' he asked, staring defiantly back at her. 'What are going to do about it?'

'It's what I won't do, Adam. I've had enough. I won't cover your bloody back again, do you understand me? Do you get it?'

'Loud and clear, Ma.' He felt a seed of rage blossom in his chest. As if she had ever done anything for him; the only person Lena Gissing was concerned about was herself. She was selfish to the core, a manipulative bitch. 'I suppose you'll miss her,' he said slyly. 'Now you've not got anyone to share your secrets with.'

'And what secrets would those be?'

Adam thought of Cato being released from jail. He thought of his dad reduced to ashes. He thought of Bo Vale floating dead in the water. 'You tell me.'

'I've no idea what you're talking about.'

'An eye for an eye. Isn't that what they say? You wasted someone I cared about. Maybe I returned the favour.'

Two spots of red appeared on Lena's cheeks. She stared at her son as if she was looking at a stranger. And then she did something unexpected. Drawing her face close to his, she gave a thin, high-pitched laugh. 'I've got news for you, sweetheart. If you did it to piss me off, you got it all wrong. You just did me the biggest fuckin' favour you could ever imagine.' And with that she turned on her heel and strode off.

Adam stood on the corner scowling as he watched her merge into the morning crowd of commuters. What the hell had that meant? Perhaps she'd just said it to get under his skin. Well, he'd show her who was boss, who was in control. Women! He couldn't stand them. They were all the same. They were all poison.

He took out his phone and called Louise. 'I need you to do something for me.' As he explained, he could hear her sighing down the line.

'And how the fuck am I supposed to do that?'

'I don't care how you do it, babe. Just make sure you do. I'll be waiting. Don't let me down.'

42

As Maddie walked past the cemetery on her way to work, she glanced through the tall wrought-iron gates at the office building. Despite the warmth of the sun, she shivered as she thought of Delia Shields. *Murdered.* It was hard to take in. Why? How? When? Rick hadn't had the answers to all her questions when he'd called to let her know last night. All he'd been able to tell her was that Delia had been killed in her home on Saturday, that she hadn't been found until Monday morning and that Adam Vasser and Lena Gissing had been arrested in connection with the murder.

'Should I go and talk to them?' she'd asked. 'The police, I mean.'

'What for?'

'Because . . . I don't know. Maybe it has something to do with Greta and Bo.'

'I wouldn't get involved,' he'd said. 'Not at the moment. Why don't you wait a while, let the dust settle?'

'You think?'

'Yeah. I'd stay out of it for now. See what happens. Well, unless you want to spend hours down the cop shop.'

Maddie had let herself be persuaded. He was probably right, although a small seed of doubt continued to grow inside her. Could it really be a coincidence, all this stuff with Lena Gissing, the threats, the revelations about the blackmail ... and now Delia Shields ending up dead? She recalled the anger in the woman's face when she'd come out of the office to confront her. *That bastard Cato!*

Still, it came as a relief to know that the two of them were safely behind bars. If Vasser had killed Delia, it was perfectly possible that he'd killed Greta and Bo too. Perhaps he would finally pay for what he'd done. She had called Solomon to tell him the news and had sensed a certain disappointment in his tone. He had been hoping, she suspected, to deal with Adam Vasser himself. And that was another reason to be glad that Vasser was off the streets. Solomon's idea of justice could send him to jail for a very long time.

She gazed along the main thoroughfare, her eyes searching for Rick, but there wasn't any sign of him. The work truck wasn't around either, which meant he must be over the other side of the cemetery somewhere. She felt a stab of disappointment. It would have been nice to see him again, even if it was only to give him a wave. With one last glance at the office building, she continued on her way.

Maddie had only gone a few yards down the road when her phone started to ring. She dug it out of her pocket and saw that it was Agnes Reach. 'Agnes, hello. Is everything all right?'

'Of course. Why shouldn't it be?'

'Oh, no reason.' These days Maddie felt like she had permanent alarm bells going off in her head. 'It's nice to hear from you. How are you?'

'I'm fine, thanks. But I just remembered something and

thought I'd better tell you before I forgot it again. You know what I'm like. I've got a brain like a sieve. It's one of the penalties of old age, my dear – thoughts come along and they're there one minute and gone the next.'

'Don't worry about it. What was it you wanted to tell me?'

'It's about Lucy Rivers,' Agnes said. 'I don't suppose it matters, but I suddenly recalled what that man's name was. It just jumped into my head while I was making a brew.'

'Vasser, wasn't it?'

'No, no, dear, that's the thing. I thought it might have been, but it wasn't – it wasn't at all. His name was Owen Vickery. It was the "V" that confused me, you see. I knew it began with that. But yes, it was definitely Vickery.'

Maddie frowned, confused by this latest twist. She'd been convinced that Brendan Vasser had been involved in some way with Lucy Rivers. 'And who was he, this Owen Vickery?'

'No one special, dear – that's the tragedy. He used to be the manager at the cemetery. We're talking way back now, thirty years or so. That's how Lucy met him. Her mother had recently died and she used to spend a lot of time at the grave. The poor girl was heartbroken and Vickery gave her a shoulder to cry on. One thing led to another and . . . well, you know the rest.'

'Right,' Maddie murmured.

'Hello?'

'Yes, sorry, I'm still here. Thanks, Agnes. Thanks for letting me know.' Maddie said her goodbyes and hung up. She stood staring along the road for a while, wondering what it all meant. 'Vickery,' she said, rolling the name across her tongue. So the married man who'd betrayed Lucy Rivers and driven her to suicide hadn't been Brendan Vasser at all. Now she was completely in the dark as to why Lena Gissing had such a thing about the girl's grave. What was it? What could it be? The only fact she did know for sure was that Delia had been in on the secret too.

Maddie gave a sigh and continued on her way. She was almost at Marigolds when her phone gave off its little jingle indicating that a text message had come in. Reaching into her pocket again, she took out the mobile and checked the inbox. The message was from Solomon. *Meet me at the LR grave. Urgent. I've got news!* She stared at the words, bemused. What was going on, and why hadn't he just called her? She tried ringing him back, but the phone went directly to voicemail. Whatever it was, he clearly wanted to tell her in person.

She glanced towards the entrance to the garden centre and then down at her watch. Talk about bad timing; she'd been passing the cemetery gates five minutes ago and now she'd have to double back, which would mean her being late for work. She dithered for a moment, wondering what to do. What could be so urgent that Solomon had to see her straight away? And why did he want to meet at the grave? It must be to do with Greta and Bo. It had to be. Maddie didn't hesitate for long. She turned and quickly headed back towards the cemetery.

As she walked, she made a call to the manager at Marigolds claiming that Zac had been taken ill and she had to go and pick him up from summer school. It was the best excuse she could think of off the top of her head. She held the phone slightly away from her ear so that he could hear the sound of the traffic and know that she wasn't sitting at home. 'I shouldn't be more than half an hour. I just have to make sure he's okay and then drop him off at his grandparents' house. I'll make the time up, I promise.'

The manager hadn't sounded pleased, but there was nothing she could do about that. Hopefully, he wouldn't sack her for it. That would be the last thing she needed, to lose this job too. She stepped up the pace, breaking into a jog. The sooner she met up with Solomon, the sooner she could get back to work.

There was no one else on the main thoroughfare as Maddie

half walked, half ran to the group of willow trees. She kept her eyes peeled for Rick, but he was still nowhere to be seen. Quickly she veered left, turning on to the narrower path that led to the older part of the cemetery. She hurried through the long grass and the weeds, sweeping aside the buddleia as she went. Her breathing was coming faster now, a product of her exertion and her expectation.

As the path wound round, she felt an extra frisson of excitement, sure that the summons heralded a major breakthrough. Whatever Solomon had found out, it had to be important. He was so big that she kept expecting to see him at any second, his huge figure looming on the horizon, but as she approached the grave, she saw that he wasn't there.

She looked all around as if he might suddenly appear from behind a tree or one of the tall stone angels with their hands clasped in prayer. 'Sol!' she called out as loudly as she dared in the quiet of her surroundings.

There was no reply.

Maddie got out her phone and tried his number again, but only got the same voicemail response. Where was he? And then it occurred to her that she had got here faster than he'd expected and he was probably still on his way. He couldn't have known how close she was to the cemetery when he'd sent the text. She considered walking back to the thoroughfare, but decided that it was better to stay where she was. She had no idea which of the two entrances he would use, and if he went off the main path, they could easily miss each other.

Frustrated, but resigned to a wait, she turned her attention to Lucy's grave. The Lady of Shallot roses were still in reasonable condition, the cup-shaped heads a soft orange-gold. She rearranged them slightly just for something to do. She thought about Lucy and the man who had betrayed her. She thought about Rick. There was always a risk to falling in love. Did she dare take a chance? Weighed against all the good stuff – the joy and the sharing – was the gaping hole left in your life when it was all over.

Five minutes later, when Solomon had still not shown up, she began to pace impatiently around the grave. When this didn't help, she went to the start of the almost invisible path and peered between the bushes at the small ivy-clad building that housed the remains of the long-dead Belvederes. She'd seen the mausoleum many times before, but today there was something different about it. Or was the light just playing tricks on her?

Frowning, she walked a little closer, leaving behind the sunshine and passing into the gloom cast by the overhanging trees. As she approached, she was aware of the sound of her own breathing, of her heartbeat beginning to accelerate. Her eyes were focused on the door and she could see a deep shadow running along the right-hand side. It was slightly open. She was sure it was. Maybe Eli Glass was doing one of his routine checks. Wasn't that what Rick had said? That Eli sometimes checked the mausoleums for damage.

'Hello?'

Her voice sounded small and tentative. She looked all around before advancing, overly aware of the stillness around her and the soft tread of her feet against the damp earth. Here, where the sun barely penetrated, the weekend rain still lay in pools. She skirted round the puddles, her ears alert to any sound that might indicate the presence of another.

Nothing.

'Hello?' she said again, stopping right outside the door. Now she could see it clearly, could see for sure that it was slightly ajar. Was there someone inside? Someone, that was, apart from the dead. She thought of the coffins, of what they contained, and gave an involuntary shudder. Maybe Eli had forgotten to lock up when he left.

For a while she just stood there, uncertain of what to do next. She was torn between curiosity and restraint. Half of her wanted to peek inside, but the other half told her not to. What she *should* do was go back to the grave and wait for Solomon. But already her hand, as if it had independently made a decision, was moving forward. Her fingertips pressed gently against the old heavy metal and slowly the door began to swing back.

It was then, as the hinge gave an ominous creak, that she sensed rather than heard the movement behind her. She half turned, but already it was too late. There was time only for a fleeting impression, a glimpse of a face, a silvery flash, before the pain cut through her skull. The force of the blow propelled her over the threshold and sent her stumbling into the heart of the mausoleum. In agony, she crumpled to her knees, her desperate cry eclipsed by an even louder, deadlier and more terrifying sound. The door was slammed shut behind her and the key turned in the lock.

43

Maddie was engulfed by blind panic, by an overwhelming terror, as she crawled on her hands and knees. Her head was throbbing, blood pouring down the back of her neck. Scrabbling about in the pitch black, she wildly stretched out her hands, feeling for the door. Where was it? Oh God. Please, God! The blow had left her dazed and disoriented. When her fingers touched dry brick, she shifted to the left, but no, that wasn't the right way. She lurched back to the right and eventually found the smooth metal panels.

Her breath came in fast, frantic pants as she hauled herself to her feet, her legs barely taking the weight of her body. With what remained of her strength, she hammered on the door with her fists.

'Help me! Let me out! Let me out!'

But there was no sound from the other side.

'Let me out!'

Bile rose into her throat as she continued to thump and yell, the sounds echoing around the small, dark chamber. She could feel the strength ebbing from her and began to shake, an icy fear twisting round her heart. Slowly her cries grew weaker, her hammering less intense, until her knees gave way and she slumped to the ground.

There was nobody there. She was on her own. Her attacker had trapped and abandoned her. Would he come back? No, she thought, her stomach churning. At least not until he was sure that she was ... But she couldn't think like that. She mustn't give up. Maybe someone else would find her. Eli or Rick? She clutched at this straw as she wrapped her arms tightly round her legs and peered into the thick black darkness.

The pain in the back of her head was getting worse, a violent throbbing ache. Tentatively she raised a hand to touch the perimeter of the wound. The flesh of her scalp felt soft and pulpy. How bad was it? By turning when she had, she had escaped the full force of the blow, but the edge of the spade had still caused some major damage. What if the blood was clotting in her brain? Already she was feeling weak and dizzy, as if the life was slowly leaking out of her.

Spurred on by fear and desperation, she forced herself back on to her feet again. For a moment she thought she was going to throw up. Her guts shifted, the taste of vomit rising into her mouth. Deep breaths. In and out. In and out. Until finally the nausea had passed. Her hands made a quick search of the door, looking for a handle, but of course there wasn't one. The people in this chamber had no need of a handle. She tried not to think of the six bodies in their coffins, or what was left of them.

The darkness was like a thick suffocating blanket wrapping itself around her. The only minuscule spot of light came from the keyhole. She crouched down and peered through the tiny gap. All she could see was the green foliage of a rhododendron.

Putting her mouth to the hole, she begged again, 'Help me! Help me! Let me out!' But her voice was thin and hoarse, not strong enough to carry more than a few yards.

She slumped back down to the ground. All she could do was wait and hope. If she stayed by the door, she would hear the footsteps if someone came down by here. But who would come? This was the old neglected part of the cemetery, rarely visited by anyone but herself.

What were the chances of Eli or Rick passing by? Slim, she thought.

The worst-case scenario began to spin through her mind again. No one would realise she was missing until this evening when she didn't turn up at Alisha's. And even then they wouldn't think to look for her here. Why would they? Nobody had seen her come into the cemetery. She had lied to the manager at Marigolds, told him she was going to pick up Zac. But Solomon would know, she suddenly thought. Her hopes soared for a second. He must be waiting for her, wondering where she was. Wouldn't he start to look around, maybe call out her name? Except . . . Her spirits instantly plunged again. Wasn't it Solomon who had lured her here in the first place? He hadn't been the one to attack her – she hadn't recognised the man who had – but he had sent the text.

But why would Solomon want to hurt her? It didn't make sense, unless . . . unless what? Maybe she had found out something that he didn't want her to know. Maybe he was working with Vasser himself. Was that possible? Christ, no. Her head was just playing tricks. Not Solomon. He wouldn't do this. Unless . . .

As she pondered on the message, her heart skipped a beat. Jesus, what was the matter with her? Her phone, her bloody phone! It was in her bag, but where was her bag? It must have slipped from her shoulder as she'd fallen forward into the mausoleum. Getting back on to her hands and knees, she began to feel her way across the dusty floor. She prayed that it hadn't landed outside. 'Please, God,' she murmured again.

The sheer density of the darkness was frightening. It was like being totally blind without even the vaguest of outlines. No colour, no contrasts, only a vast impenetrable blackness. As she flailed around, the panic began to rise in her again. Where was it? The space wasn't that big. If her bag was here, she should be able to find it. Old cobwebs brushed against her face and got into her hair as she searched by the wall. Shuddering, she tried to claw them away, but that only made it worse. The soft threads wound their way between her fingers, a vile sticky web that she couldn't escape. And then, suddenly, just when she thought it was hopeless, her hand touched on the soft leather of her bag.

'Thank you, thank you,' she muttered as she ripped open the zip and plunged her hand inside. Never, in her entire life, had she been so grateful to feel that small oblong of metal. It was her lifeline, her means of escape, her salvation. Now she could make a call and get out of here. Her fingers fumbled for the buttons and eventually the screen lit up, casting a pale blue glow. Yes! She punched in '999' and raised the phone to her ear.

Nothing.

What?

She shifted the phone back in front of her eyes and stared at the corner of the screen. Her heart plummeted. No reception. No bloody connection to the outside world. She gave it an angry shake as if sheer fury and frustration could make it change its mind. But no, either the walls of the old mausoleum were too thick, too solid, to let her gain access to a signal or she was sitting in a signal black spot.

'Shit!' she protested, moving the phone to the left and the

right. This couldn't be happening. It couldn't. Tears of frustration rose to her eyes. 'Don't do this to me.' She shook the phone again, but it made no difference. 'Come on. Please, please, please!'

The light flicked off, plunging her into darkness. She jabbed at the button to get it back. How long would her battery last? She wasn't sure. What to do next? She was starting to get cold, her teeth chattering. Bone-wrenching tremors shook every part of her body. She wondered if it was down to the temperature of the building or because she was losing too much blood.

Raising the knuckles of her right hand to her mouth, she sucked on them. They were sore, the skin broken from pounding against the door. What she needed was something hard, something metallic, with which to make a noise. She didn't want to use the phone; it would probably break and she would lose her only source of light. Maybe if she searched the mausoleum, she could find an implement that would be more suitable. But that would mean scrabbling about around the coffins. She had been trying not to think about those six bodies laid out in their boxes. It creeped her out, made the hairs on her arms stand on end. But not bodies now, she reminded herself, just skeletons. This thought didn't help much – skulls with empty eye sockets, old bones, flesh rotted away. She swallowed hard, almost expecting to hear the creak of a lid slowly opening. *It's not the living dead you need to watch out for.* Hadn't Rick said that? It felt like a long time ago.

Taking it slowly, she managed to get to her feet. Almost immediately she felt dizzy, faint, as if she was about to pass out. Crouching back down on the floor, she put her head between her knees and waited for the feeling to pass. Then she tried again. Carefully she heaved herself into an upright position. Then, using the glow from the phone, she made her way over to the right-hand side of the room.

There were three coffins here, one on top of each other, but each with their own shelf. She wondered if one of them was Harold's. Harold James Belvedere, who had been wounded at the Somme. Harold, who had only been twenty-two when his life had ended. Had they called him Harry? As her fingers reached out to pat along the length of the middle coffin, she tried to focus on this man she had never known in the hope that it would keep at bay her sense of revulsion at what lay inside the box.

There was a thick layer of dust everywhere. Her hand touched one of the heavy brass handles and she gave it a tug. It was firmly attached. No matter how hard she pulled, she couldn't wrench it out. She moved along, trying the second handle. That was the same. She wasn't strong enough to shift it. Beads of sweat were gathering on her forehead, while her heart thumped like a jackhammer in her chest.

Eventually, too exhausted to continue, she gave up. She should have stayed by the door. She had to get back there, to listen out, to wait until someone passed by. But first she had to rest for a moment. Shuffling to the side of the coffin, she leaned back against the wall, trying to catch her breath. Her legs felt weak and shaky. Slowly she slid back down to the ground.

'Move,' she murmured as sleep tried to possess her. 'Stay awake. You have to stay awake.'

But her limbs, heavy as lead, refused to respond. She was going down, sinking into mud.

Her last thought before she slipped into unconsciousness was that she was going to die here, entombed, alone. It could be weeks, months, maybe even years before anyone found her body. How often did Eli check these buildings? She had no idea. And Zac – poor Zac would think she had abandoned him. She struggled to keep her eyes open, but it was no use. With a sigh, she gave herself up to the darkness.

44

Eli Glass gazed into the back of the truck. 'Spade's gone,' he said, scratching his head. 'When did that happen?'

'Huh?' said Rick, his eyes glued to his phone.

'The spade. Someone's nicked my bloody spade.'

'Kids, probably. It'll turn up.'

'Better had.' Eli thought about what Delia would say if it didn't, forgetting for a moment that Delia Shields would never be providing another lecture on leaving tools unattended. She would never be complaining about anything again. He took no pleasure in her death, but felt no grief at it either. She had been a difficult, unsympathetic woman.

Rick continued to press buttons, a frown gathering on his forehead. 'I don't get it. Why isn't she replying? It's been hours. She must have got my messages by now.'

Eli gave a shrug. His knowledge of mobile phones was about as slim as his knowledge of relationships. Feeling in no position to offer useful advice on either, he took his tobacco from his pocket and began to roll a fag.

'Maybe I should call her at work. Do you think? Perhaps she hasn't got her phone with her.'

Eli rolled the tobacco into a skinny cylinder, ran his tongue along the thin paper, sealed it, put the fag in his mouth, struck a match, lit up and inhaled. Only then did he answer. 'Urgent, is it?'

'Adam Vasser's been released. And so has Lena Gissing. Maddie doesn't know. She thinks they're still banged up.'

Eli stared at him. He presumed Rick was talking about the girl with the long brown hair, the one who tended the graves. There was something going on between them, although he didn't know the ins and outs. All he did know was that Rick made a habit of bumping into her every time she came to the cemetery. 'I saw him, that Vasser. He was here this morning.'

'What? He was here?'

'Just said so, didn't I? He was over by his old man's grave.'

'Rick's eyes flashed with worry. 'When, exactly? What time?'

Eli pulled on his fag and gazed down at his boots. He thought back over his movements. It was after he'd cleared up that mess by the gates, so it must have been when he was emptying the bins. He glanced up again and gave a nod. 'About half nine, quarter to ten.'

Rick hesitated for a second and then punched in a number on his phone. 'Yeah. Can you give me the number for Marigolds, please? It's a garden centre in Kellston, East London.' There was a short pause and then he said, 'Yeah, put me straight through.'

Eli was beginning to feel uneasy. Some of it was down to Rick's anxiety, but there was another reason too. A thin, sad whispering was blowing through the graveyard. He walked away, inclining his head as he tried to make out the words. They drifted past him, through him, a kind of lamentation. He gazed out across the endless headstones of granite and marble. 'What is it?' he murmured, straining his ears to hear.

'Shit!' Rick said from behind him. 'Shit, shit, shit!'

Eli turned. 'What's wrong?'

'She hasn't turned up for work. She rang them apparently, just before ten, said she'd be late, but they haven't heard from her since.' Even as he was talking he was busy dialling again. 'Yeah, hello. Can you put me through to DI Middleton, please?'

And Eli knew, instinctively, that Rick was right to worry. He started to pace up and down, catching only snatches of the conversation.

'And can you send someone over to her place? I've tried the landline, but she's not picking up ... Yeah, Vasser, he was here this morning ... She doesn't know yet ... '

Eli looked up at the sky. He could tell from the position of the sun that it was almost one o'clock. If the girl was genuinely missing, then she'd been gone for over three hours. That wasn't good. A knot was beginning to form in his stomach. Had she come here this morning? He hadn't seen her, but that didn't mean anything. She could have easily turned off the main thoroughfare, taken one of the narrower paths or cut across the grass.

Rick hung up. He looked wildly around the cemetery as if she might suddenly appear. Then he turned his attention back to Eli. 'Did you see where Vasser went? Did you see him leave?'

'No.'

'Are you sure? Think about it, Eli.'

'I was clearing the bins. One minute he was there, the next ... ' Eli gave a shrug. 'You want me to help you look for her?'

'Look where?' Rick raked his fingers impatiently through his hair. 'She can't be here. Why would she be? She does the graves on a Wednesday, not a Tuesday. No, that fuckin' Vasser's got her. He must have. Christ!'

Eli began walking away.

'Where are you going?' Rick called after him.

'To check the graves, see if there are any fresh flowers.'

'I've already told you. She doesn't—'

Eli stopped and looked over his shoulder. 'You got a better idea?'

Rick screwed up his face, bouncing his fists off his thighs in frustration. For a moment, he seemed in two minds, but then he gave a sigh and jogged up the thoroughfare to join him. They checked the closest ones first, Alfie Reach and Annie Patterson, but it was clear that they hadn't been attended to that day. 'This is a waste of time.'

'Let's try over the west side.'

Rick shook his head. 'She's not doing that grave any more.'

'No harm in looking.' Eli strode on, determined and purposeful. The sun was shining, but he had a chill in his bones. Was this the time? He had always known that it would come eventually. The past was forever snapping at his heels, waiting for the right moment. Fate, destiny, whatever you chose to call it, was as unavoidable as death.

Eli's heavy boots squashed down the long grass and the weeds as he marched on. He was leaving the voices behind now; they were receding, growing fainter and fainter. The silence echoed in his ears. It was a silence waiting to be filled. Perhaps today, after all these years, *she* would finally talk to him.

The two men didn't speak again until they got to the end of the narrow path and were standing by Lucy Rivers's grave. Rick gazed down at the roses, their petals starting to curl a little in the sun. He checked out the ground, but the heat had dried out the soil, leaving nothing but dusty earth. A hissing noise slipped from between his teeth. 'She's not been here.'

Eli stared hard at the white marble headstone. He ran his palm along the smooth curved upper edge. 'I'm not so sure.'

'Those roses have been here all week.'

Eli frowned, cocked his head and put a finger to his lips. 'Do you hear that?'

Rick listened, but all he could hear was the thin breeze rustling through the trees. 'What? What am I listening to?'

'It's Lucy,' Eli said softly.

'Christ, Eli, I haven't got time for this shit! Lucy's dead and buried. She's not saying anything.'

But a strange, almost beatific smile had appeared on Eli's face. He gave a nod, his lips moving, although no sound coming out. His hand still gripped the headstone as if his fingers had become moulded to it. Forgiveness, that was all he was asking for. All these years he'd waited and now, finally . . .

Angrily Rick stormed off along the path. 'Crazy, fuckin' crazy!' he muttered. 'You think I need this now?' He brushed aside the buddleia, not knowing where he was going, not caring, just wanting to get away from the madness. He dived down into the gloom, feeling the chill as he left the sunshine behind. It was only as his eyes fell on the small brick building that it occurred to him. God, why hadn't he thought of it before? How could he have been so stupid? Quickly he scoured the muddy ground. Yes, there were footprints, two lots of prints, but there was no way of knowing if they'd been left here today.

'Eli!' he yelled. 'Here! Get down here!'

Rick ran to the door and tried the handle. Locked. Of course it was locked. He rattled the handle. 'Maddie? Maddie, are you in there?' He pressed his ear against the metal and listened. There was no sound coming from inside. He got down and tried to peer through the keyhole, but all he could see was darkness. Scrambling back to his feet, he placed his shoulder against the door and pushed. It didn't move.

There wasn't time to wait around for the key. He had to get in. He had to get in now. He ran back as far as he could, took a deep breath, sprinted back to the door and launched himself against it. He heard the splintering of wood as the frame gave way, felt the shudder and the give, the final submission as he plunged into the sour-smelling air of the mausoleum.

45

DI Valerie Middleton stood by the mausoleum, watching as the officers brought out the crates one by one and laid them on the grass. She was still irked by the fact that she'd been kept out of the loop. A major undercover op right on her patch and no one had seen fit to let her know. It was only yesterday, after the discovery of the murder of Delia Shields, when she'd finally been informed of what was going on.

And now they might have another death on their hands. Would the girl live? It was touch and go. She'd been in a bad way when the ambulance arrived, barely conscious and hardly breathing. The wound to her head was a nasty one. Add in the trauma of being locked in the pitch black with no one but the dead for company and God alone knew what the outcome would be.

Valerie turned her attention back to the crates. There was a veritable armoury here: sawn-off shotguns, automatic revolvers, machetes, knives. She wouldn't have been surprised to find a few grenades thrown in too. Adam Vasser had clearly been planning a war. As well as the weapons, there was a large supply of drugs, mainly cocaine, ecstasy and weed.

That question rose into her mind again: why the hell hadn't anyone told her? It was over three months since the stash had first been discovered by the manager of the cemetery, Bob Cannon. On noticing that the key to the Belvedere mausoleum was missing, he'd gone to check on the building, had suspicions that it might have been interfered with and called out a locksmith. Then, after finding what was inside, Cannon had made a direct call to his old mate Superintendent Saul Redding.

Valerie made a tutting sound with her tongue. It was typical of Redding to go behind her back and launch an undercover surveillance without so much as tipping her the wink. It had been decided that rather than removing the stash, they'd wait until someone came to pick it up. The Streets had been the primary suspects – Terry Street spent a lot of time in the cemetery these days – but they'd been barking up the wrong tree. It was Adam Vasser who'd been using the mausoleum as his own personal lock-up. As yet her evidence for this was purely circumstantial – Maddie Layne had been in no fit state to identify him as her attacker – but she was pretty sure they'd find his fingerprints all over the place.

There was already a warrant out for his arrest and it wouldn't take them long to pick him up. It had been bad timing when they'd let him go this morning. A couple of hours later, the computer had flagged up a match for the blood they'd found on his white shirt: not Delia Shields's, but a rent boy's in Soho who'd been beaten half to death.

Valerie raised her head as she heard a slight commotion coming from the inside of the mausoleum. A few seconds later, Swann emerged from the building. 'Well, we're falling over corpses today.'

Valerie stared at him. 'This is a cemetery, you know.'

Swann gave her a grin. 'Yeah, but this resting place is holding a few surprises. They've been opening the coffins to make sure there's nothing inside them that shouldn't be there. And guess what? Six coffins, seven bodies. So unless the Belvederes were trying to save a few bob, I reckon we've got one spare.'

She took a moment to recover from the shock. 'Recent?'

Swann shook his head. 'Nah, this one's been there for a while. Not a hundred years, though. We're looking at twenty or thirty at the most.'

46

Maddie squinted like a newborn baby. The light, hot and blinding, burned into her eyes. There was a babble of voices, noise, activity, a clattering sound in the background. Why couldn't they be quiet? Didn't they know she was trying to sleep? She'd been dreaming of Greta: the two of them walking on the beach as kids, their toes sinking into the sand, the sea rushing up and swirling about their ankles.

A sheet was laid over and around her, tight like a shroud. Was she dead? An antiseptic kind of smell. Memory came to her in flashes, disjointed images like a flickering reel of old black-and-white film: the blue glow of her mobile phone, the dense, impenetrable darkness, the thick metal of the mausoleum door. She was lying down. There was a pain in her head. She was being lifted, carried. She heard the name, David. She didn't know anyone called David.

She grasped at reality, but it slipped through her fingers. Her knuckles hurt. Eli was standing by Lucy Rivers's grave, his face raised to the sky, tears streaming down his cheeks. Why was he crying? She was floating, sinking, rising. Greta was here. Yes, she was. Leaning over, smiling, laughing, her face drawing close to whisper in her ear. But she couldn't hear what she was saying. She couldn't hear because of all the noise.

It was over a week, seven hazy days and nights, before Maddie was out of intensive care and able to start making sense of what had happened. Even then the pieces of the jigsaw didn't quite fit together. Rick came and went, feeding her bite-sized portions of information: Adam Vasser arrested ... guns and drugs ... a police stakeout ... an extra body in a coffin. The words settled around her but didn't quite sink in.

Time passed. She lay back and listened to the sounds of the hospital: the creak of wheels, footsteps on lino, a telephone ringing, the hum and beep of the machines. Alisha and Winston brought homemade soup and news of Zac. Shauna dropped by with magazines and gossip, their differences forgotten in the face of a crisis. Solomon sat on the edge of the bed and sighed. 'Hell, babe, you're the only person I know who can turn grave-tending into a dangerous occupation.'

It was on the Saturday that everything changed. Rick was sitting by her, talking again about the police surveillance on the cemetery. 'Because of the missing key, they thought someone who worked there might be involved. That's why it was all hush-hush. Even Delia Shields didn't know about it.'

'And the body?' she asked. 'The other one. Have they found out who it was yet?'

'Still trawling through the missing persons list. You'd be surprised how many people go AWOL, just walk out of the door and disappear.'

'The cigarette ends at the mausoleum,' she said, not sure why she had suddenly remembered them. Her thoughts seemed to be leaping around like jumping beans. 'Did Vasser leave them there?'

'Or one of his cohorts. He must have had help shifting all that gear. Maybe one of Tony Gissing's boys. We reckon they did some of it at night, came over the wall of one of the houses. But they probably dropped by during the day too.'

She thought of Vasser lurking in the bushes, watching and waiting. The idea wasn't pleasant. By tending Lucy Rivers's grave, she had inadvertently got a little too close to his hiding place. And then, while she was pondering on this, her thoughts shot off in another direction. 'Did you ever suspect anything? About the cops, I mean. Although, I suppose people are always wandering around the cemetery.'

He gave her an odd look. 'What?'

Maddie managed a weak smile as her hand automatically rose to her bandaged skull. 'I'm missing something, huh? Sorry – my brain is still mashed.' And then, out of nowhere, the penny finally dropped. Her eyes widened as the truth hit her. 'You said "we" just then, when you were talking about Vasser. You said "we reckon". Oh my God, you're a cop, aren't you? You were part of the operation.'

Rick gave a reluctant nod. 'Yes. I came down from Manchester. They needed someone who the locals wouldn't recognise. It was a big job, a chance to nail the Street family once and for all – except it didn't quite work out like that.' He took her hand and squeezed it. 'I'm sorry. I didn't ... I didn't mean to deceive you. But I couldn't say. You do understand that, don't you?'

She frowned, still trying to absorb the revelation. And then, with a jolt, she realised that she had fallen in love with someone she didn't know at all. A dark, sick feeling grew in the pit of her stomach. 'Is your name even Rick?'

'It's David,' he said. 'David Hampson.'

'David,' she repeated, testing the name on her tongue and feeling its oddness. Her mind flipped back through the past few months, trying to pick up on any clue, any hint, anything that might have given her reason to doubt him. But there was nothing. He had played the part of the genial gravedigger to perfection.

'I'm sorry,' he said again. 'I know it must be a surprise, a shock. But the two of us, you and me, none of that was a lie. I never meant for it to happen, but . . .'

'But it did.' She stared at him, struggling to find a way to accept, to move beyond, but her emotions were in turmoil. Who was this man? What did she actually know about him? 'You'll be telling me you've got a wife and kids next.'

She had meant it as a joke, but instantly his gaze slid away from her, his face full of guilt. Her heart sank. Just when she'd thought it couldn't get any worse . . . Quickly she snatched her hand away. 'You bastard! Get out of here. Get out of here now.'

'Maddie, I'm sorry. I'm really sorry. I didn't—'

'I don't want to hear it.' She turned her head away from him. 'Leave me alone. Go away. Fuck off and don't ever come back.'

Slowly he rose to his feet. She listened to his footsteps cross the room, heard the door open and close again. And then there was silence. What now? Tears rose to her eyes, but she blinked them away. She couldn't afford to give in to self-pity; if she started crying now, she might never stop. She had taken a chance and it hadn't paid off. Love had slipped through her fingers again.

Maddie stared hard at a thin, jagged crack running up the wall. She had to hold herself together, refuse to fall apart. She had to find a way to carry on. Terrible things had happened – too many of them – but she was still living, still breathing. Damaged, perhaps, but not destroyed. She was, if nothing else, a survivor.

Epilogue

The inside of the dark blue Mercedes smelled of leather and the musky scent of aftershave. Maddie stared out through the windscreen, gathering her thoughts for what was to come. It was almost a month now since she'd escaped death by the skin of her teeth and gradually life was returning to normal. Soon it would be autumn and the leaves would start to fall. Things carried on. The world kept turning.

Solomon drove his boss's car with an easy nonchalance, his right elbow leaning on the base of the open window. 'Any particular reason why you want to see this guy again?'

'Loose ends,' she said.

'Ah, those. Tricky things, loose ends.'

'They can be. And thanks for the lift. I really appreciate it.'

'No problem.'

'Chris Street didn't mind you borrowing the car?'

'He was the one who suggested it. Reckoned it was the least he could do. If it hadn't been for what happened to you, Vasser could have caused him a whole heap of grief. There was a goddamn arsenal stashed in that mausoleum. Man was planning some major warfare. Wouldn't have been pretty, I can tell you.'

'Well,' she said dryly, 'glad to be of help.'

Solomon grinned at her. 'Try and say it with feeling, girl. I know you ain't got much time for the Streets, but there's worse people could be running this manor. Chris may have his faults, but he ain't no psychopath.'

Thinking of Adam Vasser made Maddie shudder. She still had flashbacks to her time in the mausoleum, sudden panic attacks that left her feeling weak and helpless. She was scrabbling about in the dark again, blindly feeling her way across the dusty concrete, hammering on the door until her knuckles bled ... 'It's weird to think of all those guns in there. If I'd found them, I could have tried to blast my way out.'

'Maybe it's better that you didn't.'

'How do you figure that one out?'

Solomon's fingers beat out a rhythm on the steering wheel. 'Big, thick metal door, small space – those bullets would have been bouncing all over the place. One bad ricochet and you'd have been brown bread, hon. They'd have been scraping you up off the floor.'

Maddie hadn't considered that. 'Ah,' she said. 'Yes, that could have been something of a suicide mission.'

'Mind, if that tart hadn't stolen my phone, you'd never have been there in the first place.'

'Louise?'

'Yeah, the lovely Louise. I knew there was something dodgy about her.'

Maddie remembered the time she'd seen them together at Adriano's. 'How come?'

Solomon heaved out a breath, his mouth turning down at the corners. 'Now, I know I'm a catch, right? Ain't no denying it.

But that girl was all over me like a rash. A bit *too* keen, if you get what I mean.'

She raised her eyebrows. 'But you still slept with her?'

'Been rude not to. The girl went to a lot of effort.'

'The perfect gentleman.'

'Can't argue with that,' he said.

'So have the police charged her with anything?'

'Aiding and abetting, but she'll walk. Daddy's got her the best lawyers that money can buy. They'll claim that Vasser forced her, threatened her. They'll play the drug-addiction card and say she didn't know what she was doing. She'll go to rehab for a few months and that'll be it.' He gave a disapproving shake of his head. 'Ain't right, but that's the way it is.'

Maddie thought it ironic, even amusing, that Solomon was bemoaning Louise's lack of punishment when he worked for a family of criminals himself. She turned her head, glancing out of the side window, so he wouldn't notice the smile playing around her lips. 'I guess we both made a few mistakes on the romance front.'

Solomon released a thin whistle from between his teeth. 'You ain't wrong there, babe. Reckon you get first prize, though. An undercover cop. Shit, that was a turn-up for the books.'

'A married undercover cop,' she said.

Solomon pulled a face. 'Yeah, that don't help none.'

'I'll get over it.' She said the words with more bravado than she felt. In truth, she was still aching from the deception, still feeling completely and utterly betrayed. Sometimes she wondered if any of it had been real. She suspected now that Rick – she still couldn't get used to calling him David – had only befriended her in the first place because she was tending a grave that was close to the Belvedere mausoleum. Maybe he'd thought that she was involved in some way, using her job as a cover while she helped to stash the guns and drugs in the small brick building.

She gazed out of the window, trying to focus on the streets and the shops and the people, anything other than Rick Mallory. But she couldn't shift him from her mind. She liked to think that he'd had some genuine affection for her, that she hadn't just been used, but there was no way of knowing for sure. Love was a gamble, and on this occasion she'd drawn the joker.

Solomon gave her a glance. 'Next time we'd best be more careful, huh?'

'Are you kidding? There isn't going to be a next time. I'm sworn to celibacy for the rest of my life.'

'That's a long time, babe. Sure you want to make that kind of commitment?'

'Absolutely sure.'

They were quiet for a while with no other sound in the car than the soft, gentle purr of the engine. The miles slipped by, the districts merging, and within five minutes they were approaching their destination. Maddie felt her stomach tighten. She needed answers, but would she get them? There was only one way to find out.

Solomon pulled up the Mercedes beside the high grey wall. 'Still time to change your mind,' he said. 'We can turn round and go back home.'

'No, I want to see him. I have to.'

'Okay.'

'I won't be long.'

'Ain't no rush, hon. Take as long as you need.'

Maddie sat for a while, getting her thoughts in order. Then she took a deep breath, got out of the car, shut the door and walked through the gates of HMP Thornley Heath.

DI Valerie Middleton flicked through the slim folder as Swann did the driving. It had taken a while, but they'd finally identified the body sharing coffin space in the mausoleum. Owen Vickery had disappeared twenty-eight years ago, left the house one day and never come back. His wife had reported him as missing, but hadn't suspected foul play. Vickery, a former manager of Kellston Cemetery, had been a less-than-perfect husband, having indulged in a string of affairs during the eight years he'd been married. The last one had involved a young girl called Lucy Rivers, who had probably taken her own life.

'Not going to be easy after all this time,' Swann said. 'Whoever did it could be long dead.'

Valerie flicked through the report. 'A blow to the side of the head with a blunt heavy object. Not much to go on. I wonder what he was even doing at the cemetery; he'd resigned from the job a couple of years earlier and moved away from the area. The wife says he didn't have relatives buried there.'

'What do you reckon to her? A woman scorned and all that. Maybe she decided she'd had enough.'

Valerie thought back to their interview yesterday with Sandra Vickery. She'd seemed surprised but not especially upset by the news. She'd identified the St Christopher found round the neck of their mystery skeleton, and the white-gold wedding ring that was still attached to what remained of the third finger of the left hand. 'I don't think so. For starters, how would she have got access to the mausoleum? And even if she had, she's not a big woman. I can't see her being able to drag a body into the building, force open a coffin and then lift him into it.'

'Perhaps she had help.'

'Perhaps.'

As Swann parked the Peugeot, Valerie put the file back into her briefcase. She had the feeling that this might be one of those murders that they never got to the bottom of. Cases like these were notoriously hard to solve, but that wouldn't stop her trying. For the time being, though, she had other things on her mind.

She slid off her seatbelt and opened the door. 'Here we go again.'

'You think he's wasting our time?'

'Well, we'll soon find out.'

They walked together to the reception area, showed their ID and a few minutes later were led through the corridors to their first appointment of the day.

Valerie crossed her legs and stared hard at the man opposite her. She felt like she spent more time than was strictly healthy sitting in small, stuffy rooms while she listened to one lowlife or another feeding her a pack of lies. Today the room was in Wormwood Scrubs and the lowlife was Adam Vasser. He was currently on remand, awaiting trial for the attempted murders of Lewis Hale and Maddie Layne. There was little doubt in her mind that he had also been responsible for the killing of Delia Shields, but as yet they didn't have sufficient evidence to charge him.

'So, Adam,' she said, 'what can we do for you?'

Vasser leaned forward, laying his forearms on the table. 'I'd say it's more the other way round. I've got some information. Two unsolved murders: Bo Vale and Greta Layne. Ring any bells?'

Valerie pricked up her ears but kept her expression neutral. It was over six years now since Bo Vale had been found floating in the Thames. The body of his girlfriend, Greta – Maddie Layne's sister – had sunk without trace. They'd come up against a brick wall in the investigation and the case was still open. 'What about them?'

'Maybe I know who wasted them.'

Valerie waited, but he didn't go on. 'And?'

'And nothing,' Vasser said. 'I'm not saying more until I get some guarantees.'

'What kind of guarantees?' DS Swann asked.

Valerie shot him a look. 'We don't do deals.'

Vasser smirked. 'Sure you do, Inspector. You just call it something different, give it a fancy name and pretend it never happened. I mean, you wouldn't be here, would you, unless you were prepared for a little give and take?'

'Perhaps we had nothing better to do,' Swann said dryly. 'There's always that possibility.'

Vasser sat back and folded his arms across his chest.

Swann gave an audible sigh. 'I'm getting bored already. Just spit it out, mate. Tell us what you want.'

Vasser's gaze flicked from one officer to the other, his eyes cold and sly. Eventually, he began to talk again. 'I'm up for attempted murder, right? *Attempted.* And I reckon that's going to be pretty hard to prove.'

'I wouldn't count on it,' Valerie said.

Vasser's eyebrows shifted up. 'You think? Take our rent boy for starters. I go out for a quiet drink and get chatting to a guy at the bar: football, the state of the economy, the usual mundane stuff. The bar's about to close and he says come back and have another bevvy at my place. How am I to know that he's a whore? He makes a move on me and I lose my rag. Yeah, I shouldn't have hit him, but he took me by surprise. I overreacted, but I wasn't trying to kill the geezer.'

'And Maddie Layne?' Valerie asked, not even attempting to disguise the disgust in her voice. 'How do you account for smashing her over the head with a spade and leaving her to die in a pitch-black mausoleum?'

'I didn't hit her that hard. I just panicked when she suddenly showed up. And who said I left her to die? I was going to go back and let her out later. I didn't know how badly hurt she was. I just wanted to teach her a lesson.'

'Some lesson,' Valerie retorted. 'And she didn't just turn up. She was sent a message from a stolen phone to go to the cemetery.'

Vasser shrugged. 'I don't know anything about a nicked phone.'

'No, of course you don't. I'm sure you didn't ask Louise Cole to steal it either.'

'You drop the charges down to GBH and I'll tell you who killed Bo and Greta.'

Valerie knew that with the help of a good barrister, he could twist the truth enough to cast doubt on whether he had actually intended to kill his victims. 'I can't make that decision. It's up to the CPS.'

'So you go and talk to them and let me know.'

For the first time, Valerie saw a flicker of fear in his eyes. Vasser didn't fancy going down for a long stretch. He was only twenty-four and was looking at a life sentence with a minimum of fifteen, maybe even twenty years in the slammer. 'I need names,' she said. 'I need motive. I need to know you're not wasting our time.'

Vasser glared at her across the table. 'Okay,' he said. 'I'll give you a name. And later, if I get what I want, I'll tell you where the weapon's hidden. You can't do anything without that, anyway. Once you've got the gun, you'll be able to match it to the bullet you dug out of Bo Vale's brain.'

'There are still the drug charges, the weapons found—'

Vasser gave a dismissive wave of his hand. 'I can deal with those.'

'So?' Swann asked. 'Who's in the frame?'

Vasser paused, that sly look entering his eyes again. He left a short dramatic pause, glanced down at the table and then up again. 'Tony Gissing,' he said.

Valerie frowned. 'Your stepfather?'

'I don't know any other Tony Gissing. And my mother was in on it too. Bo was dealing for them, but he was ripping them off, taking the piss. Tony doesn't like being taken for a ride and so ...'

'What about Greta Layne?' she asked. 'Why was she killed?'

'Because she knew too much. And it wouldn't have taken her long to figure out who'd done it.'

'But why did Tony keep hold of the gun?' Swann asked. 'Why didn't he get rid of it?'

Vasser sniggered. ''Cause it cost him a fuckin' arm and a leg, and he's a tight bastard. It's a semi-automatic, a Beretta 96 in case you're wondering.' He left another short pause before asking, 'So have we got a deal or not?'

'We'll be in touch,' Valerie said as she rose to her feet.

'When?'

Swann looked down on him. 'What's the rush, mate? It's not as though you're going anywhere.'

Valerie and Swann walked in silence back through the corridors, escorted to the exit by a prison officer. It was only when they were out in the fresh air that they spoke again.

'What do you think?' Swann asked. 'You believe him?'

'Do I think he's telling the whole truth? No. Do I think Adam Vasser is prepared to grass up his own mother if he thinks it might save his arse? You bet. And Lena Gissing's going to be well pissed off when she finds out what he's up to. She might even have some accusations of her own to throw around.' Valerie turned to her sergeant and smiled. 'Do you know what? If we play this smart, we could get the whole damn family banged up.'

This time Maddie knew exactly who she was looking out for as she impatiently drummed her fingers on the Formica-topped table and waited for Jay Cato to appear. The visiting room was much quieter than the last occasion she'd been here, midweek visits clearly not being as popular as the weekend ones. There were hardly any children, for which she was grateful. She didn't want any distractions. Today she needed answers, and she wasn't leaving until she got them.

It was a long ten minutes before the door at the back finally opened and Cato walked in. There was no hesitation this afternoon. He came straight over, pulled out a chair and sat down. He looked tired. His skin was sallow, and there were dark shadows under his eyes. 'How are you?' He searched her face for a moment. 'Or are you sick to death of hearing that question?'

'I'm fine – and yes, I'm pretty sick of it.' She paused and then added, 'But thanks for asking.'

Cato grimaced and raked his fingers through his greying hair. 'I owe you an apology. I should never have got you involved in all this. If I'd known—'

'If you'd known what?' she asked. 'That Lena Gissing was a bitter, vengeful woman? That Adam Vasser was as vicious as his father? Except you did. You knew all that and you were still perfectly happy to stick me right in the middle of your crazy war.'

He briefly raised his hands and then dropped them again. '"Happy" might be too strong a word, but I take your point. And you're right. I haven't got any excuses. I didn't think it through. I just wanted to wind Lena up, get under her skin, make her think about what she'd done to me.'

'No, it was more than that. You wanted to push her buttons and make her react. And she did. Delia Shields is dead, and I ended up with my head caved in.' She left a short silence, sighed and then carried on. 'Anyway, that's not why I'm here.'

'No,' he said. 'I kind of guessed that.'

'I need to know why all this happened, to make some sense of it. Can you do that for me at least?'

'I can do that,' he said, 'although a coffee would help.'

Maddie stood up. 'Black, right?'

'Thank you.'

The queue at the counter was a short one and she was back within a couple of minutes. She pushed one plastic cup of coffee across the table and sipped the other one. Her eyes met his and she gave a nod. 'Whenever you're ready.'

Cato took a deep breath as if preparing himself for an ordeal. 'You want to know about Lucy Rivers, right?'

'I just want to understand.'

'Okay. Well ... where to start?' He glanced around the room as if searching for inspiration. A few seconds ticked by before his gaze slipped back to her and he began his story. 'I suppose what you need to know is that I didn't meet Lena for the first time ten years ago. It was way before then. It was when I was twenty-one and she was eighteen, when she was Lena Bell. I'd never come across anyone like her before. She was sweet and smart and beautiful. It was ... We were ... ' He gave a shrug, a faint flush rising to his cheeks. 'Anyway, you get the picture. Young love and all the rest of it. We wanted to be together, but ... '

Maddie peered at him over the rim of her cup. 'But?'

'Her parents had other plans for her. We knew they'd have a fit if they found out about us and so we decided to do a bunk, run off and never come back.'

'Sounds extreme.'

'You never met her father. Charlie Bell was a drunk, a womaniser, a gambler. He'd have sold Lena to the Devil for a pint of mild and twenty fags. And her stepmother wasn't much better.'

'She was eighteen. She could have just left home, couldn't she?'

'It was more complicated than that. A local thug had taken a fancy to her, more than a fancy. He was obsessed. He wanted to marry her and he was the sort of guy who wouldn't take no for an answer. Charlie owed him money and didn't mind settling the debt by pimping out his daughter. And this guy – Brendan Vasser, in case you hadn't already guessed – wasn't going to sit back and watch the object of his affections stroll off into the sunset with another man.'

365

Maddie knew how this story ended – and it wasn't with a happy ever after. But she sat quietly while he went on to explain.

'Anyway, Lena was convinced that wherever we went, Vasser would hunt her down. So we needed a plan, a way to cover our tracks and put him off the scent. It was Delia Shields who came up with the idea. Lena and I often used to meet in the cemetery – Charlie kept her on a tight leash and it was the only place locally where we could be pretty sure of not being seen together – and one of the graves there was for a girl called Lucy Rivers. She'd died when she was nineteen, only a year older than Lena. The rumour was that she'd drowned herself because of some man.'

'Owen Vickery,' Maddie murmured.

'Huh?'

She shook her head. 'It doesn't matter. Go on. Delia Shields?'

'Yeah, so Delia came up with this idea that Lena could take on Lucy's identity. If we got hold of the birth certificate, we could go up to Gretna and get married with Lena using Lucy's name. Delia reckoned we'd get away with it, that they wouldn't check the death records. And if Vasser tried to track her down, he'd come up against a brick wall. He wouldn't be looking for a Lucy Rivers . . . or Lucy Cato, as she was going to become.'

Maddie smiled thinly, beginning to understand.

Cato had a strained look on his face as if the effort of recounting the past was all too much for him. He played with the cup, twisting it round in his fingers. 'So that's what we decided to do. And from that point on, I started calling her Lucy so we could get used to it, so we wouldn't make any stupid mistakes when we did do a runner. For the last few weeks before the date we'd chosen to leave, she became Lucy Rivers. She told me that she practised at home, repeating the name over and over until it was second nature to her.'

'So what went wrong?'

'Everything,' he said. 'A few days before we were due to go, I got a letter from Lena saying she'd changed her mind and couldn't go through with it. She said it was over and asked me not to contact her again.'

'Oh,' Maddie said. 'And you didn't – try to see her again, I mean? Didn't try and persuade her to change her mind?'

'I should have, but I was young and stupid and hurt. I should have fought for her, but I didn't. I took the letter at face value and made up my mind that she'd never really loved me, couldn't have. It didn't occur to me that she might not have written it, that it wasn't from her at all.'

Maddie's eyes widened. 'What?'

'No, it looked like her writing from what little I knew – a birthday card and a couple of notes – but actually it was from someone else. Took me a long time to figure out who, but I'll get to that later. To cut a long story short, I took off, got a flight to Madrid and spent the next few years licking my wounds.'

'And then?'

Cato gave a shrug. 'I tried to get on with my life. I worked in Europe and the States, moved around, did okay. And then I made the fatal mistake of coming home. We're talking twenty years later here. I should have been over her, but I wasn't. I couldn't resist the temptation of seeing her again. And it didn't take long to track her down – she was still in Kellston and married to Brendan Vasser.'

Maddie drank the dregs of her coffee and put the cup down on the table. He must have read the expression on her face, because his lips slipped into a wry smile.

'Yeah, I should have left well alone. I know that now. But I couldn't and I didn't. And you know what happened next, so I won't bore you with the details. Suffice to say that we took up where we left off and it was all downhill from there. It wasn't the same. How could it be? We'd both changed, and I'm not sure if she ever believed me about the letter – she thought I'd got cold feet and done a runner. She thought I'd dumped her, left her to face Vasser on her own. I hadn't kept it, so I couldn't prove anything.'

'So who did send it?'

'Well, I eventually figured out that it had to have been either Delia Shields or Lena's parents. But even if it was the parents, someone must have tipped them off and provided them with my address, and the only person that could have been was Delia.'

Maddie felt a shiver run through her. 'But why would she do that? I thought she was Lena's friend.'

'Yeah, she was that all right, her thoroughly adoring friend. And at the beginning she was completely on side – anything to help Lena, anything to ingratiate herself. But then she probably realised what it all actually meant: Lena was going to go away and she was never coming back. I don't think she could bear that thought and so she decided to put a spanner in the works.'

'Does Lena know about it?'

'I told her what I thought. I don't think she went for it. Well, not back then at least.'

A silence fell between them. Maddie wondered if he was thinking what she was thinking – that Lena had maybe reconsidered and come to the same conclusion. Delia Shields was gone, murdered, bludgeoned to death by someone who was full of hate. She understood now why Delia had been so worried about Cato being back on the scene. The woman must have been terrified that the truth would finally come out.

Cato sat back and then sat forward again as if he wasn't sure what to do with himself. 'I guess that's it, the whole sordid story – unless there's anything else you want to know.'

'Only one thing,' she said. 'The gold ring, the wedding ring.'

'"For ever,"' he murmured.

She nodded. 'That's the one.'

Cato shifted in his seat again. 'I'd already bought the rings before I received the letter. I'd shown them to Lena, got her to try hers on to make sure it fitted. Perhaps I should have thrown them away too, but I didn't. I kept them for all these years. Anyway, I decided it was time to let go, to bury the ring along with the past.'

Maddie didn't entirely believe this part of the story. She reckoned he'd wanted it found, wanted a fuss so that Lena would eventually get to hear about it. 'So who put it on Lucy's grave?'

'Hayley Whittaker.'

'Your solicitor?'

'Well, she's a little more than that. She was part of my legal team during the trial. She thought I was innocent even if the jury didn't. We've stayed in touch ever since, got close.' His eyes lit up in a way that Maddie hadn't seen before. 'Everyone needs someone to believe in them, especially in a place like this.'

Maddie glanced away, not wanting to be reminded of love. It had stabbed her in the back and she was still reeling from the blow. She was glad that Cato had some hope in his life, but she hadn't been so lucky. Thinking of Rick made her stomach twist into that familiar painful knot.

'I'm sorry I dragged you into this,' he said. 'I really am.'

Maddie met his eyes again and shook her head. 'Don't be. I've spent the last six years wondering about Greta – why she died, what happened, the whole sorry mess. If it hadn't been for you, I'd never have known the half of it. If nothing else, I've finally got some answers.'

'Even if they weren't the ones you wanted to hear?'

'Even then.'

They both knew there was nothing left to say. Cato rose to his feet and held out his hand. 'Take care. Have a happy life, Maddie. Make the most of it.'

369

She took his hand – his palm was warm – and shook it. 'Thank you. I'll try.'

Eli Glass unlocked the door to the cemetery chapel and slipped inside the abandoned building. Thin slivers of sunlight slid through the stained-glass windows, casting a glow over the old tiled floor and the dusty pews. He walked slowly up the central aisle, pausing only to gaze at the cross before taking a seat.

This morning he had heard that the body in the mausoleum had been identified as Owen Vickery. He had always known that it would happen one day; secrets never remained hidden for ever. But he wasn't afraid. Not now. Lucy had spoken and that was all that mattered. After all these years of silence, she had finally forgiven him.

A smile played around the corners of his mouth as his thoughts slid back through time to those hot summer afternoons when she had come to grieve at her mother's grave. Like a bride, she had walked up the thoroughfare with a posy of flowers clutched in her hands. Her beauty had been almost ethereal, as if an angel had been let loose amid the great grey tombs and the gleaming white headstones.

He had never talked to her, not once, but he had always been watching out for her. Was that what love was – the urge to protect, to take care of another? He had guarded her from a distance, but with a fierce loyalty. And yet, in the final reckoning, he had not been able to protect her from *him*.

Eli's smile quickly faded. Owen Vickery should have left well alone. But men like that had no self-control. They had to take what was pure, what was sweet and innocent, and deliberately defile it. The bastard had taken her heart and thrown it away. It was only right that he should pay the price.

It had been two years after her death before Vickery had turned up at the cemetery again. Had his nights been sleepless, his conscience niggling away at him? Perhaps her face rose up in his dreams, distraught and accusing. Well, whatever the reason, he had come to kneel by her grave, to place a paltry bunch of flowers at the foot of her headstone.

When he'd seen him there, Eli had felt a rage he had never felt before, an anger that washed through his body and made his heart race. An eye for an eye – wasn't that what the Old Testament demanded? He had never been one for God, but in that moment he had been overwhelmed by an almost religious fervour. Quietly, softly, he had crept up on the man. The chunk of marble, broken off from a fallen gravestone, had been lying on the ground. He had bent down to pick it up, feeling its coolness in his hand.

It had all been over in a matter of seconds. Vickery had slumped forward without a sound, the blow shattering the side of his skull. Eli had stared down at him. How fast it had been, how simple. Not like Lucy's suffering. There was blood on the marble, blood and tissue. He had thrown the stone into the long grass.

And then what? There was a blurry quality to what he'd done next. He remembered dragging the body down the narrow path, his hands under the dead man's arms. Taking him where? He hadn't known, hadn't thought until he saw the mausoleum. It was as good a place as anywhere to hide him. But first he needed to get hold of the key. He must have walked back to the office, but he had no memory of it. He must have walked through the back door and along the corridor to the small room with its rows of hooks. He must have found the right key and put it in his pocket.

His recollection was clearer from the point he'd returned to the mausoleum and opened the door. He could still see the small, shadowy room with its six coffins, three on either side. He could still smell the strange musty odour. His first instinct had been to just dump the body, lock up and go, but then he'd had a change of heart. There was something wrong, disrespectful, about leaving a corpse lying around. It was only right to keep the place tidy.

He'd chosen the coffin on the right, on the middle shelf. The name Harold James Belvedere was engraved on a slim gold plaque. From the basic bag of tools that he always carried round his waist, he'd taken out a screwdriver and unscrewed the lid. There was plenty of room inside, plenty of space for company. Harold's body had long since shed its flesh and there was nothing left but bones.

Eli lifted his eyes to focus on the cross again. It had been a struggle, he recalled, hauling Vickery's body into the coffin. A dead weight – wasn't that what they called it? But eventually it had been done and the lid replaced and the evidence hidden. And then all that had been left to do was to lock the door and walk away.

'Walk away,' he murmured into the silence of the chapel.

But he hadn't been able to walk away from Lucy Rivers. Over and over he had been drawn back towards her grave, hoping for some word from her, for a sign that she'd forgiven him. Because he'd known that even as she'd plunged into the still waters of the pond, even as she'd felt the water pour into her lungs, that she had still loved the man she was dying for.

Lucy's grave. He hadn't been the only one to visit it. Less than a year after her death, there were two other people who met there regularly: Jay Cato and Lena Bell. Another doomed love affair. And Delia Shields had caught him watching, warned him off, told him to push off and mind his own business. And then all those years later, Cato had been tried and convicted of Brendan Vasser's murder. In court, at the trial, Lena had claimed that Cato was a stranger, a stalker, a man she'd barely known. And Delia had backed her up, perjuring herself too.

The two of them had lied through their teeth and a man had gone to prison.

Eli felt a weariness flow through him. His eyes, heavy as lead, struggled to stay open. He took one more look at the stained-glass windows and their soft, vibrant shots of light before giving up the fight. It was over. It was finished. There was nothing left to do. His eyes flickered shut and his breathing became shallow. His heart slowed and his head lolled to one side. His last thought as he slipped into a final sleep was of Lucy Rivers walking through the graveyard with the sun in her hair.

Maddie climbed into the Mercedes, closed the door and fastened her seatbelt. She felt tired and sad and overwhelmed. But she also felt relieved. She had done everything now that she could do. The rest was out of her hands. Maybe one day there would be some justice for Greta and Bo, but until then she would just have to get on with her life.

Solomon shot her a look as he switched on the engine and moved smoothly away from the kerb. 'So how did it go?'

She hesitated. 'It was . . . illuminating.'

He didn't probe any further, for which she was grateful. She needed some time to come to terms with it all, to think it through. He put on some music, a soft rhythmic jazz. She listened to the notes, to the plaintive strains of the saxophone as she stared out of the window and watched the streets pass by. It was only when they'd left the prison far behind that she finally felt able to repeat the story that Cato had told her.

Solomon tapped his fingers on the wheel. 'This love stuff,' he said. 'Strikes me that it's been the cause of a problem or two.'

'You could say that.'

'Probably worth avoiding.'

'Yes.'

'Unless it's the family kind.' Solomon cleared his throat and glanced at her. 'I was thinking, maybe, perhaps, we should do something together, you, me and Zac.'

She looked at him, surprised. 'What, just the three of us?'

'That a problem?'

'No, no, of course not. Where were you thinking of?'

Solomon's big shoulders lifted in a shrug. 'Beach, theme park, cinema. I'm easy. Just anywhere there ain't no dinosaurs.'

'Okay,' she said. 'Why not? It's a date ... Well, not a date exactly, but ...'

Solomon grinned. 'No need to spoil the moment, hon.'

She sat back, letting the music flow over her. So much had happened, so much grief and pain and sorrow. But she couldn't carry it around for ever. It was time, she knew, to try and leave the past behind and move into the future.